Prologue

2014

'OK . . . here's how we do it. Now pay attention, Brian. Pay very close attention . . .'

The older one was speaking, the one who'd been so indescribably vicious all night.

It was a strange thing, but as recently as one day ago, if you'd asked Brian Kelso which of two desperate criminals you'd expect to be the most unrestrainedly violent – the older one, or the younger one – he'd have opted for the younger one every time.

But of course, the last nine hours had not just changed his views on that – it had changed everything.

'Are you listening?' the guttural voice wondered.

Again, the guy sounded as if he was from East Yorkshire. Again, Kelso made a mental note to remember this, so that he at least had something he could tell the police, though both he and Justine needed to survive this ordeal first.

'Yes, I'm listening,' he told the throwaway phone they'd supplied him with.

'Drive out of the north end of town along Welton Road. You know it?'

'Yes . . . I know it.'

'You'll see a bus stop at the junction with Horncastle Lane. Slow down when you get there, and stop. That's when you'll receive further instructions.'

'OK.'

'Before you set off . . . how much did you manage to get?'

'Erm . . .' Kelso's mouth, already flavoured like mud after what seemed an age without even a sip of water, went fully dry. He glanced over his shoulder at the four heavy haversacks, now zipped and buckled tight on the rear seat of his Peugeot. 'About two hundred . . . I think.'

There was a protracted silence.

'Two hundred?' came the eventual response. 'I thought we'd agreed three at the very least?'

'Look . . . I was on my own, OK? The staff were due within the next hour. I got as much as I could in the time available. Surely you understand that? It's not like the Dunholme branch is crammed with cash anyway.'

'I suppose it'll have to do.' The tone was deeply grudging. 'But I'm not happy with you, Brian. I'm not happy at all.'

The line went dead.

'Wait, please!' Kelso shouted. 'Is Justine all right?'

Only the dial tone purred back at him.

Just about managing to suppress the cry of emotional agony set to burst its way out of him like a piece of actual anatomy, he dropped the phone onto the passenger seat next to him, and slumped forward, his forehead striking the steering wheel.

Justine, whom he'd been married to for the last twelve years, had never hurt anyone in her life. She was good-natured, kind-hearted; she rarely nagged him or got crotchety, and God knows, there were times when he'd deserved that from her. Even though she'd been so grief-stricken to learn

2

Paul Finch is a former cop and journalist, now turned full-time writer. He cut his literary teeth penning episodes of the British TV crime drama, *The Bill*, and has written extensively in the field of children's animation. However, he is probably best known for his work in thrillers and crime. His first three novels in the Detective Sergeant Heckenburg series all attained 'best-seller' status, while his last novel, *Strangers*, which introduced a new hero in Detective Constable Lucy Clayburn, became an official *Sunday Times* top 10 bestseller in its first month of publication.

Paul lives in Lancashire, UK, with his wife Cathy. His website can be found at www.paulfinchauthor.com, his blog at www.paulfinch-writer.blogspot.co.uk, and he can be followed on Twitter as @paulfinchauthor.

By the same author:

KISS OF DEATH

PAUL FINCH

avon.

Published by AVON
A division of HarperCollins*Publishers* Ltd
1 London Bridge Street
London SE1 9GF

www.harpercollins.co.uk

A Paperback Original 2018

1

A catalogue copy of this book is available from the British Library.

ISBN: 978-0-00-824398-2

Set in Sabon by Palimpsest Book Production Limited,
Falkirk, Stirlingshire

Printed and bound in UK by CPI Group (UK) Ltd, Croydon CR0 4YY

MIX
Paper from
responsible sources
FSC™ C007454

This book is produced from independently certified FSC™ paper
to ensure responsible forest management.

For more information visit: www.harpercollins.co.uk/green

For my wife, Catherine, who has always been my rock.

that she couldn't have children, she'd refused to let it get her down, determinedly continuing with life, filling what might otherwise have been a yawning desolation for both of them with her bubbly personality and busy demeanour, looking after herself to the nth degree, looking after him, looking after their detached, four-bedroom house, ensuring that it was permanently like a new pin.

And now those bastards had . . . had . . .

Kelso shook his head, hot salt-tears coursing down his cheeks as he struggled to negotiate the icy surface of Market Rasen Road. Whatever the outcome today, he knew that he'd never forget the image now branded into his mind's eye: of his lovely soulmate, stripped naked and bound X-shaped with pairs of her own tights to the lower banisters of their staircase, her head drooped, her chestnut hair unbound and hanging in long, ratty hanks, her slim, marble-white body mottled with bruises, streaked with blood.

'You have to understand,' the older one had said some time around three that morning, by which point Kelso sat stiff and sweat-soaked in the dining room chair they'd brought into the hall and tied him to with the hoover flex, so that he could watch. 'We couldn't do any of this to *you*. Because just before dawn, you've got to go down to that bank you manage with your best suit on and your keys in your pocket as if everything is normal. A bit earlier than usual of course, but not so much . . . and not in any kind of state that'll make anyone who sees you suspicious. But even so, we had to make it absolutely clear what you'll be facing if you try to fuck us over. You see, my young pal, here . . . he's going to tail you down to the bank. And he's going to park across the road till you've gone inside. Now, up until that moment I reckon it's safe to say we'll have full control over you. But we're under no illusions: once you're in there, things are different. There'll be nothing to stop you picking the nearest phone up and calling the filth.

Except the knowledge that we've still got your missus. And that nasty little question that'll be niggling away in the back of your head . . . if *that* was the way they treated her when I hadn't given them any grief, what in Christ's name will it be like if I try to double-cross them?'

Kelso shuddered at the memory of those cold, reptilian eyes fixed on him from the two slits in the bright green balaclava. It was too easy to imagine that there was nothing human behind them.

'So . . . you won't try anything stupid, will you?'

'I swear it,' the captive had said. 'Please . . . just don't hurt her any more.'

'You know . . . I actually think I trust you, Brian.' This might have sounded more convincing had the older one's pistol not been jammed so hard into Kelso's right temple that his entire head was crooked painfully to the left. 'Just don't give me any fucking reason to regret that judgement, yeah? Because if you do, what happens after that will be un-fucking-imaginable.'

By the time he was on Welton Road, it was past eight, and the veils of frozen fog were thinning and clearing. The two hoodlums would like that, because, as they'd continually reminded him, they'd be watching his progress and keeping a sharp lookout for any anomalies, like so-called members of the public displaying unusual interest in his activities or maybe a helicopter hovering in the near distance. Not that there was any possibility of this, because Kelso, though he'd been tempted on entering the bank, had eventually made no phone call. What would have been the point? In the short time available before the villains became suspicious, the police wouldn't have been able to mount any kind of response other than sending uniformed officers scrambling to the house and the bank – which would have achieved nothing, because the older villain was unlikely to still be at the former location, and though the younger one had tailed Kelso down here, he'd vanished after that, presumably secreting himself somewhere nearby, to watch. Both of them would have been able to get away relatively easily, maybe taking Justine with them, which would have been the end for her.

So, Kelso had complied.

Naturally he'd complied.

But he still had no idea what to expect next.

As he approached the junction with Horncastle Lane, he saw the bus stop in question, though nobody was waiting there. Rush hour was now upon them, as indicated by the increasingly heavy traffic, but this was a rural area, and the few commuters living in the villages round here were more likely to travel by car.

Before Kelso had set out that morning, they'd searched his vehicle for a tracker, and had even advised him that, when he got to the handover site, he'd be searched again, just in case he'd somehow managed to fit a wire and had been feeding covert info to the police all along. If that was the case, he'd never see his wife again, or anything in fact, because he'd be shot on the spot. The older one's preferred method, or so he'd boasted, was a slug through the back of the neck.

Kelso would have laughed had the predicament not been so critical. A tracker? A hidden wire? They clearly overestimated the facilities available to modern-day bank managers, but the implicit message was clear: they weren't taking any chances and no untoward behaviour on his part would be tolerated even for a second.

Trying not to think about that, he pulled into the layby opposite the bus stop, switched off his engine and sat waiting. As the seconds ticked by, he grew increasingly nervous.

He wasn't on a time clock here, but he'd assumed that they wouldn't want this thing dragged out, and that the longer it took, the twitchier and more dangerous they'd become. But what was supposed to happen? Surely someone should have shown up by now? The younger one who'd followed him to the bank, maybe – though perhaps he now had another role to play in the scheme. With the engine off, the interior of the car was cooling fast. Kelso pulled on his leather driving-gloves and zipped his anorak over his dishevelled suit. He'd tried to dress the part this morning, but it had been impossible to do a proper job.

Outside, a police traffic patrol eased past in the sluggish flow of vehicles. Kelso shrank down, only just resisting the urge to duck out of sight altogether, gabbling prayers that they wouldn't swing around and park behind him to see what the trouble was. If one of the gang was observing and they spotted that, they'd never believe it a coincidence.

Thankfully that didn't happen, though the mere sight of the police Range Rover with its hi-vis blue and yellow chequerboard flanks had touched Kelso with a new sense of despair. He'd been a bank manager for fifteen years, but he had no clue how his actions would be viewed when this was all over. Surely people would understand that he'd acted under duress? But the fact would remain that he'd robbed his own bank of £200,000. And if the hoodlums got clean away, how would people know that he hadn't been in cahoots with them? The brutalising of Justine wouldn't disprove that on its own. So, he'd be a suspect at the very least.

He sat up straight and pivoted around, to see if there was anything he ought to have responded to that he'd failed to notice.

On his left there was a stile, and beyond that a farm field, which, now that the mist had cleared, lay flat and white. Across the road, behind the bus stop shelter, stood a clutch of trees, their leafless boughs feathered with frost.

His eyes roved across the bus stop itself – and that was when he saw something.

He'd registered it on first arriving here but had barely thought about it. From across the road, it was a simple sheet of paper inserted into a ragged plastic envelope and taped to the bus stop post. He'd assumed it a reference to some proposed development in the area, a request for viewpoints from the local community, or similar. But now he clambered from his car, and crossed the road, weaving through the slow-moving vehicles. When he reached the bus stop, he saw that the paper bore a message composed from snipped-out newspaper lettering:

GO NORTH UP HORNCASTLE LANE
THAT IS OPEN COUNTRY
SO WE'LL BE WATCHING
ANY SIGN YOU HAVE COMPANY
YOU KNOW WHAT HAPPENS
BRING THIS NOTE AND THE PLASTIC

Kelso ripped the envelope down, and scampered back to his car, jumping in behind the wheel and, at the first opportunity, pulling into the traffic. He swerved onto Horncastle Lane and headed north. As directions went, these were vague, but he felt absurdly relieved, almost as if this whole tribulation had suddenly been resolved for him.

As he'd been advised, and already knew, this was a big agricultural area, expansive acres of farmland rolling away to every horizon under their coat of winter white. The sun was now up and sitting low in the east, a pale, ash-grey orb, while the sky itself was clear of cloud, but, in that eerie way of raw January days, was bleached of all colour. Suddenly, Kelso felt as if he was away from the hubbub; there were few, if any, fellow road-users on this quieter route.

The phone began to ring, and he slammed it to his ear. 'This is Kelso.'

'I know it's you,' that familiar, confident voice replied. 'So far you've been a good boy. Looks like we're really going to do business, doesn't it?'

'I hope so. Please can you tell me . . . where's Justine? Is she all right?'

'It's good that you care about your wife, Brian. I always knew you would. That's why this plan was foolproof from the start. You don't need to worry, pal. You'll see her again. Just continue to do exactly as you're told, and we'll be fine.'

'All right, well . . . please, let's just get this over with.'

'Take your next left.'

That, in itself, was unnerving. It meant they really *were* watching him. Who knew where from – they could be standing on a barn roof, using binoculars, for all Kelso was aware. Whatever it was, they were bloody well organised.

'And where will that bring me to?' he asked.

'Oh, no . . .' the voice hardened. 'Now don't spoil it by asking stupid questions. I thought we'd already established that once we hook up again, we'll be searching you . . . just to make sure that, by some miracle, you and your friendly neighbourhood PC Plod didn't get a chance to secrete some kind of communication device on you.'

'I haven't done that!' Kelso blurted. 'Come on . . . I was only in the bank ten minutes. How could anything like that have been arranged? You were watching anyway, weren't you? You'd have seen if a police officer had arrived there.'

There was a long, judgemental silence, and then: 'Like I said . . . take your next left.'

The line went dead.

Kelso shuddered, briefly feeling as if he needed to vomit, but instead he slammed his foot to the floor, accelerating from forty miles an hour to fifty. As instructed, he took a left-hand turn, but at reckless speed. It was a few seconds later, when common sense kicked in and he slowed right down again. It might seem quiet along here, but the last thing he wanted was to catch the eye of some lazy copper idling around in the back-country hoping to bag some boy-racers.

He pressed on more cautiously for perhaps another three or so miles, passing a farmhouse on his right, though it was boarded up. Fleetingly, he was taut with anticipation, recognising this as a possible spot for the handover. But he'd soon bypassed the old farm, driving steadily north, and still there was no call.

'Come on, come on,' he said under his breath, frantic and frustrated at the same time. 'Please . . . soon, good Lord in Heaven, let this be over soon.'

The phone buzzed. He snatched it up, and saw that he'd received a text:

Next right

The car was warming up again, but the sweat on his brow owed nothing to the temperature.

When a right-hand turn approached, he swung around it, paying almost no heed to the conditions. The Peugeot slithered sideways across a road so slick with ice that it might have been double-glazed. He now found himself following a single-track lane, which hadn't even been tarmacked, his wheels jolting amid rock-hard tractor ruts. It was a terrifying thought that he was being lured further and further from civilisation, but that had probably been the appeal of the Dunholme branch in the first place; he was nobody – just an everyday bank manager, but his bank was located on the edge of extensive countryside, from where it would be quick and simple for the robbers to vanish into the sticks. Yet more evidence of how well planned this whole thing had been. But none of that mattered right now. His overwhelming desire to feel Justine in his arms again – no doubt shivering and whimpering, teeth chattering from the cold, numb with shock, but at last safe – rendered any qualms about how isolated he was null and void.

Up ahead, he could see trees: not exactly a wood, more like a copse. The narrow lane bisected it through the middle, running on straight as a ribbon.

Maybe that would be the place? It was the first change of scenery Kelso had encountered on this drear landscape in the last few minutes. In that respect, it surely signified something. And indeed, as he passed into and among the trees, he couldn't resist accelerating again, bouncing and rocking on the ridged, hard-frozen surface – and, as such, almost crashing head-on into the white-painted pole with the red, circular signpost at the top, which stood in a concrete base and had been planted in the dead-centre of the thoroughfare.

When the Peugeot finally halted, having slid nearly twenty yards, the signpost stood directly in front of him, only its circular red plate visible over the top of his bonnet. A single word was stencilled in black lettering in the middle of it:

STOP

Kelso climbed out and stood beside the car, his breath pluming in the frigid air.

Initially, there was no sound. He glanced left and right and saw to his surprise that he'd halted on a narrow bridge. He'd been so focused on the stop sign that he hadn't noticed the rotted, flimsy barriers to either side of him. Not that it was much of a bridge. By the looks of it, it didn't lead anywhere in particular; it was probably for the use of livestock.

'Kelso!' a harsh voice shouted.

He turned full circle.

'Kelso!' the voice shouted again, and, realising where it was coming from, he scrambled around the front of his Peugeot to the left-hand barrier.

Some twenty feet below, he saw what he took to be a derelict railway cutting, except that this also had been adapted into a farm track, because, almost directly underneath him, a flatbed truck was waiting. Its driver, the younger of the two hoodlums, a taller, leaner figure than the older one, but mainly identifiable because, instead of a green balaclava, he was wearing a black one, had climbed from the cab.

'Throw the cash down!' he called up. 'Do it *now*!'

'Where's my wife?' Kelso shouted back.

'Throw it now, or you'll never see her again.'

'All right, for God's sake!'

Kelso returned to his car and, one by one, humped the loaded haversacks to the barrier, dropping them over. Each one landed with a shuddering crash, bouncing the truck on its shocks. From twenty feet up, fifty grand in used banknotes made quite an impact. The younger hoodlum had clearly anticipated this, because he stood well back in case one went astray. However, when all four had landed, he hurriedly lowered the tailgate and jumped on board, opening the zips on two of them to check their contents, before climbing back down and scuttling to the driving cab.

'Hey!' Kelso shouted. 'Hey . . . *what about my wife?*'

The guy never once looked back. The door slammed behind him, the vehicle juddering to life, before roaring off along the cutting, frosted leaves and clumps of frozen earth flying behind it.

'What the . . .' Kelso's voice almost broke. 'Good . . . *good God almighty!*'

'Hey,' someone behind him said.

He spun around, and almost collapsed in gratitude at the sight of the older villain, who had evidently sidled out of

11

the trees beyond the signpost and now approached along the lane.

As before, he wore overalls, heavy gloves and a green balaclava.

Also as before, his pistol was drawn.

'I've done as you asked.' Kelso limped towards him, arms spread. 'You saw me.'

The hoodlum pointed the gun at his chest. 'Yeah, you've done as we asked.'

Kelso stumbled to a halt. 'OK . . . please let's not play this game any more. Just let me have Justine?'

'Worried about your wife, eh?'

Despite his best efforts, Kelso's voice took on a whining, agonised tone. 'Please don't do this. Just tell me where she is.'

'Where she was before. Back at your house. Why would we bring her with us?'

'OK . . . so . . . is that it, then?'

'Yeah, that's it.' But the hoodlum didn't lower his firearm. Kelso was confused. 'So . . . I can go?'

'Eager to see her again, eh?'

'What do you think? Just let me go, and I'll drive back.'

'Nah. I can send you to her a quicker way.'

'What . . .?' After a night of extreme horrors, Kelso, who'd thought he'd be rendered immune to this sort of thing for the rest of his life, now felt a deeper, more gnawing chill than ever before. 'What do you mean?'

The gaze of those terrible eyes intensified. He imagined the bastard grinning under his balaclava; crazily, maniacally, a living jack-o'-lantern.

'Oh, no . . .' Kelso simpered under his breath. 'Oh no, please nooo . . .'

'Oh, yes,' the hoodlum chuckled, firing twice into the bank manager's chest.

12

Chapter 1

Present day

The church of Milden St Paul's was located in a rural haven some ten minutes' walk outside the Suffolk village of Little Milden. It sat on the edge of a quiet B-road, which ostensibly connected the distant conurbations of Ipswich and Sudbury but in truth saw little activity and was hemmed in from all sides by belts of gentle woodland and, in late summer, an endless golden vista of sun-ripened wheat.

The atmosphere of this picturesque place was one of uninterrupted peace. Even those of no religious inclination would have struggled to find fault with it. One might even say that nothing bad could ever happen here . . . were it not for the events of a certain late-July evening, some forty minutes after evensong had finished.

It began when the tall, dark-haired vicar came out of the vicarage and stood by the wicket gate. He was somewhere in his mid-thirties, about six-foot-three inches tall, and of impressive build: square across the shoulders, broad of chest, with solid, brown arms folded over his pink, short-sleeved shirt. His hair was a lush, curly black, his jaw firm, his nose straight, his eyes a twinkling, mischievous blue. To pass him in the street, one might think it curious that such a masculine specimen had found his calling in the cloth. There had to be at least a chance that he'd have certain of his parishioners swooning in their pews rather than heeding his sermons, though on this evening it was *he* who'd been distracted by something.

And here it came again.

A third or fourth heavy blow sounded from the other side of the church.

Initially, the vicar wondered if the warm summer air was carrying an echo from some distant workplace. On the church's south side, you could see the roof of Farmer Holbrook's barn on the far southern edge of the wheat field next door. But that was the only building in sight, and there wasn't likely to be much work under way on a tranquil Monday evening.

When he heard what sounded like a fifth blow, it was a sharper, flatter sound, and louder, as if there was anger in it. The vicar opened the gate, stepped onto the path and walked towards the church's northwest corner. As he reached it, he heard another blow. And another, and another.

This time there was a smashing sound too, like wood splintering.

He hurried on to the church's southwest corner. Yet another blow followed, and with it a grunt, as of someone making a strenuous effort.

On the building's immediate south side lay an untended part of the grounds, the weathered slabs of eighteenth-century gravestones poking up through the long summer grass. Beyond those stood the rusty metal fence cordoning off the wheat field. It might be a sobering thought that, once you were on this side of the church, you were completely screened from the road and any passing traffic, but the vicar didn't have time to think about that. He rounded the final corner

14

and strode several yards along the south-side path, before stopping dead.

A man with longish red hair, wearing patchwork green/brown khaki, was striking with a wood-axe at the vestry door. He grunted with each stroke, splinters flying, going at it with such gusto that he'd already chopped a hole in the middle of the door, and very likely would soon have the whole thing down.

The soles of the vicar's black leather shoes had made barely a sound on the worn paving stones, but the man in khaki had heard him; he lowered his axe and turned.

The mask he wore had been chiselled from wood and depicted a goat's face – but it was a demonic kind of goat, with a humanoid grin and horns that curled fantastically. The worst thing about it, though, was real: the eyes peering out through the holes notched for them were entirely human, and yet they burned with living hatred.

The man came down the step from the door and approached, axe held loosely at his side. The vicar stood his ground and spoke boldly.

'What are you doing here? Why are you damaging church property?'

'You know what we're doing here, shaman!' a voice said from his right.

He glanced sideways: three more figures had risen into view, each from behind a different headstone. They too largely wore green; he saw old ragged jumpers, ex-military combat jackets. They too were masked: a toad, a boar, a rabbit, each one decked with additional monstrous features, and each with the same hate-filled eyes glaring out.

The vicar kept his voice steady. 'I asked what you are doing here?'

'You know the answer, you holier-than-thou prick!' said a voice from behind.

When the vicar spun backwards, a fifth figure had emerged around the corner of the church. This one also wore green, but with brown leather over the top. His wooden mask depicted a wolf, and as he advanced, he drew a heavy blade from a scabbard at his belt; a hunting knife honed to lethal sharpness.

The vicar looked again at the threesome in the graveyard; Toad now smacked a knotty club into his gloved left palm; Rabbit unhooked a coil of rope from his shoulder; Boar hefted a canister of petrol.

'In the name of God,' the vicar said, 'don't do this.'

'We don't recognise your god,' Wolf replied.

'Look . . . you don't know what you're doing.'

'Oh, very good,' Wolf sniggered, as they closed in. 'Very fucking saintly.'

'This is sanctified ground,' the vicar advised them. 'Use more blasphemies here, and I'll be forced to chastise you.'

'Really?' Wolf was so surprised by that, that he almost came to a halt. 'I can't wait to see how you do it.'

'I warn you, friends . . .' The vicar pivoted around. 'I'm no martyr.'

'Funnily enough,' Wolf sneered, 'the ones before you didn't go willingly to it, either.'

'Ah, now I know who you are,' the vicar said.

'Always a good thing to know thine enemies.'

'You're on your final warning.'

'Perhaps your god will strike us down?' Wolf was only five or so yards away. 'Maybe throw a thunderbolt this fine summer evening.'

The vicar nodded solemnly. 'I fear one's coming right now.'

A rasping chuckle sounded behind the lupine mask. 'You've got balls, I'll give you that.'

'I also have *this*.'

From out of his trouser pocket, the cleric drew an extendable autolock baton, which, with a single jerk of his brawny wrist, he snapped open to its full twenty-one inches.

Before Wolf could respond, the baton had struck him across the mask in a backhand *thwack*. The carved wood cracked as Wolf's head jerked sideways and he tottered, dropping his knife. As the rest came to a startled halt, the vestry door burst inward and the figure of a man exploded out, launching at Goat from behind. This figure was neither as tall nor as broad as the vicar, just over six feet and of average build, with a mop of dark hair. He wore blue jeans and a blue sweatshirt with a police-issue stab vest over the top, but he also carried an extended baton, which he brought down in a furious, angled swipe at the elbow joint of Goat's right arm.

The axe clattered to the floor as the target yelped in disbelieving pain. He grappled with his injured joint, only for a kick in the backside to send him sprawling onto his face. His assailant leapt onto him from behind, knees-first, crushing the air from his lungs.

The vicar swung to face Toad, Boar and Rabbit, holding aloft a leather wallet, displaying his warrant card. 'Detective Inspector Reed, Serial Crimes Unit!' he bellowed. 'You're all under arrest on suspicion of murdering John Strachan, Glyn Thomas and Michaela Hanson!'

Wolf fled towards the southwest corner of the church, only to slam head-on into another huge figure, this one even more massive than the vicar. He too wore jeans and chest armour, and he greeted Wolf with a forearm smash to the throat.

As Wolf went down, gagging, a deep Welsh voice asked him: 'What time is it, Mr Wolf? Time you weren't here? Too bloody late for that, boyo.'

The other three ran energetically towards the boundary fence, only to be stunned by the sight of more police officers, some in uniform and some in plain clothes, all armoured, rising from the wheat and spreading into a skirmish line.

'You don't have to say anything,' Reed intoned, watching the fleeing trio as, one by one, they were overpowered, unmasked and clapped into handcuffs, 'but it may harm your defence if you do not mention when questioned something you may later rely on in court. Anything you do say may be given in evidence.'

'You're also under arrest for being a sacrilegious little fuck,' the big Welsh cop whispered, leaning into Wolf as he fastened his hands behind his back.

'We don't fear your god,' Wolf hissed in an agonised voice.

'You shouldn't.' The Welsh cop yanked the fractured mask off the lean, sweaty features underneath. 'My God's merciful. Problem you've got, boyo, is . . . there's a long, hard road before you get to Him.'

Beside the vestry door, the cop in blue snapped a pair of cuffs onto Goat, who, without his mask, was gaunt and pale, his carroty red hair hanging in lank strands as he cowered there.

'Get up,' the cop said, standing. His accent was Northwest England.

'Shit . . . think you . . .' Goat's voice became whiny, frantic. 'Think you broke my arm.'

'No, I didn't . . . just whacked you on a nerve cluster.' The cop kicked him. 'Get up.'

'Can't feel anything under my elbow.'

'You're facing three murder charges.' The cop grabbed him by an armpit and hauled him to his feet. 'A dicky elbow's the least of your problems.'

'Christ!' Goat screamed. 'My arm's broke . . . *God-Christ!*'

'Thought you boys didn't believe in Christ?'

'It's killing me, mate . . . for fuck's sake!'

'Sucks when you've come to hurt someone and found it's the other way round, eh? Who *are* you, anyway?'

18

'Sh . . . Sherwin . . .' the prisoner stammered.

'First name?'

'That's my first name. Last name's Lightfoot . . . Oh *shiiit*, my fucking arm!'

'Sherwin Lightfoot? For real?'

'Yeah . . . oh, *sweet Jeeesus* . . .'

'Fair enough. You're also getting locked up for having a stupid name.'

'Everything all right, Heck?' Reed called.

'Heck?' Lightfoot said. 'Look who's bloody talking . . .'

'Shut up,' the cop called Heck retorted. 'Everything's smashing, sir. Why wouldn't it be?'

'Easy, Sarge.' Reed ran a finger round the inside of his clerical collar but made such a dog's breakfast of loosening it that its button popped off. 'I was only asking.'

'I *have* done this before, you know.'

'Good work, everyone,' a female voice interrupted.

Detective Superintendent Gemma Piper was never less than impressive. Even now, in jeans, a T-shirt and body armour, and clambering over a rusty farm fence, she cut a striking figure. With her athletic physique, wild mane of white-blonde hair and fierce good looks, she radiated charisma, but also toughness. Many was the cocky male officer who'd taken her gender as a green light for slack work or insubordination, or both, and had instantly regretted it.

'This lot been cautioned, Jack?' Gemma asked.

'They have indeed, ma'am,' Reed said.

'Responses?'

'The only one I heard was this fella.' Reed indicated Boar, who, having had his mask pulled off, resembled a pig anyway, and now was in the grasp of two uniforms. 'Think it went something like "fuck off, you dick-breathed shitehawk".'

'Excellent. Just the thing to win the jury over.' Gemma raised her voice. 'All right, get them out of here. I want separate prisoner-transports for each one. Do *not* let them talk.'

'Don't worry,' Wolf sneered, still gripped by the large Welsh cop, though he seemed to have recovered some of his attitude. 'No one's talking here except *you*. And you've got quite a lot to say for a slip of a tart.'

Gemma drew a can of CS spray from her back pocket and stalked towards him.

'Ma'am!' Reed warned.

DSU Piper was renowned, among other things, for almost never losing her cool, and so managed to bring herself to a halt before doing something she might regret. She stood a couple of feet from the prisoner, whose thin, grizzled features split into a yellow-toothed grin.

'Don't say nothing!' he shouted to his compatriots. 'Do you hear me? Don't give these bastards the pleasure. Say nothing, and we've got plenty chance of beating this.'

'You finished?' Gemma asked him.

He shrugged. 'For now.'

'Good. Take a long look at your friends. This is likely the last time you'll see them till you're all on trial. And very possibly on that day, one, or maybe two of them, could be looking back at you from the witness stand. How much chance will you have then?'

Wolf hawked and spat at her feet.

'Let's move it!' Gemma shouted. 'Someone get the CSIs in. Tell them the scene's clear for examination – I want this ground going over inch by inch.'

Chapter 2

It wasn't always the case that suspects arrested by the Serial Crimes Unit were brought back to London for processing. As part of the National Crime Group, SCU's remit was to cover all the police force areas of England and Wales, and as such they most commonly liaised with local forces and tended to use their facilities. But on this occasion, to Detective Sergeant Mark 'Heck' Heckenburg at least, it felt like the most sensible option. Little Milden was only fifty-eight miles from London, and only seventy-two from Finchley Road police station, where extensive adaptations had been made for the confinement and interrogation of just such highly dangerous groups as the 'Black Chapel'.

Finchley Road was now classified as one of only two high-security police stations in London. The first one, Paddington Green, was primarily for holding suspected terrorists and as such was more like a fortress than a regular police office. Finchley Road was physically much the same, but primarily for use against organised crime. To all intents and purposes, it was a normal divisional police station in that it was nondescript and open to members of the public twenty-four/seven. But the reinforced concrete barriers around its exterior might indicate that it had other purposes too, while additional, less visible defences were also in place, such as bulletproof glass in its windows, outer doors of reinforced steel with highly complex access codes, and the presence on the premises of permanently armed personnel. It had an ordinary Custody Suite for use in day-to-day police operations, but there was also a Specialist Custody Suite on a lower level, which was completely separate from the rest of the building's interior and hosted twenty cells and ten interview rooms, all of these viewable either through video link or two-way mirror.

It was through one such viewing port that Heck now watched as Rabbit, aka Dennis Purdham, was interviewed. Of all five suspects, he had been the most visibly distraught on arrest. Aside from their leader, Wolf, also known as Ranald Ulfskar, the others – Sherwin Lightfoot (Goat), Michael Hapwood (Toad) and Jason Renwick (Boar) – had also registered surprise and shock when the police showed up, but as with any cult, and that was what Heck felt they were dealing with here rather than a conventional criminal gang, they'd drawn strength from their leader's stoicism, and were obediently keeping their mouths shut.

Purdham was the exception.

Like the rest of them, he'd struck Heck as an outsider: unshaved, long-haired, pockmarked. The clothing they'd seized from him mainly comprised oil-stained hunting gear and mismatched bits of army surplus wear. But, at the age of twenty-three, Purdham was much younger than his confederates, and possibly only involved in the murders as a bit player – or so his solicitor was seeking to intimate. He'd wept when they'd booked him in, and wept again when they gave him his white custody suit. As such, while the others were left to stew in their cells, it wasn't long into Purdham's interview before he'd begun to talk.

22

The interviewers were Gemma Piper and Jack Reed, who, by prior agreement, was adopting an understanding guise. It was this that Purdham had responded to, gradually regaining his confidence.

'At the end of the day, Christians are a set of vile bastards,' he said in broad Staffordshire. 'Everything about them stinks. Their hypocrisy, their dishonesty . . . they're a bunch of fucking control freaks too.'

'Someone give you a hard time when you were young, Dennis?' Reed asked. 'A priest maybe?'

'You mean was I kiddie-fiddled?' Purdham shook his head. 'Nah . . . never happened to me. But there are lots it did happen to, aren't there?'

'So, you and your friends were responding to sexual misdo-ings?' Gemma said. 'Is that what you're saying?'

Purdham hesitated, unsure how to reply.

He wasn't as stupid as he looked, Heck thought, because to admit to this would be to admit premeditation.

'Because in case you did,' Gemma added, 'I can tell you that there's never been any suspicion about those three people. Or about the Reverend Hatherton, who is the incumbent at Milden St Paul's.'

'That means he's the one I stepped in for tonight,' Reed explained.

'Look . . .' Purdham scrubbed a hand through his lank, mouse-brown hair. 'I don't think anyone was specifically targeted. It's what I said before, Christians are . . . just shit-arses.'

'You mean Christians in general?' Gemma asked.

'Lots of people agree with me on this.' Purdham's eyes widened; he became animated. 'You only need to go on social media. Everyone's always saying it.'

There was a soft *click* in the viewing room, as a door opened. Heck turned and was surprised to see the squat, bull-necked shape of DCI Bob Hunter come furtively in. Hunter acknowledged Heck with a nod and signalled that he didn't want to interrupt.

Heck turned back to the mirror, beyond which Gemma was in mid-reply.

'It's worth remembering, Dennis,' she said, 'that social media is an echo chamber.'

Purdham regarded her confusedly.

'Every mother's son on the planet uses it to sound off about stuff that bugs them. They may have genuine issues with religion, even with Christianity specifically . . . but just because they gob off about it online, most of them are not even so hyped about it that they stop celebrating Christmas. So, I'd say it's a near certainty that what happened at St Winifred's in the Marsh, for example, would be right off their agenda.'

The killing of the Catholic priest, Father John Strachan, on March 21 that year, had been the first murder in the Black Chapel case. The victim had answered a knock at the presbytery door just after 11 p.m., at his church, St Winifred's in the Marsh, up in rural Cambridgeshire – only to receive an axe-blow to the face, which had killed him instantly.

'Look . . . I've admitted I was there,' Purdham said, tingeing red. 'But . . . I told you, I didn't participate.'

'Neither did you do anything to prevent it.'

'It happened in a flash. I didn't even know Ranald was armed.'

As Heck listened, he thought again about Ranald Ulfskar. It was a cute name he'd given himself. In real life, he was Albert Jones from Scunthorpe. He was the spiritual leader of this weird group. At fifty, he was the oldest, and though also the scrawniest and most ragbag, he was, without doubt, the toughest and had led the most lived-in life. And yet it was through Ulfskar/Jones that Heck had first learned about the so-called Black Chapel. Ulfskar had spent several years as a roadie for a very successful black-metal band from Scandinavia called Varulv. One of his fellow roadies at the time, Jimmy 'Snake' Fletcher, someone not quite as besotted with Varulv's dangerous Nordic vision, had later become one of Heck's informants. And once it had become apparent to Fletcher that the East Anglia priest killings were a series, and that they were in synch with certain dates in the calendar, he'd got on the blower.

'We also strongly suspect you were there at the murder of Reverend Glyn Thomas,' Gemma said.

Purdham hung his head and said nothing.

The second cleric to die had been a Church of England minister, the Reverend Glyn Thomas. On the night of April 30 that year, he'd been alone at his church of St Oswald's, out in the Norfolk back-country, when, just before midnight, intruders had forced entry to the vicarage. He was hauled out in his nightclothes and forced to watch as both the vicarage and the church were set alight. He was then bound, hand and foot, and had a wire noose tightened around his neck, which was attached to the tow bar of a vehicle. After this, the Reverend Thomas was dragged at high speeds along isolated country lanes for fifteen miles, before his body, or what was left of it, came loose of its own accord. It was found in a roadside ditch the next day, but only several hours after the blazing ruins of St Oswald's had drawn the attention of early-morning farm workers.

'And what about the murder of Michaela Hanson?' Gemma wondered.

Purdham still said nothing.

In the case of the Reverend Michaela Hanson, it was mid-evening on June 21. She'd been alone in the Church of Our Lady on the outskirts of Shoeburyness in Essex. As with the incident at Little Milden, it was shortly after evensong, and the congregation and altar servers had gone home. Reverend Hanson was collecting the hymnals from the pews when intruders entered through the sacristy door. Her naked corpse was found the following morning, spread-eagled on the altar table. She'd been slashed across the throat with something like a billhook and pinned to the wood with a pitchfork.

'There was even a sexual element in that one, wasn't there?' Reed said, referring to the fact that the Reverend Hanson's lower body had also shown signs of being violently attacked.

'Which at least is in keeping with this Odinist fantasy,' Gemma said.

Purdham looked up sharply, as if to mouth a protest, but managed to restrain himself.

'Why don't we talk about that Odinist angle, Dennis?' Reed said.

Still, Purdham held back on a response.

'Those Vikings had a pretty violent attitude to life, didn't they? Rape, pillage . . .'

'They get misrepresented by films.' Purdham hung his head again; he almost seemed embarrassed to be mounting a defence.

'Maybe, but blood rites are a part of Odinism, aren't they? I've been reading up on it. Normally, it was animals that got sacrificed. But certain Viking leaders, to really curry favour with the gods, used to offer humans too, didn't they?'

Again, Purdham said nothing.

'You have to talk to us about this bit, Dennis,' Gemma said. 'We're not really interested in the mythology, or how Ranald Ulfskar managed to tie it in with some modern-day Aryan master-race gibberish. What we really want to know is what you saw happen on these awful nights, and what part you played in it.'

Still, nothing.

'What about the dates?' Reed said. 'If you're genuinely interested in the Viking religion, you must've known about the dates . . .'

'March 21,' Gemma reminded him. 'April 30, June 21 . . . how about today, July 31?'

He glanced up weakly. 'Look . . . I knew they were relevant, yes. But I didn't know we were going to kill people.'

'OK, let's go with that?' she said. 'Let's assume that was true the first time. But what about the second, third and fourth?'

'Surely, you didn't think you were just going to rough these guys up?' Reed said. 'Or scare them? How would that have gone down with Odin and Thor?'

'That's the point,' Purdham moaned, seemingly deeply troubled. 'It's cruel . . . I know, but you can't deny the deities. Once you've promised something, you've gotta deliver . . .'

Heck shook his head as he watched.

'Deities?' said a disbelieving voice. Bob Hunter had come forward to the mirror. 'Odin and Thor? These twats ripping the piss, or what?'

'Not totally,' Heck replied. 'Odinism was a real thing.'

'Wouldn't have thought there was much call for it in the twenty-first century.'

'Where've you been, sir? This is the age of the hate crime.'

'Yeah, but when it comes to white-power nutters, I thought Muslims were the hate figures of the moment.'

'Me too,' Heck agreed. 'But I suppose some clowns just can't get over that slap Sister Mary gave them when they were being cheeky to her all those years ago in Junior School. How are you anyway?'

'I'm good.'

'Congratulations on the promotion.'

'Cheers.'

DCI Bob Hunter had once been DI Bob Hunter of the Serial Crimes Unit, in which capacity he and Heck had worked together on several enquiries. Ultimately though, Hunter, who had moved to SCU from the Metropolitan Police's Flying Squad, had adopted a cowboy approach to law enforcement, which its overall commander, Gemma Piper, had never been comfortable with. In due course, after one dispute too many, Hunter had returned to the Met and his beloved FS – or 'Sweeney', as it was known among London's armed robbery community, whom it exclusively tackled – where he had now, much to Heck's surprise, been promoted.

'Listen, Heck . . . do you need to be in here?' Hunter asked, seemingly conscious that several other SCU officers were also present, no doubt earwigging. 'Or can we step outside for a minute?'

Heck threw a grudging glance through the mirror at Reed, who again was making headway with the suspect, before shrugging. 'I don't think they'll miss me.'

'Who's Prince Charming, anyway?' Hunter asked, noticing the object of his annoyance.

'DI Jack Reed.' Heck opened the door and moved out into the Custody corridor. 'Transferred in from Hampshire about three months ago.'

Hunter followed him out. 'What did he do down there?'

'I don't know. Some crap job . . . probably undeserving of praise.'

Hunter looked curious. 'You're not a fan, then?'

'It's nothing, I'm just being cynical.' Heck walked through the Charge Office and tapped out a code on the door connecting to the Custody team's Refs Room.

'If he's that bad how did he finish up in SCU?'

'He used to work for Joe Wullerton in the Critical Incident Cadre.'

Hunter chuckled. 'Bit of nepotism in the National Crime Group? Never.'

'Nah . . .' Heck shook his head glumly. 'He's good. I mean, he's so clean he squeaks when he walks, but I can't pretend he doesn't know his job.'

'Well . . . this is all very interesting, but how about that chat?'

'Yeah, sure.'

They went into the Refs Room, which currently was empty, and got themselves a coffee from the vending machine in the corner.

'Sounds like everything's peachy in the Flying Squad,' Heck said.

'To be honest,' Hunter replied, 'when I rejoined, I didn't think I had much of a future.'

'I always thought it was your natural home.'

'Yeah, but sometimes it isn't a plan to go back where you started, is it? Not that Gemma bloody Piper left me much choice. No offence, by the way.'

'None taken,' Heck said.

It had been well over a decade since he and Gemma had been an item, and had even, briefly, set up home together; they'd been young detective constables at the time, working divisional CID at Bethnal Green. But much fire and water had gone under the bridge since then, not to mention Gemma's meteoric rise through the ranks. On first arrival at the Serial Crimes Unit, Heck had never expected to find himself subservient to his former girlfriend. They'd worked together ever since, almost eleven years now, but not always cosily.

'The Squad's been good to me, though, as it's turned out,' Hunter added. 'It always has. I mean, it's not fucking perfect . . .'

'Give over, Bob.' Heck sipped his coffee. 'What're you moaning about? There are lads all over the Met who'd kill to get into the Sweeney.'

'How about you, Heck? Are you one of them?'

Heck snorted. 'Not in the Met any more, am I?'

'Jesus, so what? You've swapped forces at least three times already to my knowledge. And it's not like NCG's got a great future.'

Heck couldn't deny that. In this age of austerity, the police services of the UK were taking a real hammering. It would only be a matter of time before specialist squads started to feel the pinch as well, and rumours were now rife at Scotland Yard, where the National Crime Group's HQ was located.

'And the Flying Squad has?' Heck wondered.

Hunter barked a laugh. 'Come off it. *We've* survived everything from machine-gun attacks to corruption charges. A few cutbacks aren't gonna do for us.'

'Bob . . .?' For the first time, Heck wondered where this conversation was leading. 'Are you offering me a job, or something?'

'You've surely heard that we've got a vacancy for a new DI?'

'And it's down to *you* to find someone to fill it?'

'I'm running Squad North-East now. There have to be some perks.'

'There's one problem with this. You're looking for a DI . . . I'm a DS.'

'Come on, Heck . . . I think we can make *that* happen.'

'Just like that?'

'Yeah, just like that.' Hunter laughed again. 'Don't be too hard on yourself, pal. With your record, you've got credit in the bank. Or have you still got this daft, self-defeating ideal about not wanting to join the brass because you'd rather be a soldier?'

Heck had been offered promotions in the past but had rarely given them a second thought, always insisting that he preferred the front line, and that he'd rather be an investigator than an administrator – though, deep down, and Gemma had once mentioned this to him, he couldn't help wondering, being the 'rogue angel' he was (again, Gemma's phrase, not his), if it was more a case that he simply didn't fancy the extra responsibility of DI.

Times changed, of course. And so did attitudes and ambitions.

As he sipped more coffee, he thought again about how comfy the handsome, debonair Jack Reed was in his new role as DI at SCU, which in effect made him Gemma's deputy. And how comfy Gemma apparently was to have him there.

And it wasn't as if the Flying Squad itself wasn't appealing. Heck had worked Tower Hamlets Robbery once, though that had been a smaller role – mainly he'd found himself going after muggers and other street bandits. The Sweeney pursued the big boys. For that reason, there'd always been a certain glamour about it – they were regularly in the press and on TV. Their reputation for being wideboys, just a bit too close in spirit to the East End villains they often investigated, had always put him off in the past.

But again, things changed.

'Not that Squad DIs don't do a bit of soldiering themselves from time to time,' Hunter added. 'Just think, you can make your ultimate fantasy real . . . you'll be Regan Mark II, a displaced Manchester lad working over the blaggers of London.'

'Who'd I be replacing?' Heck asked him.

'Ray Marciano.'

'*Come again . . .?*'

Hunter shrugged. 'He's left us, Heck.'

Heck was astounded. 'Ray Marciano's left the Flying Squad?'

'Not just the Squad, pal. The job.'

The term 'living legend' was often overused in police

circles, but Ray Marciano, the Flying Squad's quietly spoken detective inspector from Sevenoaks, Kent, had proved to be the exception to that rule. For the last nineteen years, he'd led one successful campaign after another against the capital's legion of bank robbers, taking down more firms than anyone else before him, securing hundreds of years' worth of convictions for major-league faces. He wasn't just considered a brilliant detective, he was also better connected and therefore better informed than almost anyone else in the Met, which was all the more remarkable given that he wasn't a London boy by origin. There was scarcely a snout in the city he didn't have a working relationship with, barely a villain who didn't know him well. In fact, it was gang leader, Don Parry, whom Marciano had arrested in connection with the Millennium Dome raid and sent down for twenty years, who had christened him, with a degree of grudging respect, 'Thief-Taker No. 1'.

'Would you believe he's gone working for a defence solicitor?' Hunter said.

Heck was vaguely aware that his jaw had dropped. 'You're telling me Ray Marciano hasn't just chucked it in, he's chucked it in to go and be a case worker for a brief?'

'Not just any brief. It's Morgan Robbins.'

'Robbins . . .' Heck tried to recall; the name sounded familiar.

'He's the one who got Milena Misanyan off,' Hunter said.

Heck *did* remember it. Last year, the City of London Police had charged some female oligarch from Turkey or somewhere, who was newly settled in the UK, with various highfalutin white-collar offences: embezzlement, fraud, tax evasion, that kind of thing. Apparently, they'd done months of work on her before striking, only to see her defence, organised by Morgan Robbins, take them on at every turn and defeat them. It had been all over the papers for several months.

Heck seemed to recollect a photo of Misanyan on the cover of *Time* magazine: it was a portrait of an archetypical eastern beauty, complete with dark eyes, thick lashes and ruby lips, a fetching silk scarf woven around her head, her expression a bland but enigmatic smile. That item had come well *before* the recent court battles; he thought it had been in celebration of her joining the ranks of the world's female billionaires – the headline had been something like *From Hell to Heaven* – but he hadn't bothered reading the story.

'Thanks to the Misanyan case, Robbins is no ordinary lawyer these days,' Hunter said. 'He's a big fish, a real whopper.'

'Even so . . .' Heck shook his head. 'Hearing that Ray Marciano would rather be a case worker than a cop is like hearing Kim Jong-un's up for Man of the Year. It doesn't compute.'

'He's not really a case worker, is he? More like their lead investigator. Look . . . don't be surprised, Heck. Ray's still doing what he loves, only now there'll be no more pissing around with Met politics, no having to cover his back all day, no having to mind his Ps and Qs or watch what he says in case he upsets some fucking snowflake back in the office. On top of that, he'll be on massive money. Way more than *we* can afford to pay.'

Heck arched an eyebrow. 'You're not exactly selling the Squad to me, Bob.'

'Look, Heck . . . we're all pig-sick of the changes in the job. Everyone's pissed off about their pensions. We've had lads slogging their guts out for twenty years, waiting for promotion, only to see chinless wonders brought in from Civvy Street as direct-entry superintendents. It's not just us, it's you lot in NCG too . . . I know you're feeling it. But there are still some oases of common sense here and there, even in London.'

They were alone in the Refs Room, but Hunter lowered his voice conspiratorially.

'Heck, you know that with me as your guv'nor, you'd get a lot more leeway than you do under Her Ladyship. And I'm only answerable to Al Easterbrook, which basically means I'm answerable to no one.'

Alan Easterbrook was Senior Commander of the Flying Squad, a man once famed but now with a reputation for being a distant, remote figure, whose main ambition in life was to get through each day without any underlings bothering him with details.

'Until Easterbrook retires,' Heck said.

'Why would he retire?' Hunter replied. 'They want us all to stay on. And he's got the cushiest number ever. It's me who does the donkey work. He just gets the credit for it.'

'Look, Bob . . .' Heck threw his half-empty cup into a bin. 'I don't know if I'm even qualified to replace Ray Marciano.'

'You must be joking, pal. Ray never did anything you don't. You're bang on for it.'

Before Heck could argue further, the door swung open and Gemma came in, followed by Jack Reed. They headed to the vending machine, deep in conversation about how to pitch the next interview, though Gemma was visibly distracted by the sight of Heck and Bob Hunter, particularly Hunter.

'You don't have to decide now, pal,' Hunter said quietly, when the other two had resumed their discussion. 'But I'll have to make a decision in the next few weeks. Can't leave a vacant DI desk for too long. Not with all the bloody nutters we've got lining up to do jobs.'

Heck pondered. The offer had come from left-field and, even if other things hadn't been preoccupying him, would have left him a little dazed, not to say doubtful. It wasn't just the personal ties he had at SCU, he'd been with the unit eleven years now. In some ways, he'd almost become insti-tutionalised. It was difficult to imagine being anywhere else.

'I'll get back to you, Bob,' he said.

'Give it some serious thought.' Hunter leaned again into his personal space. 'SCU's a good gig, but anyone who stays in the same place for too long gets stale. Plus, I'll say it again ... National Crime Group's on rocky ground. You don't believe me ... wait around and see.'

He glided away, leaving the Refs Room without a backward glance.

'What's Bob Hunter doing here?' Gemma wondered, coming over.

'Dunno,' Heck replied. 'Suppose he's got some case in.'

'Thought his new patch was the East End?'

'Flying Squad, ma'am. If anyone makes good use of this nick, it's them.'

By the look on her face, she didn't believe this for one second, but decided to let it pass.

'Purdham given us a full confession yet?' he asked.

'In the end,' she said. 'I actually believe him ... somehow or other, they railroaded him into participating in these crimes. It's amazing what you'll do to become part of a club. But yeah, to answer your question ... if Ulfskar and his cronies don't get thirty years apiece, no one ever will. Once we get the forensics in play, it's over for them.'

She walked from the room with coffee in hand.

'OK, Heck?' Reed asked, edging after her.

'Fine, sir,' Heck replied stiffly. 'You?'

'Never better. You can call me Jack, you know.'

'That's all right, sir. I always think we've got to earn the right to use first names.'

Reed smiled as he left. 'No one's earned that right more than you.'

'Who's talking about me?' Heck said under his breath.

Chapter 3

The impending threat to the National Crime Group felt as if it might be real. Heck was in no position to judge, or even voice opinions on the matter – but there was rarely smoke without fire, and there was an awful lot of smoke at present.

Almost certainly, there'd be pay and recruitment freezes, people would be expected to work longer hours for less, resources would likely be slashed, and maybe staff too. If the worst came to the worst – and certain folk were saying that the crisis was actually *this* bad – entire departments could be disbanded, and all personnel reassigned. On the face of it, the latter would seem unlikely, but it would be a sure way to make an awful lot of savings in one fell swoop. And in that regard, the National Crime Group, thus far untouched by the cutbacks, had to be a prime target.

It comprised three specialist branches: the Kidnap Squad, the Organised Crime Division and the Serial Crimes Unit. In the eyes of many, these were all luxuries the British police could ill afford, as they monopolised manpower and funds for relatively small gain. Even Heck had to admit that it didn't look good in the stats when an SCU detective made maybe only four or five arrests per year. What matter that these were nearly always repeat serious offenders – serial murderers, rapists and the like – who may already have ruined countless lives and had the potential to continue doing exactly that? It was still only four or five villains off the street each year, compared to the forty or fifty that a divisional detective might account for, never mind the hundred or so claimed by the average uniform.

He tried to put it from his mind as he worked his Megane through the heavy mid-morning traffic in Dagenham, but it frustrated him no end. Several days had passed since the Black Chapel sting and yet the ominous stories about the unit's potential fate continued, seemingly unaffected by these recent positive results. In the words of DS Eric Fisher, SCU's main intel man, 'Why should we expect preferential treatment just because we do our job?' Heck supposed that Fisher had a point, but it was a job that few others could do.

Again though, he tried to dismiss it all. He'd always sought to ignore the internal politics of the police, especially high-end politics like this, mainly because it was hardly the sort of thing you'd expect of a 'rogue angel'.

This unusual status referred to the roving commission Heck was often accorded during SCU enquiries. Another name for it, again of Gemma Piper's invention, was 'Minister Without Portfolio'. In a nutshell, this meant that he was rarely attached to any specific part of the investigation but instead was authorised to develop and chase down his own leads. This was a privilege he'd earned over many years, on the basis of having felt numerous quality collars on the back of his own analysis and intuition. But whether it would have happened under any other supervisor than Gemma was questionable.

Not that Gemma was his best friend at present, and he couldn't quite put his finger on the reason why. It was certain that the menacing sounds from the top floor had put her on edge. She'd been brusque and indifferent with him recently, if not downright vexed. Neutral observers might argue that this was their normal relationship – there'd been many times in the past when it felt like they were at daggers drawn, but this was usually because of procedural disputes, not as a matter of course. Lately, she'd been actively and protractedly cold with him, much more than was normal, and much, much more than she was with anyone else.

Heck puzzled over it as he left the A13 and joined the Heathway.

He hadn't done anything especially wrong, as far as he knew. Quite the opposite, in fact. His own intel had laid the Black Chapel on a plate for them, for which he'd received minimal gratitude. He wondered if it could be down to his lack of enthusiasm for the recently appointed DI Reed, though on that front Gemma was more than making up for it herself.

He shook that thought from his head, aggravated in ways he couldn't explain.

He was now on the edge of the Rimmington Hall estate and, inevitably, his mind moved to other things. St Agatha's Roman Catholic Church was easy enough to find. It faced onto Rimmington Avenue from behind a tall wire-mesh fence. There'd be a car park behind it somewhere, but as this was August and the junior school next door was closed, there was nothing to stop him parking on the main road at the front.

St Agatha's was an industrial-age structure, stark and functional, its brickwork ingrained with the smoke and soot of generations. After recent investigations, especially the pursuit of the Black Chapel, Heck felt as if he'd been spending a lot of time in and around churches. But the lichen-clad tombstones and ivy-hung chancels of rural Suffolk were a world away from this place. Not that St Agatha's grim appearance made it seem any less incongruous that Jimmy 'Snake' Fletcher now hung out here, though it wouldn't have been the first time in Heck's experience that a half-hearted soul had only needed to be exposed once to the full viciousness of his chosen team before he went scuttling off to join the opposition.

That said, Fletcher was still lucky that the local parish priest had been sympathetic.

Heck didn't bother trying the front door but walked down a side passage into a small yard at the back. On one side here stood the entrance to the presbytery; on the other stood St Agatha's Church Hall.

The latter was a free-standing building, a single-storey with a prefab roof, and walls coated in white stucco. It was in regular use, and in fact its main entrance stood open now, so Heck ventured inside. Here, a door on the right led into the hall itself, an open space of bare floorboards and scattered school chairs. A door on the left revealed a short corridor with signposts for toilets. A whitewashed brick arch stood directly in front and, beyond that, a stairwell dropped out of view.

Heck descended. At the first turn in the stair, he saw a startling piece of graffiti on the facing wall. Some vandal had used venom-green paint to daub the words:

Abandon hope, all ye who enter here . . .

And underneath it:

. . . if you had any in the fucking first place

Heck understood the meaning of this when he looked right, to where the final flight of steps descended three or four feet, before connecting with a corridor built from bare brick and smelling strongly of mildew. Exposed piping, unlagged but dangling with cobwebs, ran the full length of it. Heck could just about see this thanks to the illumination provided by a series of grimy light bulbs mounted every ten yards in wire-mesh cages crusted with limescale. Some forty yards ahead, a pair of doorways led off opposite each other, and a little way beyond those, at the corridor's far end, stood a closed door made of what looked like solid steel.

Heck walked forward, footsteps clicking on damp cement.

On reaching the facing doorways, he glanced into two squat brick rooms, in which massive cisterns churned quietly. He strode on towards the steel door. It was heavy, full of rivets and had no visible handle.

Just as he reached it, it slid open on its greased runner.

Snake Fletcher stood there, the eyes inscrutable behind the bottle-thick lenses of his heavy-framed glasses.

'Welcome,' he said.

'Some welcome,' Heck replied. 'What's wrong with the pub, or a park bench?'

'I told you, Heck . . . I'm not going topside at the mo.'

'Never had you down as the sort who scares easily.'

'Then you don't know me as well as you think, eh?'

That was most likely true, Heck conceded, as Snake withdrew into the dank chamber beyond the heavy door.

Some informants were interested in one thing only: the money they earned off the scalps of those fellow criminals they sent to their doom. Others were trying to pay off scores or remove rivals. But Snake didn't seem to tick any of those boxes. And that had always troubled Heck about this case. If you couldn't work someone out from the word 'go', if you'd never been able to fathom their purpose . . . how could you really trust them?

He'd first encountered the guy while working in Tower Hamlets Robbery. He'd pulled in a desperate youngster, Billy Fletcher, Snake's little brother, for participating in a string of corner-shop stick-ups. There wasn't much down for Billy at the time, but Heck had managed to persuade his colleagues that the young idiot had been drawn into the crimes through his heroin addiction. He'd also persuaded Billy to turn evidence, thus saving himself both from prison and under-world retribution. Snake hadn't seen his brother for fifteen years now, as he was safely inside a witness protection scheme, but that didn't matter to him. At least, the kid was still alive. And after that, Snake had always felt that Heck, of all the coppers in London, was someone he could trust.

But still . . . you could never afford to be totally sure of an informant's motives.

It wasn't as if Snake Fletcher was the most prepossessing-looking bloke.

The first time Heck had seen him, he'd made him for an over-the-hill metalhead: early forties, bespectacled, ratty hair and beard, faded tats on his gangling arms, ragged, oily denims. Now, fifteen years later, his image hadn't changed much, except that he was thinner and greyer and had ditched the proto-biker gear for a set of dingy caretaker's overalls. For all that, he still smelled strongly of cig smoke and sweat.

'You having a cuppa, or what?' he asked.

A bare bulb showed that his room was built from brick and crammed with unidentifiable clutter. If Snake himself had been pungent, the reek of dirty underclothes and soiled sheets, which spilled out of the subterranean hovel, was eye-watering.

'I'll come in,' Heck said. 'I'm not so bothered about the cuppa though. Nice welcome for all the God-fearing church folk, by the way.'

Snake chuckled. 'You mean the "abandon all hope" thing? Yeah, some skank broke in about three weeks ago. Father Wilkin, he's the parish priest . . . he asked me to clean it off, but I need to get some paint. It's not a priority. He never comes down here, never mind any of the parishioners.'

Which was undoubtedly a good thing, Heck decided.

From its various mops, buckets, brushes, bottles of bleach and boxes of random junk, the room was clearly a caretaker's lock-up. But Snake had also adapted it into a living space, even though it was small and windowless. He'd dragged in a truckle bed from somewhere (its sheets in a rumpled, filthy state), a few bits of second-hand furniture, and even a chemical toilet, though by its stench, this was sorely in need of emptying.

Snake sidled to a rickety sideboard on which streaky tea-making things sat among crumbs and puddles of spilled milk. 'So, tell me . . . did you get them all?'

'We've charged five men with various offences relating to the priest murders,' Heck said. 'They're all been remanded in custody.'

Snake nodded, as he plugged his kettle in. 'Names?'

'Sherwin Lightfoot – still can't get over that one – Michael Hapwood, Dennis Purdham, Jason Renwick and Ranald Ulfskar, aka Albert Jones. That's all of them, yeah?'

'Far as I'm aware.'

'Well . . . they won't be darkening any church doors in the near future.'

Snake spooned coffee granules into a mug. 'I'll be laying low for a while, all the same.'

'No one knows you gave us the tip, if that's what's bothering you.'

'They'll be watching, though. Wondering.' Snake shook his grizzled head. 'If I'm not dutifully despondent about what's happened to our worshipful leaders, they'll ask themselves why.'

'Who's *they*?' Heck asked. 'You just said we'd got them all.'

'You've got the hardcore. The fanatics. But there're others.'

'You mean other activists?'

'Nah, there are no more priest killers. The rest are just gobshites. But . . . if Ulf and his nutters get off for any reason, someone'll tell them what I've been up to.'

He continued to make his coffee. Heck watched him, curious.

'Snake . . . you certain there's no one else we should be looking at?'

'No one who scares me as much as Ulf and his cronies. Sure you don't want one?'

Heck shook his head and checked his phone, noting that he'd received a text from Gemma.

ETA office?

That had been nearly five minutes ago now, which meant she'd shortly be ringing him. He turned the device off and pulled up a chair. There was a crumpled magazine on top of it. It was a five-year-old edition of the extreme metal mag, *HellzReign*, now suitably dog-eared and stained with motor-bike oil.

On the cover, father and son black-metallers, Karl and Eric Hellstrom, aka Varulv, posed in full concert regalia. The older looked particularly demonic, his craggy features eerily pale, a complexion offset by his flowing black hair and dense black beard and moustache, not to mention his sunken, green-tinged eyes. Only his head and upper body was visible, but he was clad in dark leather armour with roaring bear faces sculpted onto its shoulder pads, and in his left hand, he clutched a blood-spattered human skull. It was pure hokum, a Hollywood costume designer's idea of how a Viking should have looked. The younger Hellstrom stood behind him. His hair and beard were blond, but he too wore black, sculpted leathers, and held his clenched fists crossed over his chest, a leather bracelet dangling with Gothic adornments

– skulls, inverted crucifixes and wolf heads – encircling each brawny wrist. Behind the pair rose a curtain of flames, and over the top of that, in jagged, frozen letters, arched the headline: *Real songs of ice and fire.*

Ordinarily, you could write this off as typical rock band posturing, a bad-boy outfit doing their best to look mean and moody, with a bit of mysticism woven in to underline their high-fantasy credentials. The very name 'Varulv' was Old Norse for Werewolf. But there'd been nothing fantastical about the violence their malevolent influence had allegedly unleashed.

Heck glanced up. 'How long were you involved with these guys?'

Snake lowered his mug. 'Couple of years. I told you before . . . to me it was just music.'

Even now, with Snake's intel having paid off, it occurred to Heck that he'd never really understood how it had taken the guy as long as it had to learn that the rock band he'd once idolised and, in fact, had road-crewed for, were so swept up in their Nordic-Aryan anger that they or their followers might actually have posed a genuine threat. Song titles like 'Make More Martyrs' and 'Berserk, I Rule' hadn't hinted at a sweet and inclusive nature.

Heck flicked his way through the mag, finally coming to a full-page advert for Varulv's first and apparently seminal album, *Asatru*. He wasn't averse to listening to a bit of hard rock, himself, though his own preference was for the older-school style, not the consciously dark-hearted material of more recent times. Almost from first hearing about these guys, Heck had disliked Karl Hellstrom and his son as a pair of professional rabble-rousers who probably didn't even believe the bigoted nonsense they preached. On the sleeve of *Asatru*, the artwork depicted a Catholic nun, naked, save for her wimple and cowl, nailed to a cross upside-down, while, behind her, horn-helmeted silhouettes raised axes against a backdrop of forked lightning strikes. If Heck remembered rightly, the album had been withdrawn from a number of British and American chain stores because of concerns about that cover, but this had only enhanced the record's notoriety, and it had reached a huge audience via the underground circuit, cementing the band's reputation as a major black-metal act.

He put the mag down. 'You sure we shouldn't be going after Varulv too?'

'Be my guest,' Snake said. 'But you'd be wasting your time. You heard what happened up in Norway?'

Heck had, of course. In 2014, two Norwegian teenagers, and avowed Varulv loyalists, had set fire to an eleventh-century timber church near Tromsø, beating to death the site's elderly custodian with a bat. Pinned to his body was a note calling for a war against 'Christ-lovers and Semites' in the form of direct quotes lifted from Varulv's lyrics, putting the band deep in the spotlight.

'They might have inspired that crime, but they weren't physically connected to it,' Snake said. 'That was just head-cases reacting badly to their message. And it took all sorts. Look at Ulfskar . . . he wasn't some extremist metalhead. If anything, he came from a punk background. Varulv chucked their net widely. Some hard-line metallers, sure, some bikers, but skinheads too, white supremacists, all kinds of hyper-masculine malcontents. That Black Chapel business . . . that's more Satanic than Odinist. Look at those four clowns who got locked up with Ulf. They weren't roadies, like us . . . they weren't even followers of the band. They were Ulf's followers. I told you . . . coked-out dickheads lost in some dark fantasy. That shows how mixed up it's all got.'

Heck didn't take issue with this. It was true that Varulv had never been officially accused of involvement in the

Tromsø outrage, not even as instigators. They were put under pressure by the Norwegian press, but they weren't investigated to any serious degree.

'If I recall,' he said, 'the band haven't accepted any responsibility for the Tromsø incident, and they certainly didn't offer an apology.'

Snake looked troubled by these notions, as if he too had been wondering about it and had not yet found a satisfactory explanation.

'Maybe they didn't lower themselves to respond,' he finally said. 'I mean, it happened in the States, didn't it? Metal bands of an earlier era getting unfairly blamed for sending bad vibes, causing suicides and the like. It's just bloodsucking lawyers trying to cash in on tragedy.'

'And yet Varulv were forced to leave Norway.'

Snake shook his head. 'That's a myth. They still own property over there. They just settled here in the UK when they retired. Seems Karl Hellstrom always wanted a hunting estate up in Scotland, and now he's got one. And it was after they settled up there when all this bad stuff really kicked off. I mean, that was in 2015. We'd all gone our separate ways by then, and it was three years later when I heard about these priest murders. It never entered my head that the band might actually be involved.'

'But you had no hesitation in suspecting Ulfskar?'

Snake pondered. 'He was always the most extreme of us . . . plus these killings were down in East Anglia, and that was his home patch. He'd gone back there, as far as I knew. The first priest, the one who got axed . . . I thought, nah, that won't be Ulf. Probably just a robbery that's gone wrong or something. But the second one . . . that was a bit nastier, wasn't it? And then the third one, the woman . . . fuck me! After that, I felt certain Ulf was involved. He'd said stuff in the past, you see . . . about drugs, sex and rock and roll just being hedonistic crap. About talk being cheap. About no one believing we really hated these bastards until we took action against them. Back then, I thought it was just more talk . . .'

Heck had heard this story before, of course.

After the gruesome death of the third victim, Michaela Hanson, Snake, rather bravely, had made an effort to re-acquaint with Ulfskar. He'd still had a contact number for him and had called, saying how empty his life was after the band. Ulfskar had replied that he would soon be down in London on business and was happy to hook up.

An uproarious drunken night had followed, much of which Snake captured on a concealed Dictaphone. There would always be questions about whether such non-approved evidence of private conversation would be admissible in court, but the tape, when Snake finally took it to Heck and Gemma, had been more than sufficient to catch their interest.

The conversation the cops listened to was very telling.

Initially, the twosome reminisced about the good old days on the road with the band, feasting on babes and booze, wild times when they'd got high and did crazy things. But they also recalled the firelit meetings they'd attended in woodland groves, and the ancient sites where they'd venerated long-forgotten northern gods. Then they expressed their enthusiasm for the right-wing forces marching in Europe and the US, and expressed hope that the white races of the world were finally getting their act together. It was around this point when Ulfskar first hinted at the existence of the Black Chapel, explaining that he and a few other like-minded guys were now taking direct action. He and Snake had once dreamed the dream, he said. But now he was making it real, following the creed to the letter – and if it didn't kick off a revolution on its own, that wouldn't matter. At least, it made them feel better.

'*Hey, I want in!*' Snake blurted on the tape.

'*You want in, Snakey . . . just like that?*'

'*You were right. We dreamed it . . . but we never actually did it.*'

'*I can't take you on the next job, Snake. Not yet. I need you to sober up and think it through. Just steer well clear of Little Milden in Suffolk, on July 31.*'

That had been all Snake had needed to know. After playing the tape to Heck and SCU, he'd told them about *Ostara*, an ancient Viking festival which fell on March 21. That was the night the first cleric had died. The other two murders had coincided with other pagan Nordic celebrations, *Valpurgis* on April 30 and *Midsumarblot* on June 21. They now had the date of the fourth one as well: *Freysblot*, which was July 31. And the location, Little Milden, where there was only one church: Milden St Paul's.

Heck glanced again at the lurid cover to *HellzReign*.

'But nah,' Snake said again. 'The Hellstroms aren't involved. Why would they be? Much better to be the gurus who sit on the mountain and get the kudos without taking any of the risk. Anyway, when do I get paid?'

Heck tossed the magazine aside. 'Soon as the Black Chapel get convicted.'

'Look, Heck . . . don't fuck this up, all right?' The ex-roadie looked vaguely troubled. 'We don't want those five nutters walking free again. Let 'em rot in jail, so any other rootless, confused idiot toying with the same idea might realise that murder isn't some bloody joke.'

'Good luck with that,' Heck said, standing. 'We might have cleared the new Vikings off our streets, Snake, but I'll tell you . . . there are people out there even as we speak, who, in their own minds at least, will have perfectly sound reasons for the total bloody mayhem they're about to unleash.'

Chapter 4

Heck got back to SCU at Staples Corner, in Brent, early that afternoon. The first thing that struck him were how many more vehicles there were than was usual on a Monday. He prowled the crowded bays before managing to locate a parking space. It was just his luck, of course, after he'd manoeuvred his Megane into it, to realise that the car on his left was Gemma's aquamarine Mercedes E-class, and not only that, that the detective super was currently on her way across the car park towards it, with one of the civvy secretaries.

As he watched them through his rear-view mirror, they opened the boot of Gemma's Merc and humped out a couple of sealed boxes of paperwork. The secretary set off back across the car park, carting one of these. But Gemma waited with her arms folded.

Sighing, Heck climbed out.

'And where've *you* been?' she asked. 'I've only been trying to contact you since lunchtime.'

'Thought it might pay some dividends if I went to see a grass,' he replied.

'I gauged that from the scruffs.'

Heck hadn't yet had time to change out of the paint-stained

jeans, sweatshirt and work boots that he'd worn for the meeting with Snake.

'Unofficially?' she asked. 'As in . . . on your own?'

He shrugged. 'I was out and about, but I just had a thought to go and see him.'

She considered this, before nodding at the box by her feet, turning and heading back towards the personnel door.

Heck picked the box up and tagged along after her.

'Who are we talking about?' she said. 'Wait, let me guess . . . Snake Fletcher?'

'Of course.'

'For crying out loud, Heck . . .'

'Partly it was to reassure him. He was very happy that we've made his intel count.'

'So would a lot of lowlifes be if all they had to do to get paid was drop dimes on their mates.'

'Thing is . . .' Heck knew he had to choose his next words carefully. 'I don't know . . . I thought it went too well, to be honest.'

She glanced at him quizzically. 'What do you mean?'

'The takedown at Little Milden,' he said. 'The Odinists turned up when Snake said they would. All five of them. We nabbed them. Each one banged to rights . . . we had enough evidence to charge them almost straight away. By the time we get to trial, we'll have even more. They haven't got a chance.'

They reached the personnel door, and Gemma tapped the combination into the keypad. 'Murder cases aren't always complex, you know.'

'I understand that. I just can't help feeling that we might have missed something.'

'Is this your natural pessimism talking?' she asked, as they went inside and she summoned the lift. 'Or did Snake say something?'

'No, he thinks we've got everyone.'

'So you have no actual grounds for this concern?'

He shrugged.

'I thought so.' She folded her arms as they waited in the small lobby. 'Heck, as always, your determination to bottom out every single job does you credit. But sometimes you make too much work for yourself. And for everyone else, including me. Which, as you can imagine, is not always appreciated. Now, it may be that something else comes up in due course regarding the Black Chapel, and if it does, we'll follow it to the end of the line. But in the meantime, we've got another, equally big job on our desk. Heard about Operation Sledgehammer yet?'

'Erm . . . Sledgehammer?'

'I had a meeting at the Yard over the weekend, and another one this morning. We're going to be doing some work with the Met's Cold Case team.'

'Oh . . .?' Heck wasn't sure he liked the sound of that.

'Gwen Straker's coming in on it.'

'Oh . . . right.' This was better news.

In the late 1990s and early 2000s, when Heck and Gemma were at Bethnal Green, Straker was their DI, and an able and affable boss she'd been. He hadn't seen much of her in recent years, but from gossip she was still one of the most popular supervisors in the Met. Heck was sure that the next question Gemma expected him to ask would be about this mysterious Operation Sledgehammer, but the good news about Gwen Straker notwithstanding, he wasn't yet ready to dismiss the case they'd only recently closed.

'I keep thinking about this black-metal band, Varulv,' he said.

She regarded him carefully. There were lots of things about Heck's reckless style of policing that worried Gemma immensely, but she'd learned through hard experience that his instincts could often be trusted.

'*Former* black-metal band,' she said. 'Aren't they in retirement?'

'Yeah. Apparently, they live as country gents in the Highlands of Scotland.'

'You are aware they were fully investigated by *Kripos*?' she said. 'I mean for that church-burning incident in Norway and the murder of the caretaker?'

'I understand they were interviewed,' Heck replied. 'Not necessarily investigated.'

'Either way, they were cleared of suspicion.'

'I agree that, as far as we know, they didn't commit any crime,' he said. 'But have you seen some of their song titles . . . some of their lyrics? It wouldn't take a religious zealot to consider them a fairly malign influence.'

'Heck . . . *you're* a malign influence. Young detectives see the corners you cut, and they think "wow, this job's a doddle". And then they pull the same stunts, and because they don't enjoy the luck of the devil, like you do, they end up wearing tall hats again. But ultimately, *you* never get hauled over the coals for it. You know why? Because you never *told* them to behave that way. It's one hundred per cent their own fault. And it's exactly the same with devil-worshipping idiots like the Black Chapel. Now, the cult leaders have all been charged, and like I say, if something else comes up . . . if one of them wants to do a deal, drop a few more names our way, we'll be all ears. Until then, we've got other business, OK?'

'Yeah, but I'm just wondering if I should do some follow-up work on this one.'

She regarded him blankly, unused to a lower rank – even Heck – completely ignoring her expressed viewpoint.

'On the basis of what . . . a hunch, a wing and a prayer?'

'Just let me run with it for a couple of weeks. See if I can dig anything up.'

'Heck, you can't touch Varulv anyway. They live in Scotland, they're outside our jurisdiction.'

'They may be outside our jurisdiction, but I can still touch them.'

'No, no.' She shook her head adamantly. 'None of that. As it stands, the case against Lightfoot, Hapwood, Purdham, Renwick and Ulfskar is watertight. I'm not having you mucking things up by chucking your weight about in a foreign land.'

'If nothing else, Varulv have encouraged all this. Ulfskar was one of their roadies. Should they just be allowed to go on as if . . .'

'Heck, what don't you understand about "no"? I *need* you here. In fact, I needed you here a couple of hours ago!'

The lift doors slid open. They stepped inside, and Gemma hit the button for the third floor, where SCU's command suite and her personal office were located.

Heck stood alongside her and said nothing, but as they ascended, he pondered again the dark, black-metal entity that was Varulv. Powerful music could be a potent force, especially among the disenfranchised. But he'd never quite known anything like this, where a message of anger had been taken to such extremes. It was difficult to imagine its originators, who appeared to have spent their entire adult lives hatching this creed of hatred, simply sitting to one side while their minions were defeated, and taking no further action. After all, they'd first spread their deadly message in Norway, and having got away with it there, had moved to the UK, where the same thing had happened again, only worse.

'You still with us?' Gemma wondered.

'Sorry,' he responded. 'I just don't think this'll be the last we hear from these guys.'

She visibly tried to keep a lid on her vexation.

'And when we *do* hear from them again,' he said, 'I think it's going to be *seriously* nasty.'

'Unfortunately, Heck, serious nastiness is not in short supply at present. Which is what Operation Sledgehammer is all about . . . and as we're reduced to having to do it in twos, that's all the more reason why you can't be spared.'

'Sledgehammer?' Heck was finally distracted from his ruminations. 'We're . . . we're doing it in twos?'

'Yes. That's how few people we've got available. And you, meanwhile, want to waltz off into some distant Scottish sunset to collar someone purely on sus?'

'Sorry, ma'am . . . what do you mean, we're doing it in twos?'

'That's why I wanted you back here. Your new partner's been waiting in my office for the last two hours or so.'

'Partner?' Heck tried not to sound too appalled by this.

'Yeah. Now there's a shocking concept, eh?'

The lift doors opened again, and Gemma strode onto the top floor, where many more bodies than usual were flowing back and forth, a lot of them tooled-up techies wandering in and out of the conference room.

'That's going to be the MIR,' she said, as they walked past it.

'Sledgehammer's a major enquiry then?'

'It's pretty major for us, yes.'

Still carrying the box, Heck followed Gemma down the corridor to her office.

'And I've got a new partner?' he said. 'As in someone from outside SCU?'

Gemma glanced back. 'She's just joined SCU, as it happens. She's been trying to come to us for ages. She dropped *your* name half a dozen times during her last application. Don't look so worried. You're not being asked to puppy-walk someone. DC Honeyford's been a fully operational detective for several years now. She's clocked up some excellent arrests.'

54

'DC Honeyford,' Heck said slowly.

'You ought to remember her. That time you were assigned to work down in Surrey, she was your right-hand man.'

'Yeah, she was.'

'She also has a rep for not taking any bullshit. Which also makes her the ideal choice to be paired up with you.'

'Ma'am, she's spiky as hell.'

'Like I say, ideal.' Gemma halted by her office door. 'Yet, funnily enough . . . when I interviewed her, she said that you were the main reason she wanted to leave Surrey and come to the National Crime Group. She said that when she worked with you on the Laurel and Hardy murders, she learned more than she has from all the rest of the detectives she's met put together.' Gemma registered the disbelieving expression on his face. 'I know, I kind of doubt that too. But we are where we are.' She pushed the door open. 'Come and say hello to her. Let's hope she's not died of old age waiting for you.'

Chapter 5

'DC Honeyford,' Gemma said, 'DS Heckenburg apologises for his tardiness. The fact that he doesn't look very apologetic is to be ignored. He doesn't do apologies often or convincingly. However, on this occasion, despite all appearances to the contrary, he means it.'

Gail Honeyford looked much the way Heck remembered when he'd last seen her, which was just over two years ago: she was still slim and attractive; a cool brunette, with hair down to her shoulders, dark hazel eyes and a pale, 'peaches and cream' complexion. She wore a powder-blue trouser suit and blue heeled boots and was sitting in the chair facing Gemma's desk. A raincoat was folded alongside her, and an empty coffee cup sat on the desktop.

'Yeah,' Heck said. 'Sorry I'm late, DC Honeyford.'

She replied with a polite nod.

Gemma indicated that Heck could dump the box of paperwork in a corner, and slid behind her desk, which was a complex operation in itself, given how little room there was in here. Unlike some senior officers, Gemma had never been given to displays of power. Though she was commander here at Staples Corner, head of the Serial Crimes Unit and second in authority at the National Crime Group only to the director, Joe Wullerton, himself, her office was a cramped, closet-like space, half of it filled with filing cabinets, the rest overhung with shelves groaning beneath the weight of packed files and dog-eared legal manuals.

'Right . . .' She selected a beige folder from her wire basket in-tray. 'Seeing as Operation Sledgehammer goes live at eight tomorrow morning, there isn't a great deal of time for us to discuss the niceties of what'll be expected of you as a Serial Crimes Unit detective.'

DC Honeyford, having realised that she was the one being addressed, sat up straight.

Gemma glanced at her. 'Except to say that if you needed to learn anything, you wouldn't be here. So, you're not on probation. You understand that?'

'Of course, ma'am,' the new recruit replied.

'There's a serious job needs doing, and in SCU we do it to the best of our abilities,' Gemma said. 'If any one of us fouls up, and that includes me, we're out. But it may even be worse than that.' She sat back, watching her new charge carefully, probing her with that penetrating blue-eyed gaze. 'In this department, we deal exclusively with violent psychopaths . . . that means we can't afford any errors. Lives, including our own, DC Honeyford, may depend on it.' She paused again. 'And . . . that's it. That's the whole of the introductory pep talk. Sorry if it wasn't what you were expecting, but we're all a bit short of time at present. You've got exactly half a day to get settled in. Because after tomorrow morning's briefing you'll all be expected to hit the road straight away in pursuit of the various actions that will have been allocated to you as part of Operation Sledgehammer.'

'I'm ready to go now, ma'am,' DC Honeyford said.

'Good. That means you can spend the rest of the day familiarising yourself with *this*.' Gemma pushed the beige folder across the desk. 'Consider that a welcome-to-your-new-job present. It's a perk of sorts . . . no one else will know what case they're being allocated until tomorrow morning.'

At last, Heck understood why they were being deployed in twos.

There were clearly several investigations that needed working on at the same time, most likely of historical significance rather than dating to the here and now. So that was Operation Sledgehammer: it sounded dramatic, as if it was something right up SCU's street, but in actual fact one of the most experienced and productive special investigations units in the British police service was being used to adjust the clean-up rates.

'And, Heck,' Gemma said, interrupting his thoughts, 'let's make this thing work.'

He nodded, trying not to look as half-hearted about it as he felt.

'OK . . . off you go.' She waggled them away with her fingers.

'Thank you, ma'am,' DC Honeyford said, standing and tucking the file under her arm.

Heck dawdled after she'd left the room, edging the door closed behind her.

When he spoke, it was quietly. 'Ma'am, I—'

She halted him with a raised palm. 'I don't want to hear it.'

'Look, there's something you may not know . . .'

'I said I don't want to hear it.'

She'd already opened her emails, her manicured fingers rattling on the keyboard.

'Gemma . . . *come on!*'

Two things you never did with Gemma Piper was raise your voice or lose your temper. Even though Heck felt that, on occasion, he might have earned the right, he hadn't intended it to slip out quite so abrasively. But rather to his surprise, her reaction was mild.

'Don't get *too* cocky, Sergeant.' Her voice remained level; she didn't even look up. 'You may find this thing more of a challenge than you think.'

'You don't know the half of it,' he muttered, leaving the room and half-blundering into Jack Reed outside.

'Sorry, Heck,' Reed said. 'My fault. Don't worry, I wasn't eavesdropping.'

Heck had never known such politeness in the police environment as he routinely heard from Reed, especially not from a supervisor to an underling. It surely had its origins in the Officers' Mess, though Heck had never enquired about the DI's background, and never would – as that would imply that he was interested in getting to know the guy.

'It's OK, sir,' Heck grunted. 'Nothing to hear anyway.'

'I've told you, mate . . . it's "Jack". I don't do formalities.'

'Yeah, no probs.'

Gail Honeyford was waiting a few yards along the corridor, picking through the folder's contents. He stumped towards her. Behind him, he heard Reed tap on Gemma's door.

'Busy!' she called out. 'Unless it's exceedingly important.'

'It's me, ma'am,' Reed replied. 'Can I come in?'

Heck was now too far away to hear her muffled response, but whatever it was, Reed went in.

'You don't look very pleased to see me,' Gail said, as they walked side by side down to the detectives' office.

'I'm not displeased.' Heck tried not to sound tetchy, though it was a struggle. The truth was that he rated Gail as a police officer. How could he not when he owed his life to her? But there were other issues here, which, frankly, he didn't think he could deal with at this moment. 'I'm just . . . surprised.'

'I gave you a heads-up that I was going to try and join SCU,' she said. 'Roughly around the same time you said you'd try to give me a leg-up. Just because I didn't hear anything else from you, that doesn't mean I didn't stick with my ambition.'

'In a way, I *did* give you a leg-up,' he said. 'You name-dropped me during your interview.'

'Yeah, funny that. When I reminded DSU Piper that I'd worked with you before and that we got on well together, she said something to the effect of: "Ordinarily, that would be a reason for me *not* to appoint you." What do you think she meant by that?'

'She plays games,' he grunted. 'Likes to keep us on our toes.'

'I hear they call her "the Lioness".'

'That's true.'

'Why?'

'Muck up this enquiry, and you'll find out.'

Gail nodded as she pondered this.

'Anyway,' he said. 'Why did she?'

'What do you mean?'

'She told you that "ordinarily" she wouldn't have appointed you. What changed her mind?'

'Oh . . . she also noted that aside from that one case you and me worked together, my career's been pretty straight-laced and that I've had some good results, all of them by the book. She added that she was certain the experience of this, plus the passage of time, would probably ensure that I've got over any bad habits I might have picked up from you.'

'Might have picked up from you, *Sergeant*,' he corrected her.

'Sorry, yes . . . *Sergeant*,' she agreed primly.

That was one bad habit she'd dispensed with, he noted.

The previous incarnation of Gail had bridled at the merest hint that she was under someone else's control, especially a male's. This was explainable by the tough time she'd had with some of the idiot men in her life, but it hadn't been likely to do her any good in the long run. At the end of the day, rank was rank.

They went into the detectives' office – or 'DO' as it was known – to find the place reorganised in terms of its furniture. Heck's own desk had been moved several feet from its south-facing window and turned around ninety degrees. Another desk, previously empty, had been drawn up to face it. It wasn't hugely inconvenient. All Heck's electricals were still plugged in and he could still reach his shelves and filing cabinet. But the fact that everything had been shifted around, without his even being consulted, was the last thing he needed on a day like today.

The bloke responsible was still in the middle of it.

Approaching his late fifties, DS Eric Fisher had outlived his usefulness to SCU as an outdoors man, and if his age hadn't been against him, his colossal girth could have done the job on its own. But as an analyst, intelligence officer and now the unit's official account manager for HOLMES 2 – the latest IT system used by UK police forces for the investigation of serious crime – Fisher was second to none. In case that wasn't quite enough in this new age of extreme cost-efficiency, Gemma also had him double-hatting as a kind of unofficial office manager – a role he was currently occupying comfortably, as he issued orders to DCs Quinnell, Rawlins, Cunliffe and Finnegan, who, with much clattering of tables and scraping of chair legs, were trying to pair up their own furniture.

'What's all this?' Heck demanded.

Fisher scratched his beard. 'We're working Sledgehammer in pairs. Haven't you heard?'

'Yeah, I heard.' Heck toed irritably at his desk. 'But, given the option, I might have wanted to do things slightly differently.'

'Fair enough.' Fisher pushed his glasses back up his sweat-greased nose. 'How many permutations of two desks do you want me to go through before you settle on one you like?'

'I'm sure this'll be all right,' Gail said, throwing her coat, bag and the Sledgehammer file onto the empty desk facing Heck's.

Fisher turned to Heck and arched his caterpillar-thick eyebrows.

'It'll do for the moment,' Heck grumbled. He cleared his throat and raised his voice. 'Everyone . . . listen up. Meet our newest recruit, DC Gail Honeyford.'

The rest of the men – and they were exclusively men at present – gathered, grinning, catching as much of an eyeful as they dared in the twenty-first century. A lot had changed in British policing, even during Gail's relatively short service, but boys would always be boys.

'DS Eric Fisher,' Heck said, sticking a thumb towards the big man.

'Please to meet you, love,' Fisher nodded genially, which belied his barbaric appearance.

'DC Gary Quinnell,' Heck said. 'He's our conscience.'

Quinnell nodded too. Gail nodded back.

Heck then went through the rest of them: Andy Rawlins, who was short, tubby, balding on top and possessed of a beard as scraggy as Eric Fisher's – he smiled shyly; Burt Cunliffe, who was squat and solid, with a grey buzz cut and a tan that indicated he'd recently been abroad for his holidays; and Charlie Finnegan, who was lean, with black, slicked hair and an odd foxy look about him.

'There are a few more of us, of course,' Heck said. 'Out on the job, scattered around the building. We have actually got a few other women on the plot. You've met Gemma. DI Ronni James is on leave. Up to last year, we had DC Shawna McCluskey . . .'

'Big shoes to fill there, girl,' Quinnell interrupted; he'd been a particularly close friend of Shawna's, even more so than Heck.

'Promoted?' Gail wondered.

'Shot,' Charlie Finnegan said matter-of-factly. 'And savagely beaten.'

Gail glanced at Heck. 'Fatality? Only I didn't hear anything . . .'

'No,' he said. 'But she went on a full medical. She's OK. The Federation looked after her.'

'Yep,' Finnegan said. 'There's always that consolation. If you catch a few bullets . . . the Federation will look after you.'

'There but for the grace of God go all of us,' Gail said, pointedly unfazed by his sneery smile.

'Sounding like my kind of girl already,' Quinnell guffawed, slapping her shoulder. 'Don't worry, though . . . I'm already spoken for.'

The others laughed and continued to straighten the new-look office. But when Gail went into the adjoining room to find the locker Eric Fisher had allocated her, Finnegan slid over.

'Lucky bastard,' he said to Heck. 'Don't know how you fucking do it.'

'You wouldn't want to work with Gail, Charlie,' Heck replied. 'She'd be too much of a distraction. You know how hard you have to focus just to get the basics right.'

'Aha,' Fisher interrupted, leafing through the Sledgehammer file Gail had left on her desk. 'So, you two are going after Creeley.'

'Don't know,' Heck replied. 'Haven't looked at it yet.'

'Eddie Creeley. He's a rough customer, I'll tell you.'

Heck seemed to remember hearing something about him. If recollection served, Eddie Creeley was an offender from the North-East suspected of armed robbery and murder.

'I don't know much about Sledgehammer yet,' he admitted.

'A new initiative,' Fisher explained. 'We've received a list of bad guys who've so far eluded arrest and, thanks to info provided by Interpol, are still believed to be in the UK. We're the ones who are charged with rounding them up.'

'Us and Cold Case?'

'Well . . . they're mostly older cases, so the Coldies are providing intel and back-up.'

Heck took the file and glanced through it himself. Immediately, he was struck by a mugshot of Eddie Creeley, who'd probably been somewhere in his early thirties when the pic was taken. He was an archetype: not a bruiser as such, but cold, cruel, with a lean, aquiline face, greased-back black hair, black sideburns and small, dark eyes. Just flicking through a few more documents, the huge extent and heinous nature of the crimes he was suspected of became clear. He was perhaps most well-known in connection with a violent £7 million armed robbery at a security company in Newark-on-Trent, during which he'd taken two employees hostage, handcuffed them and injected them with drain cleaner to disable them – one later dying and the other suffering permanent brain damage. But more recently for a home invasion, wherein he took two civilian hostages; the female occupant died after she too was injected with a toxic substance, while her husband, though he survived, was shot twice.

'Everyone's drawn cards of a similarly nasty ilk,' Fisher commented. 'There are no small-time offenders on the Sledgehammer list.'

'Two of us for each one,' Heck mused. 'How much actual support are we going to get?'

Fisher shrugged. 'As many PSOs as you can scrounge out of whichever force area you end up working in. But that'll be down to you.'

Heck glanced at him. 'For real?'

'Yeah. Times are hard all over, pal. The word is the UK can't afford coppers any more.'

They turned and saw that Gail had reappeared and had been listening to the conversation.

'No pressure then,' she said.

Chapter 6

It always struck Nan as odd that August, which so many folk thought of as the height of summer, was actually more like its end. OK, the schools were closed and people went away, and it was generally the warmest, driest month in the calendar, but the hours of daylight were noticeably shorter than they were in June, when the official midsummer fell.

It particularly took her by surprise that evening, when she opted to walk home from the Spar, having just worked the back shift, and pick up a fish-and-chip tea on the way. It was only half past eight when she left the building by the side door, but already it was going dark. Unnerved, she followed the side passage to the shop's small forecourt, where she encountered another problem: that irritating bunch of school-age hooligans who always hung out here in the evenings. Yes, they were only kids, and Nan was forty-eight, but she wasn't a particularly tall or powerfully built woman, and the age gap counted for so little these days. During her own childhood, adults had ruled the roost, way more than was even remotely reasonable. But it still felt wrong that she should be frightened of these youngsters, even if it was inevitable given their rat-like faces and their habit of using

obscene words every other sentence with no fear of consequence.

The profanity didn't bother her, if she was honest. Not
after the youthful home life *she'd* led. And anyway, you
couldn't really blame them for that when it was so routine.
Every new movie was full of it; comedians on TV used it to
get laughs instead of actually being funny. No, it wasn't the
bad language that she hated; it was the name-calling.

'Oy, Toothless Mary!' one of them shouted as she walked
away, huddled inside her anorak, clutching her handbag
tightly.

Cackles of heartless laughter sounded from the rest of
them.

She'd hoped that with it being dusk, they wouldn't have
noticed her. No such luck.

'Oy, Toothless!' one of them called again, as she crossed
the road towards the chippie.

Nan was determined not to cry, reminding herself that
this was entirely her own fault. Last February, it had been.
It was wet, miserable, bitterly cold – and she'd had the sniffles. How ridiculous of her, though, to hit a sneezing fit just
after she'd finished work. How even more ridiculous that
she hadn't fixed her dentures properly, four of them shooting
out of her mouth and scattering across the pavement the
very second she'd entered the forecourt.

They would never let her forget it.

No, she wasn't going to cry. But she wasn't sticking around
either. Through the smeary rectangle of the chip shop window,
she saw there was nobody waiting at the counter. On one
hand, that might mean that Nan would get served quickly,
but on the other it might mean that, at this time of evening,
nearly everything had gone. If that was the case, they might
have to fry her a new piece of cod, and that could take ten
minutes. There'd be nothing to stop one of those callous

young brutes traipsing across the road to amuse himself even more at her expense. It was better just to vacate the district, she decided. She'd have some bread and butter when she got home.

As it was now mid-evening, and full darkness was falling, she wouldn't normally have taken the wooded footpath known locally as the Strode, which led between the small shopping centre where she worked and her home housing estate. In truth, it sounded a bit melodramatic to call it a 'wooded footpath'. That gave the impression of a track in a forest, but it was nothing like that really; more like two hundred yards of beaten grit with a narrow belt of trees separating it from the council playing fields on the right and a wall of shrubbery on the left, with privately owned houses beyond that. Not that this made much difference in the dark, because the Strode was only served by two streetlamps, one at either end, which didn't do much to light it. As such, Nan wasn't always keen to use it even during the day. But on this occasion, she didn't think twice. She just wanted to get home, and this was the quickest route.

She pressed hurriedly on down the path. The tree trunks on her right were stanchions in deep shadow, the playing fields already invisible. The dull glow of house lamps filtering from behind drawn curtains only minimally penetrated the bulwark of vegetation on her left.

Though the end of the Strode was still a good hundred yards distant, Nan told herself that there was nothing to be frightened of. But she was undeniably alone – all she could hear was her own breathing and the steady crunch of her feet on the grit. Nervously, she peeked backward over her shoulder.

There was a figure about sixty yards to her rear.

Silhouetted against the distant glow of the streetlight, it was no more than a black, hunched outline, walking not running.

She had to look again, just to be sure.

Yes, it was only walking – though at faster-than-average speed.

Nan increased her own pace. Her breath came short and quick.

It occurred to her, somewhat belatedly, that it might be a police officer. There'd been a few of them around recently. But she couldn't see any reason why this would be a copper. Coppers usually did one of two things: they watched from a place of concealment, or they came and knocked on your door.

They didn't do *this*: follow you round at night, trying to frighten you.

She glanced over her shoulder again, walking even faster, wishing she had longer legs. Even without running, this guy might catch up before she reached the main road. However, he wasn't significantly closer. She faced forward again and saw that she only had another fifty yards to go. Unless he started running at the last minute, she ought to make it – and he surely wasn't going to do that, otherwise he'd already have done it. As she approached the end of the pathway, she looked back one more time. He was still forty yards off and still no more than a silhouette.

With a sense of relief, she emerged onto the pavement, into the yellow radiance of the streetlights. She made a sharp right and continued on her way.

Just ahead, on the other side of Orchard Park Road, there was another cut-through, 'the Ginnel' as they knew this one, which passed between the rear fences of houses before opening onto her estate. In daylight hours, it was an easy and safe shortcut home. But she certainly wasn't chancing it now; she would stay on the main road.

There wasn't a great deal of traffic about. But it didn't matter. Nothing would happen to her while there were occasional cars flitting by. She felt certain of that. You heard some bad stories, of course. If she was honest, this wasn't the best part of town to live in. But it was only at the godforsaken times of night when people Nan knew had been mugged.

Assuming that was what this was.

She'd almost given up on the idea that it could be one of those stupid kids from the Spar. If it was, he'd come an awful long way simply to laugh at her again.

She glanced back, now seeing no one on either side of the road. A break occurred in the intermittent traffic, so she crossed over. The entrance to the Ginnel was about ten or twenty yards behind her, but thirty yards beyond that, the mouth to the Strode stood in the shadow of several sycamore trees. The man could be waiting there, watching her, and she wouldn't know it. It was difficult to see where else he could have gone. Even if he hadn't been following her, shouldn't he be out here on the main road somewhere? She put the question from her mind. There was no point puzzling over something when you didn't have all the facts. He could live close by and have already gone indoors for all Nan knew.

She continued on, her breathing coming easier as she turned down a side street and entered the estate. She was almost home now. Circling a block of council maisonettes, she cut across an open green space, beyond which lay the subway – another poor choice at night, but there was no real option. After that, she'd be at Hellington Court, the horseshoe-shaped apartment house on whose first floor she lived. But then she caught movement in her peripheral vision, at the bottom end of the Ginnel in fact.

Nan hadn't taken the shortcut. But he had.

Undoubtedly, it was the same figure, though now much closer; hands tucked into his front pockets, a hood pulled down over a lowered head as though he was walking through driving rain – or trying to keep his face concealed from CCTV cameras.

'My God,' she whimpered, her heart hammering her stick-thin ribs as she broke into a run.

It was a perilous course. The green was strewn with bricks and bottles, any one of which could turn her ankle, but she stumbled on blindly, risking another glance backward. He too was on the green, head still bowed. Not running, but walking much faster, as if he couldn't allow her to get too far ahead.

'Oh my . . . my God,' Nan gibbered.

Fear applied wings to her heels. She sped on, tripping only once, but though she tottered and stumbled, she managed to right herself before falling.

Just ahead, the steps led down into the subway. She took them without hesitation.

Another quick glance showed that he was about twenty yards to her rear.

At the bottom of the steps, she dashed up the concrete passage. Of the thirty-odd lights installed along its damp ceiling, only a few worked, filling the tunnel with gloom.

With a series of echoing thumps, feet descended the steps behind her. Gasping with terror, Nan staggered on. The end of the passage was clearly visible thanks to the streetlights beyond it, but it was still some forty yards ahead. Before that stood the long-abandoned relic of a pram, nothing now but corroded framework and shreds of upholstery. She thought about grabbing it and flinging it behind her to create an obstacle. But a voice told her to act her age, because that only worked in films.

She looked back again. Incredibly, he was still walking, not running; even more incredibly, he was much closer. She could make out the details of his clothing: grey tracksuit pants; a black hoodie top with some faded insignia on the front.

With a shriek, she ran into the pram.

How ridiculous, she thought, as she seesawed over the top of it, landing hard on the wet, grimy floor. She'd dismissed the idea of using the object against her enemy because it probably wouldn't have worked and then had fallen foul of it herself.

A fastener snapped open and the contents of her handbag skittered out, but Nan didn't wait to regather them. She jumped to her feet, which was some achievement considering that she'd winded herself, grazed both her hands and hurt her left hip – the latter stung abominably where a piece of jagged metal had torn through her clothes and punctured the flesh – and lurched on, aware that he was less than ten yards behind her. When she got to the steps, she hammered up them, expecting to hear an explosion of footfalls as he finally started running.

But that didn't happen.

Was it possible, was it even vaguely conceivable, that he was innocent, just an ordinary guy on his way home after a couple of pints in the pub?

No. How bloody ludicrous are you, woman!

An ordinary man would most likely have shouted after her when she fell over the pram, to enquire if she was OK.

She reached the top of the steps, throat raw with panting. The edifice of Hellington Court loomed on her right, and she scuttled towards it. The first entrance, the one directly facing her, was no longer used by residents; it led into a series of ground-floor utility rooms which were now seen as places to dump rubbish in. Nan took that route anyway, because just entering her own building felt as if it would offer some modicum of protection. As an occupant, she ought to know her way around in there better than he did.

But, of course, it wasn't that easy.

In the first room, she tripped on a pile of rusty old bicycles, and when she fell on top of them, sharp prongs snagged and cut her again. In the next room, which she entered via an arched brick tunnel that was so dark she had to feel her way, she bounced between abandoned fridges and stacks of mouldy furniture. There was no point looking back to check on his progress now, because he could be right behind her and she wouldn't even see him.

In the third room, Nan glimpsed what looked like a row of upright bars with light shining down behind them from above. The bars were accessible through another brick passage, but when she got there, they ran floor to ceiling and left to right, seemingly closing off this entire section of the building. The light spilled down an interior set of fire-escape stairs, but there was no way through to them.

From behind – in either the first or second room – there was a *clunk* of metal.

Frantic, she worked her way along the bars, spying a gate, a steel frame filled with mesh and fitted with what looked like a garden latch – but when she got to it, it was fastened with a padlock. Nan whined aloud, her torn, sweaty hands smearing blood as she yanked futilely on it. From some non-too-distant place, she heard a breaking and splintering of wood.

That mouldy old furniture.

With vision glazed by tears of horror, she fumbled on along the bars. There had to be another way out of here; there simply had to. But this faint hope collapsed as the narrow passage she was following terminated at a bare brick wall.

Nan gazed at it, rocking on aching feet. She went dizzy. The world tilted, and she had to grapple with the bars to support herself. And by a miracle, the one she grabbed dislodged. It wasn't broken but had come loose from its concrete base. Breathless, she bent and twisted it until she'd created enough space to get past.

Unsure whether it was her imagination that a dark-clad figure advanced along the row of bars towards her – she never even looked to check – she slid her thin body through and ran to the foot of the metal staircase, almost slipping on a tiled floor covered by green scum, before haring up it. At the top, there was a concrete landing she didn't recognise. Wheezing, drenched with sweat under her ragged, blood-stained clothes, she pivoted in a bewildered circle. A single bulb shed light up here, showing a couple of metal doors leading off in different directions. Nan was perplexed as to which way she should go. But when she heard a heavy tread ascending the stairway, it jolted her forward, propelling her to the nearest door.

On the other side of that, she ran down a corridor with entrances to flats on either side. At the end, she entered another similar corridor, but now she knew where she was.

A few seconds later, she was out on the balcony over-looking the central court.

Her own door, No. 26, was only four along from here.

As she tottered towards it, she fumbled in her handbag for her keys.

Only to find that the bag was empty.

The reality of this only washed over Nan as she came to a halt in front of her flat door, which stood huge and solid and impenetrable.

'No,' she moaned. '*Nooo* . . .'

She'd been so frightened down in the subway that when she'd fallen over the pram, she'd assumed all she'd dropped was loose change, lipstick, reading glasses – not her house key!

A figure rounded the corner onto the balcony and proceeded towards her.

Nan would never know where it came from: a memory, dredged from nowhere, that before she'd left the Spar that evening, she'd dropped her key from her handbag, and had only spotted it at the last minute, bending down, scooping it up – *and putting it in her anorak pocket*. With robotic speed and smoothness, all the time aware of that dark shape encroaching from the left, she delved into the pocket, pulled out the key, and jammed it into the lock.

She turned it, and the mechanism disengaged.

Nan tottered inside, banged the door closed behind her, and rammed the bolts home.

Twenty minutes later, when Nan found the courage to unlock the bathroom and re-emerge into her narrow hall, she heard nothing.

But then she wasn't sure what she'd expected to hear.

Someone trying the front door, or someone simply idling there, muttering to themselves?

Even if this person – whoever it was – *had* been following her, none of that seemed likely. One thing you had to say about these old run-down blocks of flats, they were fairly secure. The units weren't easy to force entry to, and with everyone living so close to each other, if someone tried, they'd cause such a racket that the police would inevitably be called.

Even so, it took Nan another five minutes, still damp under her clothes, to actually approach that front door. And she only did so armed with a carving knife she'd brought from the kitchen. Even then, she was tentative. Half a foot short, she waited, listening hard – but still there was no sound.

Neck and shoulders tense, breath tightening in her narrow bird-chest, she considered leaning forward to the spyhole. She'd seen so many horror films where this happened and immediately an ice pick was driven through it from the other side, or a bullet fired into the eye of the person peeking. She didn't think that was actually possible – how would the madman know when you were looking, and when you weren't? But it was still a horrific prospect. When she finally steeled herself to do it, the fisheye lens gave its usual restricted, distorted view of the balcony, but showed nobody standing near the door. Despite this, it was another whole minute before she could sum up the extra courage to withdraw bolts and turn the main lock.

She kept the safety chain on, of course, the door opening to four inches maximum.

Now she could see much more of the balcony, and still no one was there. Night sounds reached her: the hum of distant traffic, someone laughing in one of the flats above. Encouraged, Nan loosened the chain, opened the door properly, and with knife levelled like a bayonet, ventured one step outside – just enough so that she could look both right and left.

The balcony trailed harmlessly away in both directions. There was no one there, the only movement a scrap of wastepaper drifting on the summer breeze.

Chapter 7

The life of Eddie Creeley was pretty much a blueprint for the development of a violent criminal. Born into poverty in the Hessle Road district of Hull in 1979, his mother died from a stroke when he was three years old, leaving him in the care of his older sister by ten years and his unemployed ex-trawlerman father, who sought to fill the void in his life with alcohol, and periodically took time off from this to beat his children black and blue.

On one occasion, or so the stories told, young Eddie was battered so savagely by his raging parent that he 'didn't know where he was' for nearly two days.

By the early 1990s, perhaps inevitably, the youngster had become a regular juvenile offender, with form for shoplifting, car theft, burglary and assault. In 1993, he finally dealt with his father, retaliating to yet another unprovoked backhander by breaking a bottle over the old man's head and dumping his unconscious body in the litter-strewn alley out back, where a freezing rainstorm was almost the death of him. After this incident, there were no further reports of the Creeleys' father attacking either of his children, though it was noted that he himself often sported black eyes, split lips and missing teeth.

Throughout this period, Eddie Creeley served regular time in juvenile detention, where he became well-known for his violent and troublesome behaviour. One thing he didn't like were authority figures, though he could extend his brutality to any person at any time. In 1997, for example, he beat his pregnant girlfriend, Gillian, so severely that he caused her to miscarry. On this occasion, he was sent to adult prison, where he was involved in frequent altercations with staff and fellow inmates. Only five months into his four-year stretch, in response to a sexual advance, he ambushed a much older fellow prisoner and smashed his legs with an iron bar. This brought him to the attention of Newcastle gangster, Denny Capstick. Impressed by Creeley's viciousness, Capstick took him on as muscle, and he spent the next few years, both inside jail and out, attacking and terrorising the rivals of Capstick's firm and even, or so the rumours held, carrying out several murders on their behalf.

Capstick cut him loose in 2001, when he robbed a minimarket in Sunderland and unnecessarily brutalised a female cashier. Sentenced to ten years, it looked as if Creeley was finally out of circulation, but in the end he only served seven, coming out in 2008 and returning to his native Humberside, where he cheerfully recommenced his criminal career. Using his extensive underworld contacts, he put together a ruthless team, and over the next few years they carried out several raids on banks and post offices, all of which were eye-catching for their levels of violence, with shots fired, and bats and pickaxe handles used on staff, customers and security personnel alike.

In 2010, he hit the big time when, with high-level underworld backing, he pulled off a massive score. In the middle of the night, he and six associates infiltrated a private security firm's cash-handling depot at Newark-on-Trent in the East Midlands by taking hostage the depot manager and his wife and children. On successfully entering the depot, four guards and three more members of staff were handcuffed and locked into one of the vault's cages while the actual blag, which lasted forty minutes, took place. Some £7 million in banknotes was stolen, and the thieves got clean away. It would perhaps have gone down as one of Britain's most audacious and cleverly planned robberies, had Creeley's mistreatment of two security guards not left a very sour taste even in the mouths of his underworld backers. The two guards, both ex-military, proved difficult captives, and so to punish and further incapacitate them, Creeley injected them with drain cleaner; one died as a result, while the other was subject to fits and blackouts for the rest of his life.

Disowned by many associates after this, Creeley went to ground for four years, only to re-emerge in 2014, when he and a young accomplice broke into the suburban home of a Lincolnshire bank manager called Brian Kelso. The bank manager was tied up and subjected to hours of fearsome threats, while his wife, Justine, was beaten and repeatedly indecently assaulted. The following morning, the haggard and terrified manager went to work early, and stole £200,000 in cash. He handed it over to Creeley at an agreed rendezvous point and was then shot twice in the chest. He survived by a miracle, recovering later in hospital, but his wife, still at the family home, hadn't been so lucky. Police officers found her dead; she had been injected with battery acid.

The horrifying and sensational nature of these crimes galvanised the various police forces in the East Midlands into throwing all their resources at the case, and in due course, several men were arrested and charged for the depot robbery, though Creeley wasn't among them. Yet again, he'd gone on the run, but it wasn't easy for him. Increasingly seen as a dangerous psychopath, fewer and fewer of his former compatriots wanted to work with him.

It was probably no surprise that sometime in 2015, he dropped out of sight – as in quite literally vanished, never to be seen again even by those who were close to him.

Gail Honeyford breathed out long and slow as she laid the case papers down on the pub table.

'Well . . . that's a life well lived.'

Heck, at the other side of the table, wiped froth from his lip. The Duke of Albion affected the look of an old-fashioned gin palace, but much of that was window-dressing. In truth, it was another large and typically impersonal inner-London pub, but it was close to Staples Corner, so it served. This being a Monday night and now after ten o'clock, it wasn't especially busy, though there were a few punters dotted about its spacious interior.

'I wonder where you actually get off causing so much damage to everyone around you,' Gail said. 'No wonder even his fellow hoodlums hate him.'

'He's obviously got some buddies left . . . to have disappeared so effectively,' Heck said.

'Are we sure he's even in the country?' she wondered.

He shrugged. 'If Interpol have had no leads on him, and Europol have had nothing . . .'

'I suppose we should expect a maniac like this to leave some kind of ripple. Unless he's died, of course.'

'No death of anyone even closely resembling Eddie Creeley has been reported, but that's something we may need to look into. Need to cover all bases, as they say.'

'Looks like we've got a lot of legwork ahead of us.'

'You wanted to be where the action was.' He half-smiled. 'You couldn't have arrived at a better time.'

She nodded thoughtfully.

'I'm sorry if I wasn't very welcoming earlier on,' he said.

She waved it away. 'I did come at you a bit out of the blue.'

He watched her, genuinely puzzled by the change in her personality since they'd last met. 'Gail, I don't know what it is, but you seem more . . .'

'Grown-up?'

'Not necessarily the words I'd have used.'

'When we worked together in Surrey, Heck, I took issue with the fact that I had a murder enquiry, my very first, which I thought I was on top of . . . and then you came in, kind of from nowhere, and were given seniority over me.'

'It's understandable you were peeved about that.'

'But I was wrong.' She shook her head. 'I'd been listening too much to people like Ron Pavey. Who, as you know, was a dickhead of the first order. Surrey's own version of Charlie Finnegan.'

Heck sniggered. 'Good . . . you've already got Charlie's number.'

'Ron always said that special squads like SCU, and even National Crime Group itself, were a complete waste of space. A bunch of flash gits hogging all the resources and getting all the headlines but doing police work in name only. But that was typical of him. Total crap from a total gobshite.'

Heck nodded. He'd known Pavey as a divisional DS down in Surrey, and as Gail's ex-boyfriend, which status he'd only reluctantly relinquished after giving her hell for several years. Of course, being a total gobshite was only one of Pavey's lesser vices. The more Heck had got to know the guy, the more irritated he'd been by his swaggering style and casual, brutal bullying – so much so that he'd stood and applauded when Gail herself had arrested Pavey and charged him with several career-ending offences. It had been an enormously brave move by the young policewoman, one which, now that Heck recollected it, filled him with a surprising amount of affection for her. There were lots of ingredients in the make-up of an effective police officer, and though it wasn't fashionable to discuss it in the modern era, raw courage was still one of the most important (and one of the rarest).

'Course, I didn't know any of that at the time,' she said. 'When you first arrived, I was rude and prickly, and probably came over as very arrogant.'

'Well . . . it's big of you to admit that.' Heck was so unused to people apologising to him that it made him feel awkward. 'But we should remember that *my* style is not to everyone's taste, either. You heard what Gemma had to say about me. On occasion, I like to cut corners.'

'Yeah, but it works.'

'Not always.' He felt a pang of unease. It was amazing how pertinent Gemma's warning words of earlier that day now seemed. 'Perhaps, while we're working on Sledgehammer together, it should be more a case of do as I say, not do as I do.'

Gail laughed. 'If only I'd got that on tape. I could have you over a barrel for the rest of your career.'

'Do you think anyone'd be surprised to hear it?'

'Possibly not.' She finished her drink. 'But it's something I'm still going to hold you to over the next few weeks. Anyway . . .' She checked inside her handbag. 'We're in at the crack tomorrow, so I'm off back to Cricklewood for an early night.'

'Cricklewood?' Heck was surprised. 'You've got digs up here?'

'Course. What else was I supposed to do . . . commute from Guildford every day? You know what the Orbital's like.

It'd be four hours here, four hours back. Anyway, Cricklewood's not so bad.'

'You've bought a flat, or something?' he asked.

'Rented one. I haven't sold up in Surrey just yet.'

Heck nodded, relieved. That decision had shown prudence and suggested that this wasn't totally a knee-jerk thing.

'Anyway, I've got to go.' She stood up. 'I'll be in tomorrow morning.'

'Briefing starts at eight.'

'I know, don't worry.' She slung her bag over her shoulder, tucked the Eddie Creeley paperwork under her arm and pushed her chair backward.

'Shall I take that?' Heck said. 'Line manager, and all that.'

'Oh, sorry . . . yeah.' She smiled and handed the file back.

Only when she'd left did Heck allow himself a smile, though it was tinged with concern.

Gail was clearly still Gail; she'd evidently got on top of her inferiority complex, but a hint of the old single-mindedness remained. She'd been in SCU less than a day and was already trying to make the running on their first case. On one hand that was good – she would need to be feisty in this world; Gemma was the perfect example of that. But a couple of questions still nagged at him. Firstly, how comfortably could she make the switch? Working CID in Surrey's green and pleasant land was likely to be a very different experience from the Serial Crimes Unit, where they dealt exclusively with the worst of the worst. And secondly, did he really want to be the man in charge if it started proving problematic?

Heck was looking forward to going after Eddie Creeley. He was in no doubt that he would find and collar the murderous bastard, but only by doing it *his* way rather than the approved way. Gemma would tolerate that to a degree; if she didn't, she'd never have accorded him his roving commission. Having Gail Honeyford along for that ride would be interesting. He just hoped that she was up to handling life at the sharp end.

If she had trouble coping when they were chasing this baddest of bad boys, that would be a level of complexity he really didn't need.

Chapter 8

Nan's eyes sprang open in a face rigid as wax and beaded with sweat.

She didn't think she'd ever seen her bedroom as dark as it was at this moment. Normally, yellowish streetlighting suffused through the curtain on the single small window, dappling the bare wall opposite with curious shapes. But tonight, there was nothing. Utter blackness. A void. And why was the room so deathly cold? Wasn't this supposed to be summer?

She was unable to move as she lay there, rucked in damp, tangled sheets. Couldn't budge so much as a muscle. Good God, was she paralysed? Had she become ill during the night, had a stroke or something? Dear Lord . . .

And then she heard it.

The voice. From the darkness alongside her.

'Sorry, missus,' it whispered. 'I don't like to wake you when you're having your beauty sleep and all. But you know how things are. Sometimes a man can't wait.'

Nan couldn't answer because she couldn't speak. Couldn't even utter a whimper.

'That's why I followed you home,' he explained. 'Had no choice.'

She tried to roll her eyes sideways, to visualise him. His voice was so close to her ear, his breath so rank – a mixture of onions and ketchup and something else too, a faint odour of rot – that he had to be kneeling right alongside her.

'No choice at all,' he said again. 'When the mood's on me, like. When the rest of the lads told me . . . well, that you've got a soft mouth.' He sniggered, a snorting pig-like sound. 'No teeth, they said. Nothing to chomp or chew me . . . you getting my drift?'

To her abject horror, Nan still couldn't react.

'I'll be honest,' he said. 'I couldn't think of anything more exciting. Getting a blowjob off Toothless Mary. I'd have asked you nicely, like . . . if you'd let me catch up with you. But you kept running and squawking . . . you know, like some typical fucking idiot lass who doesn't know what side her bread's buttered on. But it's all right . . . I know you're not like that really. I know you'll co-operate . . .'

She sensed rather than saw him rise to full height next to her, and then felt the weight of him across her chest as he straddled her and knelt there. With a slow, metallic slither, his zipper was drawn down.

'Won't you?' he chuckled.

Nan screeched as she leapt from the bed, arcing though the air, landing knees-first, then slamming the thickly plastered palms of her hands on the carpet.

She didn't know which was the more painful, the smarting of recent flesh wounds, or the agonising thumping of her heart. She looked up, eyes goggling, mouth drooling, sweat dabbling her brow. What seemed like an age passed before her tear-glazed eyes were able to focus on the neon numerals of the clock on the dresser. It read: 5:28 a.m.

It was still early. In winter, it would feel like the middle of the night. But this was summer, and dawn light penetrated the curtains, revealing the bedroom's meagre furnishings:

Nan's mirror, her wardrobe, the chair with her anorak draped over the back, two library books on an otherwise empty shelf.

But nothing else.

No hooded figure skulking in a corner or crouching to keep low.

A dream, then. Nothing but a dream. But good Lord . . . a dream from Hell, if ever there was such a thing!

She rose shakily to her feet, hands still smarting. A tugging at her side revealed that part of her nightie had adhered to her left hip, probably where it had caught on the Elastoplast she'd applied to the gouge wound from the old pram.

Nan had taken a long shower before coming to bed. She'd paid particular attention to that gash on her hip, because of the dirt and germs. But now she felt as if she needed another one. She brushed rat-tails of hair from her eyes as she turned to look at her bed. It was a foul nest, the sheets stained and messy. The last thing she wanted to do was climb back in there. Not, in truth, that sleep was a viable option. Not now.

It might only be half-past five, but she switched the bedroom light on and inserted her feet into her slippers. She really had to do something about her 'coming home from work' arrangements, she thought, as she opened the bedroom door. She couldn't afford a taxi home every day, though even if she could, she'd still have to go out to the front of the shop to get it, which would defeat the object. Alternatively, perhaps she could arrange to work ordinary day shifts from now on. Though that wouldn't be easy, because all the other ladies employed at the Spar were the same: they didn't like walking home late either.

Nan crossed the hall to the kitchen, to make herself a cup of tea, when she spotted something lying at the foot of the front door. Something had been pushed through the letter box.

Her breath shortened again, her chest began to tighten. She took a couple of steps forward.

The dull light from her bedroom showed a relatively small object, two or three inches long, narrow, bright green. From this distance, it resembled a cigarette lighter.

'Good . . . good God!' she stammered.

Had someone put petrol through, and then had they tried to light it? It was beyond belief, but you heard about horrific things like that happening.

She blundered forward, heart trip-hammering. But as she approached, she realised that it wasn't a cigarette lighter. Nothing so sinister, in fact. She ventured all the way up to it, and there was no mistake.

A pen drive lay on her welcome mat.

Nan wasn't the kind of person one might automatically expect to be electronically proficient. 'Dim' was one term she'd heard people using for her. She'd been regarded as a 'dunce' at school. But in fact, in adult life, Nan had become familiar with computers, the internet and such because she'd needed to while she was working at the Spar. She'd even bought herself a second-hand laptop in order to practise at home. And though she wasn't an expert yet, she certainly knew what she was doing.

She'd been so momentarily petrified by the thought of petrol that now she mainly felt relief, but she was mystified too. Why would someone stick something like this through your letter box in the middle of the night? If it was someone well-intentioned, wouldn't they have attached a note? Perhaps not if it was a friend playing some elaborate but harmless joke – but Nan wasn't friendly enough with anyone for that to be a possibility.

As she took her laptop from the shelf in the living room, it occurred to her that the pen drive might contain a virus. But she had nothing on her computer that she would miss if it was lost. She sat on the couch, set the laptop on her knees, opened it and switched it on. When it came to life, she inserted the pen drive, which immediately appeared as a smiley face icon on her desktop. When she touched it with her cursor, it opened, and she saw that it contained a single file: an MPEG, which someone had entitled: *Greetings – from the Devil's Messenger.*

Even more mystified, she clicked on it.

A window opened, and a black-and-white video commenced playing. Nan watched it for twenty seconds or so, slack-jawed.

Before she began to scream.

Chapter 9

Setting off at around six from his Fulham flat, Heck made it to Staples Corner before seven, hoping to get some breakfast in the canteen, only to find even at this ungodly hour that it was busier than usual.

Lots of people appeared to have set off early to avoid being late for the briefing. Not just from SCU, but from the Cold Case team as well, while Gemma and her joint SIO, Gwen Straker, had secured the attachment of extra personnel, both police and admin, to do the legwork and provide office back-up. This meant that the queue to the service counter stretched halfway around the room.

Disgruntled, Heck went to the vending machine instead, to get himself a coffee-to-go. While he waited for his Styrofoam cup to fill, he glanced left – and saw Gemma in the far corner, facing Jack Reed across a tabletop, conversing with him in intent but friendly fashion. The body language alone was fascinating. The twosome cradled a cuppa each and leaned towards one another – not exactly the way lovers do, though it would be easy to picture Reed reaching out an affectionate hand and brushing aside a stray lock of Gemma's flaxen hair.

Heck was more than surprised. Behaviour like this, not just in full view of her own team but of the Cold Case officers too, who'd be arriving here under the impression that their new joint boss was a hard-ass of legendary proportions, underlined the sea change in Gemma since Reed had come on board. She would never normally have been this lax in her manner. Quite clearly, other things were now on her mind.

Other things that were making her smile.

'You'll not win her favour by glaring at her in public,' a voice behind him said.

Heck spun around and found Detective Chief Superintendent Gwen Straker waiting her turn at the vending machine.

'Oh, ma'am . . .' he stuttered. 'Sorry . . . I'm done here.'

He stepped aside, and she moved forward.

'I wasn't glaring,' he said. 'I'm, erm . . . I'm actually waiting for the new DC I'm working with. Wanted a quick chat before the briefing.'

'Why don't you go and find us a table, Mark,' she said.

'Thing is, ma'am . . . I was going back to the office. Wanted to get some stuff sorted.'

'Couple of minutes won't hurt. Go and find us a table.'

This was easier said than done, so the first time a couple of seats facing each other became free, Heck pounced on them. When Gwen arrived, she sat down in neat, non-fussy fashion. Not atypically, she'd got herself a herbal tea rather than the milky, sugary coffee that Heck preferred.

One of the first black female detectives in the Met to actually make rank, Gwen was now in her mid-fifties. She wasn't especially tall, around five-seven, and the little weight she'd put on over the years gave her a buxom-to-heavy build. But otherwise, age had been kind to her; she still possessed thick, shoulder-length hair, and, unmarked by wrinkles, boasted soft, pretty features. Back during her days as Heck and Gemma's divisional DI at Bethnal Green, Gwen had favoured street casuals: denims, sweatshirts, leather jackets and the like, earning her the soubriquet 'Foxy Brown', after the gorgeous, hard-hitting heroine of the 1970s blaxploitation movie. But today, in reflection of her new, high-powered status, she wore a charcoal-black skirt suit, which fitted her snugly, though such a severe look didn't quite match her personality, which was famously warm, at times almost maternal.

Gwen sipped her brew, before grimacing.

'Ma'am, like I said, I have some stuff—'

'So, you've been getting reacquainted with Gail Honeyford?'

Heck was surprised. 'You know her?'

Gwen sipped her tea again, slowly but surely finding it tolerable. 'You worked with her once, I believe?'

'Yeah.'

'And it went well?'

'We got a result.'

Gwen pursed her lips and nodded. 'Sounds ideal . . . you and her, I mean.'

'It's hardly ideal.' He'd blurted that out without thinking; immediately regretting it. He ought to have learned from experience that Gwen Straker never missed anything.

She arched an eyebrow, intrigued.

Heck chewed his bottom lip. His and Gwen's previous relationship had been a difficult one to gauge, even at the time. While she was his DI, Gwen had rebuked him whenever necessary – sometimes spectacularly – but she was an old-stager herself. So long in the tooth that when she'd first entered the police, rules and regulations were mainly regarded as guidelines. For that reason alone, while she hadn't always approved of some of Heck's antics, she'd tacitly tolerated them if there was no serious fallout. Stranger than that, though, had been her attitude to his relatively short-lived romance with Gemma. Whereas most gaffers would have wanted the two officers concerned to work in different outfits so that they couldn't distract each other, Gwen had seemed to enjoy it; like a fond parent pleased to finally see two of her wayward children get fixed up.

Heck and Gemma *had* been her protégés, of course. Bethnal Green had been both their debut CID postings, and Gwen their first ever plain-clothes supervisor. Perhaps it was no surprise that, way back then, Heck had come to trust her to the point where he'd seek advice from her, even on personal matters, and would feel particularly lousy if he ever did anything that seriously disappointed her. It was probably as much the presence of Gwen Straker, right here in the canteen, as it was the sight of Gemma fawning over that square-jawed, blue-eyed Henry Cavill lookalike, Reed, that reminded him why a working partnership with Gail Honeyford might prove to be more awkward than he'd prefer.

'Look, ma'am,' he said, 'Gail's a great girl, and an even better detective. Spirited, tenacious. Not perfect, of course. When I first met her, she was all attitude and not enough nous. But that seems to have changed. I'm strongly hopeful she's not going to go at this case like a bull at a gate . . .'

'Well, no,' Gwen agreed. 'Two of you taking that approach would never work.'

'Listen . . . if you must know,' he lowered his voice, 'last time, we . . . as in me and Gail . . . I've unfortunately neglected to mention this to anyone, but we had a *thing*.'

'I see.' Gwen looked thoughtful. 'As in a real thing? Or as in you just ended up in bed together.'

'Well, the latter.' He reddened. 'We'd had a tough day. Got into a real scrape, in fact. We were stressed, wired, whatever you want to call it.' He shrugged. 'Guess we just needed to hit a release valve. I mean, Gail wasn't spoken for at the time. But it was still an error . . . and we both realised that afterwards.'

'You don't need to offer a defence, Mark.'

'Just filling you in on the circs.'

'You don't need to do that, either . . .' she sipped more tea, 'because I know all about it.'

Heck was astonished. 'How'd you know?'

'Gemma told me.'

'*Gemma* told you!' he almost shouted. A couple of faces turned from nearby tables. He lowered his voice again, throwing a quick nervous glance to the farthest corner of the room, but Gemma was still engrossed with Reed. 'How does *she* know?'

'Don't be daft. You can't keep anything secret in this job.'

'No, seriously . . . *I* didn't blab about it, and I'm damn sure Gail wouldn't have.'

Gwen waved that away. 'No secret's one hundred per cent, Mark. Think about it. No matter how sensitive the info, everyone trusts someone, and quite often it's someone they shouldn't. Hell, does it matter? . . . We're all adults.'

'Yeah, but . . .' This wasn't panning out the way he'd expected it to. 'Look, if . . . if Gemma actually *does* know, and she's still partnered me and Gail together, that's a bit of an error, isn't it?'

'Perhaps she just wants everyone to be happy?'

It was several seconds before Heck could process the meaning of that.

'Hell,' he said slowly. 'She wants to sweeten the pill . . . is that it? So that when she finally hooks up with Reed, I won't be too upset?' It was a shocking thought, but it made a horrible sort of sense. Heck was so thrown by it that suddenly he was thinking aloud rather than making conversation. 'Who'd have known she'd ever be so manipulative? The bloody little schemer. Well, it won't sodding work. There's nothing between me and Gail now . . .'

'Hey, Mark,' Gwen said, 'got room for some advice?'

'Sure,' he said distractedly.

'You're being a bit ridiculous.' She gave him a frank stare. 'Gemma is doing the best she can with limited resources. One of those resources is a relatively inexperienced detective . . . who, quite rightly, she's put in company with an experienced detective. And as those two detectives know each other already and have worked together previously, so much the better.'

'Yeah . . .' When Heck thought about it that way, it *did* make sense.

'I honestly don't know why you still have this hankering after Gemma's affection,' Gwen said. 'Assuming that's what it is. The way I hear it, you and she fight like cat and dog.'

'We've been through hell and high water together.'

'Tough experiences usually bring people closer.'

'Personally, I've always felt it's the job that's got in the way.'

'The job?'

'Most of our fallouts are over procedure.'

'Ah. You mean you want to use the Ways and Means Act, and Gemma wants to do things the proper way?'

He didn't bother answering that, because there was no answer he could give.

'Let me tell you something, Mark.' Gwen sat back. 'I once thought you two were right for each other. But, for whatever reason, it hasn't happened. So, for both your sakes – and for the sake of Operation Sledgehammer, I might add – *this* can't go on much longer.'

'Ma'am . . . we're fine. It's business as usual.'

'It isn't, Mark. That's the problem. We're under the microscope like never before.'

'It won't interfere with anything.'

'Just make sure it doesn't, hmm? And think about growing

up a little. You both have separate lives . . . time you started living them.'

Heck was about to respond, when he spotted the object of their conversation approaching.

Gemma and Reed had been en route to the exit, but having seen them together, Gemma now veered towards their table.

'Don't you two look cosy?' she said.

'Just reminiscing about the good old days,' Heck replied.

Reed offered his hand to Gwen. 'DI Reed, ma'am. Jack.' She shook hands with him. 'Pleased to meet you, Inspector.'

'Heard some amazing things about you, ma'am.'

'And I you. Well done on the Black Chapel arrests.'

'Well . . . it was a team effort.' Reed indicated Heck. 'I particularly couldn't have done it without this fella's ground-work.'

Heck said nothing, but inwardly seethed. It wouldn't have been so bad if Reed had been a pompous idiot, or a boring fart. But instead he was basically a good egg. The guy wasn't just tall and handsome, with a natural aristocratic bearing, he was pleasant, clever, witty, and he always gave credit where it was due. It was no small challenge when you'd set your stall out to loathe someone like that.

'Let's hope we can call on the same level of effective teamwork when Sledgehammer gets under way,' Gwen said.

Reed nodded. 'We'll all be pursuing different targets, of course. But ultimately, we're the same outfit. We can always call on each other's expertise or assistance. I was thinking we should video conference twice a day, just so we can keep each other informed.'

'We'll be doing that, anyway,' she replied. 'It's part of the strategy.'

'I don't just mean with Silver Command, ma'am. I mean all of us. Filing our updates together, keeping each other appraised of where we're at. If nothing else, it'll be good for morale.'

'I agree,' Gwen said. 'It might even boost progress. For example, Heck, if you felt that one of the other teams – I'm not thinking of anyone specifically, of course – was making real headway on their case, and you were still on first base . . .'

'I'm not sure that turning this thing into a competition between the investigation teams is necessarily the way we want to go,' Gemma said.

'Nevertheless, that's what'll happen,' Gwen replied.

Gemma clamped her mouth shut, biting down on a riposte. Heck eyed her with interest; it was rare to see Gemma voice a concern and have it so airily brushed aside. He'd been wondering how he was going to cope having Gail Honeyford along, but now he wondered how Gemma would do playing second fiddle to Gwen Straker.

'I don't think it'll be a case of competition,' Reed said, 'as much as mutual encouragement.'

'So long as it gets the best out of everyone,' Gwen replied, standing up. She turned to Gemma. 'You ready? We've got a long session ahead.'

Gemma nodded. 'I'll not be a sec.' As Gwen left the canteen, Reed sauntering after her, Gemma turned to Heck. 'How are things going with DC Honeyford?'

'Sweet,' he said. 'We went for a drink last night, and it's just like we've never been apart. I think she and me are going to get on very well.'

Gemma nodded as if satisfied to hear this. Otherwise, there wasn't a flicker of emotion.

Chapter 10

'Right . . . there's no way to sugar-coat this,' Gemma said to the assembled staff of Operation Sledgehammer. 'You all know the crisis we're facing in the police service at this present time. And you know that it's a very serious crisis indeed.'

There were over seventy of them crammed into the conference chamber, and on a hot August morning like this, it was an uncomfortable crush. Fans whirred overhead, but it was stuffy and stale. Many jackets and ties had been removed; foreheads gleamed with sweat.

Gemma Piper, not atypically, seemed oblivious to this, looking cool and unruffled as she pirouetted back and forth in her slacks and heels, her only concessions to the temperature that her blouse's sleeves were rolled to the elbows and her collar button unfastened.

In contrast, Gwen Straker was seated on a stool to one side, next to the conference room's large VDU, fingering her collar uncomfortably. Alongside her, sat Director of the National Crime Group, Joe Wullerton. In his late fifties now, burly in shape with thinning salt-and-pepper hair and a thick if droopy moustache, he normally preferred cardigans and open-neck shirts to the grey suit he affected currently. It was smart enough, but it wasn't ideal for these conditions and made him look awkward and restless.

'In short,' Gemma said, 'money is tighter than a duck's you-know-what. There are cutbacks everywhere. Many forces haven't recruited since what feels like the Stone Age. People are having to work longer and longer just to get their pensions. And, inevitably, sections like ours are under ever greater pressure to produce, and I quote, "impressive results".'

She paused. There was silence, the entire room, the brass included, paying rapt attention.

'Now, you people here may consider that pretty unfair . . . I certainly do. Only a couple of days ago, the Serial Crimes Unit concluded the first part of its investigation into the Black Chapel. Not too long ago, we helped to halt a string of brutal underworld slayings and apprehended a notorious hitman.'

Heck listened alongside everyone else. He still felt the bruises from that last one.

'I would certainly call those results impressive,' Gemma said. 'And you Coldies have an equal track record. In case any SCU officers are uninformed about this, in the last twelve months, Cold Case, under the command of Detective Chief Superintendent Straker here, have brought charges against eight individuals believed to be connected to historic homicides. But it seems, ladies and gentlemen, that none of this is quite enough.' She paused to tuck ringlets of blonde hair behind her ears. 'I recently attended a meeting at the Yard, wherein representatives of the National Police Chiefs' Council put it bluntly to me that the Serial Crimes Unit either had to find some clear and visible way to reduce its overheads, or it had to increase its arrest and conviction rate dramatically, or, preferably, both. One other alternative was laid out for me – we discontinue operations.'

Mumbles of anger sounded, even though they'd all known this was coming.

'What's more, the whole of National Crime Group is under similar pressure.' She glanced at Wullerton. 'You want to say something about that, Joe?'

Wullerton sat stiffly upright, arms folded. 'No, it's fine, Gemma . . . you carry on.'

'Director Wullerton is too self-effacing to mention it,' she said, 'but he's been putting up a hell of a fight on our behalf. He recently put a forceful case to NPCC that if we lose the Kidnap Squad, the Organised Crime Division and the Serial Crimes Unit . . . all at the same time, then in one go we'll have left our society significantly weakened in its battle against some of the most serious threats currently posed by the criminal underworld . . .'

There was silence again. Clearly, no one disagreed.

'Unfortunately, it cut no ice,' Gemma said. 'However, two days after my meeting at Scotland Yard, I received a phone call from Detective Chief Superintendent Straker here, who advised me that she and her Cold Case team at the Met were facing an identical crisis. Do you want to take it from here, Gwen?'

'Thanks, Gemma,' Gwen said, standing up.

She peeled off her suit jacket and hung it from a hook on a shelf.

'I won't elaborate on any of this,' she said. 'We all know we're under the microscope. However, our two units are in a more invidious position than most because we can't just send staff out onto the streets to bump our stats the easy way. At least . . .' she paused, 'that was what I thought. But then it occurred to me that maybe there actually are some offenders out there, still at large, whose pursuit and appre-hension would comfortably fall within the remit of the people gathered in this room.'

There was a stir of interest.

Gwen nodded to one of her Cold Case detectives, who hit some keys on his laptop. The VDU came to life, initially depicting a gallery of twenty thumbnail mugshots.

'Unlike the FBI, in the UK we don't keep an official list of the Most Wanted,' Gwen said. 'But that doesn't mean there aren't a number of fugitives from British justice wanted in connection with some very serious crimes who may still be living here – either in hiding, or under false names and identities.'

She turned to the screen.

'My proposal, which I first made to DSU Piper and then to NPCC, was that SCU and Cold Case pooled their resources and drew up a list of the twenty Most Wanted fugitives from UK justice who were still believed to be in the country. And once we'd established that list, that we rekindled and pursued those particular enquiries. In short, that we made it our very next job to go after the twenty worst of the worst.'

Heck eyed the rows of faces on-screen. On their way in, everyone present had been handed a bundle of paperwork relevant to their own particular part of the enquiry, but also providing overarching information about Sledgehammer as a whole. No doubt, all of these mugshots, and the rap-sheets attached to each one of them, would be included in said packages, but it was interesting to see the faces all on-screen together.

'You won't need me to tell you,' Gwen said, 'that if, within a reasonable timeframe, we can arrest and convict even half of the names on this list – because each one of these is an open sore which NPCC is both angry and embarrassed about – we will massively boost our value for money in the eyes of the people who matter.'

She paused again, to let it sink in.

'So, people . . . welcome to Operation Sledgehammer. DSU

Piper picked the name, because we're going to bring the full weight of the police service of England and Wales down on these scattered nuts, who are likely to be much more fragile than they realise.'

There were several satisfied snickers.

'In the first instance, as some of you are already aware, we're assigning two detectives to each individual. I know it doesn't seem like a lot, but that's only for the initial phase of the enquiry. Once you've made substantial ground on your case, Silver Command – that's myself and DSU Piper, we will joint-SIO this investigation from the Command Centre here at Staples Corner – will provide all the technical, financial and personnel back-up you require to see it through to the end. We've already made preliminary contact with the various force areas in which your enquiries are to be focused, and in most cases, you'll find that local CID have already done some groundwork on your behalf.

'I'm not going to waste time giving you a pep talk,' Gwen added. 'You're all experienced police officers, and you'll have heard about these individuals before. You may even have encountered them. But just reappraising yourself with the offences they are suspected of committing ought to be enough to motivate you. For example –' she indicated a mugshot '– I'm sure you're all familiar with Leonard Spate, who is wanted for raping and beating to death a woman he picked up at a Workington nightclub, and who later escaped from custody and then raped and murdered a prostitute in Carlisle. The latter victim's two children also died because, after finishing with the mother, Spate burned down the house where they were sleeping.'

Disgusted mutters rippled across the room.

'How about Terry Godley?' Gwen said, moving on to the next target. 'He's wanted in connection with an armed carjacking in Nottingham several years ago. There were two teenage boys in the vehicle at the time. Both were later found dead, having been made to kneel before being shot through the back of the head, execution-style.

'And let's not forget Christopher Brenner, who went on the run four years ago after three missing prostitutes were found chained in his Luton cellar – they'd been tortured, raped repeatedly and were emaciated to the point of near death.'

And so it went, name after name, their atrocities never less than despicable. But for all that, Heck was worried. It was clear to him that, despite these diabolical crimes – and Eddie Creeley was as bad as any of them – this still felt like a desperate ploy. It was no small task the detective duos were facing here.

'So you see, people . . .' Gwen fixed them all with a flat stare. 'You're not just going to be saving our skins by doing this. We pull in half of this lot . . . hey, we pull in even as few as a third, and we'll be doing the world a big favour. Now, neither DSU Piper nor I are going to pretend that this is some kind of easy option. But at least it means that our communal fate is still in our own hands.'

Heck was in the DO, inserting new photos into his scrapbook, when Gail found him.

From their headshots, Father Strachan and the Right Revs Hanson and Thomas looked like thoroughly decent people; the first of them avuncular and jovial, the second prim and refined, the third pleasantly mischievous. There were some dodgy characters in the clergy these days – there was no doubt about that. But these three had apparently led blameless lives, and so made sad additions to his collection. The scrapbook resembled such an item in name only now. Its spine had gone, and its cover was more sticky tape than cardboard, having fallen apart and been repaired so often, but the record it contained – a photo gallery of all those murder victims Heck had managed to gain some kind of justice for – had remained intact through thick and thin. In fact, there were more faces in there now than the book had ever been designed for, so he'd needed to add extra pages.

'I heard about this,' Gail said, looking over his shoulder.

Multiple faces gazed up at her as he flicked through, looking for spare space. Some were passport shots, some cut-outs from photos taken at functions or family gatherings. They depicted all ages, races, sexes. None looked unhappy, of course, and why would they? When these pictures were taken, they were very much part of this world, with no clue that disaster was slowly creeping up on them.

'Just the victims, is it?' she said.

'Well, they're the most important,' he replied. 'The crims can go and rot, for all I care. In most of these cases, I'm glad to say, that's exactly what the bastards are doing . . . either in jail, or in the ground.' He closed the book and slid it into his drawer.

'You seem stressed,' she said.

He looked up at her. 'I'm not stressed. But this is a big job. We'll need to focus.'

'I'm assuming it's a case here of "last in, first out"?'

'What?'

Gail sat at her desk. With the briefing over, officers were bustling back into the DO. Most were now preoccupied, but even so, she lowered her voice.

'During my interview and application process, no one in SCU told me we were dangling by a thread.'

'We're not dangling by a thread,' he said. 'We've heard this sort of thing time and again.'

'You don't believe that. I can tell from the look on your face.'

'Listen, Gail . . . every time we have a tough case, we hear

104

the same thing: "Sort this one out quick, the future of the squad depends on it." And what happens? We sort it out and life goes on.'

'That's as may be, but I can't help thinking that if Gemma really is forced to make cuts, I'll be on the first train back to Surrey.'

'Well . . . what you have to do is prove to her that it won't be necessary.' He stood and handed her the Creeley file. 'And in that regard, this is very timely, don't you think?'

'Like you said,' she replied, 'big job.'

'Like *you* said . . . no pressure.'

Chapter 11

When the night of the shooting got under way, Spencer Taylor had no reason to assume that it wouldn't go as smoothly as usual.

Dante Brown was nothing if not a creature of habit. Ever since he'd stepped away from the Stamford Toreadors, got himself a job delivering Domino's Pizza, and moved in with pregnant girlfriend, Carolyn, you could set your watch by his schedule.

His weekday shift always finished at 10 p.m., and then he invariably hung around the shop an extra fifteen minutes while the kids who worked there made him a pizza on the house, or in lieu of his wages, or some such shit. After that, distinctive for the red hoodie top he always wore, he'd walk home down the Seven Sisters Road with the box tucked underneath his arm, reaching St Ann's at about 10:30 p.m., at which point he'd turn left into South Tottenham. As home was a flat above a burglar alarm shop on Tottenham High Road, he would now almost have reached his destination. Once indoors, he and the lovely Carolyn would spend the rest of the evening in their undies, slumped in front of their portable TV, chomping contentedly through a delicious twelve-inch Margherita.

If only . . .

As Spencer waited in the shadowy alcove between two caged-off shopfronts thirty yards west of the corner with High Road, he shook his head in mock-regret.

If only Dante had not forgotten who he was.

If only he'd not been so weak-willed as to let Carolyn talk him into finding a so-called 'better way' purely because he wanted to hump her brains out.

If only Dante, having insisted that, at twenty-nine years old, he was past all this and that the Toreadors were big enough to stand on their own two feet, had at least done what he'd told them he was going to do – which was retire to private life.

If only in the last two weeks, he had not commenced clandestine meetings with undercover officers from Operation Trident, the Metropolitan Police's special unit for investigating gun crime and murder within the city's Afro-Caribbean community.

That latter had been unexpected, Spencer had to admit.

Dante, as elder statesman, hadn't once just been spiritual leader to the Toreadors, he'd been a solid trooper, a real marine. And it wasn't as though, if he'd ever suddenly decided to talk, he'd easily have been able to conceal his own past. Dante had pulled the trigger at least twice, as far as Spencer knew. Long in the past now, of course, though this was doubtless the reason why Dante was now contemplating singing. The pigs must have him over a barrel. They were ready to nail him for his own indiscretions, so he'd offered them a deal, and in all honesty, what could you really use to trade away two premeditated gang hits? Well, how about a whole lot more premeditated gang hits. Ten, fifteen . . . maybe the entire twenty that Spencer was aware the Toreadors had been involved in over the last two decades. He wasn't even sure if that was the full tally. At nineteen years old, he was a relative baby. But Dante would have the full skinny on all the crew's activities going way back.

But it was strange, the state of mind you could fall into when someone you'd once idolised could overnight become the means by which you yourself might obtain star status.

To take down a player, or even an ex-player, like Dante Brown, would have been an onerous thing for any of the Toreadors. He'd put their crew on the map; he'd done personal stuff for all of them in the past; his leadership had inspired each and every one to great things. So even though he was now a grass it would have felt wrong on every level to put his candle out.

But someone had to do it.

And come the hour, come the man.

When Spencer had put his hand up, they hadn't regarded him with awe as much as surprise, probably thinking who the fuck does this snot-nosed rugrat think he is?

His two previous hits had seemingly counted for nothing, but why wouldn't they? On both occasions, he'd been part of a three-man team. The first time, blasting from a moving car at a queue outside a kebab shop, he was certain that of the three who'd gone down, he'd been the only one to put rounds into their intended target, the one in the middle – but there'd been no way to prove that. The second time, pumping lead through a hairdresser's window, he'd only winged the target, the elder sister of a rival who'd previously accounted for two of their own; but the rest of the team wouldn't have been able to finish her off if she hadn't fallen clear from her bunch of girlfriends, landing full length on the carpet of shattered glass. Again though, he couldn't expect to be singled out for praise; they'd hardly hung around to check whose piece had fired the slugs that did most damage.

But this was the one that was going to change all that.

After this, no one would spot him walking around the

neighbourhood and wonder who he was; no one would ever question his credentials again.

Spencer was distracted from these dreams of glory by the sudden unexpected sight of his target strolling casually into view.

The fuck . . .?

Initially Spencer was dumbstruck.

What time was it? He couldn't even take his phone out to check, because the two or three seconds that would entail might enable Dante to pass him by. The guy was already directly opposite on the far side of St Ann's Road. He was clearly distinctive, not just for his tall outline, but for his reddish hoodie with its hood pulled up, and for the square pizza box tucked under his arm.

Spencer realised that there was no time to quibble with himself about why Dante was early. He zipped his jacket to the throat, jammed his gloved hands into its front pockets and emerged from the recess, falling into step parallel to Dante but on his own side of the road. As usual, there was traffic, but it was now 10:25 p.m., so it was only coming in dribs and drabs. A gap appeared, and he was able to veer onto the tarmac, crossing diagonally towards the unsuspecting figure about ten yards ahead of him.

'Hey, bro!' he shouted. 'Yo . . . Dante, man!'

The hooded shape didn't look round, but continued walking.

Eager to get home to his gorgeous girl, no doubt, and his sumptuous pizza. Well . . . the first of those two treats might soon be Spencer's, he thought, with eager anticipation.

He drew the Bulldog .44 Special from its place of concealment across his belly.

'Yo, Dante!' he called.

Spencer reached the pavement. His target was no more than five yards ahead, but still hadn't looked back – which

109

was inconvenient, because Spencer didn't want to do it from behind. But there was no time to ponder.

He opened fire.

Once, twice, three times.

The Bulldog had more recoil than he'd expected, but from this range he couldn't miss. The first slug impacted on the left side of Dante's neck, jolting his head to the right. The second took him in the upper left shoulder. The third struck the back of his skull. This one did the most visible damage, smashing out a huge divot of hair, bone and fabric.

At first, it was all flickering, unreal imagery, but as the stricken figure corkscrewed its way down to the pavement, Spencer saw three key things: a pair of earbuds flew loose – Dante had started doing music again, which explained why he hadn't heard the shout; a big square book, like a college text, clattered to the ground, pages fluttering, rather than a box of exploding pizza – which bamboozled Spencer, because he'd never had Dante down as a scholar; the hood, though rent apart like the skull beneath, remained in place, so that even when the body hit the floor, he only *glimpsed* the face.

But that was enough to show him that it was white.

Spencer stood rigid, gun arm cocked, eyes bugging frog-like in features suddenly dotted with sweat.

'The fuck . . .?' he muttered.

Frantic thoughts fell over themselves inside his head.

It didn't matter . . . this was OK . . . it wasn't the end . . . it had happened before . . . tough shit . . . mistaken identity . . . casualties of war . . . collateral . . .

'*The fuck!*' His voice turned hoarse as the question struck him like an anvil: if he hadn't just downed Dante Brown, where the hell *was* the guy?

Spencer turned and gazed back along the pavement.

Dante – the *real* Dante – had come to a stupefied halt some forty yards behind him. He was wearing his red hoodie top, yes, but not doing music. He wasn't carrying a book under his arm, but the usual pizza box.

And he wasn't alone.

A buxom black girl in a vest, slacks and fluffy slippers had come out of the shop alongside him. Drawn by the sound of gunfire, she too stared along the pavement. Further back along the road, others were doing the same. But Dante was the first to move; slowly backtracking, taking longer and longer steps, before dropping his pizza, turning and running for his life.

Spencer ran a couple of yards after him before common sense kicked in.

Dante was older, taller, stronger. He also had longer legs. There was no possibility of catching up to him.

'Try outrunning a bullet, motherfuck!'

Spencer aimed two-handed like he'd seen in American cop shows. He still had three bullets left. He wouldn't miss.

But he did.

The first went awry somewhere. The second whacked the black girl in the throat, her chin flying up as she staggered backward.

Even in the midst of his panic, Spencer was wise enough to know not to waste the third.

He spun around, looking for the pickup crew. Not that they'd be keen to admit knowing him now that Dante – who had seen him, had locked eyes with him in fact, clearly recognising him – had got away.

Oh, Jesus . . . oh JESUS!

Spencer pelted across St Ann's Road, zoning in on the mouth to the alley, where the pickup car, a stolen Ford Mondeo, was due to meet him. On cue, the Mondeo was waiting. The youngster on the mountain bike should be there too, the wannabe with the open haversack on his back, into which Spencer could deposit the gun, the gloves, the jacket.

But he was still twenty yards from the meet-point, when he saw the wannabe pedalling away fast down Tottenham High Road, his backpack empty.

So young and yet so wise, so neatly equipped with hair-trigger survival instincts.

The pickup crew didn't wait either. When Spencer was ten yards short, the Mondeo pulled off.

His protracted cry narrowed to a tortured, despairing screech.

But the Mondeo accelerated away.

This had nothing to do with them. They were just a couple of guys out for a late-evening drive. They hadn't even seen what had happened.

Not that it would be quite so easy for them when the Trident pigs visited later, carrying a whole checklist of names because suddenly Dante Brown had reached a decision that it was no longer worth his while holding anything back.

Spencer Taylor ran down Stamford Hill, sweat blinding his eyes, breath sawing at his ribs, his world collapsing around him in a quake-style cataclysm.

Chapter 12

'We don't take the fact that Eddie Creeley's sole living relative is on our patch lightly,' DC Barry Hodges said.

'No?' Heck replied.

'No way.' Hodges shook his head as he drove them onto the housing estate. 'Even before all this, we were keeping an eye on her. He robbed a lot of banks here on Humberside.'

Hodges was young for a detective, even by divisional standards, fresh of feature, with short-cropped blond hair and a trim blond moustache. He was one of Heck and Gail's two official liaison officers, and from the moment they'd been introduced to him he'd seemed eager to please. Most likely this was because he was still young and naïve enough to be intrigued by the prospect of attachment to a specialist operation like Sledgehammer. But it made a nice change; it wouldn't have been the first time Heck had arrived in 'Counties', as certain NCG officers liked to refer to the UK's provincial police forces, and been greeted by a wall of unhelpful indifference.

As such, it didn't concern him that Hodges' affability had been counterbalanced by the more traditional attitude of the other official liaison, DS Vic Mortimer, currently riding in

the front passenger seat. Mortimer had said nothing of consequence since Heck and Gail had first shown up here, and
even now, as they were chaperoned around the infamous
Orchard Park estate, he seemed uninterested in conversing.
Mortimer was somewhere in his late forties, and of a squat,
heavy build. His face was pale and pitted, his greying hair
collar-length and greased back. Whereas Hodges was
regulation-smart in blazer, crisp, clean shirt and pressed tie,
Mortimer's tie was loose, his collar unfastened, and his leather
jacket crumpled.

'That's where she lives,' Hodges said, pointing.

Heck and Gail, both in the back of the Jag, glanced left.

One block of low-rise flats in this rather desolate district
looked much like another, but this one was horseshoe-shaped,
and Heck recognised it from the intel file.

'Hellington Court,' Hodges added, rather unnecessarily as
Heck and Gail had both been able to go through the fine
details of the case while taking turns to drive up here from
London. 'Nanette Creeley lives at number 26.'

'How much attention have you been paying to the place?'
Heck asked.

'Well . . . more since we heard about Sledgehammer,'
Hodges said. 'We keep tabs on her on and off all the time,
though. Normally just to see if there's any sign her brother's
been around.'

'What does "keep tabs" involve?' Gail wondered.

She and Heck turned to watch as the grotty block of flats
fell slowly behind them.

'We've had obbo points on the surrounding roofs,' Hodges
said, turning down a side street. Heck assumed he was
doubling back so they could see Hellington Court from the
rear. 'Lots of good vantage round here. We've tailed her
sometimes too, when she's been out and about . . . you know,
in case she was going to meet him, or something.'

'So . . . nothing intelligence-led?' Heck said.

'Well . . .' Hodges' cheek reddened, 'it's only in the last week it's become a priority. This is a high-crime area. We have lots of other stuff to do.'

'Have you made a lot of drive-bys like this?' Heck asked.

'Three or four times a day this last week. Nothing to report thus far.'

'Why?' Mortimer wondered, sounding suspicious of the question.

They approached Hellington Court again, now from a different angle. It sat beyond a litter-covered green, and from this side, its bleak façade was little more than a towering, pebble-dashed wall with numerous TV aerials along the top.

'Because it seems to me,' Heck said, 'that if you've suddenly started making regular drive-bys in a divisional car, it's likely the local hoodlums will have spotted it ten miles off. I'm guessing there are quite a few living round here?'

'More than average,' Hodges admitted. 'They make the proper residents' lives a misery.'

'The point is,' Heck said, 'if they've clocked you, which they almost certainly will have done, word could now have reached Creeley's sister that there's more police activity than usual in the vicinity of Hellington Court. Which may mean that if the offender *has* been around here recently, he won't be now.'

'Creeley's not around here,' Mortimer said simply. He didn't bother looking at them as he spoke. '*We've* got inform-ants too, you know. And he hasn't been seen for two years. Not in this neck of the woods, not anywhere.'

This much Heck already knew, so he didn't comment.

'What about the sister, Nanette?' Gail asked. 'What's her pattern of behaviour like?'

'Fucking dim-bulb,' Mortimer commented.

'What does that mean?'

Mortimer smirked. 'What I say. You can tell just by looking at her.'

'Bit of a lonely soul, too,' Hodges chipped in. 'Whenever we've obbed her . . . apart from going to see the old lady next door, she never seems to interact with anyone.'

'She must go out sometimes?' Heck said.

'She works at the local Spar. So, there's that. Like I say, she sometimes goes around to assist her neighbour, an infirm old girl called Maggie Stoke, who's bedridden most of the time. Apparently, Maggie gave her a spare key. That's usually first thing in the morning. In the evening, Nan goes to the pub.'

'Which pub?' Heck asked.

'*This* one.'

They looked right and saw a red-brick building standing alone on a street corner with wasteland behind it. It looked as if it had once been physically attached to a row of houses that had all now been demolished. The shield over the front door depicted a faded image of a figure in a sou'wester, and said that it was called The Crewman. As they passed it, a burly woman with short dark hair, and tattoo-covered arms exposed by a sleeveless vest, came out with a watering can to tend the boxes of flowers under the frosted windows.

'That's her local, eh?' Heck said.

'It's the only pub left in the neighbourhood,' Hodges replied.

'She goes in there at night, you say?' Gail asked.

'Has been doing lately.'

'Most nights?'

'Near enough every night recently. And she's regular as clockwork – it's nearly always eight-thirty. I know, because I tailed her a few times last week.' Hodges appeared to sense Heck's scepticism about this. 'You don't need to worry, Sarge. I dressed down for the occasion. She didn't clock me.'

'She's too fucking dim to clock anyone,' Mortimer grunted.

'Does she speak to anyone when she's in the pub?' Heck asked.

'Nah. Never. That's what I mean about her not interacting. Stands on her own at the end of the bar, same place every night . . . has half a bitter and writes a letter.'

Immediately, the oddity of that struck home.

'How do you mean "writes a letter"?' Gail asked.

'Well . . . she doesn't always do that,' Hodges admitted. 'She did it a couple of times last week. Tuesday and Thursday. The other nights she just stood there on her own.'

'And she didn't talk to anyone?'

'Only to order her drink.'

'Just the one drink?' Heck said.

'That's all I've seen her with. She makes it last about an hour.'

'She literally stands at the bar and writes a letter?'

'Yeah. Posts it on the way home. Least . . . she did on those two occasions.'

'It has occurred to you lads that this is off-the-wall behaviour?' Heck said. 'So off-the-wall that . . . I dunno, maybe she's writing letters to her brother?'

'Way ahead of you,' Mortimer said, sounding smug. 'That's why in the early hours last Friday morning, before the dawn collection, we got a warrant and opened the pillar box.'

'Good thinking,' Gail said.

'Trouble is, we found nothing useful.'

'Every letter in there was addressed to a legit party.' Hodges pulled off the estate onto a main road. 'We checked them all on the voters' roll, cross-checked with the database and so on. None of them even had form, let alone links to Eddie Creeley.'

Heck and Gail pondered this as they rode back towards Clough Road police station.

'There's no law against writing letters,' Gail eventually said.

'No,' Heck agreed, but his suspicion was firmly aroused. One would normally write letters at home, though he supposed it wasn't impossible that certified 'lonely soul' Nanette Creeley might go to the pub in the evenings to find some company or a cheerful atmosphere, and just happened to write her letters while she was there.

'You say this pattern repeats itself?' he said. 'I know she doesn't write a letter every night, but she always goes at the same time and stands in the same place?'

'Well, we've only been watching her closely this last week or so,' Hodges said. 'But it's been more or less the same, yeah.'

'Sounds weird enough to warrant some further investigation,' Heck said.

'Time for a front-on approach?' Gail suggested.

He glanced at her. 'What do you mean?'

'Nanette Creeley's got no form. If she's a law-abiding citizen and she's been drawn into this through misguided family loyalty . . . I don't know, maybe she'll talk to us?'

'This is her brother. You think she'll collaborate in sending him down under a full-life tariff?'

'Maybe. When she hears what he's done. I mean, it's some of the vilest crime I've ever heard of. The murder of that bank manager's wife in particular . . .'

Mortimer chuckled aloud. 'She already knows what he's done. She won't help.'

'Maybe *I* should try?' Gail said.

The DS chuckled again. 'Think that southern softie accent will win her over? Be my guest.'

'Eddie's her only surviving relative,' Heck said. 'She isn't going to gift-wrap him for us.'

'She must know this can't go on.'

118

Mortimer shook his head, even more amused.

'They never think that far ahead,' Hodges replied. 'None of them.'

Gail said nothing else, but looked frustrated rather than abashed.

It struck Heck again that she had plenty to learn. Except for a brief interlude in London, when he and she had ended up making arrests in a pigsty of a flophouse, she'd so far spent all her service in Stockbroker Land. OK, there were villains there, and not just the white-collar sort. But she couldn't have experienced inner-city sprawls like this very often, where the code of silence was all-consuming, mainly through a kind of underclass loyalty, but also through fear – in districts like this, you turned your fellow oppressed over to the oppressors at your extreme peril.

There was no further conversation until the Jag pulled up in the personnel car park at Clough Road, which itself was a bleak, soulless structure. They got out and Hodges locked the car, but as Mortimer trudged away, the younger Humberside cop hung around.

'Me and Vic have just put a full shift in, but we're at your disposal so long as you need us,' he said. 'So . . . just wondering what your plans are for this evening?'

Heck glanced at his watch. 'Well . . . we've got a Skype conference with Silver Command before anything else. That'll be fun.'

'Thing is,' Hodges said awkwardly. 'DCI Bateson's our gaffer. He's been wondering how long we need to keep tabs on Nan Creeley for. The overtime's costing us an arm and a leg.'

'You can't charge it to Sledgehammer?' Gail asked, surprised.

'Maybe . . . I don't know.' Hodges shrugged.

Heck knew that they could and would charge all overtime

to Operation Sledgehammer, but that Hodges was only doing what Mortimer had primed him to: looking for an evening off. It wasn't completely unreasonable of them. If they'd been putting in lots of extra hours watching Nanette Creeley's flat, they might rightly have expected the reinforcements from SCU to take at least some of the weight.

Which, of course, they would – because this was also what Heck was looking for.

'We don't need any of your lads tonight,' he said. 'We'll take care of the obbo.'

Hodges looked surprised, though not displeased. 'You'll need some support, though . . .?'

'As long as divisional Comms know where we are, we'll be OK. We're just sussing the lay of the land.'

'You're certain about this. I mean . . .'

'They're sussing the lay of the land, Bazzer,' Mortimer called from over near the personnel door. 'That's what they do. They're experts at it. So, let 'em crack on.'

'OK.' Hodges shrugged again. 'Your call.' Mortimer had already gone inside, but the personnel door was still open, and Hodges edged towards it. 'Make sure you check some radios out, and that Comms and the duty officer know what you're doing.'

Heck nodded.

Once the two liaison officers had gone, Gail sniffed with irritation. 'That Vic Mortimer's the biggest wanker I've ever met.'

'Only at local level,' Heck said. 'Trust me, there are bigger ones at Scotland Yard.'

'So . . . we're running the obbo ourselves tonight?'

'Nah, we're going to the pub. Let's see the Nan Creeley show, eh?'

She pondered this. 'You think that's a good idea, going alone?'

'We won't be alone. We can call support if we need it.'

'We're strangers here, Heck . . . don't you think it's a bit of a risk?'

'The trade-off is we won't have the local lads involved.'

'And that's a good thing?'

He headed for the personnel door. 'Course it is.'

She fell into step alongside him. 'Hodges and Mortimer know this territory way better than we do.'

'Yeah, and the local crims know them way better than they know us. Listen, Gail . . . this is one area where being new faces gives us an edge. We can go where we want on this plot, so long as we dress the part and you keep your BBC English to yourself. No one'll bat an eyelid. But these lads are the neighbourhood fuzz. So, even if none of the firms in this neck of the woods have heard a dicky bird about Sledgehammer—'

'How can they? We haven't gone to press with it.'

'Don't be green . . .'

'I'm not being green!'

They entered the building and headed past a row of lockers towards the canteen.

'The thing is,' he said, 'even though there's a press embargo on Sledgehammer, the word's likely to get out. It always does somehow. But even if it doesn't, Mortimer, Hodges and co. have already made it obvious that something's afoot. It's not just the daily drive-bys in known CID cars. There've been spotters on the roofs surrounding Hellington Court, and yet there are windows just about everywhere round there. Hodges even followed this Nan Creeley to the pub. Don't get me wrong, he seems like a willing lad, but he's another one who sticks out like a sore thumb. If the bad boys of Hull aren't thinking by now that there's a bit more police activity on Orchard Park than usual, then they're not worthy of the term "bad boys" . . . and something tells me that won't be the case.'

121

Gail sat at an empty table, while Heck went to get them some tea.

As he waited to get served, he glanced back at her, sitting alone, lost in thought. Despite everything, the partnership was working out OK thus far. Gail had been co-operative and observant, and had asked only intelligent questions. She was clearly a long way from the go-it-alone rebel she'd once been. It was understandable that she'd query him on *this*; that was only what any responsible person would do. In due course though, experience would teach her to read people and situations more subtly, to look a little further down the road, to know which corners to cut and which gambles to take. If she managed all that successfully, and maintained her other skill sets, she likely had a great career ahead of her.

She still looked doubtful when he returned. 'Isn't it a bit irregular to have no back-up?'

He sat down. 'We're only obbing the woman. We won't be challenging anyone.'

'We'll still be short-handed . . . and in the depths of enemy territory.'

'Course.' He pushed a mug across the table towards her. 'Welcome to SCU.'

Chapter 13

For the first few days of Operation Sledgehammer, Heck and Gail hadn't left their desks.

Instead, they'd rummaged through the life and crimes of Edward Jason Creeley via the online intelligence files of all those relevant police and prison agencies in England and Wales. They'd also spoken on the phone, and at some length, to various police officers and legal representatives who'd had dealings with him. The general consensus seemed to be that, while Creeley had been admired for his undoubted proficiency as a career criminal, his popularity had gradually waned among his own kind due to his ever-increasing propensity for extreme violence.

This was confirmed for Heck and Gail in the middle of that first week, when they went to interview John Fowler, one of Creeley's fellow blaggers, who'd worked with him on the Newark job. He was now doing twenty-five years in Wormwood Scrubs, and he wasn't best pleased about it.

'Good luck finding the fucking lunatic!' he'd ranted at them. 'But if you do, try and get him sent *here*, eh? The law wouldn't have come down on the rest of us so heavy if he hadn't got his jollies hurting people.'

The other thing that most of those who knew Creeley personally were quick to point out was how efficiently he could go to ground. That was another reason why his fellow blaggers were no longer so affectionate towards him. While other participants in his various bank raids had eventually been arrested, he'd simply vanished, leaving everyone else to their fate.

Ultimately, this was why Heck and Gail were now on Humberside, Creeley's home patch and presumably the place he was most familiar with and where he felt most secure.

As agreed, they met in the lobby of the Premier Inn they were staying in at 8 p.m. that evening. Also as agreed, they'd dressed down, though Gail had gone to more trouble than Heck. Whereas he wore jeans, trainers, a T-shirt and a scruffy Wrangler jacket, Gail emerged from the hotel lift wearing a black leather miniskirt, black tights, black spike-heel boots, a black vest and black leather jacket with tassels. She'd frizzed her hair and added green extensions, affecting the 'punkette' look. With green eyeshadow and a slash of vermilion on her lips, she looked every inch a wild-hearted babe on the prowl for a good night out.

'Well?' she said, as they strode to his Megane.

'Not bad,' he responded. 'I'm not sure they get too many girls looking like you in The Crewman, but at least you don't look like a copper.'

'If it's any consolation, you look a right yob.'

'Yeah, but I get that when I wear a suit too.'

'Don't worry about it.' They climbed into the car. 'It's part of your charm.'

'I'd hope you wouldn't treat a real girlfriend to a night out in a place like this,' Gail said quietly, as they selected a table with a clear view of the bar.

'One thing about this job,' Heck replied, peeling off his

jacket, 'it makes you a connoisseur of the world's crappest pubs.'

'Well . . . we're not really here for the beer, are we?'

'Nevertheless, we're drinking. Got to make it look right.'

While Gail sat down, he walked to the bar.

If, from the outside, The Crewman had looked like the forlorn remnant of a demolished neighbourhood, inside it consisted of a single room with lino on the floor, benches around the edges and a few tables and chairs in the middle. There was a blackened fireplace, which clearly hadn't been lit since last winter, and red flock wallpaper, some parts of it frayed and loose, others tinged brown. To be fair to the place, it wasn't completely odious. The tables were clean, the beer mats fresh and only a very slight whiff of stale beer tainted the air. Two or three locals were present and had struck up a low hubbub of conversation. One old boy leaned against the bar, nursing a pint of Guinness, and chatted amicably with the tattooed barmaid they'd seen earlier that day.

Heck bought a pint of bitter for himself and a white wine for Gail.

He settled alongside her, furtively scanning the other occupants of the room. No one looked especially tense or edgy. And aside from a couple of admiring looks thrown in the direction of the sexy rock-chick who'd unexpectedly turned up, no one was paying much attention to the newcomers, so their disguises were holding out.

'Be just our luck if she doesn't come in tonight,' Gail murmured, noting the clock behind the bar, which was approaching 8:30 p.m.

'If so, we come back tomorrow.'

'And in the meantime, what? A whole day gets wasted. That wouldn't be music to Silver Command's ears.'

'Silver Command mean well, Gail, but the schedule they've set is impossible.'

'If she doesn't show tonight, why don't we come back tomorrow during the day, and sequester the pub's security videos? They should have two or three days' worth. Let's see if we catch anything that way.'

'Yeah, and by the day after tomorrow, the entire neighbourhood will know . . . and Nan Creeley will have cancelled whatever plans she's making with her brother.'

Gail tutted. 'There's a lot of supposition there.'

'We'll see.'

'Heck, I . . .' Her words broke off and she grabbed his wrist.

Nanette Creeley had entered the pub.

They knew her instantly from the surveillance photos in Eddie Creeley's file: a small, thin woman, with short, dark hair greying at the edges, carrying a large handbag and wearing a beige, zip-up waterproof which came down to her thighs. According to the file, she was only forty-eight, but she looked a good ten years older; her face wizened and colourless, emaciated to the point where her eyes seemed to bug. She shuffled straight to the bar and purchased, as they'd been told, a half a bitter, before moving along the counter to its farthest end, close to the Ladies', where she took up her normal post. There were plenty of chairs and tables free in the pub, but she made no attempt to go to any of those.

Heck wondered if it was a protection issue. With the bar-top to her left, and the wall next to the Ladies' behind her, that meant she only had two directions to keep an eye on; if anyone approached her, she'd see them in good time. In addition, there were no chairs or stools at that end of the bar, so no one could plonk themselves down in a position that she might feel crowded her.

'Perfect place to write a letter she wants no one else to read,' he muttered.

Gail sipped her wine as she covertly watched.

A minute passed, during which the woman took occasional pecks at her drink. Then, abruptly, she opened the handbag at her hip, taking out what looked like writing materials. It was difficult to be absolutely sure, because though they had an open view of her position, she was in the opposite corner of the pub, a good twenty-five yards away. It looked as if she had a pen in hand, and had laid at least one small, squarish piece of paper on the bar-top. She now bent over this, partially shielding what she was doing, and began to write.

'Don't suppose you fancy paying a visit?' Heck said quietly.

Gail took another sip of wine, stood up and sauntered across the room. Making a beeline for the Ladies', she veered closely past the woman, who, in a very unsubtle gesture, leaned right over what she was writing. The same thing happened when Gail re-emerged from the toilets and crossed back towards their table.

'Well,' she said, as she sat, 'that was instructive.'

'Yeah? Do tell.'

'She made sure to cover what she was actually writing. But she must have written out the envelope, and stamped it, beforehand. Because that was lying on the bar-top next to her.'

'And?'

'It's addressed to Maggie Stoke of 27, Hellington Court.'

'Isn't that . . .?'

'Yep.' Gail glanced round at him. 'Heck . . . why is Nan Creeley writing a letter to the old lady who lives next door to her? The same one she goes to visit every morning.'

Heck thought long and hard. 'The only explanation . . . is that she *isn't* doing that.'

'I don't need my eyes checking. I assure you that was the address . . .'

'I believe you.'

127

Again, he pondered the conundrum, still watching their target, who now seemed to have finished writing, because she was in the process of licking the envelope, sealing it and slipping it into her coat pocket.

'Who'd have thought it?' he said. 'Seems Nan Creeley isn't as dim as our pal, Vic Mortimer, thinks. She probably isn't as dim as Vic himself.' He leaned into Gail's personal space. 'Suppose what you've just seen over there is a diversion?'

'What you mean?'

'Nan's not sure if anyone's watching . . . but just in case they are, she wants them to think she's written a letter.'

'She *has* written a letter. We just saw—'

'No.' He caught her hand under the table and squeezed it. 'No . . . we saw her write *something*.'

'Yeah, and then she sealed the envelope and put it in her pocket.'

'That's the clever part.'

Gail still watched the woman but was looking and sounding tetchy. 'I still don't follow.'

'Listen . . . as far as the world knows, Nan Creeley's just written an everyday letter, which she will soon go off and innocently post. Yes?'

'OK . . .'

'But suppose she's not written an everyday letter, and that envelope is in fact empty?'

'How'd you get that?'

'Something weird's obviously going on. Like you say, why bother writing a letter to a neighbour she sees all the time? Even if she's fallen out with that neighbour and will only now communicate in writing, why not save the price of a stamp and shove it through the letter box? Anyway, we know she's already written several of these letters.'

'Yeah, but . . .' Gail shook her head, 'why bother sending empty envelopes?'

'Because they're dummies, designed to distract people like us.' He paused to think. 'Though I suppose that begs the question why not send them to her own house?'

'Now you've totally lost me,' Gail said.

'Most likely, it's down to our clodhopping friends, Hodges and Mortimer, who've been all over this neighbourhood like a rash.'

'You mean she's clocked them?'

'Totally. They might as well have walked around Orchard Park with megaphones. Nan Creeley probably already knew who Hodges was when he tailed her into this pub.'

'Now I get it,' Gail said. 'She knew he'd see her posting letters, and was worried that he might get a warrant to open the post box?'

'Exactly. Which is what he did. But none of the letters or packages in that pillar box were of interest, were they? All the names got checked . . . and none of them rang any alarms.'

'Whereas, if she'd addressed the dummy envelope to herself, that might have aroused at least some suspicion,' Gail said.

'Exactly. That's why she addressed it to a completely innocent party, nice old Maggie Stoke who lives next door.' Heck sat back. 'So, there you go – dead end.'

'But what would Maggie Stoke think, receiving empty envelopes through the post?'

'She won't think anything. She's infirm, or so we've been told.'

'Heck, we don't know how badly . . .'

'She doesn't get around easily. That's what Hodges said. OK, doesn't mean she's completely immobile . . . but Nan Creeley has a key to her flat, provided by Maggie herself, because she needs quite a bit of assistance. Is it such a stretch to assume that bedridden Maggie can't get down the hall easily to pick her mail up?'

'There's a lot of assuming going on here.'

'But it's logical. Nan Creeley goes next door every day, first thing in the morning. Ostensibly, to help Maggie out. But maybe to recover the empty envelope too.'

Gail still looked doubtful. 'That's going to an awful lot of trouble.'

'Yeah, but it worked.' Heck never took his eyes from the near-stationary figure in the corner, fascinated to know what the next move might be. 'It certainly threw Hodges and Mortimer off the trail. We can check anyway. They'll have kept a record of all the letters that search warrant turned up in the pillar box.'

'Sounds vaguely plausible, but . . .' Gail shook her head, 'the real question is, if whatever she wrote over there hasn't gone into that envelope, where is it now?'

'Probably still over there. On the bar.'

Gail tried not to look as puzzled as she clearly felt. She couldn't see if there was any paperwork still on the bar-top and said as much.

Heck shrugged. 'To be fair, Gail, you yourself admitted that you couldn't see what she was actually writing, or what she was writing it on. Could have been the back of a bus ticket, for all we know.'

'Heck . . . let's be realistic.'

'OK, but it doesn't have to be a sheet of foolscap, or something we'd see easily.'

Gail pondered. 'If all this cloak-and-dagger stuff is real, and not pure imagination, that suggests she's writing to her brother, doesn't it?'

'It also suggests she's meeting someone here who knows where he is,' Heck said.

'Again, that seems like a stretch.'

'Just eliminate the other possibilities. If she still intends to post that note, whatever it is, why not just write it at home, where no one can see and no one will be suspicious? No . . . she's here because she's meeting someone, and she wants to put it into their hand personally.'

'So why not just pass it to someone out on the street? You know, she's walking one way, he's walking another . . . seemingly accidental contact.'

'That doesn't work if you're as conscious that you're being watched as Nan Creeley is. She knows the cops are onto her. So, coming in here serves two purposes, firstly to create the diversion, secondly to somehow pass the real message on.'

'So, the next person she talks to . . .?'

'Uh-uh.' He shook his head, as though suddenly doubting his own thesis. 'Can't be that obvious, even *with* the diversion.'

'So, how the hell is she going to do it?'

'I don't know. We just need to keep obbing her. But don't make it too obvious. She doesn't know us from Adam . . . but this is a locals' pub, so that alone may cause her to be suspicious.'

In response, Gail took a compact from her bag, and though she continued to keep watch, made a show of fixing her make-up. Heck, meanwhile, sank some more beer. Not that Nan Creeley seemed in any way suspicious. She wasn't looking back at them, and in fact barely seemed to have registered their presence. Now that her letter was written, she stared into space, a worried and preoccupied look on her face.

'She doesn't look too happy,' Gail observed.

'No,' Heck agreed. For the first time, he wondered why it was that the woman might be attempting to contact her estranged brother.

Gail stood up. 'Shall I get us another round?'

'No. She's already had a gander at you. I'll go this time.'

He strolled over to the bar. The hour was getting on, and

the pub filling up. The licensee had now appeared alongside the barmaid. He was an older man with a squat build and square shoulders. Despite his shirt and tie, he possessed a thuggish aura. His grey hair was thinning, but sideburns adorned both his cheeks, and he had a snarly, hangdog face. Because there were now two staff on, Heck was served quickly and didn't get much of a chance to survey the lone figure at the end of the bar, or the bar-top alongside her. It also struck him that time was running out. Hodges had told them that Nan Creeley normally stayed in The Crewman for an hour – she'd arrived at 8:30 p.m. and it was now 9:25.

'We're not getting anywhere here,' Gail said, when he sat down again. 'Sod this, Heck . . . we need to know what we're looking for. I'm paying another visit.'

Heck said nothing as she stood up and crossed the pub. This time, a couple of loutish individuals stopped her, both semi-inebriated and passing ribald comments on her sexy attire. The Gail Honeyford of their previous association would have bristled with outrage, but tonight she stayed in character, exchanging a few flirty quips with them. She even managed to put on an amateur-dramatics-standard northern accent.

Heck continued to watch Nan Creeley, who, in somewhat desultory fashion, sipped away the last suds of her bitter and commenced buttoning her coat. Gail also noticed this and broke away from the two men with a comment about desperately needing to pee.

She passed the woman as closely as possible, before ducking through the entrance to the Ladies', where she halted and hovered, never allowing the target to leave her eyeline.

Nan Creeley snapped the last button into place and set off across the pub.

Heck watched her hawkishly, looking for any last-second contact with someone.

But she met no one en route to the door.

Once she'd left the premises, Gail re-emerged from the Ladies', checked the bar-top on the off-chance something had been left there and returned to their table.

'Nothing,' she grunted. 'No notepaper, no bus ticket. If there ever was, she's taken it with her.'

Heck stared at the distant corner. 'Nothing at all?'

'Nothing but the beer mats.' Gail was visibly restless. 'Shouldn't we get after her?'

'Just wait.' On the surface, the obbo had failed, but some sixth sense was telling Heck that this thing wasn't over yet.

'Look, Heck, if she's going to meet someone—'

'If that's the case, why did she come in here first and risk drawing attention to herself? Hang on, whoa . . .' He turned to look at her. *Beer mats?*'

'That's all. Just a couple of . . .' Gail's eyes widened. 'Did she write that note on a beer mat?' She stood up. 'I'll go and look . . .'

'Wait.' Heck grabbed her arm.

'Christ's sake . . . we need to *know*. All I have to do is—'

He pulled her back into her seat. 'We don't want the beer mat as much as the person who picks it up. And if he's in here now, watching, you go and fiddle with it and he won't show.'

Reluctantly, Gail remained in her seat, fingers interlocked to stop her hands trembling.

Heck could tell that she was deeply frustrated. Fleetingly, he remembered the reservations he'd had about Gail a couple of years ago: that she was sharp, keen and dedicated to the job, but that she lacked patience.

'Listen,' he said quietly. 'If she's been leaving notes on the beer mats that would explain a lot.' He pushed her half-finished drink across the table to her. 'Let's give it another few minutes . . . see if anyone picks one of those beer mats up, yeah?'

Slowly, getting a grip on herself, Gail nodded.

They watched again, absorbedly, though no one came anywhere near the now-vacated farthest end of the bar.

'It would be so easy for me just to go over there and check,' Gail said. 'I feel like we're doing nothing, Heck. And yet we have a suspect who may be about to meet a contact . . .'

'I've told you—'

'I hear all that. But look at these people. Is anyone behaving furtively? Does anyone look wrong for this place?'

It was true. Almost to a one, those other people in the pub were now engrossed in laughter and conversation.

'Gail . . . Eddie Creeley is very good at evading the law. That's not going to happen for him if he uses amateurs.'

But briefly he wondered if Gail was right. What did they have so far that was solid? Nothing. And it was amazing how often you could delude yourself into believing that 'nothing' actually meant 'something'.

He shook it from his head.

This was only the first night of the ground-level investigation. They could afford to be imaginative.

'She's been gone five minutes now, Heck, and no one's making any kind of move.'

'Perhaps they're wary of us . . . we're newcomers, after all.'

'Heck . . . no one's even watching us.'

'Eddie Creeley doesn't do obvious. That's why his old muckers don't even know where he is.'

'Look . . .' She made to stand up again.

'*Wait*!' he hissed.

She glanced over and saw the tattooed barmaid mopping down the bar-top in the area where Nan Creeley had been standing. And then start rearranging the beer mats – one of which she took away with her.

'Good God,' Gail breathed. 'Is that barmaid the contact?'

'It would make sense,' Heck said. 'That would explain why Nan's been coming in here and not going anywhere else.'

He lurched to his feet.

'Heck?'

'Stay here, I'll not be a sec.'

He walked quickly to the bar. The barmaid was down by the till. She no longer had the beer mat in hand, but it seemed to Heck that she'd just slipped something into the back pocket of her jeans.

'What can I get you?' the landlord asked.

'Oh, erm . . .' Heck glanced towards the barmaid again; various packets of nuts and crisps hung on the display stand next to her. 'Bag of salt and vinegar, please.'

The landlord turned. 'Fee, chuck us some salt and vinegar, will you, pet?'

The barmaid did as he asked. Heck paid and moved back to the table.

'Feeling peckish?' Gail asked.

He sat down. 'Think she slipped something into her back pocket, but I didn't see what.'

'You know, that mat might just have been dirty or torn. It's probably in the bin.'

'The landlord called her "Fee".'

'And that's relevant because . . .?'

'Because it's all we need.' He grabbed his phone and stood up.

'Where are you going now?'

'Calling Eric Fisher. But I can't have that conversation in here. You hold the fort, yeah?'

'Hang on, Heck . . .'

'Keep watching Miss Tattoo. Stuff may still happen.'

Gail muttered with irritation but remained in her seat.

Heck walked through the pub's rear door and out into the darkened car park. Only one or two vehicles were present, but he wandered around to ensure there was nobody loitering inside any of them. Then he put the call through.

'Yello,' Eric Fisher said, on answering.

'Hi, mate.'

'Thought it might be you. Especially when I saw it was almost ten o'clock at night.'

Heck glanced up at the pub's first-floor windows to ensure that no one was eavesdropping from on high. 'I need something very fast, Eric. Really fast.'

'Don't we all,' Fisher said. 'Preferably blonde, 38-24-38 . . .'

'No time for pipe dreams, mate.'

'All right . . . let's hear it?'

Heck heard Fisher's fingers bang the keys of the laptop that habitually sat open on the coffee table in front of him when he was watching TV in the evening.

'White female, early thirties,' Heck said. 'Red-brown hair. Heavy build, scuzzy tats on both arms. Humberside region . . .'

'Define scuzzy?' Fisher said.

'Could be prison tats, but you never can tell these days. One distinctive tat on the left bicep. Only saw it from a distance, but looks like a Chinese dragon.'

'Any names?'

'Only one. Could either be a street name or a nickname. "Fee".'

A brief silence followed, and then Fisher exhaled with satisfaction. 'Try this for size . . . Fiona Birkdale, 13, Crawford Crescent, Bransholme, Kingston-upon-Hull, thirty-three years old. Sound like her?'

'Could be. Keep going.'

'Well-known. Form for drunk and disorderly, possession,

dealing, wounding, theft. Sounds like a rum 'un. Not currently wanted, no outstanding warrants. Sorry if that means you're not going to get the leverage you doubtless need.'

'I'll find some leverage, mate,' Heck replied. 'Don't you worry.'

Chapter 14

The picture texted to Heck's phone by Eric Fisher left them in no doubt that the woman behind the bar was Fiona Birkdale. It was a custody photo and a couple of years old, depicting a female with longish dark hair. But aside from that, she hadn't changed.

They remained at the pub table, having another round of drinks, and continued to watch her as the clock ticked towards closing time.

'We'll wait till she leaves, and pull her on the way home,' Heck said. 'If she's got wheels, we'll take her at her front door. If she's on foot, we can find somewhere a bit quieter.'

'Heck . . . I appreciate it's a promising lead,' Gail said. 'But let's be honest. We *can't* pull her. This isn't even circumstantial.'

'That's sadly true,' he agreed.

'So why don't we do it all lawful-like? We go back to the nick and report to Gemma. And we come back here tomorrow with Hodges and Mortimer, and even DCI Bateson, if he's so keen to see where his money's being spent . . . with a warrant, based on the suspicion that she's been assisting an offender. We turn her pad over, we're bound to find something . . . we arrest her, and we're on our way to striking pay dirt.'

'Or alternatively just dirt.'

'Why?' she asked.

Heck glanced sidelong at her. 'Because if we lock her up, she'll give us absolutely squat. Look, Gail . . . whatever message was written on that beer mat, it'll be in code or couched in non-incriminating language. It's certainly not going to include directions to Eddie Creeley's hideout. Those directions will be safe inside Fiona Birkdale's head. And she won't give them to us. Why would she? We'll ultimately finish up charging her with possession or handling, or whatever Mickey Mouse offence it is that we finally drag her down to Clough Road for. And she'll take that on the chin, even if it means doing a little time. You know why? Because even that is better than being known as a grass.'

'And instead, we do what?'

'Waylay her and have a private chat. That way, no one will know that she's told us anything. We actually give her a reason to help us.'

'So, what you're saying is we'll be granting her some kind of immunity from prosecution . . . even from having to give evidence?'

'Basically, yeah.'

'And are we authorised to do that?'

'Course we aren't.'

'Hell, Heck . . .' She shook her head. 'I don't see how this is going to work.'

'I know. Give it a bit of time, though. And you will.'

Before Gail could object further, the object of their interest, having briefly disappeared into a back room, now reappeared wearing an anorak.

'Off, Harry,' she shouted.

'Tomorrow, pet!' he replied, barely looking up from the

conversation he was having with one of the few locals left in the pub.

Heck glanced at the clock, which said that it was quarter-to-midnight. He swilled down the last of his beer, grabbed his jacket and stood up. Gail finished her wine and did the same. Outside, they at first saw no sign of the barmaid, which caused brief consternation, but then spotted a figure walking quickly away down an otherwise deserted side street, hands jammed into front pockets.

'Good, she's walking,' Heck said. 'Can you get after her, just in case she takes a side passage, or something? I'll drive ahead . . . try and cut her off.'

'Why do *you* get to drive?'

'Because I'm in charge.'

'Seriously, Heck?'

'Do you really want a debate, Gail? Think it through. I'm a bloke. If she sees me following her at this time of night, what do *you* think'll happen?'

'OK . . . I suppose . . .'

'Yeah, exactly. She may not run off, shouting for help. But she may shout. Do we need that kind of hullabaloo?'

Gail hurried off in pursuit.

Heck jumped into his Megane and gunned it to life.

Had Gail not known better, she'd have suspected that her quarry was deliberately leading her into dangerous territory. She followed her at about fifty yards, along several streets comprised of nothing more than boarded-up council properties. Only a few of the streetlamps here worked, so it was a tale of unremitting gloom. A couple of times, she thought that the chunky shape ahead glanced back at her, but these were fleeting, and in the restricted lighting it was difficult to be sure.

The barmaid then turned a corner and crossed a wasteland

littered with demolition rubble. This was particularly awkward going for Gail in her high-heeled boots, but Birkdale didn't gain much ground. Beyond the rubble, she veered down a passage between blocks of flats. These structures were occupied, most of their upper windows showing lights. It made Gail feel better, though the passage was long, perhaps seventy yards, and narrow. Its walls were sheer, and as it wasn't overlooked by any of the apartments, the only light leaking into it came from the far end, though that wasn't reassuring, as Gail had expected to see the diminishing form of the barmaid silhouetted there, and yet, suddenly, there was nobody.

She stumbled along more quickly but found that old furniture and mattresses, and numerous sacks of festering rubbish, had been dumped the full length of the alley.

'Shit,' she muttered, struggling to clamber around or over it all, and wondering where the hell Heck had got to.

At which point a burly form stepped out of a recess directly in front of her. Gail came to a shocked halt.

'Looking for me, love?' a voice asked.

It was hard, guttural. But it was also female.

'Don't bother answering that, pet,' the barmaid said. 'I saw you giving me the eye in the pub. So, I suppose the next question is . . . you looking for some action?'

Gail was so taken aback that she couldn't initially respond.

Even in the half-light of the alley, Fiona Birkdale was a singularly unattractive presence; broad and heavily built, with pale, doughy cheeks, a low brow and small eyes. Her reddish hair had been slashed into a severe crew cut.

'I don't know,' Gail said warily. 'Maybe.'

Birkdale switched her phone light on, bathing the police-woman in a dazzling glow. A lingering silence followed, during which Gail realised that she was being assessed.

'Think you've got me wrong, pet.' Birkdale switched her

141

light off. 'Probably the tats and the haircut, eh? I don't normally do birds. But looking at you, fuck . . . maybe I can be flexible.'

'Excellent,' came a male voice behind her. 'Just what we like to hear.'

Heck had advanced from the far end of the passage and caught both of them unawares.

Birkdale swung around. Her hand stole into her anorak pocket, where possibly she kept a weapon. 'What the fuck is this?' she barked.

'Relax, Fiona.' He displayed his warrant card. 'We're police officers.'

Birkdale remained where she was, hand in pocket, as if unsure whether this revelation was reason enough to stand down. Only slowly, with barely concealed curses, did she relent, her hand coming back into view, empty.

'Fuck,' she said. 'Fuck, fuck, fuck . . .' She rounded on Gail, doubly furious with herself for being taken in. 'Nice outfit, love . . . must've taken a while to doll yourself up till you looked human. Pity it was all for nothing.'

'That depends on whether you consider gathering evidence of serious crime nothing,' Heck said.

Birkdale swung back to face him, baring manky teeth. 'I haven't committed a serious crime.'

'Really? What would you call obstructing a murder enquiry, assisting an offender?'

'I've no fucking clue what you're talking about.' She hunched her shoulders and tried to brush past him.

'Hang fire.' He pushed her back, unceremoniously. 'Don't force me to arrest you.'

'I've not done nothing.' But her tone had now turned querulous. She was undoubtedly tough, but she was also frightened.

'That beer mat in your pocket says different,' Heck said, taking his first big chance of the night. Birkdale's inability to answer this encouraged him to take another. He held his phone up. 'I've got you on film picking it up from the bar-top after Nan Creeley wrote on it and putting it in your back pocket.'

Gail said nothing, but, even having worked with Heck before, she was amazed by the audacity of that line. He hadn't taken any film during the pub stake-out.

'Look,' the barmaid said, her voice breaking, almost becoming a whine. 'I'm just delivering a message.'

Gail glanced at Heck with thinly suppressed fascination; he'd been right all along. He didn't acknowledge this, though. It was no time for triumphalism.

'I never ask any questions,' Birkdale said, her voice having gone from aggression to weakness so swiftly that it verged on the ridiculous.

'That won't work, Fiona,' Gail said. 'Eddie Creeley isn't just wanted in connection with one of the biggest armed robberies of the twenty-first century, he's a two-time murderer who injected his victims with corrosive fluids. Do you really want a court to think you're his protector?'

'I'm not his protector.' Tears glinted in the barmaid's lashes. 'I'm just a messenger girl.'

'Fine,' Heck said. 'Give the message to us. And then you can take a walk.'

'They'll kill me.'

'Why would anyone kill you? No one'll even know about it.'

'You've collared me in the middle of the street . . .'

'No,' Gail said, 'we've collared you in an alleyway.'

'But we can easily march you out into the street and have this conversation at the tops of our voices, if you want,' Heck said.

'You've got nothing on me.' The barmaid straightened up bullishly, trying to regain control. 'So, I'm not saying fuck all.'

'OK.' He took the cuffs out. 'In that case, I arrest you. DC Honeyford then searches you . . . and finds the beer mat on which Nan Creeley wrote that message to her brother. The upshot: we get the message anyway, and you get charged.'

'No . . . no!' She shook her head angrily. 'That's where you're wrong. The message isn't for her brother. Nan doesn't know where he is, and neither do I.'

'Why don't you cut the crap,' Heck retorted, 'and show us what it says.'

'It won't mean anything to you. It doesn't mean anything to me.'

'Show it to us anyway.'

'Look . . .' She glanced from one to the other, wet-eyed. Her anger had ebbed again, almost as quickly as it had risen. She was either a consummate actress, or she really was this emotionally unstable. It could have been either as far as Heck knew; not that he cared.

'You've got three seconds to decide, Fiona.'

'You'll seriously let me go?' she said. 'I give you this note and walk away, and no one ever knows?'

'Not unless you tell them yourself.'

She evidently wasn't as stupid as she looked, and realising that this was the best deal she was going to get, she reached to her back pocket and drew out a folded beer mat.

'First thing you should know . . .' She handed it over. 'Nan Creeley's a sad cow.'

'You don't say,' Gail replied.

Heck studied the beer mat by torchlight.

'She's written three of these the last few nights,' Birkdale added. 'They always say the same thing.'

Heck handed it to Gail. She too read the scribbled hand-writing:

Contact me
Ed in trouble
Scared

Heck's immediate thought was that this message possibly referred to the extra police effort being put into locating Creeley since the launch of Operation Sledgehammer, but he quickly dismissed the idea. The robber-turned-murderer lived on the lam because the cops were *always* after him. This was clearly something else. But it was still the link they'd been looking for.

He eyed the woman so intently that she hung her head.

'You told us this message wasn't for Nan's brother,' he said. 'Quite clearly that's true, which is a big tick for you, Fiona. But it begs the question *who* is it for?'

She shrugged but kept her head down. 'Eddie Creeley used to have lots of contacts on Humberside, but not so many now. Only one, really. You know Cyrus Jackson?'

'Remind us,' Heck said.

'Eddie's mate. His bosom buddy from way back. Like . . . they knew each other when they were kids. Even did time in reform school together.' Her eyes were moonlike with worry. 'But Cyrus is bad news too. An out-and-out crim. Truth is, they're both as fucked up as each other. That's why they get on so well.'

'And Cyrus knows where Eddie can be found?'

'Dunno. Nan thinks that. Or she can't think of anyone else to turn to. One or the other.'

'So, you've been delivering these notes on beer mats to Cyrus?' Gail asked.

The barmaid nodded.

'And each one says the same thing?'

Another nod.

'And Cyrus doesn't think that's weird?' Heck said.

'Don't think he's arsed about them. But I give them to him because I don't want to be the one who fails to deliver a message that matters, if you know what I mean.' She shook her head, looking tearful again. 'Wish Nan'd pack it the fuck in. I didn't ask for any of this.'

'What do you mean when you say he's not arsed about them?' Heck said.

'I put them in his hands, he looks at them, bins them. Carries on as normal.'

'Why would that be?'

'Look . . .' her voice turned shrill again, '*I don't fucking know! No one tells me anything!*'

'So, you don't know whether this Cyrus Jackson is in contact with Eddie Creeley, or not?' Gail sought to establish.

'No, and I wouldn't dare ask.'

The cops exchanged glances. Several seconds ago, this had felt like a live lead. But now they weren't so sure.

'How do *you* know Cyrus?' Heck asked her.

She squirmed under his gaze. 'All you wanted was the message. I've given it to you, so let us go, eh?'

'What's so embarrassing about knowing Cyrus Jackson?'

'I don't want to talk about it, that's all.'

'Oh dear, Fiona . . . now you've got us intrigued.'

'Used to deliver stuff for him, if you must know.'

'Let me guess . . . drugs?'

'Course, drugs!' she snapped. But again, just as quickly, she lowered her voice and hung her head. 'Was a user too. I needed stuff . . . did what I needed to, to get it.'

Heck regarded her carefully. 'What does he hook you up with?'

'Nothing. I'm clean.'

'Spare me, Fiona. If you weren't still using, you wouldn't be seeing him regularly enough to give him Nan Creeley's notes. We're not going to tell your boss down at the pub, if that's what's worrying you.'

'We're not here to arrest drug addicts, Fiona,' Gail added.

'So why are you interested in what *I* get up to?'

'Because we need to know what we're dealing with,' Heck said. 'Tell us everything.'

'On the pipe, aren't I!' She glared at Gail. 'And I'm not the only one round here, so don't look at me like that . . .'

'I'm not looking at you like anything.'

'Yes, you are, you snotty bitch. You're fucking judging me . . .'

'Ease off with the aggression,' Heck cut in. 'You've got no power here, Fiona.'

'It's like I'm the shit on her fancy shoes.'

'What do you expect, when you're protecting a drug dealer?' he said.

'I'm not protecting no one. Just told you who he is, didn't I!'

'Well, let's see . . .' Heck paused, mainly for effect. 'The fact is, I'm not interested in you or Cyrus Jackson. As far as I'm concerned, you're both tiddlers. But if your mate, Cyrus, knows where Eddie Creeley is, I'll have to speak to him.'

'Hah, some chance!' She seemed genuinely amused. 'You won't find Cyrus a pushover like me. He'll do time rather than dob his mate in.'

'Which is why I'm going to need to catch him doing something he shouldn't be.'

'What?'

'Like you say . . . I can't just knock on his door and expect him to talk.'

The penny dropped, and her eyes bugged even more.

'I'm not fucking giving you Cyrus. You can forget it. My life wouldn't be worth living.'

'We're getting him anyway,' Heck said. 'Doubtless, we'll have his details on file. And now that we know he's the man, all we need do is watch him till he crosses the line. And when he does, just think what a shame it'd be if I let it slip that *you'd* told me he's been in touch with Eddie.'

She looked appalled. 'But I haven't . . .'

'Yeah, but you see . . . I'm a Lancashire lad, and Cyrus is from Hull, and how often the truth gets lost in translation, eh?'

Now she was crying for real. 'This is blackmail, you pig bastard!'

'No, it's not,' Heck said. 'It's your only way out of a real fucking mess. Now, you tell me where and when we can catch Cyrus in the act, and your name never even needs to come up. In fact, I'll even return this . . .' To her bemusement, he handed back the beer mat. 'Now, you can carry on and give it to him as if this meeting never happened.'

She regarded it dully, before shaking her head. 'He'll still sus me. I'll be looking over my shoulder for the rest of my life.'

'Don't be so melodramatic,' Gail said. 'There are probably junkies all over Humberside who owe everything they are to Cyrus Jackson. You really think you're the only one who's likely to peach on the guy? When it comes to getting even, he won't know where to start.'

Again, the barmaid's sniffles seemed to dry up. She glanced from one to the other, as if hoping to find a chink of mercy. But Fiona Birkdale was nothing if not pragmatic, and she knew a get-out when she saw one.

'The new thing is changa,' she said.

'You mean spice?' Gail replied. 'The zombie drug?'

'That's what they call it. It's a kind of synthetic cannabis. Knocks the shit out of the users.'

'We know what it is,' Heck said. 'You're telling us Jackson's peddling spice in Hull?'

'He runs all sorts. But that's the new one. He's got a few dealers doing it.' She glanced over her shoulder, as if belatedly checking that one of these self-same villains hadn't somehow crept up on them. 'They work the parks and playgrounds at night.'

'The playgrounds?' Gail said.

'Who do you think are keenest to try new stuff? It's always kids.'

'Cyrus Jackson is selling spice to teenagers?'

Birkdale looked genuinely puzzled by the female cop's disgusted tone.

'If he's got dealers doing this for him,' Heck said, 'when does he get his own hands dirty?'

'Look, if anyone finds out this has come from me . . .'

'You still won't be going to prison for the next few years, which you will be if you don't give us something useful.'

'Aiding and abetting a two-time murderer,' Gail reminded her. 'Just think about that.'

'Perverting the course of justice,' Heck said.

'Assisting an offender to avoid arrest,' Gail added.

'All right! All right . . . for fuck's sake. Look, he's got a collection point.'

Birkdale paused again, nervously pondering the wisdom of what she was doing.

'Keep talking,' Heck said.

'It's where he goes to collect the cash. He goes there every Tuesday and Friday night. Tuesday's the biggest, 'cause that includes the weekend take.'

'What time?' Heck asked.

'Ten on the dot. Lasts about twenty minutes. He doesn't hang around.'

'Cyrus collects it personally?'

'Yeah. He doesn't like having too many middlemen. More chance they'll skim.'

Heck looked at Gail. 'Ten p.m., Tuesday night. How convenient, tomorrow being a Tuesday.'

'How do we recognise him?' Gail asked her.

'Drives a white Audi A4.'

'Registration?'

'Do me a fucking favour . . .'

'Attitude, Fiona,' Heck warned her.

'I don't know his registration. Anyway, you won't need it. It'll be the only car there. It'll be the only car anywhere near the fucking place.'

'And where is "the place"?'

'St Andrew's Dock. Derelict spot on the riverfront. Off Clive Sullivan Way.'

'Will he have muscle with him?' Heck asked.

'No, like I say—'

'He doesn't trust people. Yeah, we heard.'

'Bit risky for him,' Gail said.

'You haven't met Cyrus.'

'Will he be armed?' Heck asked.

'Never known him carry a shooter. Like I say, he doesn't need one.'

'He's really that much of a badass?' Gail sounded sceptical.

Birkdale snorted with contempt. 'You have no idea, love. You really have no idea.'

Chapter 15

'Everything OK?'

Barry Hodges seemed a tad puzzled that it was halfway through another day, and yet their guests from Operation Sledgehammer didn't seem to need any assistance from their official liaison. He knew that Heck and Gail had done a late stint the previous night, which explained why they'd only clocked on again just before noon. But it was now two o'clock, and still neither he nor Mortimer had received any kind of report or update.

'We're fine,' Heck said, looking up from the desk he'd been allocated in a corner of the Clough Road DO. Gail, on the other side of it, said nothing.

'Anything last night?' Hodges asked.

Heck thought it through. 'Not really. We made some enquiries around Nan Creeley . . .'

A few yards away, Vic Mortimer shuffled paperwork at his own desk. He smiled to himself and shook his head.

'Nothing doing there so far,' Heck added.

'OK, what's the plan for today?' Hodges wondered.

Heck shrugged. 'Just some follow-ups. Nothing too promising, but I'll let you know.'

Mortimer threw a quick glance in their direction. He still looked amused, but also irritated, as if he couldn't believe departments still existed in the cash-strapped police service of England and Wales where detectives could afford to spend day after day dawdling through unpromising leads. A couple of minutes later, he and Hodges left the office on other business, and Gail spun her chair round to face Heck.

'Lying comes discomfortingly easy to you,' she said tersely.

Heck didn't look up from his notes. 'Do you believe in God, Gail?'

'What?'

'Simple question. Do you believe in God?'

'I'm a twenty-first-century person . . . why would I?'

'Then zip it.'

Half a second of surprise passed, before she sat up straight. 'Excuse me?'

'Lying's not a crime, it's a sin . . . and you don't believe in God, therefore you don't believe in sin. End of conversation.'

He still didn't bother looking up, as he emailed his latest dispatch to Silver Command.

'Cute logic,' she snapped. 'But at the end of the day, what really matters here is not whether I believe in God, it's whether we go out there tonight minus back-up. I mean, last night was one thing, but this is something else again. And, for the record, I want it writing down on paper that I've expressed that opinion.'

'I told you . . . back-up means awkward questions.'

'You mean they'll want to lock Cyrus Jackson up for selling spice, whereas all we're interested in is Eddie Creeley?'

Finally, he glanced at her. 'That's what we're up here for, isn't it?'

'Heck . . . some crimes we can turn a blind eye to. But this is deadly serious.'

'Tonight, we're only there to observe. Let's see what happens. For all we know, Miss Tattoo might have fed us a load of baloney. You want to send the whole of Humberside on a wild goose chase?'

'We're just observing? Definitely?'

'Definitely,' he confirmed. 'We'll probably shoot some footage, too . . . to strengthen our case. Now is that OK with you?'

She sat back again, only vaguely placated.

'And just to be on the safe side,' he said, 'I've got some spare bits of body armour in the car. Some of it should fit you.'

Outside on the car park, Heck stood by his open boot and rummaged inside a bulky blue travel-bag. Gail waited in silence, her face written with doubt.

'Heavier duty gear than normal tonight,' he said. 'An ordinary stab-vest might not cut it. No pun intended.'

'Heck . . . why do we need heavyweight body armour if we're only observing?'

'Think this'll fit.' He tossed her an undershirt made from thick layers of white, tightly woven Kevlar fibres. 'You should know by now, Gail . . . surveillance can be one of the most dangerous jobs there is. Try these too.' He handed her a pair of shin guards, before rooting out some equipment for himself.

'Will I need a gumshield as well?' she wondered acidly.

'If you don't already have one, you need to rectify that.'

'Heck . . . I'm not a rookie, OK. Surveillance is *not* one of the most dangerous jobs there is, if you do it properly.'

'In which case, as *I'll* be in charge tonight, you'll have nothing to worry about.'

'You're gonna go for it, aren't you?' she said. 'If Cyrus Jackson shows up, you're gonna try and grab him?'

153

Heck gave her a tired stare. 'Gail . . . we're strangers in a strange land. Two police officers on foreign soil, pursuing a dangerous criminal who is not just native to this region, but has all kinds of connections here. That means, at the very least, that we need to be adaptable. If I have to make snap decisions when we're out in the field, if I have to change plans on the hoof because a good option has unexpectedly arisen . . . I'm not going to apologise to you for that.'

'Heck . . . we may be strangers, but we've got a whole police force at our beck and call.'

'You've already seen how uninterested they are. And, frankly, I don't blame them. What are we, Gail . . . homicide specialists, serial killer experts? No, I'll tell you . . . as far as this lot are concerned, we're the only two units our ailing, underfunded outfit can spare, and like everyone else in Operation Sledgehammer, at present we're part of a last-gasp, scattergun effort to prove to the top floor that we are worth our elite status. Meanwhile, like divisional forces up and down the country, Humberside are struggling to keep nicks open and man everyday shifts.'

'OK,' she said. 'I get that. But we still don't need to do this thing on our own.'

'If it goes pear-shaped, they'll only be a radio call away.'

'Late on a Tuesday night? How many are likely to be on? We'll be lucky if we get any more than a pair of bored beat-lads.'

'They're an urban police force, Gail.' He slammed his boot closed. 'They don't have time to get bored.'

Though a lot of the Hull riverfront was undergoing modernisation and redevelopment, the St Andrew's Dock area, despite its central location, was still in need of some TLC.

Much of it was barren, wild grasses and weeds growing along its disused roads, flat demolition land where warehouses

154

and other installations had once been. The skeletal timber structures of a few disused piers, protruding out into the lapping brown waters, were a melancholy reminder of better times past.

There were various spots here where Cyrus Jackson could have chosen to park up and await his couriers, and none would have been any more conspicuous than the next, because though it was a relatively open place, there was very little else here. There was no reason for anyone to visit, especially after darkness had fallen, as there was no streetlighting. Even so, Heck and Gemma had finally got Fiona Birkdale to be specific about where the exact spot was before letting her go and had learned that it was an empty, litter-filled parking bay in front of the chain-link fence blocking the entrance to Pier No. 6, another dilapidated relic of the local fishing industry, which, according to the notice on the chain, was 'Unsafe'.

They parked a considerable distance away on a nearby retail park and then recced the area on foot early that evening, finally locating the spot and discovering that, directly across the deserted road from it, there was a tumbledown red-brick wall, beyond which lay only scrub-thorn – which made a perfect observation point. By nine o'clock that evening, a balmy dusk had fallen, the sky burning a dim orange over the distant south shore. At the same time, the sounds of the city gradually diminished until, by 9:30 p.m., they were almost non-existent. The water sloshing around the decayed pilings of No. 6 was eerily audible.

Heck and Gail were appropriately 'scruffed out' in jeans, sweatshirts and trainers. They'd also brought along light-weight anoraks in case it rained, but that possibility had dwindled while they'd been here, and the unused waterproofs lay on the broken stones alongside them, along with a small haversack containing their radios, a flask, some sandwiches, a torch, a CS canister and a pair of expandable batons.

Heck fitted his Canon XF100 night-vision camera into a niche between the dislodged bricks, and lay full length to peer through it, adjusting its super-zoom lens until it was squarely trained on the parking bay opposite.

As he did, the phone began to vibrate in his pocket. On seeing that the caller was Gary Quinnell, he put it to his ear. 'Gaz?'

'How's it going?' the jovial Welsh voice asked.

'We've got a sniff of something,' Heck replied. 'I think.'

'How's your new sidekick coming on?'

'We've had some differences of opinion . . .' Heck glanced at Gail, who stuck her tongue out. 'But, at present, common sense is prevailing. How's everyone else doing?'

'Not good, from what I'm hearing. Reed thinks he's got a lead, but no one's holding their breath. Sounds like he's in High Wycombe, pressuring Hallahan, the McDonald's shooter's estranged daughter . . . even though she hasn't spoken to the bastard for years.'

Heck wasn't sure whether it was right to feel smug about that, or not. Patrick Hallahan had killed three people during his attempted robbery of a Slough fast-food outlet some four years ago. Bringing that piece of scum to justice was surely a higher priority than seeing Jack Reed with egg on his pretty face, but sometimes you couldn't help your inner feelings.

'How are you getting on in Shropshire?' Heck asked.

'Odd one, really.' Quinnell sounded bemused. 'John Stroud's girlfriend, Darlene Stewart's been helpful . . . because she reckons she's worried about him.'

'She should be. He's facing two life sentences minimum . . . assuming something doesn't happen to him on the way to court.'

Heck was only half-joking. In 2013, one-time gangster and escaped convict, John Stroud had ambushed and shot dead two police officers who'd originally given evidence against him; among members of Operation Sledgehammer, and the wider police family, he was easily one of the most hated targets on the list.

'I don't mean like that,' Quinnell said. 'She's admitted he stayed with her for a while when he was on the run. She also claims to have been the last one to see him, except that there was some bloke looking for him around the same time, who wasn't a copper.'

'Yeah?' Heck was briefly distracted by what might have been the rumble of an engine somewhere close by. He listened out, but it faded again. 'Did she give a description?'

'Fair hair, late thirties or early forties.'

'Piece of piss finding him, pal.'

'It's vague, I know. But Stroud had apparently been crashing in the back room of some snooker joint that her brother managed. Sounds like he was sleeping under one of the benches. It wasn't ideal. The local fuzz were poking their noses around. Kept missing him by inches, by the sounds of it.'

'Great work, West Mercia.'

'Anyway, one day she takes some stuff round for him, clean undies and that – and this blond fella's sat down and chatting to him.'

'Did Stroud make an introduction?'

'Nah. She glimpsed them through the door, but didn't go in. Said they were like old mates . . . said she hadn't seen John looking so relaxed in months.'

'I'm so glad,' Heck said. 'Always cheers me up to know a cop killer's feeling good about himself.'

'Yeah, but the thing is . . . next day he wasn't there.'

'What do you mean?'

'Gone. No trace of him.'

'So he got his ticket out.'

'Yeah, but Darlene doesn't know where to. She's het up

157

about it. Says he didn't leave her a note or a forwarding address, or anything . . . says that would be very unlike him.'

'She *is* aware we're talking about a suspect in the murder of two police officers here? And that she could get seriously done for her involvement in harbouring him?'

'Oh yeah, but like I say, she's really worried. I mean seriously.'

Heck was about to pass another disparaging comment about the inability of a certain type of deluded person to see any evil at all in the deeds of their loved ones, when something struck him that gave him pause for thought.

'When was this?' he asked curiously.

'Middle of last Feb. Says she hasn't seen the blond bloke since.'

Heck didn't get a chance to question him further, because now he heard that engine again, and this time it didn't fade. Gail glanced around, trying to locate it in the twilight.

'I've got to go, Gaz.'

'Yeah, all right. Take care, boy.'

'Speak later.' Heck shoved the phone into his pocket, pushing all other thoughts aside.

The rumble was growing louder, the vehicle responsible clearly approaching. Heck and Gail dropped from sight, scrambling to the crevices they'd selected as vantage points.

Half a second later, a white Audi A4 cruised slowly by.

Heck waited until it had passed and vanished along the barren shore.

He stuck his head up. 'By anyone's reckoning, that's got to be Jackson?'

'Isn't it a bit early?' Gail asked.

'He's making a drive-by. Checking there are no odd-bods around.'

She glanced over her shoulder, feeling vulnerable and wanting to ensure that none of Jackson's associates were encroaching from the rear. But the only movement came from a coastal breeze rippling through the straggly vegetation.

They waited a little longer, keeping low as a distant hum gradually resolved itself back into the rumble of the engine. As they watched through their respective crannies, the white Audi returned, this time wallowing into place on the parking bay, and halting. With a clunk, a handbrake was applied, and the engine was turned off. In the rapidly dying light, only the vague outline of the driver was visible, despite him powering down his window.

Heck pressed a button, and the camera began to record.

'Got your pocketbook?' he whispered.

'My pocketbook?' Gail whispered back.

'You need to take notes, Gail. Contemporaneous . . . everything that happens, OK?'

'Aren't we filming this?'

'Yeah, but notes taken at the time are the best corroboration there is. Don't worry, I can countersign them later. So that'll be two witnesses as well as the footage.'

She slid over the stones and grass to the bag, groped inside and brought out her pocketbook and a pen. Another three or four minutes passed, dusk entering its final stage, the blue-purple twilight dissolving into the full blackness of night.

'Won't be able to see much,' she muttered.

'I think we can see enough,' Heck replied. 'Our pal, Cyrus, isn't as cautious as he should be. That motor stands out a mile.'

This turned out to be truer even than Heck expected, because almost immediately after that something happened which took them both by surprise. A figure on a mountain bike materialised from nowhere, hurtling up to the car from behind and skidding to a halt alongside the open window, framing itself perfectly on the white bodywork.

Heck leaned down, to get a better view through the night-vision lens.

The cyclist looked like a kid, or, at the most, a teen. His features were hidden beneath a cagoule with the hood pulled up, but he was small in stature and lean of build.

As they watched and filmed, he produced what was quite clearly a substantial wad of cash, wrapped together with elastic bands, and offered it to a hand that had half-emerged from the window. The cash disappeared, but, just as quickly, the hand reappeared with a smaller roll of notes, which the cyclist shoved into one of his cagoule pockets. Words were exchanged at a mumble, before the hand appeared a second time, this time with a plastic bag of grassy-looking resin. The cyclist thrust it into another capacious pocket and pushed himself away from the Audi, scooting into the blackness.

'I take it we got all that?' Gail said.

'We got it, all right,' Heck replied. 'Quick and efficient, this operation . . . but we got it.'

They waited another minute or two, and the same thing happened again, a young cyclist appearing along the road from the rear of the car, handing over a pile of money, receiving payment for himself and then another portion of product, which he pocketed before pedalling off into the night.

It happened a third time as well.

And then a fourth.

'Amazing, the villainous use pushbikes can be put to, eh?' Heck said.

'Never have believed it if I hadn't seen it with my own eyes,' Gail replied. 'Can it really be as simple as this?'

'Simplicity's good . . . if you want to get up close and personal.'

He pulled his anorak on and zipped it, before crawling to the haversack, taking one of the expandable batons out and shoving it into the back of his jeans. Rising to a crouch, he scampered away.

'Where are you going?' Gail hissed.

'Stay here. Keep clocking everyone who comes.'

'Heck, you're not doing anything stupid!'

'Just do your job, DC Honeyford. Let me do mine.'

Still keeping low, he shuffled further and further from the obbo point, until the Audi was some distance behind him, at which point he rose up and moved at a stooping run along the edge of the road, weaving around clumps of vegetation, vaulting fragments of dockside architecture. With no streetlamps around, he was navigating by starlight, just about able to distinguish the pale ribbon of tarmac denoting the road, and the flat sweep of the river beyond that. Eventually, when he'd put some three hundred yards between himself and Pier No. 6, he halted and squatted beside a brick post.

He waited, breathing hard, mopping sweat with the sleeve of his anorak. His blood began to slow, his heartbeat to recede.

And then he heard it: the approaching *whirr* of bicycle wheels.

He couldn't see it as it sped towards his position, which was a problem; it meant that he'd have to judge purely by sound, and he'd need to be accurate. If he timed this thing incorrectly, his one chance of getting something useful out of Cyrus Jackson without the entire Humberside Police breathing down his neck would be gone. He jumped to his feet, perambulating out into the middle of the road.

As he did, a blurred form emerged from nowhere.

Heck glimpsed a figure slouched back in the saddle, pedalling fast but casually, one hand gripping a pair of extended handlebars.

He jammed his left arm out, muscles tensed, fist clenched. When the cyclist spotted him, it was too late.

161

The impact caught him across the chest. By his high-pitched yelp, he really was young; maybe no more than sixteen or seventeen. He catapulted backward, the bike flying out from under him, clattering away along the aged tarmac.

By the brutish exhalation of air as the kid hit the deck, he was badly winded.

Heck ran up to him.

'Fucking little shit!' he snarled in his best 'nasty bastard' voice. 'Gimme the cash, or I'll rip your fucking gonads off. Every penny . . . you fucking little shit!'

Wheezing with pain and fear, the kid crab-crawled away, and then jumped up to his feet and started running.

'Your boss is nothing!' Heck growled, chasing. 'Nothing, you get it! He's lying back there in an open grave . . . which is exactly where *you'll* be! Gimme the fucking money!'

At least the kid was loyal. He didn't give up the money as he ran, though that could easily have been because he was already thinking two steps ahead – if Cyrus really *was* dead and some other firm had moved in, some right set of bastards, he might need to go to ground, and for that he'd need some green. On top of that, he was swift on his toes.

Heck landed one swiping kick on his backside, eliciting another yelp, before the youngster put his burner on and accelerated into the night.

Satisfied, Heck slowed to a halt, turned and headed back to look for the bike. He found it lying half over the kerb. In the dimness, he couldn't tell whether it was damaged or not, but when he pushed it forward and leapt into the saddle, it rolled freely enough.

His feet caught the pedals, and soon he was pumping back along the riverside road.

In no time, the sleek white shape of the Audi slid into view.

Heck braked and pulled up next to its open window. With no headlights or interior lights switched on, Jackson would be blind as to who exactly this was, though, in return, Heck couldn't see much of the drug dealer. Thanks to the faint red glow of the dashboard clock, he thought he could picture an immense barrel torso, a short-sleeved Hawaiian-patterned shirt, the glint of neck chains, the black bush of a beard.

But Heck wasn't really looking at the driver. What he was looking for, he found straight away: the keys dangling from the ignition. Jackson said something, but Heck wasn't listening. Instead, he reached down and snatch-grabbed the keys, shoving them into his anorak pocket.

'Hey . . .?' the dealer blurted, only for Heck's hand to reappear with a wallet in it, which he flipped open, showing his warrant card.

'You're locked up, pal. Suspicion of possessing drugs with intent to . . .'

With a roar of bestial rage, the driver kicked his door open.

It slammed into Heck's side, and as he was still astride the bike, he toppled over, landing full length on the road. Jackson, who was spry for such a big man, sprang out after him. Heck glimpsed a huge, bowling-ball-shaped figure, immense shoulders, but also a hefty gut straining under that luridly patterned shirt. Before he could see more, Jackson landed on him with both knees. The guy weighed twenty stone at least, so it was a crushing impact, impressing the frame of the bike into Heck's left leg with such force that he thought it would cleave straight through. A heavy punch from a ham-fist descended. That might have done equal damage, had Heck not deflected it with his right forearm and tried to grab the bastard by the beard. Jackson tore himself loose and, with another animalistic roar, stumbled away across the road as he sought an escape route. Heck saw that he was carrying some kind of sports bag, which he'd presumably taken from the front passenger seat. But panicked though he was, the dealer slid to a standstill, one meaty forearm jammed across his eyes, when dazzling torch-light blazed into him.

'Serial Crimes Unit to Bravo Comms,' Gail shouted into her radio. 'Immediate support required at Pier No. 6 off Clive Sullivan Way. Officer down and injured, suspect resisting arrest, over.'

Heck kicked the mangled frame of the bike away as he extricated himself. As he did, he saw more of Cyrus Jackson. The big man was swarthy-skinned, as though of Mediterranean or Middle Eastern origin, and truly enormous. His neck barely existed, his huge, shaven bullet-head sprouting straight from his ox-like shoulders. When he turned to run the other way, Heck saw wild eyes in a sweat-soaked face, the lower half of which was covered by a black beard worthy of an Old Testament prophet.

The giant lumbered back towards the car, perhaps thinking he could stomp Heck some more and retrieve his keys to affect a higher-speed getaway. But Heck was now back on his feet, albeit wobbling on his left leg, which was fleetingly deadened. He snapped the baton open and assumed the posture.

'Give it up, bonehead!' he shouted.

Swearing hoarsely, Jackson veered left, tottering around the Audi's front end. Heck threw himself across its bonnet to try and snag him, but again, the guy was faster than he looked, evading Heck's reach by several inches.

They crossed the parking bay together, Heck only a couple of feet behind but still limping. Jackson turned, swinging the sports bag like a wrecking ball. It struck Heck on the right shoulder and sent him reeling left. Jackson ran on, only to again find the bright spear of Gail's torch penetrating to the backs of his eyeballs. She'd circled around the rear of the Audi, and now he was cut off: a cop in front, a cop behind.

Only one option remained.

With panting grunts, he cleared the chain-link fence in a single clumsy stride, his footfalls resounding like drumbeats as he thundered away along the derelict pier. Thirty yards further on, almost as an afterthought, he flung the bag over the side, sending it cartwheeling into the darkness.

'*Shit!*' Heck shouted, straddling the chain. 'Gail . . . something tells me we need that bag more than we need Jackson.'

'You can't tackle him on your own.'

'Just get the bag.'

He lurched along the pier, feeling it quaking beneath him, planks cracking and slipping as he trod on them. He slowed to a walk, not so much because of this, but because the further he drew from shore, the more the dim light faded. Soon, there was no sound either, save the hiss of a stiffening coastal breeze.

At forty yards, Heck stopped altogether.

The silence seemed ominous.

It meant the guy could be very close, lying flat perhaps, or crouching beside one of the two barriers, hoping not to be noticed but ready to launch a vicious attack if he was.

Heck advanced again. Even the distant south shore, a line of lights previously, was now partly blotted out. He hadn't noticed it earlier, but midway along the pier there was a structure of sorts, something like an old boatshed. He edged towards it, and when he drew close, saw a square of deeper blackness in its wooden, weatherboarded front. An open door – which might explain how Jackson had suddenly disappeared.

Heck closed on it quickly, but before he'd gone a couple of yards, a missile came twirling out and struck him on the left side of the chest.

A heavy spanner clattered to the planks.

The point of impact was cushioned by Heck's undershirt armour, though it was still sufficient to hurt him and send him toppling sideways.

He reached the shed at a stagger, flattening himself against the wall next to the door.

It was anyone's guess how many more such abandoned tools-turned-weapons Jackson might find in there. Maybe a handful, maybe none – but why make it easy for him?

Heck probed at his side. It was tender but tolerable. Thanks to the Kevlar, there'd only be a little bruising there.

He held his breath to listen.

Then heard a clumping of feet and a scraping of timber – it sounded like a stiff door being lugged open. The bastard was working his way through the boathouse to the other side.

'Where do you think you're escaping to?' Heck shouted. 'You're not going to swim the Humber, you thick twat!'

There was no response.

Heck shook his head and followed.

The interior of the shed was rank. It stank of mildew and stagnant water. With a slimy floor underfoot and stands of cobweb draped over him, he bored through cavernous darkness towards the uber-dim oblong of another open door. A violent attack could come from either side; the sound of that door being opened might have been a feint. But it was a chance Heck had already taken.

He made it to the other side unharmed and poked his head out.

The first thing that struck him was that he was almost at the end of the pier, only thirty or so yards of it remaining. It had once been longer than this, maybe by another couple of hundred yards, but years of disuse had seen the seaward end collapse. The footway now terminated at a precipice delineated by stubs of rotted, broken planking. Beyond that, two lines of blackened, tooth-like projections trailed out into the silt-black water, until they too submerged. As before, there was no sign of his quarry.

Heck held his breath, straining to listen, his eyes slowly adjusting.

Further objects emerged. Some ten yards in front, a steel pole protruded up through the middle of the footway, standing to a height of about thirty feet. Maybe there'd once been a flag on it, or a lantern. Either way, there was no possibility someone could hide behind that, not someone of Cyrus Jackson's girth. But ten yards to the left, square against the east barrier, was a small hut, the size and shape of a sentry box. Heck padded towards it, but the closer he got, the more apparent it became that its frontage had been kicked in and that there was nothing inside.

He backtracked to look at the rear of it – but it was fast against the barrier. No one could be hiding behind it.

'Damn it!' he hissed.

He turned, scanning the immediate area – and completely failed to notice the immense shadow rise to its feet up on top of that small hut.

Cyrus Jackson was about four feet above Heck's head. Not a huge distance, but given his weight, he knew that if he landed on the cop from up here he would crush his target flat, slamming him into that unyielding woodwork with a force that could pulverise flesh and bone alike.

Chapter 16

It was Jackson's colossal weight that was his undoing.

He'd risen to a crouch and was just levering himself fully up when a dull *creeeaaak* split the air. Heck spun around as the entire arthritic structure of the hut gave way, sagging sideways and then crashing downward, every joint splintering apart.

He leapt back as the massive shape of the fugitive descended. Jackson had still partly managed to jump, but it was wild and uncoordinated. He landed on the flats of his feet about half a yard to the left of the steel pole, but it was a huge collision, which dropped him into a squat, his ankles smashing upwards into his backside, causing him to choke in pain.

Meanwhile, the planking he'd landed on exploded down, and he passed through it like a cannonball. But not completely. He lodged halfway.

'Shit!' he gasped. '*Oh shiiit!*'

It looked as if gravity would now do the rest, tugging on him inexorably. Jackson scrabbled at the shattered boarding, trying to get a purchase as his bulk slowly sank.

'*Help! For Christ's saaake!*'

'What's up?' Heck asked, standing over him. 'Can't swim?'

'*You pig bastard!*' Jackson's voice rose to a falsetto shriek.

'Relax . . .' Heck bent down. 'Gimme your hand.'

Jackson reached up with a desperate paw – only to feel a handcuff snap around its wrist.

'What the fuck you doing?'

'The other one,' Heck instructed him.

Jackson held it back, trying to brace himself with his free elbow.

'Give me the other one,' Heck said, 'or I'll chain you to this flagpole and let you hang.'

'Fuck you!' the fugitive snapped, but he offered his other hand anyway.

Heck grabbed this one rather than cuffed it, and stepped behind the pole, where he locked the two hands together.

'What . . . you said . . .'

'I'm getting you up. Stop your whingeing.'

Heck strolled around to the back of him, crouched, reached down through the jagged hole and, grabbing Jackson by the belt of his pants, hauled him up. It wasn't easy; the guy weighed a ton, and with his arms bound around the pole, he couldn't exactly assist.

'Jeez,' Heck said, with much puffing and grunting. 'Could do with getting some flesh off, Cyrus. Or would that make you look too much like your customers?'

Jackson said nothing. But when he was up on his knees, he clambered to his feet, panting. He yanked at the cuffs, but they were good and tight. He looked up; the old flagpole was solid – it didn't so much as sway when he tested his bulk against it.

Heck watched him impassively. 'I'm disappointed, to tell the truth. I thought you were supposed to be a living legend. Expected a lot more trouble from you than this.'

Jackson glared at him balefully, before a slow smile curled his fat, wet mouth. 'There are different ways to win, pig.'

And with a ringing impact, he drove his forehead against the steel pole. He did it three times at least, and when he'd finished, blood trickled down his face from two deeply lacerated eyebrows.

Heck watched, thoughtful.

'Shit,' Jackson chuckled dazedly. 'Look what you did to me. Brutalising me while I was under arrest. My brief'll have a fucking field day.'

'No, mate. It was all in self-defence.' Heck stepped up to the pole, and headbutted it, himself, twice.

Like all heavy blows to the skull, the initial impacts sounded worse than they felt. The pain would come later – once he'd stopped seeing stars. He rocked backward on the balls of his feet, as warm liquid dribbled down the left side of his face. Poking gingerly, he found that only one of his eyebrows had split, but this too was deep.

When he glanced at Jackson, the criminal was gaping.

'You seriously think there's anything a clown like you can do that I'd can't do better?' Heck said.

'You're fucking nuts.'

Heck dug his phone out and flicked the light on. He used it to examine the prisoner's wounds, which would probably need stitches, as his own doubtless would.

'You've got a couple of extra gashes on me,' Heck said, prodding his eyebrow gingerly. 'But *one* is all I need. They'll put the discrepancy down to me being a better fighter than you.'

'Jesus wept . . .'

'Not for you.' Heck stared back towards the boatshed. 'But that reminds me . . . I'm going to check my partner's OK. If, by any chance, she's drowned . . . so will you.'

'Hey, fuckhead . . . you're not leaving me here!'

But Heck was already walking back.

He met Gail on the landward side of the boatshed. Even in the dark, he could see that she was plastered in mud. Not just her feet and legs, but her body and arms. It even smeared her face and hung clotted in her hair. But at least she was carrying the muck-caked sports bag.

She immediately noted that he was dabbing at his brow with a bloodstained handkerchief. 'Oh, God . . .'

'It's nothing, don't worry. Well done on that.'

She hefted the bag, which she'd clearly already unzipped and checked inside. 'Low tide, thankfully. It's full of gear, by the way.'

'That's what I like to hear.'

'You sure you're OK . . . that looks nasty?'

'The nastier, the better.' Heck took the bag and looked into it. Even at first glance, it contained bundles and bundles of string-tied money, and at least ten additional bags of greenish resin.

'I presume you got him?' she said.

'Sure did.'

Gail looked uneasy. 'Is he hurt too?'

'No worse than me. Come on.' He zipped the bag up again and set off back. 'Did you get a response from local Comms?'

'Hardly. I was only play-acting.'

He glanced at her with new respect. 'Really?'

'I knew you didn't want the world and his wife here. Plus, I thought I'd try and put the willies up Jackson.'

'Well, it worked. Good girl.'

'Please don't patronise me, Heck. I'm giving you the benefit of the doubt on this occasion, because, so far, your instincts have been right. But we'd better get this case back on the straight and narrow damn soon, or I'm going to be very upset with you.'

'Fair enough.' Heck handed her the bag back. 'You carry this, if you don't mind. Let me lead the questioning.'

Jackson was still waiting on the other side of the boatshed when they got there. He hadn't managed to free his hands from the cuffs and was now sitting on the floor.

'Get up,' Heck said, approaching.

The prisoner did so, but sullenly. 'I want my fucking brief.'

'I'll bet you do.'

'You almost fucking killed me,' Jackson said, already trying his bogus assault claim now that a newcomer had arrived. 'They'll rip you apart in court, you smart-arse bastard.'

'Going to court, are we, Cyrus?' Heck asked him.

'Well . . . *you* are. Not sure about me.'

Heck appraised him. 'Does this bravado ever get you places? I mean, I'm genuinely interested to know. Do coppers round here actually quake in their boots when a moron like you threatens to sue them?'

'You forced entry to my car,' Jackson stated. 'I thought you were trying to rob me, so I ran. You followed, kicked the shit out of me. End of . . . that's your career, I mean. End of your fucking career.'

'Sounds as if he's done us like kippers, DC Honeyford.'

'Fucking right,' Jackson snorted. 'You got all mucky for nothing, darling.'

Heck looked at her. 'Did you get mucky for nothing?'

'I don't think so, DS Heckenburg.' She produced the sports bag from behind her back. 'You didn't reach the waterline, Cyrus. It was sitting on a mudbank.'

Jackson tried to brazen it out. 'What's that supposed to be? Someone's squash kit?'

'Good question,' Heck said. 'But as you're under arrest on suspicion of possessing Class A drugs with intent to supply, the law empowers us to have a good rummage inside.'

'Don't try it, pig . . . that's not my bag.'

Heck took it off Gail and unzipped it again.

'We both saw you throw it, Cyrus,' she said.

'Be a laugh trying to watch you sell that in court,' he retorted. 'One look at your two faces says you're stitch-up merchants from way back.'

Heck pulled out a handful of tens and twenties. 'So, if we set fire to this pile of cash . . . you're OK with that?'

Jackson's expression tightened, but he clamped his mouth shut.

Heck pulled out two or three more handfuls. 'There must be four or five grand here, Cyrus. Wouldn't half go up with a flash.'

'Not mine. What does it matter?'

'Don't worry.' Heck threw it back in the bag. 'No fires tonight . . . not when this all needs to go to the lab. It's come straight from the dealers, hasn't it? Which means it's likely impregnated with trace evidence. As, no doubt, is the inside of that flash motor of yours.'

'That'll also be going to the lab, Cyrus,' Gail said. 'Did we plant *that* on you too?'

Jackson's mouth stayed shut.

'Where are those trusty middlemen when you need them, eh?' Heck said.

'You won't make this stick.'

'We might make *this* stick.' Heck pulled out a couple of bags of resin. 'Is this the spice of life, or what?'

'I don't know what that is,' Jackson replied.

'Let me enlighten you.' Heck examined the plastic sacks closely. 'This is a form of synthetic marijuana. It's the same stuff that's rotting the hearts, minds and souls of people all over this country, turning once happy members of society into the living fucking dead. You feel me, bro?'

Heck just about managed to restrain himself from slapping the pugnacious face in front of him.

'While you were driving round in your swanky A4, this is the stuff that's destroyed lives, broken up families and ruined dreams. And yet . . .' Heck shook his head, as though bewildered at where this business had taken him, 'even now . . . after all that, I might be prepared to let you off the hook.'

Jackson arched one of his wounded eyebrows – especially when he sensed Gail stiffen.

Heck shrugged. 'Really, Cyrus? No snappy comeback?'

'Who do I have to kill?'

Heck chuckled without humour. 'Suppose it's no surprise that's the way a rodent like you would think. But, actually, it's going to be *worse* than murdering someone.'

'Pig bastards,' the prisoner breathed.

'I'd save your anger till you hear the offer,' Gail advised him. 'Because it's a lot more than you bloody deserve.'

'I want Eddie Creeley,' Heck said.

There was protracted silence, before Jackson snorted with derisory laughter. 'You and everyone else.'

'The difference between me and them, Cyrus, is they haven't got you on a dealing-to-children charge,' Heck said.

'Eddie's gone, all right. He did a runner two years ago. And when Eddie does a runner, he *really* does a runner.'

'How unfortunate.' Heck regarded him stonily. 'For *you*.'

'You seriously saying you want to trade?' Despite his scorn, Jackson seemed interested.

Neither of the cops replied; they simply stared at him.

The prisoner snorted again. 'You can't think you've got a bang-up case against me here or you wouldn't be doing this.'

'We caught you in the act,' Gail said, adding the lie: 'We filmed some of the dealers you've got selling in the parks. We followed them all the way here.'

'You're totally fucked, pal,' Heck said.

'I don't know where Eddie is. I swear it.'

Heck frowned. 'That really doesn't work for me.'

'But I can give you *something* . . .'

Jackson left it hanging there, glancing from one to the other.

'Make it good,' Heck said quietly.

'Eddie's sister's been trying to get in touch with me.'

'His sister?' Gail said, play-acting again.

'Nanette . . . stupid fucking name for a loser like her.'

'We know Nanette Creeley,' Heck said. 'We've already checked her out. She's got no form.'

'No, but she's recently heard something.' Jackson now seemed animated, increasingly eager to cut himself a deal. 'Or she thinks she has.'

'What do you mean?' Gail asked.

'She's been trying to get in touch with me. Sending me notes, keeps saying Eddie's in trouble, can I help her, and all that stuff.'

'Why did she come to *you*?' Heck said.

'Same reason *you* have. She thinks I'm the fucking man.'

'Well, don't worry, we'll soon strip her of that misconception.'

'I've not responded anyway.'

'Why not?' Gail asked.

Jackson barked with laughter. 'Eddie's a bad lad. I don't want a piece of that.'

'Well, of course,' Heck replied, 'you being pure as the driven snow.'

'No one wants to touch him these days. He's a right nutter.'

'So, what are you saying?' Gail said. 'You ignored these notes Nanette Creeley wrote?'

'Course I fucking did. I binned the lot of them.'

'But you think she knows something?'

'*She* thinks she does. I couldn't tell you what it is. I'm not fucking interested either. And that's it . . . that's absolutely all I know.'

Heck and Gail pondered this, before Heck finally nodded. 'I believe you, Cyrus . . . you know why, because you'd have absolutely nothing to gain if that was a lie.' He turned to Gail. 'Call Comms. Ask them to send prisoner transport. We've got one in custody for possession with intent to supply.'

'Hang on!' Jackson blurted. 'We just made a bargain.'

'Uh-uh.' Heck shook his head. 'The bargain was I let you go if you give me something good. You didn't.'

Chapter 17

When they booked their prisoner in at Clough Road, the custody sergeant was bemused, especially when he saw the filthied state Gail was in. But when the evidence was presented to him, which included the footage Heck had shot, the bag of drugs and money and the spanner Jackson had thrown, there was no way he could refuse detention. However, it was plain to him that both Heck and the prisoner needed medical treatment. A couple of uniforms were called in to escort Jackson to Hull Royal Infirmary, while Heck opted to drive himself there, though before going outside, he had Gail photograph his split eyebrow and bruised ribs.

Out in the car park, he said: 'I don't know how long I'll be, but while I'm at the hospital, can you get in touch with our liaison officers. Apologise to them for the hour and tell them we've got a prisoner in for offences unconnected to Eddie Creeley. We could do with contacting the Humberside anti-drugs team too and letting them know what's happened. That's a formality really, but with any luck they'll come in and take Jackson off our hands. In the meantime, we also need those substances sent off to the local lab . . . fast-tracked, if possible.'

She nodded. 'I'll sort it.'

He opened the car.

'Heck,' she said.

He glanced back.

She smiled awkwardly. 'Sorry for doubting. I should've realised you wouldn't let a scrote like Jackson walk.'

Heck shrugged. 'If he'd given us something really useful, it would have been difficult. I've got a rep for being someone the hoods know they can make deals with. Don't want to turn that on its head at this stage of the game, but you're right . . . some of these animals cross the line once too often.'

Before setting off, he checked through his contacts, found the one he wanted and called it on his hands-free. It rang out as he set off driving, and continued to ring out until he expected it to switch to voicemail. At which point it was answered, the rural East Anglian tones of DC Andy Rawlins filling his Megane.

'Bit bloody late, isn't it, Sarge?'

'Don't tell me you were in bed, Andy,' Heck replied, hearing the laughter and clinking of glasses going on behind him. 'Sounds more like a pub to me.'

'Hey, we're allowed some downtime at the end of a busy day.'

'Relax, I'm not checking up on you. I want to pick your brains.'

'Yeah?' Rawlins sounded genuinely surprised – it was a red-letter day indeed when Heck asked someone else their opinion.

'Where are you and Burt up to with Terry Godley?' Heck said, referring to the Nottingham carjacker who, several years earlier, had executed a teenage driver and his young male passenger.

Rawlins mused, taking the opportunity to sip some beer. 'Nowhere much. We've been talking to a few faces he's allegedly wronged.'

'I'd imagine there are plenty of those to choose from.'

'There's one crew in particular who are out for his blood. Three lads and their self-appointed leader . . . name of Kenny Donovan. About three years ago, Godley ripped Donovan off over a drugs deal. They've been looking for him ever since he did a runner. They're after the reward, obviously, but they want to take it out of Godley's head in the process. Donovan's currently doing a year and a half for intent to supply. We went to see him in Doncaster. He said that him and his lads got close to Godley last spring. They'd had word he was dossing in some railway sheds in the St Ann's district of the city. They went up there tool-handed, but when they forced their way in, nothing.'

'Bullshit intel?'

'No, they said he *had* been there. Some food cartons, tatty old sleeping bag, pillow . . .'

Heck pondered this as he drove. 'Seems odd he didn't take the sleeping bag with him?'

'That's what we thought. We went and had a look. Stuff was still there. There was even a rucksack with bits of clothes in it – all gone green with mould. A flask too, couple of old paperbacks. He'd left all that behind. But that's what you've gotta do, isn't it . . . when you're on the lam? You get a hint that *we're* round the corner, and you go for it.'

'Yeah, but he didn't get a hint you were round the corner, because you weren't.'

'Well . . . us or this Donovan guy.'

'Where does Donovan think he went to?'

'No clue, but that's why he was prepared to talk to us. Said he wanted to put the record straight that Godley's disappearance was nothing to do with him and his boys.'

Heck found that puzzling as well. 'Why would Donovan assume we'd think it was?'

'Dunno. Just said it was a bit spooky.'

'Spooky?'

'His words, not mine.'

'What did he mean?'

Again, Rawlins mused. 'I suppose the way Godley was there one day and gone the next. Whoever it was told Donovan he was hiding in these sheds, they had no clue where he'd gone after that. But that's what you do, isn't it? You get word the heavy mob's coming and you don't just drop everything . . . you cut all ties, so *no one* knows where you've legged it to.'

'Suppose so,' Heck said, though for some reason he didn't feel entirely convinced by that.

An odd thought had occurred to him earlier that evening, just before they'd sprung the trap on Jackson, though he hadn't really had time to sit and think about it until they'd got the drug dealer back to the station. Gary Quinnell had casually mentioned that John Stroud's girlfriend was worried something bad might have happened to him while he was on the run. In itself that had meant nothing – who wouldn't be worried if their loved one was sleeping under benches? Except that Nan Creeley had also been concerned that her brother, Eddie, was in some sort of additional danger. And now, he learned that former criminal associates of Terry Godley, another fugitive, were claiming that whatever had happened to him, it wasn't down to them.

Whatever had happened to him.

'You still there, Heck?' Rawlins wondered.

'Erm, yeah. Sorry.'

For the first time, the DC sounded curious. 'Something we should know about? Something new maybe?'

'No, not really.' Heck pulled into the Hull Royal car park. 'Shots in the dark, mate. But one last question. Did Donovan say anything about a blond bloke hanging around? Forty years old . . . ish. Did he mention anyone like that at all?'

'A blond bloke?'

'I know it sounds daft, but that's all I've got on him.'

'Never mentioned it.'

'It's all right . . . like I say, shots in the dark. Keep digging, eh? I'm sure something'll come up.'

He cut the call, parked and strolled across the car park towards A&E, advising himself that he had plenty other things to be thinking about, not least the apprehension of Eddie Creeley, without inventing a few conspiracy theories to add to the mix.

'Oh . . . so *you're* the dumb fuck?' a harsh voice said.

It was shortly after one, and Heck had only just re-entered the DO at Clough Road. The office was largely empty, aside from Gail, who slumped at her desk, looking dispirited and sallow-faced, and Hodges and Mortimer, who, though they were both at their own desks, were in scruffs, having clearly been called in off-duty. There was one other person, a woman. She was in her forties and about five-seven, but with a solid build, a strong, weather-beaten face and a head of wiry, grey curls. She wore jeans, sandals and a leather jacket over a ragged, shapeless sweater, and now strode belligerently across the room, only stopping when she'd invaded Heck's personal space.

Heck shrugged. 'And you are . . .?'

'This is DI Warnock,' Gail said sullenly. 'Drug Squad.'

'Morning to you too, ma'am.'

'You realise we've just done four months' work on Cyrus Jackson?' DI Warnock said. 'Four whole months. And now it's all gone up in smoke because of your cowboy escapades.'

Heck felt puzzled. 'Sorry, ma'am . . . haven't I just served him up for you?'

Warnock glanced at Hodges and Mortimer. 'Is he always this fucking dim, or does he have to work at it?'

Mortimer smirked. 'Don't think he has to work very hard.'

'Shut up!' Gail snapped at him. 'If *you'd* been more helpful, none of this would have happened.'

Warnock glared at her, for the first time seeming to notice the dried mud caking her clothes. Aside from washing her hands and face, Gail hadn't been able to fix herself up yet.

'Who are *you* again?' the DI demanded.

Gail stood up. 'DC Honeyford, ma'am. Serial Crimes Unit.'

'Oh great, another fucking glory boy. Or is it a glory girl, or a glory person? It's bound to be some fancy, politically correct bullshit down in London, isn't it?'

'Sorry, ma'am,' Heck interrupted, 'I'm still confused. Jackson was a clean pinch. What's more, I've given you enough evidence to put him away for ten years.'

'Oh yes, all your evidence is good. That's why he'll be charged. But it wasn't Jackson we were after. It was his suppliers . . . and now we won't get anywhere near them.'

'We didn't know you had Jackson under surveillance,' Gail replied.

The DI shook her head in disbelief. 'Yes, DC Honeyford, but it's my understanding that you didn't inform anyone about what you intended to do. If you had done, we could've told you to leave Jackson alone.'

'Ma'am,' Heck said. 'If you had Jackson under observation anyway, how come you didn't intercept us at the time and tell us to back off?'

'It just so happens, DS Heckenburg, that you people at NCG are not the only fucking ones who can't mount operations as fully manned as they'd like. But we were on top of it, for Christ's sake! Another couple of weeks and we'd have had the lot of them. Jackson, all his little bike-riding chums, and the overarching power that's been fuelling them.'

Heck gave her his most sincere frown. 'I can only offer you a heartfelt apology.'

'You'd be better offering it to all my team's wives, husbands and kids, and anyone else who hasn't seen them for weeks on end.' She produced a paper cup half full of coffee, but, taking a big swallow, grimaced and threw it away. 'I don't know what it is with you fucking people. You think you can just swan in from Scotland Yard, taking over . . .'

'Strictly speaking, ma'am, we're not from Scotland Yard any more,' Gail said.

Warnock scowled at her. 'Are you looking for trouble, DC Honeyford?'

'No, ma'am.'

'Because I'm telling you . . . I'll give you all the trouble you can fucking handle. How long have you been in the job?'

'Seven years, ma'am.'

Warnock, who'd clearly made an assumption based on Gail's non-battle-hardened looks, seemed taken aback by that. But she didn't let it knock her off her stride. 'You want to stay in, you keep your mouth shut when I'm talking. You'd also be advised to distance yourself from *this* fella.' She turned back to Heck. 'I've spent the last hour doing some checking up on you, Heckenburg. You really are a law unto yourself, aren't you?'

'Ma'am, I can appreciate that you're genuinely upset,' he said, 'but *our* enquiry's serious too.'

'So serious that you didn't even take your local liaison with you?'

He didn't reply.

'Let me guess why . . . so you could beat the info you wanted out of Jackson with none of us there to intervene.'

'It wasn't quite like *that*.'

'Don't pull my pisser, Sergeant. I've heard about the state he was in.'

Heck indicated his own left eyebrow. 'What about the state I'm in?'

183

'No doubt a lamppost came in handy for you.'

'Seriously?' Gail said, now hot-faced. 'You believe Cyrus Jackson, but not Heck?'

This time, Warnock didn't bother looking at her. 'Shut it, darling.'

'I'm not your bloody darling!'

'Gail,' Heck warned her. 'It's OK . . .'

'It's not OK.' All of a sudden, the feisty Gail Honeyford he'd worked with down in Surrey was back. Her eyes flashed as she advanced from her desk. 'Who is this, anyway . . . the gobshite queen of Humberside?'

Tough though she doubtless was, Warnock looked startled.

'We're after an armed robber and two-time murderer, who happens to have committed a load of his crimes on *your* patch!' Gail stated flatly. 'And you're giving us a world of shit just because we were there when Jackson got caught dealing and you weren't? Yeah, it's a cock-up, but Heck said he's sorry. We couldn't *not* arrest him, could we!'

'Gail, enough!' Heck said.

'And if you're such a bloody hardcase, ma'am . . . why don't *you* go and knock some intel out of Jackson? He's still in custody. You can use the excuse that Heck did all the damage – I mean, that's what you're going to do anyway.'

'*Enough!*' Heck shouted. '*Put a sock in it, all right!*'

Gail shut her mouth but glared at Warnock defiantly.

Warnock responded with a cool smile. 'Too late, I'm afraid, DS Heckenburg. When I get onto the top floor about this, I was going to go easy on this colleague of yours . . . on the grounds that she's way too pretty and well-spoken to be a real fucking copper. But now I can see that she's as big a fucking reprobate as you are.' She paused for malicious effect. 'So, trust me, you two are *both* in for the high jump.'

'Ma'am,' Heck said hastily, 'I'd like to put it on record that DC Honeyford objected from the outset to my tactics concerning Cyrus Jackson. She didn't think we should even put an obbo on him without informing local command. And she certainly didn't think I should have moved in when I did. She only participated because she thought I was in trouble.'

He let that hang, scanning her granite-hard features for any hint of conciliation.

'Nice try,' Warnock said, turning to the door. 'Save it for the disciplinary.'

After she'd gone, Mortimer switched his laptop off and stood up, chuckling.

Gail rounded on him. 'You should be glad we *didn't* let you know, Mortimer. Being the dickhead you are, you'd probably have gone along with it without telling Drug Squad either.'

Mortimer was pulling his jacket on. He looked sharply round. 'You've got some mouth on you, girl.'

'Oh yeah,' she retorted. 'Well—'

'*I said leave it!*' Heck interjected. He locked eyeballs with Mortimer. 'And that includes *you* too, pal. Toddle off.'

Mortimer's mouth twisted into a snarl. For several seconds, he returned Heck's gaze. But maybe seeing something there he didn't totally like, he finally relented, smiled again and stumped across the office, letting its door swing closed behind him.

'You too, Bazzer,' Heck said. 'I'm sure it's past your bedtime.'

Hodges, who'd been a fascinated observer, stood up uncertainly.

'If you'd just let me know,' he said, 'I could've run some checks for you.'

Heck sat at his own desk and opened his laptop. 'Like Gail says, it's a good thing you lads didn't get involved. It's a clusterfuck, and it's best if only *I* carry the can for it.'

Hodges grabbed his jacket and moved to the door. 'At least you got a result . . . of sorts. Whatever Diane Warnock says, we've been looking to put Jackson behind bars for ages.'

'There is that, I agree,' Heck said.

Strangely apologetic, Hodges left.

'And that's the important thing.' Heck swung round in his chair to face Gail.

'What is?' she wondered disconsolately.

'We got a result . . . just not the one Barry Hodges thinks.'

'You mean Nan Creeley?' She pulled a face. 'It's hardly gold-plated.'

'It's a new lead, and any new lead is good. And the fact that I took Warnock's bollocking on the chin means we ought not to have outstayed our welcome on Humberside just yet.'

'Are you joking? We'll be persona non grata up here on an epic scale.'

'Only to the Drug Squad.'

'Isn't that enough?'

Heck sat back. 'Why should it be? Division are providing our liaison.'

'But Warnock's going to whinge to everyone.'

'Gail . . . do the maths. Warnock screwed up. We caught her boy with bags of gear, openly distributing. Sure, she might have been banking on him leading her to some higher powers. But there're drug dealers all over Humberside like him. Any one of them could provide the same intel . . . and she knows it.'

'So . . .?' Gail didn't look as if she quite believed this. 'You *don't* think she's going to raise a big stink?'

'Not unless she wants to be redder-faced than she already is.'

'What if word gets to Gemma?'

'She'll do nothing.'

'Nothing? This is the Lioness we're talking about. You know, bites people's heads off?'

'The trick with that is to grow another one.'

'It doesn't surprise me *you* have that ability. But I'm not so sure about me . . .'

'Gail, for God's sake. Gemma's on the run too. Sledgehammer needs results . . . but it sounds to me like *we're* the only ones even close to nabbing our suspect.' He allowed himself a sly grin. 'Jack Reed, for one, has gained no ground.'

'Jack Reed's got nothing to do with it. She'll still call us in, bollock the living crap out of us.'

'No. She'll bollock *me*.'

'Not just you. Not this time.' Regret rippled across Gail's wan features. 'I shouldn't have cheeked Warnock like that.'

'Admittedly, that wasn't very clever. But you were clearly provoked.'

Gail gave a puzzled frown.

'You heard her,' he said. 'Casting doubts on your ability just because you're a female.'

'Heck . . . *she's* a female.'

'So what? That doesn't mean anything. Plus . . .' he leaned forward with an air of outrage, 'she mocked the Met's progressive culture. That won't go down well at Scotland Yard.'

Gail still looked bewildered. 'Are you saying the odds are actually in our favour?'

'Well . . .' he mused, 'we'll get the piss and wind. I mean, a bit more of it than we've already had. But if we've also got Eddie Creeley . . . what will it matter?'

Chapter 18

'Who is it?' came a voice from the other side of the weather-worn door.

'Police officers, Nanette,' Gail replied. 'We need to come in and speak to you, please.'

'There's no one called Nanette here.'

'Come on, Nan, love,' Heck said. 'We know we've got the right place.'

Fumbling movement followed. Assuming the householder was looking out through her peephole, the two cops held up their warrant cards. In addition, they were now suited and booted as per the manual, and that could only help.

'I'm Detective Sergeant Heckenburg,' Heck said through the door. 'This is Detective Constable Honeyford.'

'I don't know you,' the voice responded.

'We're from the National Crime Group, specifically the Serial Crimes Unit. That means we go after very bad men indeed . . . which means that though you don't know us, you can probably guess why we're here.'

'Eddie's not here. He hasn't been here for ages. I haven't heard from him.'

Silence followed. Heck glanced over his shoulder. Though

it was August, the air was cool, the early-morning light a dim grey as it spilled over the motionless flats opposite.

'Can you open the door please, Nanette?' Gail said. 'It's getting silly, this.'

'I don't want to talk to you. Whatever my brother does is nothing to do with me.'

'Nan . . .' Heck leaned against the door. 'Cyrus Jackson is *not* going to help you. First of all, he can't. He's in police custody, and he's unlikely to get bail. Chances are, Nan . . . you aren't going to see Cyrus again. Secondly, he isn't inclined to help you anyway. You know how I know that? Because he told me himself.'

Another thoughtful silence followed.

'Nanette . . .' Gail said, 'Cyrus Jackson may not be able to help you, but we possibly can.'

More silence.

'Up to you, love,' Heck said. 'But if it's more important to you that people don't think you a snitch than it is getting your brother out of trouble . . . you're not much of a sister.'

Metal clunked as a catch was turned, and wood thumped as a bolt was drawn back. The door opened on a dark hallway. When they stepped through, Nanette Creeley was standing just to the left, a spectral, pale-faced figure with unruly 'bed' hair, wearing a quilted, neck-to-floor dressing gown. She closed the door after them.

'I don't know anything,' she said stiffly, regarding them with frightened eyes.

'Nan, let's not go through this whole rigmarole, OK?' Heck said. 'I'm sure you saw us in the pub the other night.'

Her eyes bugged as a faint recognition dawned.

'That's right,' he said. 'We've been watching you for some time.'

She contemplated this, before turning and traipsing to an open doorway. They followed, exchanging a quick, meaningful glance. They'd agreed beforehand that they wouldn't mention the beer mats at this stage, if they needed to at all. Firstly, because they'd promised to protect Fiona Birkdale's role in this, but also because it was always more desirable that info came voluntarily than as a result of someone being pressured.

'You're right, Nan,' Heck said, as they entered a small neat living room. 'To all intents and purposes, you're a law-abiding citizen. We never expected that you'd be hiding your brother. So, we decided to look up some of his other acquaintances, and Cyrus Jackson, it seems, is not so good. When we arrested him last night, he tried to make a deal with us . . . he told us you've heard that Eddie is in trouble and that you were trying to enlist him to help.'

'And like we say,' Gail added, 'he also told us that this was a non-starter. That he wouldn't help you under any circumstances.'

The woman showed no emotion as they told her this, aside from working her thin, grey lips together. She stood in front of a small television set, narrow shoulders hunched, arms folded tightly.

'Whatever trouble Eddie's in,' Heck said, 'he'll be facing it on his own. Because his best mates don't want to know him.'

'He doesn't have best mates any more.' Nan shook her head pointedly. 'He doesn't have *any* mates. Cyrus was the closest, and he was never up to much.' She swallowed and a brief flicker of pain crossed her face. 'You see . . . you see, Eddie's not a full shilling. He's sick . . . I mean in the head.' She looked at them pleadingly. 'You must realise that? No one would do the things he's done if they were sane.'

Gail gave a gentle shrug. 'That's for an investigating medical authority to determine. If we can take him into custody, that may well be the outcome. He could go to a hospital rather than prison.'

But the woman didn't seem to be listening. 'They called him all kinds of terrible names, those newspapers. I mean, for heaven's sake . . . a poor mentally ill man.'

'He may be mentally ill, Nan, but he's a criminal too,' Heck reminded her. 'A very, very active one. And he's certainly of sound enough mind to go to ground when he wants to.'

She gazed at Heck bleakly. 'Stealing's one thing, but hurting people the way he did? You can't think that's normal?'

'What I think is irrelevant. No one else is going to help Eddie, Nan, so it's best for all of us, him included, if you tell us what's been going on and where we can find him to assist him.'

She sniffled. 'I think he's maybe beyond any assistance now.'

'Why don't you let us decide that?' Gail said.

The woman's face was a picture of pain as she assessed them.

'Nanette, whatever trouble your Eddie's in,' Gail said, 'I can tell it's serious, because if it wasn't, I doubt you'd have endangered him by speaking to anyone, even Cyrus Jackson. *We* are the only hope he's got.'

The woman didn't reply, just moved to the mantelpiece, took something off it and threw it down on the carpet. It was small and bright green, and it looked like a pen drive.

The cops glanced at each other again, and then at Nan, who stood back against the mantel, shuddering, as if this was as close as she dared to get to it.

'That came through the front door the other day,' she said.

'You mean like a letter,' Heck said, 'in an envelope with a stamp?'

'No. Just like that. Someone stuck it through the letter box.'

'OK . . . who?'

'I . . .' Her voice fell to a near whisper. 'I didn't see his face.'

'Just tell us what happened,' Gail coaxed her.

So, Nan did, the whole thing – from the moment she left the Spar a week and a half ago, the mysterious hooded figure following her all the way home, to her waking up in the middle of the night, only to find this object on her doormat.

'If that man who followed me wasn't the one who delivered *this*,' she said, face even whiter than before, eyes now red and moist, 'it's quite a coincidence, don't you think?'

Heck crouched alongside the pen drive, but he hadn't yet touched it. 'You've obviously opened this thing, Nan?'

'Oh yes . . .' She swallowed hard, as though her mouth was full of bile. 'I opened it.'

'OK . . . what's on it?'

'You should look for yourself.'

'I'm not sure it's a good idea to do that here,' Gail said. 'We need the techs for that. I mean, it could carry a virus, or something.'

'You should look at it,' the woman insisted.

Heck stared at the object. 'This fella who came after you . . . was he following you like he wanted to catch up with you?'

'He was coming fast,' she confirmed.

'So, he could have been trying to put this thing in your hand?' Gail said.

'Why would he do that? Wouldn't I have seen who he was?'

Heck straightened up again. 'Why do *you* think he was following you, Nan?'

'Why else . . . to find out where I lived. So he could deliver this later on that night.'

Heck pulled a disposable glove from his pocket. 'Who else has touched it since it arrived?'

'No one. Only me.'

'Nanette . . . tell us what's on it,' Gail said.

The woman shook her head, dumbly. Tears surged into her eyes.

'Whatever it is, don't be frightened . . . even if it's a demand for money or something. We'll find this man who followed you. And even if he isn't the one who delivered this, we'll have a good old word with him.'

'For . . . *God's sake!*' Colour flooded the woman's wizened cheeks. 'You need to do more than have a word. You watch what's on that drive! I mean now! *Here!*' She bent to a shelf underneath the television and brought out a laptop. 'Do it with this.'

Gail glanced at Heck uncomfortably.

'I'm not telling you what's on there,' the woman reiterated firmly. 'You have to look for yourselves.'

Heck pondered this, and then took the laptop from the woman's hands. As he stepped back around the pen drive, Gail leaned to his ear.

'Heck . . . if we damage vital evidence by doing this . . .'

'You want to risk plugging some killer virus into the Humberside Police computer system?' he replied. 'We're not their favourite people, as it is.'

He handed her the computer and reached down for the drive.

'I'm not watching it again,' Nan Creeley said, crossing the room. 'I'll be in the kitchen.'

Heck sat alongside Gail on the couch. She rested the laptop on her knees and switched it on. Heck inserted the drive, careful to handle it only with his gloved hand and making contact with it only at either tip.

Neither commented when the 'Devil's Messenger' file appeared, though that alone felt ominous. Gail moved the cursor and activated it.

At first, it wasn't entirely clear what they were seeing. The laptop didn't possess a large screen, and the image was typically grey and grainy, the figures moving around in it little more than an indistinct blur.

But then, very quickly, they resolved themselves into greater clarity.

The footage looked to have been shot from above and to the side, which actually gave a good, clear view of three men: one in the middle, and two others circling around him belligerently. The man in the middle wore only a pair of Y-fronts, and was grubby and lean – unhealthily lean, as if slightly emaciated. He wore a grizzled beard and moustache and a mop of stringy, dark hair. He was also armed with a baseball bat, which he gripped with both hands and hefted to his shoulder, as though to ward off an attack.

More important than any of this, though – he was recognisable.

'Is that . . .?' Gail stuttered. 'Good Lord, that looks like Eddie Creeley.'

The other two men in the film were much burlier, though this may have been down to the body armour they were wearing. They sported black, heavy-duty breastplates, shoulder pads, shin and forearm guards and thick padded gloves. They also wore black ballistic helmets, with opaque, mesh-covered visors pulled down. They too carried weapons.

The taller of the two had a chain in his left hand, with a heavy padlock on the end of it, and in his right, something like a lug wrench. The other one held what looked like a football sock, which extended down from his hand because there were weights inside – Heck remembered the old snooker balls routine – and an upgraded cat-o'-nine-tails, literally a stiff-handled whip, with nine leather straps attached, each one embedded with nuts and bolts. If that wasn't enough, the duo also wore body harnesses, in which other weapons were installed. Even though the figures were moving quickly, Heck saw a knife hilt and the vicious head of a claw hammer.

For all this, it was Creeley who got in the first shot. Taking a full two-handed swing with his bat, he caught the shorter of his two opponents across the side of the helmet with what would ordinarily have been shattering force. But the helmet was clearly solid, because though the shorter guy tottered and reeled away, he remained on his feet. However, in making the first move, Creeley had left an opening, which allowed the taller one to counterattack. He struck at Creeley's exposed ribs with his wrench, the meaty *smack* of which penetrated through the poor sound-system, as did Creeley's choked squeal of agony. He flopped down like a puppet with its strings cut, but to his credit, he wasn't falling entirely through injury – it was mainly to make a getaway. He tumbled head over heels to evade the follow-up swipe with the chain and padlock. And just about managed it.

'What the hell is this?' Gail stammered. 'Is this for real?'

Heck couldn't answer; on the screen there were no clues to help. The floor of the fighting area looked as if it was made of coarse metal and the encircling walls, only glimpsed fleetingly by the jerkily moving camera, of some corrugated material, but because the image was black and white, it was impossible to be sure in either case.

Creeley was now back on his feet, but clearly hurt, inclining to one side as he tried to back away from his tormentors, still hefting his bat. They stalked after him, maintaining a good distance between themselves, which meant that he could only go for one at a time.

Perhaps Creeley was gambling on the one he had hit already being groggy with pain, or maybe he was just drunk on it himself. But he lurched awkwardly towards the same guy, barely thinking about defending his rear. The bat came up and over his head, in an arcing downward smash. His intended target raised an armoured forearm. It didn't totally absorb the blow, which bounced off it, deflected down onto the guy's shoulder, though that was well-padded too.

In the meantime, the taller opponent swept down with the weighted chain, lassoing Creeley's extended left leg, wrapping it tight, the padlock cracking against the side of his kneecap – and yanked it from under him.

Creeley landed chest-down on the metal floor, with such force that he dropped the bat.

Despite the horrible pain, some instinct for survival kept him going. He tried to crawl away, but his left leg was still snared, and he was hauled backward by the taller guy, which left his entire body unguarded. The other one now let loose on the naked, flailing figure on the floor, using his weighted sock and his cat-o'-nine-tails alternately. *Smacking* impacts again sounded across Nan Creeley's living room, along with semi-muffled howls of agony. With the fourth or fifth blow, the sock exploded, scattering what looked like batteries over the steel floor. No doubt it had already smashed several ribs and maybe vertebrae. But the cat-o'-nine-tails was still wreaking havoc, rending flesh and muscle to bloody ribbons.

It was the taller one who put a final end to it. Striding forward, he raised his lug wrench in both hands and brought it down with tremendous force on the back of Creeley's skull.

The crunching impact was horrifically audible, and Heck felt Gail jerk with shock.

It had lasted less than a minute, and yet the two victors had put so much effort into their combined assault that their chests and shoulders heaved as they stood there surveying the pulped and ruined form. Finally, they slotted what weapons they had left into their respective harnesses, casually high-fived each other and strode off-camera.

What remained of Eddie Creeley didn't so much as twitch. At which point, the film cut out.

'I should be sick after watching that,' Gail said, her cheeks ashen. 'But I'm too numb.'

Heck stood up. 'Not exactly a fair fight, was it?'

Gail closed the laptop, pulled out a latex glove of her own and extracted the pen drive.

Heck went through to the kitchen.

Nan Creeley was waiting at the far side of the small room, braced between two worktops. She watched him intently, lips quivering, eyes still brimming with unshed tears.

'Nan,' he said, 'that's your brother on that film, yeah?'

'*Was* my brother,' she corrected him.

'You're absolutely sure about that?'

A single tear snaked down her right cheek. 'You're asking me if I don't know my own brother?'

'He looked different from all the pictures we have of him.'

'Course he did. He's been on the run two years. That means roughing it, hiding God knows where, eating one meal a day if he's lucky.'

Gail now appeared. 'Nanette,' she said softly. 'None of us really knows what it is we've just watched. For all we're aware, it might not have been your brother . . . just someone who looked like him.'

'I know my own brother,' the woman repeated.

'We can't be sure he's dead . . .'

'Then why did whoever sent me that thing call themselves the Devil's Messenger? Answer me that.' Nan's voice rose to a despairing wail. 'I mean, where else do lads like our Eddie go when they're dead . . . except to the Devil?'

Chapter 19

'Yeah, we're watching it now,' Gemma said.

'OK,' Heck replied, having to press the mobile to his ear, to block out the noise of the Humberside Central Control Room. 'And?'

'Heck . . . you have considered the possibility that this horror show has been staged?'

'Yeah, that's what DCI Bateson up here at Humberside said.'

But though the DCI may indeed have said that, and though he'd additionally blown his top at Heck because DI Warnock had been in *his* ear too about the 'Cyrus Jackson fuck-up', it still hadn't prevented him authorising Heck and Gail's entry to this electronic hub of Humberside Police operations, so that they could avail themselves of the city's CCTV.

It was a busy unit, both uniforms and civilian staff beavering away at monitors, phones ringing constantly, live feeds from all over the city hitting the big screens overhead. A few yards away, Gail and Barry Hodges shifted back and forth between the three operators they had permission to exclusively use that morning.

'It's a valid argument, Heck,' Gemma said. 'There are

198

people out there who are good at this sort of thing. And if Eddie Creeley's recruited them to make it look as if he's been killed, and has sent the footage to his sister, knowing full well it would eventually end up in our hands . . . that would work very well in his favour.'

'I'm aware of that, ma'am. But if that's the case, it makes it even more important that we catch his delivery boy, this Devil's Messenger character . . .'

'*Whoa!*' Barry Hodges shouted. 'Think we've got something here.'

Heck told Gemma, and she replied that he should get on with it. He cut the call and joined Hodges and Gail, who were now leaning over one particular VDU, a young policewoman controlling the flow of imagery on it, which consisted entirely of material recorded on the night of Monday 7 August.

'I think this is our man,' Hodges said.

Initially, he hadn't been optimistic that the town's CCTV would have caught anything useful, primarily because Nan Creeley's run-down home neighbourhood wasn't massively endowed with cameras. However, Heck had suggested they locate the moment their suspect commenced the pursuit – there was surely camera coverage on the forecourt in front of the Spar? – and run it backward, to find out where he'd come from.

On screen, the man Hodges referred to was seated on the bench in a bus stop shelter, reading a newspaper.

'This is opposite the Spar?' Gail said.

'Yeah,' Hodges confirmed. 'See . . .'

The young policewoman ran the image forward, the clock in the top right-hand corner, advancing fast from 20:30 to 20:33, at which point the unmistakable figure of Nan Creeley walked quickly past as she crossed the road, wearing an anorak and clutching her handbag.

'Watch,' Hodges said.

Another half-minute passed, before the figure rose to its feet and followed. Previously seated behind the newspaper, it had been completely indistinguishable. Even now, no face was visible, but it wore grey tracksuit bottoms and a black sweatshirt with the hood pulled up – which perfectly matched the description that Nan had given them.

'We lose it from here, because Nan takes a cut-through between housing estates,' Hodges said. 'After that, she's into Orchard Park, and there are very few cameras there anyway. Certainly none on Hellington Court. But, like you said, we can at least see where the bastard's come from.'

Heck nodded. 'Go for it.'

The policewoman ran the footage backward, and the hooded shape resumed his seat in the shelter. And there, it seemed, he'd sat for the best part of the evening. They'd scrolled back to 18:00 and he was still there, still reading his paper.

'Man on a mission, isn't he?' Gail commented.

'He was certainly determined to wait for her,' Heck said. 'He knows there's a camera there too, which is why he's holding that paper in front of his face.'

'Think that means he'll be savvy to all the other cameras?' Hodges asked.

Heck shrugged. 'Just don't expect him to take his hood down.'

They continued to watch, and it was 17:04 before the figure rose to its feet again, and backtracked away, newspaper rolled up, retreating from frame. From here, the operator had to work some computer jiggery-pokery as she danced about between different streets and various camera angles. They caught up with him again, still hooded, as he walked backward through neighbouring housing estates, though always, it seemed, taking longer than was necessary, making odd turns, doubling back on himself, sometimes going in circles.

'He took a meandering route,' Hodges said.

'Trying to ensure he's not leaving an electric vapour trail,' Heck replied.

Gail snorted. 'He seriously thought that'd work?'

'It might do yet,' the operator put in. 'I've seen this before . . . all it takes is a couple of streets or squares with no cameras, and that's it. They're gone.'

On this occasion, that didn't happen. They'd been standing by the young policewoman's desk a good half-hour, working their way back and forth across central Hull without any apparent rhyme and reason, when the object of their interest suddenly backed in through the front door of a high street cafeteria called Nico's, and it swung closed.

The clock in the corner of the screen read 16:15.

'He went for his tea first,' Gail said.

They watched the front door of the café for a considerable time, scrolling back through the footage at high speed until 13:00, at which point there was still no sign of the suspect arriving, and Heck asked the operator to stop.

'He was really there all afternoon?' Hodges sounded more than sceptical.

'What is that place?' Heck asked.

'Greek restaurant,' Hodges said. 'Not particularly salubrious.'

'Could he really sit in there all afternoon and not draw attention to himself?' Gail said.

'We don't know whether he drew attention to himself or not,' Heck replied, 'seeing as we haven't been over there to ask. But I don't want to go stampeding in, because there's one other possibility. Suppose this guy is one of Nico's staff . . . or Nico himself?'

'Suppose he's neither of those things,' a gruff voice said

from behind. 'Suppose he didn't want a sit-down dinner, he just wanted a kebab?'

They turned and saw that Vic Mortimer had come in, with jacket draped over shoulder.

'Surprised to see *you*,' Heck said.

'It's under sufferance, believe me,' Mortimer replied. 'But I've no choice. From now on, it seems I've got to keep a beady eye on you all the time you're here.'

'What do you mean, he might have fancied a kebab?' Gail asked.

Mortimer nodded at the screen, where the shopfront was still frozen in place. 'The lad who owns this place is Nico Karamanlis . . . or Nasty Nic, as they call him. He also runs a kebab shop on Albion Row.'

'That's the next street over,' Hodges said.

Mortimer shrugged. 'Yeah, but all these old buildings are interconnected. There's a passage through to the other side, so the proprietor can move back and forth between them.'

'Punters can walk through it as well?' Heck asked.

'Not normally, because it goes through the kitchen. But if someone knows Nico well enough to ask, don't see why not. Nothing too suspicious, if it's your mate. Quick shortcut from A to B.'

'So, you're saying he could have entered the premises through the kebab shop, and then exited via the restaurant?' Gail said.

Again, Mortimer shrugged.

'That'd be one way to lose the surveillance,' Heck mused.

He turned to the young policewoman, but she was already two steps ahead and had pulled Albion Row onto the screen. When she scrolled to around 16:12 on the same day, they almost immediately caught an image of the same figure as he entered the kebab shop. He was dressed as before in grey tracksuit trousers and black tracksuit top. The only difference this time was that the tracksuit top's hood was down.

They watched in silence as the operator again tracked the suspect's progress back, freeze-framing on a street corner, where his face was fleetingly visible between a red beard and longish, greasy red hair.

'Shit . . . don't know him,' Hodges muttered.

'Yeah, but I do.' Mortimer chuckled. 'Who'd have thought it . . . Tim Cleghorn. Don't know what his connection to all this is, but he's got plenty form. Mainly for indecency.'

'Bad?' Gail asked.

'He's done time, yeah.'

She glanced at Heck. 'Perhaps the pen drive didn't come from him? Maybe when he followed Nan Creeley home, he was planning to attack her?'

'Only one way to find out, isn't there?' Heck turned to Mortimer. 'Does he work?'

'He wasn't working that Monday, was he? It'd surprise me if he *ever* worked, shithead like him.'

'Good.' Heck shrugged his jacket on. 'That makes it easier.'

'Easier?' Gail said.

'Yep. It's grabbing time.'

Chapter 20

Tim Cleghorn lived at 33, Trafalgar Road, a terraced street just east of the town centre and perhaps half a mile from the riverfront. This was an area that had seen better days; some of the houses were boarded up, but others were occupied and, here and there, cars sat along the kerb. It was mid-afternoon, and while the rest of the city was humming with life, this particular nook lay quiet, though that was perfect from Heck's point of view. Deprived inner-city neighbour-hoods weren't always the easiest location for police operations: the misguided belief that the denizens of these districts were all in the shit together and shared a common foe in law enforcement could often lead to interference with arrests, or, at the very least, warnings being shouted beforehand. That wasn't the case across the board, but the mere fact that it *could* happen meant you had to approach with caution.

As such, Heck didn't request any uniformed close-support, merely informed the afternoon shift what they were doing, and advised that neither he, Gail, Mortimer nor Hodges wear any kind of identifying insignia: no high-profile windbreakers or chequer-banded caps, no radios in hand or visible appoint-ments like handcuffs and batons.

They made the approach just after two o'clock, Heck and Hodges approaching No. 33 from the front, Gail and Mortimer working their way into the alley at the rear.

The house was in a poor state, the front door scabby and flaking, ragged, dingy curtains drawn behind dusty windows. From all accounts, Cleghorn had once lived here with his wife and baby daughter, but the marriage had ended after his most recent conviction for indecent assault.

Heck knocked loudly, and almost immediately the curtain in the bay window alongside them twitched open. The figure behind it was male and in his early forties. He was clad in black tracksuit bottoms and a ragged green jumper, the sleeves pushed back to the elbows, exposing thin but tattoo-covered forearms. As Heck had seen on the close-circuit video, Cleghorn wore a scraggy red beard and a mop of collar-length, dirty red hair. Hodges flashed his warrant card and pointed at the front door, to which Cleghorn's response was to dash out of sight.

Heck threw his shoulder at the door; it was a bruising impact, but the woodwork resisted.

'Whoa!' Hodges protested. 'Shouldn't we give him a chance to open it?'

A loud *thud* resounded from inside.

'That's the back door, isn't it?' Heck said.

Hodges' face fell. 'Yeah . . . shit!'

Heck rammed the front door again. 'Get onto Gail and Mortimer . . . warn them.'

Hodges put his radio to his lips, as Heck battered the door. It crashed inward on the fourth impact, the jamb flying apart in fragments.

They were confronted by a dim, foul-smelling hallway, its crumb-impacted carpet strewn with discarded underwear. Directly ahead, the hall opened into a kitchen, at the far side of which a back door stood wide open. Gail and Mortimer were visible through it, out in the rubbish-filled yard, but encroaching at speed. Cleghorn, who'd now run back into the house, slid to a halt at the sight of Heck and Hodges.

They advanced two-abreast.

'Easy, Cleghorn,' Heck warned him. 'You're not going anywhere.'

But even Heck was surprised by what happened next.

The felon reached left and, from an ironing board standing out of sight, hefted an iron, which he flung overarm along the hall towards them. It tumbled through the air, striking Hodges in the face with a massive *clank*. For a split second it was like something from *Tom and Jerry*, Heck half-expecting the flat appliance to leave an equally flat visage underneath. But there was nothing comical about the way Hodges, his nose now mashed to a froth of blood and cartilage, fell into a lifeless heap.

'You bloody maniac!' Heck dropped to one knee, checking the carotid artery in Hodges' neck. The pulse was normal, but the young cop lay out cold. 'DS Heckenburg, Serial Crimes Unit,' Heck shouted into his radio, jumping back up. 'Urgent message. Ambulance required at 33, Trafalgar Road. Police officer injured and in a collapsed state, over.'

Cleghorn, meanwhile, veered right and vanished, his heavy feet clumping away up a staircase.

Heck pursued, still jabbering into his radio. 'The injured officer is DC Barry Hodges. He's out for the count, but he's breathing and his pulse appears normal. Get someone here quick. And send us some support units. Suspect, Tim Cleghorn, is resisting arrest with extreme force, over.'

'Heck!' Gail shouted from the kitchen, but Heck was already mounting the narrow stair.

'One of you needs to stay with Bazzer!' he called back.

He was halfway up when Cleghorn reappeared at the top. He had what looked like a portable television in his hands.

Heck halted, stunned, before the heavy device came spinning and crashing down, tubes and circuitry flirting in all directions. He flattened himself against a wall as it somersaulted past, only just evading it, and continued ascending.

Cleghorn had already vanished again, so when Heck got up there, he found himself with two immediate choices: go left, into a bleak bedroom with no curtains or furniture; or right, along a short, narrow passage to a bathroom and another bedroom. But on second glance the decision was taken for him: what looked like a full-size Welsh dresser sat in the middle of the passage, and above it, a skylight yawned in a slanted section of ceiling.

When Heck climbed onto it, the dresser was every bit as heavy as it looked; Cleghorn could not have dragged it out in the last minute or so. It clearly lived in this corridor.

'Bastard's ready to skip at the first sign,' he said out loud, as he reached for the edges of the skylight and, standing on tiptoes, poked his head through.

A tilting hillside of roof slates ranged off in both directions, broken at even points by TV aerials and chimney pillars. Amazingly, Cleghorn, who'd gone right, was already two or three houses away. He ran awkwardly, his right foot landing higher up than his left, so he constantly had to brace himself against the roof with his right hand. All the time, slates broke beneath his feet, smashing into the guttering eight or nine feet below, or into the street, twenty feet below that.

Even so, he made a rapidly dwindling figure.

Heck put his radio to his lips again. 'Suspect in the police assault at Trafalgar Road is Tim Cleghorn. Male, IC1, red hair and beard. About six foot tall, well known to us. Currently making his getaway along the roofs on the north side of Trafalgar Road, heading in an easterly direction. In pursuit, over.'

Heck had expected what followed to be difficult, but it was actually much worse.

To start with, while his quarry was wearing trainers with rubber grips, Heck was in leather, lace-up shoes. He slipped constantly as he scampered along, and at least twice, he found himself sliding towards the precipice below with nothing to gain a purchase on, save more slates, which were often slick with moss. In addition, there was the damage Cleghorn had done. Several times, Heck encountered areas of roof where patches of slates had already gone. These presented real pitfalls, because all that remained was lagging and skeletal joists.

A couple of times as he proceeded along, muffled roars sounded from the buildings underneath him. None of the householders knew what was going on, of course, though police sirens now approached from several directions, and there were shouts in the street. Meanwhile, the much-diminished form of Tim Cleghorn kept looking back as he fled, and when he saw Heck chasing, seemed to run even faster and more recklessly. One particular bound appeared to carry him several feet. Even with his trainers on, he went slithering downward on a raft of broken slates when he landed, though again he managed to stabilise himself and scramble on.

Heck understood why, when he reached the same point.

There was a gap in the terraced row. He dropped to a crouch, peering down into a weed-filled passage.

When a diminutive voice called his name, Heck realised it was the radio in his jacket pocket – they wanted to know his status. But he wasn't going fishing for the device now.

He backed away and rose to full height. It was a five-to-six-yard gap. He'd no doubt that, with a proper run-up on a flat surface, he could clear that distance easily. But when the stakes were as high as this . . .?

He looked up again, fixing on the distant Cleghorn, little more now than a toy man.

Heck's breath hissed through clenched teeth.

Then he lunged forward, taking long, rash strides.

When he launched into mid-air, it took less than a second to cross the gap. Halfway over, he knew that he was going to make it. The only problem was that there was nothing to land on. Cleghorn had already bludgeoned a dozen slates loose, and Heck crashed straight into the resulting hole. A green waterproof sheet exploded beneath him, dust and filth filling his eyes and lungs. He'd have gone clean through into the loft, had a sturdy wooden joist not caught in his right armpit, but it was a sickening blow.

He hung from the joist in a fog of pain, before swinging his legs up, finding another joist with his left hand and levering himself out of the hole. Then he was off again, pummelling the rooftops.

The distant shape of Cleghorn stopped again and looked back.

The figure visibly sagged, as if unable to believe that the chase was still on. But then, to Heck's bemusement, it crouched, and, inch by inch, disappeared from sight. The bastard was climbing down something . . .

Again, Heck skidded and tumbled as he ran, a couple of times sliding almost to the bottom of the slope, nothing but the old guttering to prevent him going clean over the edge. And yet, somehow, limping and battered, he made it to the end of the row. He was now well aware of the chaos caused by the pursuit. Blues and twos filled the entire street, though its epicentre, he felt, was some distance behind. In front of him, meanwhile, a long way down, was what looked like a builder's yard. Stacks of bricks alternated with piles of timber, and a couple of cement mixers stood against a single-storey prefab office. Two or three vehicles spattered with dry mud were parked against a high brick wall separating the yard from Trafalgar Road.

It was along the top of this wall that Cleghorn was executing the latest part of his escape.

The wall connected to the gable of the last house. It was a good fifteen feet below Heck's perch, though Cleghorn's means of descending to it was self-evident: a bundle of cables snaked down like vines; no doubt, it had once been fixed to the brickwork with brackets, but the weight of the climber had torn them loose.

Heck wasn't sure how loose, but he had no option but to chance it.

He turned, got a firm grip on the thickest of the cables, lowered his body over the edge and, hand over hand, began to descend. Whatever he was anchored to above, it didn't hold for long. With a *thunk*, something snapped free, and Heck was falling at what felt like light speed – only to jerk to a halt again as a mass of twisted, broken aerial overhead snagged. It was only a few feet from here to the top of the wall, so he dropped the final distance – though even then he almost fell off, having to windmill his arms to rebalance himself.

Breathless, he pivoted around and tightrope-walked his way forward.

Cleghorn was only about thirty yards ahead. Clearly, he was a less confident customer on this wall than he had been on the roof. He glanced over his shoulder again, almost by chance, and was visibly astounded to see Heck as close as he was.

In a panic, he looked left – but it was ten feet down to the pavement. However, when he looked right, he was directly above one of the vehicles parked in the yard. It was a scruffy old Toyota van, and it had an orange rubber dinghy on its roof rack. The instant Cleghorn saw this, he jumped, legs jutted out in front. He landed inside the dinghy on his backside, only to bounce back up, arms flailing, and come down hard on the grit alongside the van.

But in Cleghorn's adrenalised state, that impact didn't do nearly enough damage.

Heck, less than fifteen yards behind, saw him get straight up again and lurch to the Toyota's front offside window, which was open. Its driver was presumably inside the builders' office – because its keys were still dangling from the ignition.

Cleghorn yanked the van's door open, jumped in and the engine grumbled to life.

'*No!*' Heck shouted.

He hunkered down, took a fingertip grip on the edge of the wall and dropped the remaining distance. His impact with the ground was heavy. He fell sideways, rolled and climbed dustily to his feet – just as the van's rear bumper disappeared through the gate. He stumbled forward, digging in his pocket for his radio, only to find that it now wasn't there.

He skidded to a halt, bewildered.

It was possibly no surprise that he'd lost it. Maybe when he'd half fallen through that hole in the roof, or just scaling down the gable wall into this yard.

He gritted his teeth with frustration. This meant he wouldn't even be able to pass on the VRM – not in time for support cars to give chase.

From beyond the wall, there was a screech of tyres and a hefty *clunk* of metal.

Heck ran again. He skidded out onto the road, where a Ford Focus had jammed its anchors on but had still collided with the stolen van, which now stood skew-whiff across the middle of the tarmac. As a large woman jumped out of the Focus, shouting, Cleghorn threw the van into reverse, pulled it to a better angle and burned rubber as he accelerated down

211

the backstreet opposite. The woman's shouts became shrieks as Heck pounded in pursuit.

'Call nine-nine-nine!' he yelled at her. 'Tell them where the bastard's headed to.'

But this was something Heck had dreaded all along. Any town could be a jungle if you didn't know your way around, especially an old, industrial town like this, with lots of alleys and narrow, terraced streets.

At least the Toyota wasn't gaining ground on him. It was about forty yards ahead, but as the backstreet was dotted all the way with blue wheelie bins, it had to bullock past them.

Heck found himself leaping over falling, rolling plastic and mounds of freshly shed rubbish, but he was catching up. He was exhausted, racked with pain, and the more corners they turned, the more difficult it became to work out where he was. If he'd still had the radio handset, Humberside Comms could have tracked him through its inbuilt APLS, but now both he and they were flying blind.

A half-second later, he emerged onto a bigger road, right in the midst of teeming traffic.

The van had barrelled straight through and was already shooting down another side street opposite. Heck jumped back as a Vauxhall Corsa screeched to a halt, its horn yowling, before weaving his way forward through a river of slow-moving but nevertheless impatient vehicles. More horns tooted, more tyres squealed.

He tumbled across a bonnet, a beery voice bellowing profanities behind the windscreen, and hammered down the next side street, threading between warehouses, workshops and fenced-off yards, trying to memorise the route in case he had a chance to stop and use his phone. He spotted no street names that he could recognise, but if nothing else, the open sky ahead indicated that they were heading down towards the river. All he could see of the fleeing van, meanwhile, was its bumper and tailpipe as it vanished down another alley. It was a certainty that Heck wasn't going to be able to stick with him much longer. They'd soon hit a major road from where his quarry could make a proper escape. But as Heck emerged into open space again, now with derelict land on either side, he saw the Toyota flattening a wire-mesh barricade and dipping down a slip road into a tunnel.

That surely could only lead to one place – the waterside.

With his last reserves of strength, Heck ran on.

The tunnel was made from damp concrete and strewn with bricks and bottles, which were perilous in the half-light. Heck hared through it anyway. Where was the maniac going?

And then it struck him.

'*You've got to be bloody kidding!*' he shouted.

The Toyota was at least a hundred yards ahead when it fishtailed out into the blot of light at the end of the tunnel and hit its brakes hard. Heck saw Cleghorn jump out and grapple with the bungee cords holding the inflatable boat on the roof rack. Halting, Heck dug into his pocket for his phone, but as he was underground, he couldn't get a signal. Frustrated, he shoved it back and belted forward again.

It seemed like minutes later when he emerged into sunlight, a vast rippling riverscape stretching in front of him, though immediate access to it was blocked by the abandoned van. They appeared to be on a litter-strewn beach of mud and shingle, which was narrowed by fences of high, rusty steel on either side. Above the fence on his right, only the Humber Bridge, majestically crossing the skyline, provided any kind of geographic reference.

Ahead, screened from view by the van, a motor churned to life.

Heck threw himself bodily over the dented vehicle, but on the other side, landed in black/green slurry. His feet flew from beneath him, and he hit the ground with his backside. It was a furious thud, and it knocked the wind from him, as well as smearing him with filth.

Swaying exhaustedly back to his feet, he scrambled forward over rubble and broken stones, but when he reached the water's edge, both the dinghy and Tim Cleghorn were some forty yards from shore, cutting a broad if meandering wake through choppy brown wavelets. Cleghorn was clearly new to sailing, but all he'd had to do was sit at the back of the dinghy, lower the propeller and man the tiller.

Heck sank to one knee, sweat-soaked, ragged and muddy. Fleetingly, he was too tired even to feel disappointed.

The bastard surely wouldn't get far. He'd know that he wouldn't have enough fuel to reach the south shore. He might still put distance between himself and his pursuers, perhaps by aiming for another derelict quay a bit further along the front. But if Heck could get some support out here, they might still be able to locate him.

He fished the phone from his pocket, only to discover that the device was now clogged with mud. He urgently tried to claw this away, while Cleghorn drew further and further out.

Heck glanced up, wondering if some air support might be homing in – a chopper would resolve everything. But if any such thing had been deployed, there was no sign of it yet. He tried to put another call through, when a deafening noise shattered the afternoon.

A tugboat with *KLS Ship Repair & Dry Dock Ltd* stencilled on its hull rounded the headland on the right, engines throbbing as it towed the steel leviathan of a midsized cargo ship. The tug had sounded its siren because Cleghorn's dinghy had almost strayed into its path.

Heck watched incredulously.

The connected vessels, which were sending an enormous backwash shoreward, were about two hundred yards out, while Cleghorn was probably just over half that distance. He ought to have been safe, but as Heck had already seen, the fugitive wasn't handy with a tiller. He attempted to turn, pulling the flimsy rubber craft in a tight semicircle, which meant that he'd brought his port side about-face to the approaching surge.

Calling out so shrilly that even Heck could hear it, Cleghorn rode high, before tilting sideways, at which point a crosswind caught the craft and completed the job, flipping it clean over. The inexpert steersman vanished beneath the foaming surface.

Heck continued to watch, spellbound. The ship-under-tow hadn't even passed when Cleghorn re-emerged, spluttering and coughing, splashing the water like a terrified child.

Swim back, Heck said to himself. *For God's sake, just swim back*.

But Cleghorn continued his frenzy, finally turning in Heck's direction, long hair plastered over his face as he slapped the sloshing surface. When he went under again, he was waving a desperate hand.

Heck swore aloud, ensuring that his phone was slotted back into his jacket, before peeling it off and wading forward.

The river was bitingly cold and bobbing with all kinds of shoreline debris. He was waist-deep before he dived and commenced a strenuous front-crawl. The backwash from the ship hit him in the form of several huge waves. With a massive effort, he managed to crest them, though foul-tasting water gushed up his nose.

'Can't . . . I can't swim . . .' Cleghorn screeched some distance ahead.

Heck strove on hard, his arms already feeling like lead.

He could see the guy about twenty yards away, stuttering

and choking. They made contact a few seconds later, Heck grabbing the idiot by the collar of his sweater as they trod water together.

'Listen!' he spat.

Cleghorn gasped and gibbered, his strained, white features still pasted with streaks of red hair.

'You listening?'

The fugitive responded with a short, terse nod, though his eyes were glazed, his teeth chattering in his grimacing mouth.

'I've no inclination to save your worthless life, OK?' Heck said. 'But I'm not chasing you halfway across Hull to get nothing out of it.'

Cleghorn began struggling again, arms windmilling.

Heck tightened his grip on the guy's neck. 'Pack that in and listen! *Are you listening?*'

Cleghorn gave another tight nod.

'When I get you ashore, you're going to fucking talk to me. Yeah?'

Another nod.

'*Say it!*'

'Yeah . . .' Cleghorn coughed out a wad of filthy water. 'Yeah!'

'OK . . . so I'm going to put a hand under your chin, and I'm going to tow you in on your back. You understand that?'

'My back . . .?'

'On your back. All you do is float. But keep still. The more you struggle, the harder it is.'

Another nod.

Heck hooked the fugitive under his jaw and, frog-kicking backward towards the shore, hauled the guy behind him. Frightened though he was, Cleghorn at least had the sense to follow instructions, flattening himself on the surface. That made it easier, but it was still a laborious effort. When Heck's heels touched the muddy riverbed, he hadn't felt as relieved in ages.

He dragged the fugitive ashore, still by the scruff of his neck, and dropped him, then stood over the prone figure, breathing heavily, dripping.

'You heard me out there,' he panted. 'I don't swim the rivers of England for nothing.'

Cleghorn lay on his side, back heaving, hands clutching the surrounding sludge as if he'd never leave dry land again. But he managed another nod.

'Before we do anything else,' Heck said, 'you don't have to say anything, but it may harm your defence if you do not mention when questioned something you later rely on in court. Anything you do say may be given in evidence. You're under arrest, of course . . . to start with, for taking a vehicle without the owner's consent, for assaulting police officers . . .'

Cleghorn nodded a second time.

'. . . and for conspiracy to commit murder.'

'Whaaa . . . *no!*' This seemed to bring the guy to his senses. 'No, no . . .' He squirmed over into a sitting position. 'I've nothing to do with no murder.'

Heck kicked him. 'I thought we'd agreed that you being straight with me is the only reason you're still alive.' He reached down, grabbed Cleghorn's collar and hauled him to his feet. 'You tell me what I want to know, or I'll drag you out to midstream again.'

'You . . . you can't do this?' the prisoner spluttered. 'You've just cautioned me.'

'Well, one of the advantages of not having a clue where I am on this riverfront is that no back-up's arrived. So, there's no one to say whether I've cautioned you or not, is there?'

They eyeballed each other from two or three inches apart. Cleghorn was around the same height as Heck, but older.

Any remaining belligerence drained away as Heck's no-nonsense gaze bored into him.

'Your choice, pal,' Heck advised him.

'OK, look, look . . . I'll cough to the other stuff, but I'm nothing to do with these murders.'

'Sorry . . .?' Heck thought he'd misheard. '*What?*'

'It's just what I've seen on the videos, that's all.'

'Murders? As in . . . *plural?*'

Cleghorn's fearful expression shifted to one of bemusement. 'Isn't that what this is about?'

Heck scanned his prisoner for any undue body language, any sign of deceit, but saw none. 'Tell me about Eddie Creeley?' he said.

'Nah . . . no way, mate.' Cleghorn suddenly seemed to sense that he had more power in his corner than he'd realised. 'If you don't know nothing, I've nothing to say. You can kick my arse, drag me back in the river . . . I don't give a shit. I'm saying nothing . . . not till I've got my solicitor present.'

'You know what, Tim . . .' Heck released his collar but instead placed him in a wrist-lock and produced the handcuffs from his back pocket. 'I think getting yourself some legal rep would be a very good idea at this moment.'

He fastened Cleghorn's hands behind his back, snatched his discarded jacket and marched the prisoner back up the beach.

'Can't say I'm not grateful for you hauling me out of there,' Cleghorn coughed. 'Nightmare, that river. Thought I was a goner.'

'Just don't count your chickens, pal,' Heck replied. 'You may still be.'

Chapter 21

'I hear you've had a busy day?' Gwen Straker said.

'Could say that, ma'am,' Heck replied.

He was slumped in an armchair in the Clough Road rec room, his laptop open on the coffee table in front of him. Both Gwen and Gemma's faces were visible on-screen, in separate boxes. Neither commented on his appearance; though he'd managed a quick shower and had changed into jeans and sweatshirt, he looked beaten-up and sallow-cheeked.

'Anything that's going to annoy us?' Gemma wondered. 'I mean, we might as well get the bad news out of the way first.'

'Well . . .' Heck gave it some thought. 'You're going to get billed for some roof repairs.'

'Roof repairs?'

'Yeah . . . some houses in the Trafalgar Road area of Hull.'

'Houses, eh?' Gwen chuckled without humour. 'This is something of a destruction upgrade, Heck, even by *your* standards.'

'You'll get a bill for my best suit too.'

'Excuse me?' Gemma already sounded irritated by his offhand tone.

'I ruined it in the line of duty, ma'am. I'm sure you don't want me representing National Crime Group looking like a scruffy urchin for the rest of the enquiry.'

'Now listen, Sergeant Heckenburg—'

'Just tell us what happened,' Gwen cut in. 'And keep it relevant. And less lip, if you don't mind. No doubt you've had a tough day, Heck, but you're not the only one.'

Heck made a show of sitting painfully upright. 'I locked a bloke up this afternoon, name of Timothy Cleghorn . . . for various superficial things, but basically on suspicion that he was the character who posted the pen drive through Nan Creeley's letter box.'

'And?' Gwen said.

'He's put his hand up to it.'

'He has?'

Both women's expressions visibly changed.

'Yeah, but that's all he's putting his hand up to,' Heck said. 'In terms of Eddie Creeley, that is. If we want more, we've got to make a deal.'

Gemma shook her head. 'You know we don't do that.'

'Ma'am . . . we *do* do that,' he said wearily. 'We may not *like* doing it, we may not comfortably *admit* to doing it, but—'

'*Tone,* Heck!' Gwen interjected.

Heck leaned forward. 'Look, the situation is that Cleghorn may have a lot to give us. Something much bigger than an armed robber who's gone missing. On top of that, we don't have too much to lean on him with . . . Let's be honest, with nothing but that pen drive to go on, we'll be lucky to make a conspiracy-to-murder charge stand.'

He let that hang.

'Keep talking,' Gwen said.

'I interviewed him for a bunch of petty offences. He's coughed to them all, so he'll be charged with those later. He's also claiming that he stole that pen drive.'

'Who from?' Gemma still sounded sceptical.

'That's where it gets tricky.'

'I'll bet it does.'

'Cleghorn tells me he's a member of a porn club.'

'Isn't every fella, these days,' Gwen said.

'Yeah, but in Cleghorn's case I think it's a bit different from the norm. He says the club is, quote, "a cinema of the extreme".'

'Which means what?' Gemma asked.

'You name it, it's there.'

'Are we talking paedophilia?' Gwen wondered.

She rightly sounded worried, because if a bargain needed to be struck, it would be much harder to convince the powers that be when it might mean someone evading a child-exploitation charge.

'No,' Heck replied. 'Surprisingly. He says it's definitely not that. But it's still pretty reprehensible. We're talking rape, torture, horrific violence . . .'

'The real thing?'

'Apparently. And by the sounds of it, it's all non-consensual.'

There was a protracted silence in the MIR. From where Heck was seated, he could see that various other staff had gathered behind the SIO and her deputy to listen.

'Murder . . . by any chance?' Gwen asked.

'Cleghorn thinks so,' Heck said. 'Says they've been getting quite a few videos recently which appear to depict real-life killings.'

'*Appear* to depict?'

'We've seen one for ourselves.'

'Creeley?'

'Correct. Cleghorn says there've been several of these. A kind of crude gladiatorial combat. Men stripped to their undies, put in a sort of arena, given street weapons, pipes, bats, chains and stuff . . . fighting for their lives against these

human tanks in body armour. It always ends the same way
. . . nastily.'

'So, Cleghorn's a member of a snuff movie club,' Gemma
said. 'And he thinks we're going to do a deal with him?'

Heck shrugged. 'If it means we get the people running the
club and making the films . . . perhaps we should.'

'This club's online, presumably?' Gwen said.

'No, that's the thing. None of this stuff is on the internet.
Seems they're quite nervous about leaving electronic trails
that might lead back to them. So, it all takes place in some
kind of renovated basement that they're using as a cinema,
with a projector and a big screen, and even a nice old lady
to sell ice lollies at the interval . . .' He shrugged. 'Well, I
don't know about the last bit, but you get the picture. Only
proven members get in, and they pay handsomely for the
privilege.'

'How did Cleghorn get a copy of the film?' Gemma
asked.

'As I say, he claims to have nicked it. When I say
"projector", I mean a laptop wired to a big widescreen telly.
Seems they have a meeting every so often, and watch all
these movies one after another. But Eddie Creeley's farewell
performance only got a lukewarm reception – I guess because
he didn't put up much of a fight. At the next break this
particular pen drive got shoved onto a shelf with a few
others. Cleghorn kept an eye on it, and as soon as no one
was looking, he slipped it into his pocket. Reckons it was
so unpopular with the punters, it probably hasn't been missed
even now.'

'We must never disappoint the paying public,' Gwen said
wryly.

'Why did he steal it?' Gemma asked.

'Simple . . . or so he says.' Again, Heck delicately adjusted
his position. 'Cleghorn's a local lad, Hull-born, and he recog-

nised Eddie Creeley straight away. Seems our Ed used to beat him up when they were at school together, steal his lunch money, all the usual scrote stuff. And one day, when Cleghorn went round to their house with his mum, to complain, the only person there was Nan Creeley, who would never hear a bad word against her kid brother and sent them off with a flea in their ear. Cleghorn reckons he's owed them one ever since, and this was just too good to be true.'

Another silence ensued.

'And do you believe this story?' Gemma asked. 'Seriously?'

'Like I say, ma'am, we won't know what to believe until we get some further info. And that's the part Cleghorn's sitting on. We searched his house after arrest, and found these . . .' He held up a transparent evidence bag containing stubs of paper. 'Train ticket receipts . . . in an unemptied bin. London and back. Lots of them, over several months. So, it's fair to say this club is based in London, but he won't say whereabouts specifically, he won't tell us how you gain access to it, he won't tell us who's running it.'

'What are the other offences he's committed?' Gwen asked.

Heck listed the charges pending against Cleghorn – TWOC and police assault, as he'd promised during the arrest, though he'd now added a few extra: causing grievous bodily harm, theft of a boat, leaving the scene of an RTA and driving without insurance.

'The Hull copper he GBH'd is a lad called Barry Hodges,' Heck said. 'He's got a broken nose and two fractured cheek-bones, so I think Cleghorn's going down . . . especially as he's already got lots of form. That gives us a bit of leverage, but not enough apparently.'

'If this club is based in London, wouldn't it better if we just put our own grasses on it?' Gemma said.

'We can do that,' Heck replied, 'but it sounds like this

thing is one of the best-kept secrets. And our clock's ticking, isn't it?'

They considered the situation.

'I'm sure I don't need to say it,' Heck added, 'but if this thing is kosher, and other folk like Eddie Creeley are dying in this home-made arena, it's not impossible that we might find out what's happened to more of our missing fugitives.'

The women almost looked shocked.

'What on earth makes you think that?' Gwen asked.

'It's only a theory,' Heck replied, 'but . . . no one's getting anywhere, are they? Or so I'm told. Not even DI Reed, apparently . . .'

Gemma was about to interrupt, but he carried on regardless.

'Gary Quinnell's hit a dead end in Shropshire. Same seems to have happened to Andy Rawlins and Burt Cunliffe in Nottingham. In both cases, local informants told them it's weird . . . like the targets have just vanished.'

'Of course they've vanished,' Gwen said. 'They're facing full-life jail terms. It's a miracle they didn't vanish years ago.'

'You'd certainly think that,' Heck replied. 'But, for whatever reason, this particular bunch have been dumb enough to hang around in the UK, in some cases for years . . . until the last few months, when suddenly they've all started disappearing.'

There was a brief, contemplative silence.

'But as I say,' he added, 'it's only a theory. The main thing, if this lead's a goer, is that we might have cracked a vigilante firm who are organising gladiatorial combat to the death. How effective will our respective outfits look then? Especially when we make sure the dailies get the story first.'

'And the price of this win-win is that we don't connect Cleghorn in any way to this cinema club, or to any of the murders?' Gemma said, still sounding unimpressed.

Heck nodded. 'That's about the strength of it. Says he'll give us everything we need to close them down. If we can offer him protection, he'll even witness for us. Give us a full statement, offer testimony in court, the lot.'

'What do the local brass think?' Gwen asked.

'Well . . . DCI Bateson's blazing about the injury to one of his detectives. I get the impression he's the sort of bloke who blazes quite a lot, but on this occasion with some justification. And CPS are doing what they usually do, sitting there like lemons, unsure. But if one of you two was to have a word . . .?'

Neither of the SIOs initially responded.

'I take it Cleghorn's got full legal representation?' Gwen eventually said.

'Oh yeah,' Heck said. 'His solicitor's onside. The idea probably came from him. He knows his dipshit client could finish up in big trouble here.'

'We need to tell Cleghorn and his solicitor that he's not out of the woods yet,' Gwen said. 'If this snuff club turns out to be fantasy, for any reason . . . I mean, even if it was there once but isn't there any more because someone involved has got wind that we're onto them, that won't be good enough.'

'I can tell them that, ma'am, but I think it'd be better coming from you.'

Gwen nodded. 'That's OK. Do we actually need to come up there?'

'I don't think so. If you get what you want on the phone, me and Gail will probably be coming down to you.'

'I'd say excellent work, Heck . . .' she shifted her chair backward, 'but first of all, I want to see how big those roof-repair bills are.' And she left the conference.

'Upon which subject,' Gemma said, 'despite the *bloody rudeness* of the way you said it, you can submit the claim

225

for your suit, and I'll give it due consideration. But if this turns out to be another wildman caper, Heck . . . I mean it, you can pay for the damn thing yourself.'

'I'll pay for it, ma`am,' Heck said sourly, '. . . on the day I see a receipt proving that Jack Reed paid for his dog collar.'

Then, he too left the conference.

Heck found Gail in the canteen. It was mid-evening, so she sat there alone, sipping coffee.

'You're going to get us both canned, Heck,' was all she said.

'What do you mean?'

'Talking to the Deputy SIO like that.'

He sloped to the vending machine. 'Listening in, were you?'

'Firstly, I could hardly fail to hear as you were only in the next room. Secondly, I wasn't aware it was supposed to be a private conversation. It's not like it doesn't involve me.'

He returned with a coffee for himself. 'You are aware we've just broken the case?'

Gail sat back. 'I'm aware of no such thing. We've made ground, yeah . . . and we've made two very good arrests, but at least one of them has got nothing to do with the enquiry and might still have negative consequences for us.'

'We're not going to get canned, OK?' Heck slumped down on the other side of the table. 'We're well on.'

Gail mulled this over, and said: 'What is it with you and her, anyway?'

'Now what are you talking about?'

'Gemma. I get it that you two were together once, but that was ages back, wasn't it?'

'Certainly was.'

'OK, so . . .? I mean, she's the Lioness. She's got a rep for

226

eating mouthy male officers for breakfast. But somehow, with you she's . . . well, "tolerant" would be one word.'

He shrugged and sipped his drink. 'She knows I get results, that's all.'

'That is such a fucking cliché, Heck.'

'Clichés are clichés because they tend to be true.'

'Clichés are clichés because people trot them out without thinking too hard.'

'Look!' he said. 'I don't know what the explanation is. Gemma probably feels she's had her claws pruned by being made second fiddle to Gwen Straker.'

'Well, if that's true it makes you a pathetic bully, doesn't it?'

He stared at her, askance, the mere thought that anyone could believe Gemma Piper was capable of being bullied leaving him dumbfounded. 'Sorry . . . *what*?'

'She's had her confidence knocked, and your response is to stick the boot in. That's particularly despicable.'

Heck didn't initially reply. Was it conceivable? That Gemma – supercool, super-efficient Gemma, so used to being in command – was now so shaken to see her normal SIO role usurped by an older, more senior officer, that she was losing her roar?

'So, what is it?' Gail asked him again.

'I said I don't know. Look . . .' he tried to wave it away, '. . . we've known each other a long time, and we're having problems. It happens.'

'No, *you're* having problems.' Gail stood up. 'I'm not dumb, Heck. You've got to sort your head out where DSU Piper's concerned, all right?' She marched from the canteen, but half a second later came marching back in. 'And for God's sake, Jack Reed has got no relevance to our case. So, stop bringing him up.'

'He's all show, you know.'

'I don't bloody believe this.'

'Gemma's not being forthcoming about it, but he's chasing a case in the Home Counties, and it sounds to me like he's getting nowhere.'

Gail leaned down. 'You know, if she fancies him . . . she fancies him. That's just tough shit, and you'd better deal with it, Heck, because getting into SCU was my dream, and I'm not seeing it screwed up because you've got a schoolboy beef with someone who's probably destined to rise twenty ranks higher than you whatever happens with Operation Sledgehammer.'

She marched out again.

Heck knew that he should go with her, so they could get on with interviewing a prisoner who was allegedly ready to sing like a canary. But for a moment or two, he sat alone, pondering the events of recent days.

It ought to be easy to shrug off this thing that was relentlessly bugging him. To admit, even if only to himself, that Jack Reed's presence wasn't that big a deal, and that Gemma Piper was a grown woman, *and* a singleton – she could tap off with whoever she wanted to.

But he couldn't shake his mystification that, all these years down the line, she never had.

Ever since their own break-up, Heck had never known or heard of her dating anyone else. He hadn't even known her get especially friendly with anyone. He'd always put this down to the steely thing she'd become over so many challenging years; to her wilful, hard-headed nature; to her turbocharged policewoman persona. Not many blokes outside the job would go for that, though with Gemma's looks she still should have been able to take her pick.

Was there a deeper reason, then?

She wasn't the one who'd wanted to break up, after all. Or so she'd said. Was it conceivable that, even after so long, she still carried a minuscule flame for him, and that, deep down, he'd always known this?

He gulped his coffee and stood up, determined to shake that idea off.

Unrealistic hopes were the bane of so many men's lives.

For all kinds of reasons, a romantic entanglement wouldn't work between them these days, the biggest of all being that they didn't dovetail professionally.

But even so, when he tried to tell himself that he didn't care, when he snorted dismissively and decided that he was merely irritated by Jack Reed's effortless charisma, was it anything more than bravado?

Maybe that knot of tension inside him was all about fear.

Fear that the door was finally closing.

Fear that when Reed eventually popped the question, even if it was something as chaste and demure as 'fancy coming out for a drink', Gemma would say 'yes' . . .

'Bollocks!' he said, throwing his cup into the bin and setting off down through the station towards Custody.

Let them go for a drink. Sod it . . . let them hit the sack and shag like demons. It was nothing to do with him.

But then he thought about swimming out into the Humber, those filthy, ice-cold waters, to save Tim Cleghorn, a piece of trash whose sole facility was perhaps that he *might* put them onto Eddie Creeley's killers.

That was a mystery too.

They kept using phrases like 'the clock is ticking', but it wasn't like there was a *real* urgency about this case. It wasn't as if the lives of anyone Heck cared about depended on it . . . or the lives of anyone society cared about, if he was frank.

So why would he put his life on the line in that way?

Why the hell was he running around like a blue-arsed fly, headbutting posts, climbing roofs, disrupting other police

229

operations . . . pushing himself and his partner to the maximum limit?

In truth, he knew the answer without needing to say it.

In truth, he'd known it for some time.

'Damn it, Gemma, you're a torment,' he said under his breath. 'But any chance, no matter how bloody small, is better than none.'

Chapter 22

'So, Spencer?' the voice said from the darkness. 'What's the story?'

At first, Spencer Taylor thought he'd been dreaming. Exhausted and hungry, he was certainly half-asleep. But then he realised that someone was actually here and talking to him.

'The fuck!' he shouted, jumping up from the mound of dirt that had served as his backrest. He pulled the Bulldog from under his ragged jacket and swung it around in both hands. 'I'm fucking packing, man!'

To his amazement, there was nobody there. The subterranean water-junction, which for eight days now had been his sanctuary, looked as it always did: arched brick passageways leading off in various directions, filth and bodily waste flowing along each one. More vile fluids dripping from overhead. Rats scurrying. After so long taking refuge in this hidden place, emerging only when he needed to find something to eat, his eyes had finally attuned to a darkness which, at first, had seemed opaque. Though even now he couldn't see everything.

Certainly not whoever it was who'd just spoken.

'Tell you, man, I'm packing!' he warned again, in his distinctive Jafaican patois.

'Oh, I know you are, Bullet Boy,' the disembodied voice replied.

Spencer spun frantically, Bulldog cocked.

'Is that what we should call you from now on? Bullet Boy?'

'*The fuck!*' Spencer shrieked.

'You've got a great vocabulary, Spencer. I'm surprised . . .'

'Fuck you, yeah!'

'I thought you street guys were supposed to be inventive in your dialogue. Or is that just how middle-class academics like to portray you?'

'Don't know who the fuck you are, man, but I'm not taking no shit.'

'Wooo . . .' the voice tittered.

Spencer desperately scanned his underground refuge. The voice was weird, tinny. It seemed to be coming from everywhere and yet nowhere. Whoever the guy was, he had to be close. But Spencer needed to know for sure. He couldn't afford any more mistakes; not when he only had one round left.

'Big bad Spencer and his terrifying .44,' the voice said, still amused. 'What I always wonder, though, is how baby gangbangers like you would get on if you weren't armed?'

'The fuck are you, man?'

'Seriously, what do you think? How would you get on in the world if you didn't have a gun to stick in people's faces?'

Suddenly, Spencer couldn't reply. He was too busy gasping for breath. He'd only managed to grab bits of food in the last few days, and the odd mouthful of water. It was summer, so it wasn't cold, and yet it staggered him how tired and ill he was feeling after a week outdoors – if you could call this verminous underground hole the actual outdoors.

'Not so good,' the voice said, 'by the looks of it.'

'Hey, fuck you, man!'

'It's funny, actually. The press are calling you Public Enemy Number 1. Apparently, you're the most hated and feared gang-member in London. But me and you know the truth of it, eh? You're just a punk kid who's scared of his own shadow.'

'Step out here, man!' Spencer retorted. 'You're a gutless piece of shit . . . you won't show yourself, neither.'

'Oh, you're right there. You see . . . I think a little frightened kid with a big gun can still be dangerous. But what would you say, Spencer, if I told you I had a bead on you right now? That there's an infrared lens over here in the shadows and the crosshairs are right on your sweaty little forehead?'

Spencer had slapped at his brow, as if he could actually remove any such cherry-red speck by wiping it away, before realising the ridiculousness of the action.

'Look, man . . . I don't know what this is, yeah?' He tried to keep the despair from his voice, but he was out on his feet here, lost, frightened, sick. 'But if you wanted to pop me, you'd have done it already, yeah!'

'Sure of that, Spence?' the voice wondered. 'Maybe I want to mentally torture you first.'

'Shut the fuck up, man!'

'How's it feel, Spencer . . . being the one at the other end of the firearm?'

'I know that feeling, man . . . that's the way we live.'

The voice chuckled again. 'And if you didn't have the Toreadors to fall back on, would you still live that way? Even if you did, it'd be a piss-easier option than working for a living.'

More chuckles; in fact, open laughter, which seemed to come from everywhere at once.

'Shock horror, Spence . . . imagine that? Having to go out and break your back every day to put food on the table for the kids, maybe buy a prezzie for your woman now and then. Naw . . . I can't see it, either. You'd rather be Spencer the Big I Am, eh? Spencer the Bullet Boy.'

'I'm no camp-follower, man!' Spencer shouted, stung. 'The rest of the bluds respect me.'

'I don't know about that, Spencer. They may have once. *May* have. But they sure as shit don't now. They've denied even knowing you, though I suppose when Operation Trident get them up against a wall and it's a case of them or you, what do you think'll happen next?'

'Fuck you, man, yeah?'

'Doesn't matter anyway, does it? I mean, you've achieved national infamy. Your face is on every TV screen. You know that lady you gunned down on Tottenham High Road was pregnant. So that's three innocent lives you took that day.'

'What you doing, man?' Spencer all but screamed. 'If you're the Five-Oh, just take me the fuck in, yeah!'

'The Five-Oh? You been watching American telly down here, Spence?'

'Just fucking pack it in!'

'You may not actually believe this, Spencer . . . but I reckon I can help you.'

'What . . .?' At first, Spencer thought he'd misheard. 'What you say?'

'I don't like to think of a guy like you eking out what's left of his life down here. I mean, don't the rats and roaches of London have enough troubles of their own?'

Spencer didn't answer. Sweat stood on his brow in globules as his eyes strained at the rancid darkness. But he was listening too.

'So, here's the thing,' the voice said. 'I'm proposing to get you out of here. And not only that. I'm going to take you to the coast, smuggle you onto a boat, and ship you overseas to a safe haven. How's that sound, Spence?'

'You offering a deal, or something?'

'Deals are where I live, pal.'

'That's fucked, man. No one can get me out of this shit.' But, deep down, Spencer felt his first surge of hope since the Dante Brown disaster – and that now seemed like a lifetime ago.

'Is that so?'

'Hey man, fuck you, yeah!'

'Don't get me wrong, Spence,' the voice said. 'As far as I'm *really* concerned, you can die down here. But I'm going to try to be nice one more time just on the off-chance I might otherwise miss out on a potential earner. No one you know gives a flying fuck about you any more. Your family's disowned you, the Toreadors think you're the biggest prick that's ever walked the streets of Tottenham, and that's saying something, isn't it? There was a girl in your life, wasn't there? . . . Amazingly enough. Chantelle something or other. Well, you won't believe this . . . she's sold her story to the gutter press. Sixty grand just to tell them what a total wanker you are. All that slapping her around if she so much as looked at other fellas . . . it's backfired a bit now, hasn't it?'

'Get me the fuck out!' Spencer shrieked.

'Sure.' There was a brief pause. 'But it'll cost you a hundred grand.'

Again, Spencer thought he must've misheard. 'You smoking crack, man?'

'You seriously telling me you can't get a hundred grand, Spence?'

'I'm living in a fucking sewer.'

'Get it off the Toreadors.'

'You wavey, man? You think they'll just give it to me?'

Yet another chuckle. 'I'm not talking about *asking* them

for it, pal. But it's your call. If you don't think you can manage it . . .'

'Wait . . . wait, for Jesus's sake . . .'

But there was only silence now, and that steady *drip-drip* of the underground realm, that faint skitter of rat paws, that distant rumble of tube trains.

'Wait . . .' the kid almost wept. 'Anything, man . . . just don't . . .'

'Something I can do for you, Spencer?' the voice asked.

'I can get it, yeah. If you can really get me out of this . . .'

'Already told you, didn't I? Pay your way, and the only thing you'll have to worry about is the Far East or the Caribbean or the Middle East?'

'The fuck, man . . .?'

'Take your pick, Spence. You've got the beaches and palm trees of the Dominican Republic. You've got the hot sun of Bahrain and Kuwait. You've got the big cities with all the mod cons of South Korea, Japan. None of those countries have extradition treaties, you see. So, you get a chance to start afresh. Get a job as a barman or waiter, or something. Then, in due course, when you inevitably fuck up, we'll have to go through this whole fucking thing again. But in the meantime, the heat will be off.'

'Yeah, man . . .' Spencer nodded eagerly, desperately. 'Let's . . . let's do this, yeah!'

'Sure. But not till you bring the cash.'

'I'll get it . . . I've said I'll get it . . .'

'OK, Spence . . . it's a deal.' The voice was already diminishing, as if its owner was moving away through the tunnels.

'Hey man, I ain't even seen you!'

'You'll see me on the day.' It was now very distant.

'When? And where'm I gonna find you?'

'Don't worry, Spence . . . I'll find you.' Spencer could only just hear him. 'Wherever you are, I'll find you.'

Chapter 23

It was difficult to tell what the building on Deercot Road had once been. Some kind of a minor office block, perhaps, but with workshop premises downstairs, as indicated by the unloading bays at the front and the wagon-sized entrance doors with roll-down steel shutters. These days, superficially at least, it was nothing, litter and scraps of last year's leaf-fall blowing about in the parking bays, and dust on the insides of the windows. The properties both to the left and right – one a small industrial unit, the other a storage facility – were in a less neglected state, but were not exactly hives of activity.

'So . . . there're only two ways in and out,' Heck said, as they cruised past in his Megane. 'One midway along the entry . . .' he nodded to a passage running down the side of the empty building, '. . . which is basically the front door. And a fire exit round the back. Apparently, there's no access to the rest of the building from the cellar . . . which is where we're reliably informed this cinema is.'

Gary Quinnell who was in the front passenger seat, nodded but said nothing.

'You all right?' Heck asked.

Quinnell nodded again.

'Sure you're up for this?'

The big Welshman shot him a sideways glance. 'Always, boyo, if it's doing God's work.'

They rounded a corner and rejoined the heavy rush-hour traffic on Putney High Street.

'Yeah, well just remember,' Heck said, 'heaven helps those who help themselves. So, when you're down there, you keep your wits about you and your back to the nearest wall.'

'No worries,' Quinnell replied.

'Wish we could arm you, but they're bound to search you when you first go in.'

'Do I look like the kind of bloke who needs to be armed?'

'Just stay sharp, OK?'

'Will do. Stop pestering.'

'On which subject . . .' Heck checked his phone to see if he'd maybe missed a call, but there was nothing, 'don't suppose you've seen Gail Honeyford today?'

'Can't say I have.'

'Don't know what the bloody hell she's playing at. Hope she's in time for the briefing.'

'Well . . .' Quinnell shrugged, 'if she doesn't show, at least we'll have Jack Reed.'

A red light approached, but Heck hit the brake harder than he'd intended to. 'Reed? Since when?'

'Since last night . . . when he locked his suspect up.'

'What?'

'That's right. Patrick Hallahan, he was after. The McDonald's shooter from Slough.'

'Reed's bagged him already?' Heck couldn't believe it.

'Sounds like it. Bastard's coughed to it, too. Press were all over Staples Corner this morning. Gwen was doubly happy we're signing on at Putney. Which makes me think . . . could it be Gail doesn't know about that? Putney, I mean? Green, mate . . .'

238

Heck was so startled by this that at first nothing else computed.

Quinnell nudged him. 'It's on *green*.'

Tooting horns from the ever-impatient London traffic bottling up behind them finally caught Heck's attention. He knocked the Megane into gear and they moved forward.

'I emailed Gail last night, to remind her,' he said. 'Gaz . . . you're saying Reed's nicked Patrick Hallahan, and he's already got a full confession?'

'That's what I heard.'

The briefing commenced at six o'clock that evening and was held in the spare parade room at Putney Bridge Road police station.

From the outset, it had the air of a rough-and-ready affair. Only a handful of Sledgehammer personnel were present – Heck, Reed and Quinnell, the latter only available because his own Shropshire-based enquiry into the whereabouts of John Stroud was making such little progress that it had seemed neither here nor there if he diverted from it for a couple of days. The rest of the team, some twenty officers in total, had been seconded from local uniformed staff and the Territorial Support Group and were now convened in full crowd-control wear, including fireproof overalls, stab vests and shin and elbow pads. Those seated had their helmets on the tables in front of them, those standing carried them under their arms. Even Gwen Straker, who was hosting the event, wore a padded blue anorak over her plain clothes, with POLICE stencilled on the back in hi-vis white lettering.

'OK, listen up everyone!' she shouted.

The buzz of conversation died.

'First of all, I'd like to thank Inspector Takuma, for making this facility and his uniformed staff available to us today.' She nodded to a corner, where Cyril Takuma, a short, bespectacled officer of Nigerian origin, who, despite being duty officer here at Putney Bridge Road, was also padded up in armour and carried a riot helmet under his arm. 'Quite a few members of Operation Sledgehammer are still otherwise engaged,' she added, 'so we're reliant on local forces today – and they've really come through for us.'

Again, Heck checked his phone to see if Gail had returned at least one of his several calls. Still, there was nothing.

'Now . . . I'm sure we know what's going on here,' Gwen said, 'but let me refresh a few memories. One week ago, Detective Sergeant Heckenburg arrested a known criminal on Humberside.'

Heck remained inexpressive as various heads turned his way.

'The person concerned is one Timothy Cleghorn.' Gwen stepped aside so that everyone could see the large-screen television and opened her laptop. Tapping her keyboard, she brought up the most recent mugshot of Cleghorn. 'Mr Cleghorn was bang to rights on various offences that are likely to send him to jail. However, to minimise this, he's supplied us with some intel which could well lead us to this man . . .'

The next image, another mugshot, depicted Eddie Creeley.

'Eddie Creeley. Bank robber extraordinaire and two-time murderer. Those of you who've had a chance to scan the video notes you've all been provided with will know that he's high on Operation Sledgehammer's list of the twenty Most Wanted. Now . . . this was a good catch for all kinds of reasons, not least because last night, DI Reed here arrested another face on our list, Patrick Hallahan.'

Reed, who was standing alongside Heck, nodded as they glanced at him.

'Hallahan's already made a full confession and is prepared to take his punishment,' Gwen added. 'Which, needless to say, will spare the relatives of his victims any further grief, will save the taxpayer some money and spare the police service a load of extra work. So . . . if we play this thing properly today, ladies and gents, this week could be a very good one for British law enforcement.

'Back to Creeley . . . as you're aware, we strongly suspect that he's dead. Of course, we have no clue at this stage what the events leading up to his death involved. However, we are certainly going to investigate, because we also have reason to believe that he may not be the only person to die in these violent circumstances. They may even have accounted for several more of the fugitives on our wanted list.'

There were mumbles around the room at this, and even a snort of approval.

'Doing our job for us, ma'am,' a podgy constable chirped up in the front row.

Gwen gave him a long, appraising look. 'And is that OK, PC . . .?'

'Erm, Bunting, ma'am.'

'Is that OK, PC Bunting? That a crime syndicate, whose gig seems to be making real-life snuff movies, are doing our job for us?'

Bunting's plump face tinged red. 'No, ma'am.'

She addressed the rest of the room. 'For what it's worth, I actually sympathise with the sly satisfaction some of you are possibly feeling about what may have happened to Eddie Creeley. I've made no bones about it that the names on our list are basically the scum of the earth. But as Senior Investigating Officer in this case, I personally resent not being the one to get my hands on them first. Do we all at least agree with that?'

Mutters of 'yes ma'am' echoed around the room.

'Relax, Bunting,' she said, spotting that his cheeks still burned. 'We all let our hearts rule our mouths from time to time. But we can't afford to do that today. On with the show.'

Two further images were called onto the screen. They were surveillance shots, grainy black-and-white blow-ups of a man and a woman, both of whom had been photographed while leaving the empty premises on Deercot Road. The woman, who was somewhere in her late forties, looked attractive even in the poor-quality picture, wearing a long but light-weight raincoat, the hood drawn up, dark masses of curls framing a sensual face. The man, who wore an open-necked shirt, was older, around fifty, but nevertheless had a big chest, big shoulders and a thick neck. He had chiselled good looks, a deep tan and short grey hair.

'This is Margot Frith, and her husband, Lance,' Gwen said. 'As they are now. However, this was them back in their pomp . . .'

More images of the twosome were called up. In these, a decades-younger Margot Frith wore a flowing platinum-blonde wig, bright lipstick, massive eyelashes, fishnet stockings and a black leather basque, which did little to conceal her colossal bust; she was in the process of peeling off a long, silky black glove. Lance Frith, meanwhile, who thankfully had only been screen-captured from the waist up, was bare-chested and even more deeply tanned and muscular than now, his hair hanging backward in a permed but sweat-soaked, blond mop as he reared like a stallion, eyes tightly closed, evidently in the process of reaching orgasm.

'They're both former sex workers, as if you can't tell,' Gwen said. 'Primarily, that involved acting in porn movies. Lance Frith was known as "Lance Alot" . . . yeah, I know, you can't beat the imaginative touch. While Margot was "Miss Whiplash".'

There was a lack of reaction from the police audience, who were clearly fascinated to know what was coming next.

242

'All this was years ago,' Gwen said. 'As far as we're aware, they don't perform any more, but for the last decade at least, they've been involved in the production and distribution of legal pornography. On the *illegal* side – and here's where you guys come in – they would also appear to be running this snuff club . . . or at least we assume they are, because they own the building where it's located, and we've now observed them several times, both arriving and leaving on the Wednesday nights when the film shows are said to be held.'

The next image portrayed the supposedly empty building on Deercot Road.

'The club's got no name, of course,' Gwen said. 'It doesn't exist in any official capacity. The building isn't used for anything else, and the cinema, if you want to call it that, is located in the basement. It's strictly members-only, and though it seems that, at one time, obtaining such membership was only possible through a site on the Dark Web, that site was short-lived, only existing for a few weeks. Potential new members must now be presented to the Friths in person by an existing and trusted member. And that's going to be our way in . . . and DC Quinnell here is the lucky lad.'

Gwen turned to Quinnell, the only one of the detectives present not wearing a hi-vis jacket over his scruffs.

'We've chosen him for two reasons,' Gwen said. 'Firstly, because though Gary has been in SCU for quite a few years now, he's former South Wales Police and so isn't as well-known around London as someone like DS Heckenburg, who is former Met. Secondly, DC Quinnell, as you can see, is a bloke who knows how to handle himself.'

There were chuckles all round.

'And that may be necessary,' she said, 'because the moment he's seen enough to call the rest of us in, it's going to kick off in that basement. Now, the punters, I suspect, and probably the Friths as well, will try to get away. But we're expecting most trouble from these two . . . the establishment's so-called security personnel, who are always present on screening nights.'

The next two images were custody mugshots, the one on the left showing an older man, probably in his mid-forties, the other a much younger guy, thirty tops. Despite the age discrepancy, lives of unremitting violence were engrained into those hard-bitten visages.

'Our informant warned us about these two,' Gwen said, 'but didn't know their names. *We* do, because they have long records. The first one, the older fella, is Alfie Adamson. A good, old-fashioned East End boy and former bare-knuckle boxing champion, he's been on the fringes of organised crime all his adult life, mainly working in enforcement. The younger one is Wade McDougall. He hasn't got the same illustrious reputation as his mate, but he's an up-and-comer.' She turned to Heck. 'I think *you* know him, don't you, Sergeant Heckenburg?'

'From my uniform days at Rotherhithe, ma'am,' Heck confirmed. 'He first came to our attention as a teenager who liked to batter visiting fans at Millwall. But he went on to bigger things later. Basically another thug-for-hire, but he knows how to do a job. He recently finished a ten-year stretch for beating up an undercover Drug Squad officer so severely that he almost died.'

She nodded and turned back to the others. 'If, during the course of the raid, you find yourself nose-to-nose with either of these two . . . trust me, and I don't say this often, you'll need to get *your* shots in first. OK, questions?'

'We locking up everyone in there, ma'am?' a female PC wondered.

'If we can,' Gwen said. 'There ought to be enough of us . . . but if one or two slip the net, that won't be the end of the world for me so long as we collar the Friths and their two minders. We also need to grab their equipment, of course, especially the laptop relaying the films and the pen drives on which they're uploaded.'

'Do we make a show of arresting Cleghorn?' someone else asked.

'It won't make any difference whether we do or don't. Cleghorn will be marked for ever after as the guy who brought in the police. Even if the Friths believe it was an accident, they won't forgive him for that.'

'But if he's going to do time for these other offences . . .?' Bunting said.

'*If* he does time for them,' she replied, 'he'll do it in isolation. And he'll be thankful for it. Anything else?'

A wall of expectant faces greeted this. There were no further questions.

'OK, good. Well . . . check your notes again, pay particular attention to the visuals.' Gwen glanced at the clock on the wall. 'It's six-thirty bang on. This thing goes live at seven. You all know your particular jobs, you all know your jump-off points. Let's roll.'

Chapter 24

'I don't believe you, Gail,' Heck said into his phone.

She'd finally answered one of his calls, but he was having to shout to be heard over the hammering of boots and shouting of orders, as the team hurried across the huge personnel car park at Putney Road Bridge, scrambling into their various vehicles.

'We've worked our backsides off over the last couple of days, putting this thing together,' he said. 'And now you haven't even made it to the bloody briefing!'

'You need to talk to Gemma,' she replied, sounding tired and miserable.

'I'm talking to *you* . . .'

'Just talk to her. Don't give me any more earache.'

'Listen, DC Honeyford . . .' Before Heck could say more, he was distracted by the on-off flashing headlights of a vehicle parked directly in his eyeline. It was Gemma's aquamarine Merc. Gemma herself, wearing a hi-vis coat over her plain clothes, was standing alongside it, leaning in to manipulate the lights. When she saw that she'd caught his attention, she pointed at the front passenger seat and climbed in on the driver's side. 'Erm, yeah . . .' Heck said into the phone, thrown by this, only to find that Gail had already cut the call.

He pocketed his mobile, signalled to Gary Quinnell that he wouldn't be too long and walked across to the Merc. Gemma watched him through the windshield.

He climbed in and closed the door. She said nothing for a second or two, gazing out as the two unmarked troop-carriers ferrying the uniforms departed the car park.

'Ma'am . . . if it's about that suit business last week, I'm sorry,' he said. 'I was a bit impertinent.'

'I don't give a toss about your suit, Heck. It was a cheap and nasty thing, anyway.'

'I paid three hundred quid for that.'

'You got ripped off. Not for the first time, I might add, when it comes to your sartorial sense.'

She still didn't look at him but watched as Gwen Straker left the car park in her black Audi Q7, Cyril Takuma riding alongside her. When they'd gone, she took something from her anorak pocket and unfolded it; it looked like three sheets of printout.

'I received this rather lengthy email last night,' she said. 'From Detective Superintendent Bellman, head of the anti-drugs team up on Humberside.'

'I see.' Heck had to batten down his frustration. Quinnell and Reed were still waiting for him by his Megane.

'I take it you know what it's about?' She sounded amazingly calm by her normal standards; in fact, now that he thought about it, she sounded weary.

Heck considered again Gail's view that Gemma was not only feeling the pressure of having to fight to keep her outfit together but was struggling to cope with the relatively new experience of being ordered around by an operational senior.

'Having read this, I'd say it was quite a serious abrogation of duty on your part,' she said. 'You're very lucky that Humberside are content to leave *me* to deal with it.'

'All respect, ma'am, but I don't think luck had much to do with it. That DI Warnock, whose operation I allegedly bolloxed, struck me as a bit of a pillock, if you don't mind me saying that about one of your fellow ladies. Not that she's much of one of those.'

'Are you *serious*?' she wondered. 'An issue like this, and your response is to be disrespectful?'

'There's no disrespect intended towards you . . .'

'Towards the senior ranks.'

'I wasn't disrespectful to her at the time. Gail Honeyford will back me up on that . . .'

'Gail Honeyford has been complained about in equally strong terms to you. And I'm not having that where a junior is concerned. So, from today, she is officially removed from Operation Sledgehammer.'

Heck looked round, startled. 'Removed . . .?'

'I've transferred her back to Staples Corner, where she's currently on non-operational duties. That way, she can learn the ropes without being exposed to any unduly malign influences.'

'Non-operational. You mean she's the office dogsbody?'

'It's no less than she deserves. And keeping you on Sledgehammer is a lot less than you deserve.' She finally raised her voice, banging the printout on the dashboard. 'For Christ's sake, Heck . . . at a time when we need all the friends we can get, this is an *absolute fuck-up*!'

Heck could always tell when Gemma was genuinely upset, because she used profanities, something she rarely did in normal conversation.

'Did it not even occur to you to enquire if this Cyrus Jackson was under observation?' she asked.

'Of course it did.'

'Of course?' She blinked in disbelief.

'I had to make a judgement call. Which case was more important . . . theirs or ours?'

'So, you took a deliberate chance that you might be ruining weeks, months even, of another unit's work?'

'That's about the sum of it, yeah.'

Gemma rocked back in her seat. She let out a sigh so heartfelt that it might have implied bewilderment at the meaning of existence rather than annoyance with an underling.

'What did I do that was so wrong?' he asked.

'Heck . . . there are *ways* of doing things.'

'Ma'am, the only reason this DI Warnock cut up nasty is because she wasn't on top of her brief. Not sufficiently to keep full tabs on Cyrus Jackson.'

'Do you actually believe that?'

'I'm sure it's part of it. Anyway, I ask again . . . which is more important, whoever's supplying Cyrus Jackson with souped-up grass, or this new thing we've got wind of, where unwilling participants are being forced to fight to the death? It's no surprise that Humberside Drug Squad don't see it that way. But I had no choice, did I?'

Gemma shook her head, tired again, almost glassy-eyed.

'I especially had no choice,' he added, 'given that, from what I've been hearing, no one else on Sledgehammer is making any ground at all.'

'That actually isn't true . . .'

'I don't mean Golden Boy, of course. I hear *he's* finally made something happen. The only question there is did he fill you in in private before it hit the airwaves?'

'What . . . *what did you just say?*'

Her expression was genuinely one of someone who thought they must have misheard. But Heck was suddenly too frustrated to hold back on it.

'Do you think I don't know what's going on here?' he said. 'You're infatuated with this guy, Reed. Just because he looks like a bloody action hero.'

Again, Gemma looked too stunned to respond.

So, he kept on going, all his pent-up disappointment finally pouring out.

'He's your new star player, isn't he? Your international centre-forward. But the fact is, Gemma . . . his looks and that ridiculous urbane charm of his are seriously getting the better of you. I don't know how last night went down, but he nabbed the Black Chapel on the basis of intel *I* provided. He might be better behaved than me, he might be more of a team player . . . but his overall results are way inferior . . .'

'What is this?' she interrupted. 'An argument in the school disco?'

'You want to know why I did what I did up on Humberside? Let me come one hundred per cent clean . . .'

'That'll be a first.'

'Like you, I want SCU to survive. But unlike you, that's not because I believe in its purpose with a righteous zealotry. In fact, you press me on it and I'd probably say the whole National Crime Group could probably be broken up and its operational duties repatriated to other forces and other squads. Wouldn't make any real difference in the long run. No, I believe in it because . . .' he faltered, working his lips together, 'because I *need* it.'

She arched a quizzical eyebrow.

'Personally,' he said. 'I need it . . . for *me*.'

He let those words dangle.

'Is that supposed to mean something?' she finally said. 'Have we just had a cinematic moment, Heck?'

'I don't want to work *away* from you.' He rubbed at the back of his neck, which was rigid with tension. 'There, I've said it. Look, Gemma . . . I know you and me will never be an item again. I've accepted that. Especially now that Golden Boy's turned up. But . . . as long as we're together . . . you know, working in the same office . . .' His words petered out, his cheeks flushed. Immediately, he regretted saying all that. But sometimes the truth had to come out, no matter how weak it made you feel.

Gemma sighed again, still in something like a state of bewilderment. She glanced from the window. Thirty yards away, Reed and Quinnell were still loitering. A third party had joined them, having been escorted from the police station by a divisional uniform; it was a nervous-looking Tim Cleghorn. Gemma ran a hand through her famously unruly blonde hair. When she spoke again, it was quiet, remarkably lacking in energy.

'Maybe we should save this conversation for another time, eh?'

'So, I get no opportunity to explain myself?' Heck said. 'You know as well as I do that these mythical other times never actually arrive.'

'You really pick your moments, Mark.'

'Did I do a job for you, or not? Did I not use nous and know-how to bring you info that may lead us to a massive kill . . . a kill which, if we pull it off, might secure the future of SCU for years to come?'

She looked around at him again but didn't even try to refute this.

'Exactly, Gemma . . . I'm fighting as hard as I can to save this unit. My reasons may be different from yours, but you *will* benefit . . . you're benefiting already. So, at the very least, I should be given a hearing.'

Helpless to do otherwise, she shrugged, inviting him to say more.

'I've made a lot of mistakes in my life,' he admitted. 'I'll

251

not lie. But the biggest one by a country mile was driving you away when we were kids.'

In actual fact, they hadn't been kids when they'd set up home together back in the early 2000s. They'd been young detectives in their twenties, but it seemed so long ago that it was difficult to envisage those younger versions of themselves any other way.

'You don't think that would have happened anyway?' she wondered. 'Us separating?'

Heck couldn't deny it, much as he'd have loved to.

'Mark . . . we just weren't right for each other. After that first flush of excitement was over, we soon learned that we were completely different creatures.'

'Are you saying you never felt anything for me at all?'

'No, I'm not.' She glanced surreptitiously at the dashboard clock. It was a touch indelicate, though he could hardly blame her. They were very short on time here. 'When I first met you, you bowled me over. You jeer at Jack, but you were a good-looking lad yourself. You had physicality too . . . good Lord, you still do. But I didn't realise then that you chased the game with a fury because you were on the run from a past that you couldn't bear thinking about. Instead, I just got vexed with you all the time. I mean, it didn't take long for me to start being cruel to you, did it? And despite what you may think, I'm not a cruel person.'

'You weren't cruel.'

'I actually *was*. Your childlike energy for the job started getting on my nerves, because I preferred the slower, more analytical approach. The chances you took and the corners you cut . . . they worried and upset me because I thought that if you were brought down, I'd be brought down too. No matter how hard I tried, I couldn't persuade you to be a normal copper. I couldn't convince you that this job isn't an adventure . . . that it's a serious business.'

'If I was such a bad bet, why have you tolerated me working with you for so long?'

She waved that away. 'Work's different. There's no emotional attachment. If I have to drop you in the shit, trust me, I will.'

'Even though you *never* have done . . . and I've given you plenty cause?'

'OK . . . I like the results you bring in.' She paused to think. 'And for what it's worth, Jack Reed is *not* our star striker. Not yet. That position's still occupied. But don't take that as a compliment, please. It's merely a statement of fact.'

He tried to feign indifference to that. 'Gemma . . . I'm not content to just be *near* you all day. But it's better than being somewhere else. Which is what would happen if SCU folds and we all go our separate ways. I didn't realise that was my thinking when all this started, but I do now. *That's* why I busted a gut, and a drugs operation on Humberside, to make today's raid possible. That's why I'll keep on doing it.'

She watched him steadily, again dumbfounded that Mark Heckenburg, the loosest cannon she'd ever known in the job, was still the only police officer who could leave her speechless – usually with indignation and amazement at the sheer gall of him, though so often this was tempered by her underlying awareness that his high-risk strategies were nearly always designed to bring home the bacon for her and her team.

'So . . .' he said, 'getting back to the business at hand, if you want to bollock me, you'd better get on with it. Because we haven't got all day. There's a case to solve.'

Still, she made no reply.

He shrugged and opened the passenger door.

'For your information, Gail Honeyford will not be the office dogsbody,' Gemma said. 'She's working with Eric. He's training her up on HOLMES 2 and sitting with her on any additional case notes that come in while the rest of us are otherwise engaged.'

Heck considered this. Inside, he still felt that Gail would learn more about real policework from him, but he understood that the top brass would never get this. Plus, while Gail was still new to SCU, it would probably be safer for her to find her feet indoors.

'So, I'll have your apology for that before you get out of this car.'

'I apologise,' he said in as genuine a voice as he could muster.

'And where my relationship with Jack Reed is concerned, I have two things to say. Firstly, it's got nothing to do with you. Secondly, it's got nothing to do with you. Whoever we once were, Mark, whoever we are now, whatever our relationship is, however much you *need* to work in close proximity to me, however affected by that I am, or not, as the case may be . . . my situation with Jack Reed has *nothing* to do with you. Do you understand?'

He nodded glumly.

'Get het up about it, if you wish . . . but the only person you're hurting with that is yourself. Like I say, you may be our star performer, but at times you let yourself down with very, very, very unprofessional behaviour.'

Heck said nothing.

'Now grow up,' she said, 'and get out of my car. Let's make today another win.'

Heck crossed the car park, aware that his three passengers were watching him with interest, only briefly distracted by the sight and sound of Gemma blistering away at reckless speed. He climbed into the driver's seat. Quinnell got in alongside him, Reed and Cleghorn into the rear.

'Everyone got everything they need?' Heck asked.

'Everything except a machine gun?' Cleghorn said worriedly.

Heck put the car in gear and drove them out.

He was still vaguely numb, and couldn't decide whether he'd unmanned himself or not, baring his soul to Gemma like that. But it was better that the cat was out of the bag; it was true what Gwen Straker had said – this strained, repressed relationship between them had gone on too long and really needing fixing, one way or the other. Professionally, of course, he doubted that such raw, painful honesty – a definite rarity for him – would lead the aptly named Lioness to appreciate his efforts any more than she already did (even if she wasn't her normal unforgiving self at present), but if she didn't, it was hard bleeding luck.

They were where they were, and it was game on.

He glanced through the rear-view mirror at their informant, who wore the haggard look of a man unable to believe the predicament he'd let himself in for. Gwen Straker had certainly played hardball with him and his legal reps, advising them that simply informing the police where this snuff cinema could be found was nothing like enough assistance to make life easier for him regarding all the other charges he faced, let alone to dismiss him from any potential murder enquiries. Cleghorn hadn't liked it, but in the end had accepted the reality that the cops could not back down on this as they *needed* much more from him. They could always have raided the place without him, using a warrant and brute force, but pen drives were nothing if not quickly and easily disposable. By the time they'd battered the doors down, there might not be a shred of evidence left. So, it was imperative that they had someone on the inside to secure it.

In due course, after several futile attempts to argue otherwise, Cleghorn and his solicitor had accepted that what he was doing today was likely to be his only way out.

'Sounds like you got a result last night, sir,' Quinnell said, as they hit the traffic.

Heck glanced into his rear-view mirror, where Reed was busy adjusting his stab vest.

'We mainly got lucky,' the DI said.

'Lucky . . . how?' Heck asked.

Reed gave it some thought. 'Hallahan was last seen in High Wycombe, which is not his home patch, but his estranged daughter lives there. He'd been seen a couple of times in the district, trying to buy heroin. One sighting in the area wouldn't have been worth much, but two sightings two weeks apart suggested he was stopping somewhere close by. In both cases, witnesses said he was long-haired, bearded and dirty. This suggested he was sleeping rough. Possibly in a homeless camp or something, but I didn't think it was that – there's a reward out on him, and his face has been plastered all over the newspapers. You couldn't crash with a bunch of vagrants and expect none of them to grass on you. So, I reasoned he had to be with someone he trusted.'

Heck was even more disgruntled. Reed's deductions had been good so far; it didn't sound as if he'd been lucky at all.

'And his ex-daughter was the best bet?' Quinnell asked.

'Even an estranged daughter would likely let you sleep under her roof,' Reed replied. 'But she might not go out and buy you smack. So, when his dependency got too much for him, he had to do that himself. At least, that was my theory. We got a warrant and searched the daughter's house. She was compliant, even helpful – but even though there was no sign of him there, I felt there was something a bit fishy about it. Eventually, we had to leave . . . but this feeling wouldn't go away. I mean, the beard and long hair told us that, wherever he was, he wasn't going out much . . . to a barber's or whatever. But dirty? If he was stopping in a house, he could at least use the bathroom, the shower. So that's why, at the last second . . . before we left the premises, we pulled the floorboards up.'

Quinnell hooted with laughter. 'And that's where he was?'

'Living under her feet, would you believe. With her permission, of course. There was already a crawl space, but they'd actually widened it – made it habitable. If you could call it that.'

'He'd been down there four whole years?' Quinnell asked, incredulous. 'I mean . . . that's how long he'd been missing, isn't it?'

'Sure had,' Reed said. 'But I think he'd had enough. He came without a fight. Not that I think he'd have been up for that even if he'd wanted one. He was badly strung out and thin as a rake. He'd barely been eating. So, though it's a certainty he'll get life for those two murders, I doubt he'll be around very long.'

Heck drove on. They were almost at the lying-up point now, which was located in the rear car park of a to-let workshop located two streets from Deercot Road.

'Well, I'm not gonna say "poor bastard",' Quinnell declared. 'Even *my* Christianity has its limits.'

'You'd better remember that when we get into this place,' Tim Cleghorn piped up. 'Soon as they find out you're a cozzer, them two bouncers'll come for us . . . even if it's just to buy their bosses enough time to get away.'

'We'll have all the exits covered, Tim,' Heck replied. 'They won't get away.'

'If either of them does, my life won't be worth living,' Cleghorn whined. 'In fact, my life could be on the line anyway. Soon as they find out who this fella is,' he indicated Quinnell, 'they'll go for *me*.'

'Don't worry,' Heck said. 'DC Quinnell has only two jobs for the first minute he's in there . . . secure the evidence and protect you. The second minute, the rest of us'll be in . . . so then it won't matter.'

Cleghorn was still pale with fear. He didn't look even remotely reassured by what he'd just been told. Which was probably a fair-enough reaction, Heck thought; because they knew so little about this firm that he had no clue what level of resistance they were about to face.

Though neither, at present, did he care.

Chapter 25

Detective Constable Gary Quinnell was a conundrum to those who knew him. Six feet and three inches tall, as brawny as a bear, with thinning red hair, battered but likeable features and a gregarious personality, which, combined with a deep voice and melodious accent, made him an attractive figure straight away. He was also known as a religious guy; when he and his wife had made the move from South Wales to London, nine years ago, so that he could join the National Crime Group, he'd only done so on the condition that there'd be a Nonconformist chapel they could attend.

For all that, he was no stranger to the rough stuff. Even though he was not officially in the Metropolitan Police, Quinnell played number eight for their Rugby Union team, and if it ever got tasty he'd always be found in the thick of it. By the same token, as an operational police officer, he had a famously no-nonsense approach to law enforcement. Quinnell was only in his mid-thirties, but in some ways quite old-school. He was a rare creature these days: a vocational copper rather than a careerist. He loved being a detective, and he was quite happy to remain a detective constable, because that brought him into close contact with those hoodlums who, as far as he was concerned, made innocent people's lives such a misery. It enabled him to right wrongs personally, which he also expected to be doing on that evening of August 23, when, wearing ripped jeans, trainers, a T-shirt and a beaten-up leather jacket, he tramped alongside Tim Cleghorn down a shadow-filled entry off Deercot Road.

As Heck had said, there'd almost certainly be a body search on entry, so he hadn't been able to take either a radio or any concealed weapon. In fact, his only contact with the outside world was a miniaturised transmitter taped so high on the inside of his upper right thigh that it was snug against his scrotum.

A door appeared on their left. It was wood rather than steel – less easily defensible perhaps, but less likely to attract casual attention. There was no handle, of course; this door did not open from the outside.

Cleghorn's forehead was speckled with sweat. Nervously, he licked his lips.

'Taking me in, bruv, or what?' Quinnell asked, affecting a nonchalant stance – highly likely they were already being watched and listened to.

Cleghorn nodded, lifted a fist and gave a coded rap on the wood; three knocks, two knocks, three more, and then one. Half a second later, an invisible intercom crackled to life.

'What can we do for you?' came a cultured female voice.

'Erm . . . oh, hi.' Cleghorn filched his membership ID from the front pocket of his jeans. It was nothing more than an oblong piece of card, neatly printed with his membership number, A956B3, and his photo alongside that, the whole thing then laminated. As an indication of how long Cleghorn had been a member, the plastic coating was slightly opaque and crumpled at the corners. He held it up anyway, so that wherever the hidden camera was located, its operator would have a clear view.

'Who's that with you?' the voice asked.

'Oh, erm . . . a new friend.'

Silence greeted this. The seconds ticked by.

'He's a workmate,' Cleghorn added nervously.

Quinnell held his breath. From Cleghorn's body language alone, the proprietors would have to be stupid not to figure there was something wrong here. Rather to his surprise, though, an electric hum followed and a lock on the other side of the door disengaged.

Mopping the sweat from his brow, Cleghorn pushed forward, Quinnell following. A dim, narrow stairway led downward, so narrow in fact that they could only descend it in single file, Cleghorn leading. At the bottom, a lone bulb burned over the top of another faceless door. This one *was* made from steel; again, it had no handle. They were still two or three steps up from it when a male figure stepped from a hidden alcove on the right.

Quinnell immediately clocked him as Alfie Adamson, the one-time unlicensed boxer.

Adamson was still a professional enforcer, as his shaven head and brutish Neanderthal features clearly attested. He wasn't a tall man, probably no more than five-eleven, but he packed immense breadth into his smart black dinner jacket and white shirt. The fact that he also wore a dicky bow implied that once he was done here, he'd perhaps go on to work the doors of some other, more legit establishment.

'You're rather late, A956B3,' Adamson said, his limpid grey eyes twinkling under his heavy, shelf-like brow. 'Another five mins and we'd be locking the outer doors.'

Cleghorn shrugged apologetically. 'Had to wait for Donny, here. He's come all the way from Wales.'

Adamson appraised Quinnell with humour-filled curiosity,

which seemed so out of place that it was more than a little unnerving. 'Thought you said he was a workmate.'

'Oh, erm . . . yeah, well, I'm a driver. I deliver to a depot in, erm . . . in . . .'

'In Gabalfa,' Quinnell added, picking at random a district in Cardiff, hoping to create the impression that Cleghorn wasn't confused about which city he regularly drove to, but which part of it.

'That's right, Gabalfa,' Cleghorn said,

Adamson glanced from one to the other, before indicating that both should raise their arms.

'Cursory pat-down,' he said. 'We can't have people bringing cameras in here, or any other recording devices, can we?'

They complied, and Quinnell was frisked first.

This had always been a risky moment, given the location of his wire, but they'd banked on the search not being anything like as professional or thorough as it would be were a police officer carrying it out, and they were correct.

Adamson checked Quinnell's pockets first, extricating his mobile and his wallet, and switching the former off before laying them both on a table inside the alcove, where sundry other such goods had already been deposited. He advised Quinnell that he'd get his property back at the end of the evening, while patting him down around the body, the arms, the hips, and the upper and lower legs. He didn't go anywhere near the crotch.

The doorman stood back. 'You can't actually come in here, Taffy,' he said, 'unless you're a full member. We don't have guests. That means you've got to join.'

Quinnell shrugged. 'That's what I was told. Fine.'

Adamson's smile broadened into a dead-eyed grin. 'So . . . that's five grand.'

Quinnell feigned astonishment, which was hardly difficult. When Cleghorn had first quoted the costs of membership here, they hadn't known which to be more astounded by – the fact that Cleghorn himself could afford such sums, or the fact that anyone at all would agree to pay them. The former was explained by an inheritance several years ago, which, by the sounds of it, Cleghorn had spent on absolutely nothing else; the latter, rather more chillingly, by the overwhelming desire of certain members of the public to watch real blood being violently shed.

'Is that on top of the hundred-quid entry fee?' Quinnell asked, sounding flabbergasted.

'That's correct,' Adamson said. 'But a hundred quid every time you come here isn't very much, considering what you're getting, is it? That extra five grand's a one-off payment. Once you've been issued with your membership card, you'll never have to fork out that much again.'

'Better be bloody worth it,' Quinnell grumbled.

'Oh, it's worth it. We offer a form of entertainment here that you won't get anywhere else.'

Quinnell extended his hand for his wallet, which was duly given back to him.

'Course, if you can't afford it,' Adamson said, 'you're in the wrong place, anyway. We only cater to discerning clients.'

'I can afford it, don't you worry, boyo.' Quinnell took out a bunch of twenties and fifties, selected the requisite amount, and handed it over.

Adamson made a quick count. 'I'll take the wallet back, but you can keep what money you've got left . . . you'll need it if you want refreshments.'

Quinnell twisted the remaining notes into a roll and thrust it into his back pocket. The wallet went back on the table in the alcove.

'Excellent,' the doorman said. 'That's the necessaries taken care of. It's all easy from here, but first we'll fix you up with a card.'

Right on cue, the steel door slid open. Beyond it there was another corridor, this one painted bright red and lit by lurid red lights. As they walked down it, they passed framed photographs depicting the most extreme pornographic images that even Quinnell, as a long-serving copper, had ever seen. Every kink imaginable was on show.

At the end, they approached a pair of wooden swing-doors – the sort you saw in more regular cinemas – though before they reached them, there was an open door on the left. Beyond this sat a small office packed with high-tech equipment, including several different computer screens. A woman was in there, perched on a high stool.

Margot Frith was approaching fifty now, but every bit as glamorous as in her porno heyday. Slim but shapely, with golden-brown skin and lustrous, chestnut curls. She wore a sleeveless red evening dress, cinched at the waist, slashed at the thigh and possessed of a plunging neckline, which revealed a tantalising amount of cleavage.

She beckoned Quinnell in with a long, crimson-lacquered fingernail and bade him stand on an X painted on the concrete floor, where she surprised him with a camera flash.

'Your membership card is not replaceable for free,' she said brusquely – it was the same voice from the intercom. 'You won't get in here without it, no matter how much of a regular you become, so if you lose it, or deface it, you'll have to pay the full price for another.'

She took a rectangular cardboard slip from the desktop. A membership number had already been printed on it. She then turned to collect a passport-photo-sized image from a dispenser unit underneath the camera, tore a piece off the back of the image and smoothed it onto the card with her thumb, before running it through a lamination device.

'OK . . .' She handed the finished card over, for the first

time smiling, showing an expensive array of gleaming white dentistry. 'You're good to go.'

Quinnell went back into the corridor, where Cleghorn, who had now paid his own fee – yet more Operation Sledgehammer cash – and handed over his wallet and phone, was nervously waiting. Adamson stood watching as they strode the remaining distance to the swing-doors.

'How long's it gonna take your mates to get in here?' Cleghorn whispered.

'Shut up,' Quinnell said from the side of his mouth.

'That fucking steel door behind us has just been locked . . .'

'Shut up, I said. They know what they're doing.'

Beyond the swing-doors, they entered the cinema proper.

Reminiscent of a basement sex-club cinema in the days before the internet, it wasn't a particularly big room, about sixty feet by sixty, lit by 40-watt bulbs and boasting damp, bare-brick walls. There was no fixed seating. Instead, several rows of what looked like school chairs had been lined up and, as Alfie Adamson had said, most of the club's clientele were now gathered in them. They were exclusively men, mainly aged from forty up, and for the most part they looked well-dressed, almost refined – this was no doubt due to the prices here. But what was especially interesting to Quinnell was that there were at least a hundred guys here, probably more, and yet there was almost no conversation between them. Perhaps, deep down, they were too embarrassed about what they were doing here to want to get to know any of their fellow snuff addicts.

At the far end of the room, facing the audience, two additional chairs stood on top of a table, and on top of those was balanced a widescreen TV, at least seventy-eight inches across. Bundles of cables led away from this around the left edge of the seating, every few feet fastened to the carpet with strips of black duct tape. They eventually connected with a recess in the left wall, where the hunky, suntanned shape of Lance Frith sat on a stool and fiddled with a laptop resting on a table in front of him. Alongside this there was an array of different coloured pen drives.

The porn-star-turned-MC was almost as well turned-out as his wife, wearing pressed beige trousers, a crisp white shirt and yellow silk tie held by a gold tiepin, though all of it was covered by a black, semi-transparent plastic raincoat – as if the twosome would be going on to somewhere more salubrious later and Lance didn't want to carry any smudges from this odious dungeon with him.

Close by, leaning casually against the wall, was the tall shape of the other security man, Wade McDougall.

He was about six-foot-five, his big, spare frame with its long, rangy arms and legs fitted into a neat black suit, though he wore only a black T-shirt beneath that, and despite the dim lighting, a pair of opaque, wraparound shades. Previous mugshots had shown him as a redhead, clean-shaven and wearing a crew cut, but now he sported a thick hipster beard and moustache, which he appeared to have dyed black, while his hair, also newly black, was long and styled in a man-bun. None of these fashionable touches detracted from his face, which was long, lean and curiously pale and had been cut several times in the past; tramlines of old razor slashes ran down from his left eyebrow, connecting with both the left side of his nose and the left side of his mouth, as though whoever had done it had really tried to open him up.

Quinnell remembered Heck saying that McDougall started out as a Millwall football hooligan before graduating into organised crime – no doubt the Bushwhackers hadn't had it all their own way on Saturday afternoons.

The newcomers found two spare seats on the second-from-the-front row, both located on the right side, with Quinnell sitting next to the aisle, as he'd be the one who'd soon need to get up. No sooner had they settled than a voice sounded.

'OK, gents . . . you know the rules.'

Lance Frith perambulated into view. His accent was almost neutral but carried a vague hint of the North Midlands.

'You've all been searched on the way in,' he said, stopping in front of the television. 'But it's the usual thing . . . if any of you have managed to smuggle any kind of recording device into here, there will be an awful lot of trouble. Sorry to say it in such bald terms, gents – but that's the way it is. We can't afford any of these movies to end up on the internet. I'm sure you understand why. But aside from that, you're all paid up, you're all now present and correct, the outside doors are locked, and we're ready to go.' He rubbed his hands together. 'We've got approximately three hours of films for you tonight. I think you're going to enjoy all of them. We'll take our first refreshment break in approx. one hour's time. As always, beer and wine will be served at the usual West End prices.'

He grinned – like his wife, showing a row of no doubt very expensive pearlers.

On cue, the swing-doors at the back banged as Alfie Adamson came through carrying several crates of beer.

In front, meanwhile, Lance Frith switched the television on and sauntered back across the cinema to its left corner, where he hit the lights.

Without fanfare, the show began.

Chapter 26

That evening's entertainment was every bit as horrendous as Gary Quinnell had anticipated. Gone were the days, it seemed, when cellar cinemas like this restricted themselves to showing straightforward sex between willing adults.

Mercifully there was no soundtrack on the first film, but the visuals were bad enough. In it, two young people, a male and a female, both Orientals, fought and kicked furiously as they were hanged upside down, naked, in a derelict room, and whipped by their masked captors for minutes on end with bamboo rods, an exercise which was less like a gentle BDSM paddling and more like a Roman scourging. Gradually, as the blood and flesh flew, Quinnell felt his gorge rise and had to fight hard to keep his eyes on the screen – it would not do for him to be seen avoiding looking. Especially when he glanced sideways and saw the rest of the row of viewers, Tim Cleghorn included, rapt.

When the film ended, with the two mangled bodies left hanging there, he already felt that he'd seen enough to call in the heavy mob, but there were one or two lingering doubts. When the original movie, *Snuff*, had first appeared in 1976, it had purported to show a real murder, but in fact it had been a hoax. It was not impossible, Quinnell told himself, that he was seeing something similar here.

What followed, however, undoubtedly *was* real.

It was a compilation of video footage, almost certainly taken by police officers for the purpose of crime scene analysis. How it had ended up in the hands of private collectors was anyone's guess, but Quinnell had the dismaying notion that, most likely, these snippets had been sold on by coppers. He was more familiar with this kind of material, of course, but never when it was being offered up as a form of entertainment.

In the first movie, the camera tracked along a disordered passage in what looked like a small apartment. Everything of any value there seemed to have been smashed and scattered. The camera then veered left into a bedroom, where the bed had been turned upside down and the mattress tossed against a wall, both of them now arced with drying bloodstains. The camera panned slowly around, finally locating an adult female spread-eagled on the carpet. She wore only a short nightie, which was soaked red and plastered to her body thanks to what looked like multiple stab wounds. Her face had been covered by a pillowcase, this too drenched through with blood. When the camera panned further around, it found a man in a pair of pyjama trousers huddled, foetus-like, against the far wall. His head had all but disintegrated, as if from a shotgun blast, his blood and brains splurged in a fountain up and across the wallpaper.

The film lasted eight minutes, the crime scene tech catching the grotesque parodies of humanity from every conceivable angle in order to snag all the forensic data he could.

More films followed in the same vein, all ghastly beyond belief and yet none, to Quinnell's mind at least, qualifying as snuff – not to any certain degree.

As the eighth or ninth of these murder-scene movies rolled,

he risked another glance left. Tim Cleghorn sat as rigid as before. He might have been nervous to be here – scared out of his wits even – but he was still goggle-eyed, his mouth agape. Further along the row, other men had loosened collars or were mopping sweat from their foreheads with grubby handkerchiefs. A couple of hands had stolen to crotches and were kneading the increasingly obvious bulges there.

You're a stranger in this kingdom of shadows, boy, Quinnell told himself. *But don't you worry . . . it'll all be over soon. Please, Lord . . . bloody soon.*

As the last police video came to a halt, freeze-framed on the rictus face of an elderly woman who'd been strangled in her own bed with a hoover flex, Lance Frith called down from the back of the room again.

'OK . . . fight club time, gents.'

There were mumbled cheers; this decadent crowd might have been too shamefaced to look each other in the eye when they'd first got here, but they were relaxing now.

'Yeah . . . we know these have been popular of late,' Frith said. 'We've been getting more and more of them recently, and we've got more to come. But this first one tonight should blow your fucking socks off.'

When the black-and-white footage commenced playing, it was near enough identical to the one depicting the last fight of Eddie Creeley. However, on this occasion, the guy in the underpants put up more resistance, engaging his would-be slayers with something like a heavy, two-handed mallet. He even managed to put one of them down, though the huge advantage his assailant enjoyed – being armoured – was more than enough to save his life. And soon, predictably, as Underpants was subjected to cuts and slashes and bone-crunching blows, he weakened, staggering and stumbling between his heavy-clad opponents.

It was around this stage, when Quinnell got a proper look

at the victim's face. Despite everything, he almost shouted out loud.

It was another of their missing fugitives, if he wasn't mistaken, Ronald Ricketson, who was wanted by North Wales Police in connection with the murder of his girlfriend and her two baby daughters.

Quinnell's hands, currently resting on his legs, hooked into claws, knotting themselves into the flesh and bone of his kneecaps.

The moment had arrived. This was literally *it*.

He took a couple of deep breaths, before drawing down the zip at his crotch. He didn't feel conspicuous doing this, as it was now going on all over the so-called cinema. Shoving his hand inside, he felt around his scrotum, finally locating the strip of tape and the micro-sized transmitter. He ripped it out, just managing to avoid yelping in pain.

On screen, Ricketson weltered in his own gore as a succession of blows from a baseball bat in one hand and a spring-loaded cosh in another felled him first to his knees and then to the metal floor. Quinnell ignored it further, getting to his feet, stepping away from his chair and walking to the front of the room, crossing past the television. As the film had abruptly ended, plunging them all into a brief Stygian gloom, no one initially objected.

Quinnell strode to the light switches in the corner, flicked them all on and turned to face the audience. Rows of blank white faces regarded him. Lance Frith was one of them, leaning out of his recess in puzzlement.

Less puzzled and more aggressive was Wade McDougall, who, though he hadn't yet removed his shades, was already lumbering warily down the side aisle. Adamson did the same from the opposite corner.

'All right, gents,' Quinnell announced loudly, holding the transmitter close to his mouth to ensure there was no mistake,

'I must inform you that I am a police officer, and that you are all under arrest for aiding and abetting the disclosure of indecent and distressing images. That's just to start with, by the way. Oh yeah, and you don't have to say anything . . .'

Before he'd completed the caution, the room exploded.

Chairs flew as shocked and terrified men leapt to their feet. Cleghorn was among them, but he ran to the front of the cinema and scampered across it so that he could cower behind Quinnell's back, which reminded the big cop that one of his key jobs here was to protect their informant.

This would be a problem, because he also had to seize the evidence. But it might not be a problem for long, because, unless his ears deceived him, he could already hear the cavalry hammering at the outer doors on the upper floor. Even so, he craned his neck to look over the scene of chaos and spied the Friths – Margot had appeared alongside her husband – sliding the laptop into a satchel and cramming handfuls of pen drives in after it.

They were only thirty yards away, but it wouldn't be as simple as blundering over there; already, the cinema's security staff were closing in.

Even as the shouting clientele hurried back and forth, tripping over each other and their fallen chairs, Adamson and McDougall advanced from left and right respectively. The latter was less certain about this – he slowed to a near halt, as if unsure what the best course now was. But Adamson was brutal as he knocked men out of his way.

He was the one Quinnell turned to first, but not quickly enough to prevent the doorman's two hands clamping the lapels of his jacket.

What surprised the big Welshman from this point was that no head flew in, there was no gouging, no biting. The doorman merely drove him backward against the wall – squashing the fearful Cleghorn in the process – and tried to pin him there, his shaven head pink and gleaming with sweat, his brutish face set in a rigid mask.

Doesn't want to assault you, boy. He's not so stupid . . . just wants his bosses to get away.

Quinnell retaliated, grabbing the left side of Adamson's bull neck, sinking his fingers into the taut muscle. He slammed his right forearm into the hoodlum's jaw, and when that didn't work, into the right side of his throat.

Adamson rode it out, teeth clenched, saliva frothing through them.

They cavorted round as though dancing, banging Cleghorn against the wall again, eliciting a massive squawk from him, and then tottering the other way, crashing into the television, which fell from its chair and struck the floor with a flash of sparks. Still in Adamson's clutches, Quinnell had to spin them both to look across the room again. It was a bedlam of staggering, panicking men, though most were now cramming through the swing-doors, possibly not realising that the steel doors beyond those would still be locked.

A thunderous *BANG!* then sounded from that direction, along with a tremor-inducing *SCRUNCH* of twisting, warping metal.

They wouldn't be locked any more. Quinnell knew a hydraulic ram when he heard it.

Immediately, the frightened mob began flooding back into the cinema, armoured and helmeted cops pouring after them, carrying batons and shortened riot shields.

'You fucking Taffy bastard!' Adamson snarled.

'You fucking *Saesneg*!' Quinnell retorted, driving two massive body shots under the hoodlum's extended arms.

Ribs cracked with each impact. As Adamson staggered backward, Quinnell caught him under the jaw with a bone-slammer; the besuited figure all but launched from his feet. The cop spun around, again to scan the room. Arrests were

273

being made everywhere. Inspector Takuma stood in the middle with visor raised, looking on in satisfaction as the punters were manhandled to the floor and bound with plasticuffs. The only real problem was that Lance and Margot Frith were now nowhere to be seen.

Quinnell swore, focusing on the recess. Could it be that the fire door stood at the back of it? He glanced at Cleghorn, now cowering behind the wrecked TV.

'Stay over here, all right?'

Cleghorn's eyes widened in alarm. '*Look out!*'

Quinnell twirled, but it was too late.

The chair that had been swung up and over the top of Wade McDougall's head crashed down on him with jackhammer force.

Chapter 27

Lance and Margot Frith were already halfway up the back stairs. It was a simple fire exit and, in truth, Lance, who was at the front, had never fully expected that, in the event of a raid, the police wouldn't have this portal covered too – but on the off-chance they hadn't done their homework properly, he'd always kept his innocuous-looking but souped-up Passat W8 in the small rear yard it gave access to.

Inevitably, though, as they climbed the stairs, the door at the top erupted inward and police officers piled through. Most were uniformed and armoured, but the one at the front was in plain clothes; he wore jeans and a sweatshirt with its sleeves rolled back and a black bulletproof vest. He descended quickly, discarding the Halligan bar with which he'd busted the entrance. He was tallish, just over six feet, with a lean but strong build. He had a mop of black hair, rugged features and a plaster on his left eyebrow, and as he descended the final few stairs to their level, the most intense, steel-blue gaze that Lance Frith had ever seen. He also wore what might be described as a shit-eating grin.

''Ello, 'ello,' Heck said. 'Correct me if I'm wrong, but aren't you supposed to be under arrest?'

Before Frith could respond, Heck grabbed him by the tie knot and slammed him face-first into the opposite wall, goose-necking his left wrist behind his back. For all that the ex-porn star was a mass of bronzed, gym-toned muscle, he went as easily as polystyrene.

'Lay one undue finger on me, copper, and my lawyers'll have you,' he warned.

'It's you who's going to be had,' Heck hissed into his ear. 'Every time you go for a shower.'

He pushed him into the custody of the uniforms behind and continued down.

On seeing her husband apprehended, the beautiful Margot had retreated back down towards the internal door, only to find that also filled with police officers, watching her. The next thing she knew, Heck had grabbed the satchel she was carrying. At first, she resisted, clutching it to her body.

'Don't give me an excuse to break those lovely fingernails,' he said. 'You're another one, Miss Whiplash . . . you're gonna need a set of claws where you're going.'

She released the bag, and he passed it to the officers behind, before taking the woman's elbow and steering her into their custody too.

With the main targets wrapped up, Heck hurried on down the stairs, entering the cinema proper. The place was a mess of kicked-over chairs and struggling bodies, most now in cuffs as the uniforms hustled them out via a set of swing-doors at the other side of the room. Jack Reed was there too; standing by the doors, supervising.

Then Heck's eyes fell on Gary Quinnell.

The big guy was lying prone, Inspector Takuma and a female sergeant kneeling alongside him. A few yards away, Tim Cleghorn hovered nervously.

Heck scrambled over and dropped to one knee.

Quinnell had taken a tremendous smack to the head, just

above his hairline in fact, leaving blood all down his face. The sergeant had produced a first-aid kit and was applying a compress. When she removed it briefly, Heck saw that the casualty's scalp was not just lacerated, but swollen like a cricket ball.

'My own fault,' Quinnell mumbled.

'No arguments there,' Heck said. 'You've been asking for this for years.'

'Bloody chair . . .' Quinnell groaned in pain, though at least he seemed fully compos.

'I think he's OK, but he needs to go to A&E,' the sergeant said. 'At the very least, he's going to have severe concussion.'

Heck nodded. 'I'll sort it.'

'I've already called an ambulance,' Inspector Takuma said.

'Bollocks to that,' Quinnell grunted, struggling to his feet. 'If you don't mind me saying, sir . . . I'm not a cripple yet.'

He then turned dizzy, and Heck had to pull up a chair for him, which he plonked himself down onto. Takuma arched an eyebrow.

'We'll wait for the ambulance,' Heck agreed.

'Hold that there,' the sergeant said, placing Quinnell's own hand on top of the dressing.

Satisfied, Takuma turned away.

'Oh, sir . . .' Heck said, 'are you heading up to Finchley Road?'

'That's where all the prisoners are bound, I understand,' Takuma said. 'And where the debriefing will be held . . . so, yes.'

'Excellent.' Heck beckoned Cleghorn forward. 'Can our CI ride with you?'

Takuma eyed Cleghorn with visible distaste.

'If we're off to hospital . . .' Heck said.

Takuma sighed. 'I suppose if he must.'

The uniforms walked away, and Heck signalled Cleghorn

to follow them, which he did on hurried, nervous feet. Heck swung back to Quinnell. They were now alone.

'OK . . . who was it?'

The Welshman shook his head. 'Barely saw him . . . but, pretty sure it was McDougall.'

That came as no surprise to Heck. It was also what he'd wanted to hear. 'Did anyone else see him?'

'Cleghorn, probably . . .'

Heck nodded. 'That works. Any uniforms?'

'Two uniforms locked him up . . . but that was when he was trying to fight his way out. Don't think they saw his attack on me.'

'That works too . . . because if Cleghorn is all we've got, it's difficult. He's not going to volunteer another witness statement unless I lean on him again. And it may be that I forget to lean on him.'

Quinnell frowned through his blood. 'What're you talking about?'

Heck lowered his voice. 'Wade McDougall's only out on parole. So, he's going back to the clink whatever happens. But it's a matter of how long for. You know what he went down for last time?'

'Didn't you say he beat up . . .'

'He attempted to murder a police officer, Gaz.'

'You mean . . . like he's just done now?' A slow look of understanding came over the Welshman's pain-twisted features. 'Which means this time he'll likely get life?'

'What do you think? He got fifteen last time and served ten. That was lenient . . . but they won't be lenient a second time.'

'Unless we find a reason not to charge him with attempting to . . .'

'. . . murder a police officer. Correct.' Heck gave him a hand to help him to his feet. 'Will you mind?'

Quinnell rose weakly to full height. Fleetingly he looked dazed and had to lean on Heck. 'I don't mind,' he said. 'I don't mind anything as long as you get me to a head-doctor. Gimme a pair of binoculars and I don't think I could see straight.'

'That's where we're going now.'

It was slow progress as Heck assisted the casualty across the still-crowded basement.

'Just make sure you get something good out of him,' Quinnell said. 'Don't want a cracked noggin for nothing.'

'Don't worry, pal. You know the rules. You don't wallop one of our lot and walk off. One way or the other, that bastard's having it.'

'Ah, Sergeant Heckenburg,' Anderson Burke said in an unsurprised voice. 'Some things never change, I see.'

Burke was a tall, spare man, with short white hair and steel-rimmed glasses, and he'd been the McDougall family solicitor for at least as long as Heck had known the nefarious clan. The twosome had dealt with each other many times back in Rotherhithe, a period of Heck's career when he'd been Wade McDougall's arresting officer more often than he could these days remember.

This latest encounter came in the Custody Suite at Finchley Road, where, despite the bustling crowd of captives and captors, Heck had ensured that he was the first person the solicitor laid eyes on when he arrived.

'They certainly don't,' Heck agreed. 'Wade resisted arrest as strongly as he always used to. Once a Bushwhacker, eh? Odd thing, though . . . you and him going back as far together as you do. Thought he'd have learned something by now. Such as how dumb it is, when you're only out on parole, to be clobbering police officers with chairs.'

Burke was at the Charge Office counter, in the process of

signing himself in with the Custody Officer; now he looked round, briefly but visibly troubled.

'One person you won't be seeing tonight, Mr Burke, is DC Gary Quinnell,' Heck said. 'He was our undercover officer during the raid. He's currently having an emergency operation to elevate a depressed skull fracture.' Heck gave him a frank look. 'What a silly boy our Wade is, eh?' But then he mused, 'At least . . . we *think* it was Wade. Very chaotic down in that cellar. I didn't witness the attack, personally . . . I've got to see what the other officers present have to say first.'

'What were the actual circumstances?' Burke asked coolly.

'Here's a copy of Gary Quinnell's statement, taken before he went into surgery . . . and my initial intel report.' Heck handed him a couple of printouts. 'The latter outlines the reasons for the raid, what we expected to find there and why, *who* we expected to find there, etcetera. It's heavy stuff, as you'll see. Of course, the last thing your client needs on top of this lot is being charged with attempting to murder a police officer . . . wouldn't you say?'

Heck collected the keys from the Custody Officer and headed down the cell corridor. Burke followed, briefcase tucked under his arm as he skimmed through the documents.

'Sergeant Heckenburg,' Burke said, 'you know Wade McDougall very well. He's never been the sharpest tool in the box.'

'That is undoubtedly true,' Heck said over his shoulder.

'He's often the architect of his own misfortune. But that doesn't always mean that he appreciates the bigger picture. Just because Wade was arrested at this weird underground cinema, I wouldn't necessarily read huge responsibility into it. He's rarely been anything except a minion.'

'He'll still go back to prison,' Heck said.

'Of course, but it's all about how long for, isn't it?'

'Well . . .' Heck halted at the relevant cell door, 'I guess we'll only find out exactly how involved in the running of this cinema Wade was, or even . . .' he pondered, 'how much he *knows* about it, when we get into the interview room. Be an interesting exercise, won't it?'

'And this . . . "attempting to murder a police officer"?' Burke tried to sound amused. 'Seriously?'

Heck shrugged. 'It wouldn't be his first time, would it?'

'It would certainly be his first time with a chair.'

'With all respect, Mr Burke, you haven't seen the steel-framed chair.'

'Sergeant Heckenburg—'

'Look, as I say . . . your client may be investigated for attempting to murder DC Quinnell, and he may not. I've got to make some further enquiries on that . . . *after* we've had a chat with Wade about this cinema.'

Then he unlocked the door and allowed the solicitor access to his client.

Chapter 28

'I want to talk first about your relationship with Lance and Margot Frith,' Heck said.

Jack Reed sat alongside him. On the other side of the interview room table, Wade McDougall slouched next to Anderson Burke.

The prisoner shook his head. 'Don't have a relationship with them.'

'We arrested you working in their unlicensed cinema, Wade,' Heck replied. 'Excuse me if I struggle to keep a straight face in response to that.'

'I mean I don't have . . . like a relationship with them. You know . . . as in a *relationship*.'

'You work for them, though, don't you?'

'Oh that . . . yeah.'

'How long have you worked for them?'

'Eight months. About.'

'So, you started not long after the last time you got out of prison?'

'Soon after, yeah.'

'What has that job involved?'

'Security. I'm just a glorified doorman really.'

'Glorified.' Heck considered that. 'Funny use of the term, Wade. Bobby Moore was glorified when he lifted the World Cup in 1966. The Virgin Mary was glorified when she entered heaven with no sins on her soul. *You* worked in a club that showed snuff films.'

'That's yet to be established,' Burke cut in.

'Did you ever watch the films that were being shown there, yourself?' Reed asked.

'I saw some of them, yeah.'

'What did you think?' Heck wondered. 'Good stuff?'

McDougall grimaced. 'No . . . fucking horrible.'

'Damn right, Wade,' Heck said. 'Damn right. Because this isn't just porn, is it? I mean, this stuff's really nasty. So, I'll tell you what . . . given that you were working for these people, helping them make money out of providing this "fucking horrible" service – to quote you exactly – once this interview is concluded, we're going to be looking at you for disclosing indecent and distressing images. Now, you may not be too worried about that . . . even though I happen to know you're at a stage in your life where you're really supposed to keep your nose clean. But . . . there might be some heavier stuff coming down the line too. Because you and me also know that, whether we can accurately classify that place as a snuff club or not, a lot of those movies depicted sequences which look, on the surface, to contain real-life rape, torture and murder. True or not?'

'I wouldn't know.'

'You must have an opinion, Wade? I mean, you're not *that* dense, are you?'

'Sergeant, please . . .' Burke said.

'What do you think, Wade?' Reed asked. 'Didn't they at least *look* real? Certainly, the customers who went in there thought they were . . . I mean, they were paying top dollar.'

McDougall shrugged. 'They looked like they were real, yeah.'

'We've now had the chance to skim through a few of those films, ourselves,' Heck put in. 'And, quite clearly, not all of them are home-made. Some look like they originated overseas, some looked quite old. So, I'm guessing that Mr and Mrs Frith bought those in?'

McDougall shrugged. 'They bought them *all* in.'

Heck and Reed glanced at each other.

'Do you want to elaborate on that?' Reed said.

The prisoner looked reluctant to say more. Many career criminals were snake-like in the treachery they showed to each other; but some – the soldier caste, like this one – never found it easy. Only in extremis would they consider informing on comrades, and as Heck had already indirectly reminded McDougall's solicitor, this situation was potentially the very definition of 'extremis'. But before the prisoner could say more, Burke cut in.

'Perhaps, Sergeant . . . I could have another consultation with my client?'

Heck met his gaze. The only thing that surprised him about this interruption was that the interview had actually been allowed to start, but again, that was probably down to McDougall's mulishness. Now, however, he'd clearly changed his mind.

'No problem. Interview suspended, 10:19 p.m.' Heck flipped off the tape machine. He then gave the solicitor and his client a long stare. 'You guys got a statement for us?'

'I'm still a tad concerned about this chair incident,' Burke said.

Heck shrugged. 'As I say, there may be nothing in it.'

Reed sat listening to this in fascination, but he kept his mouth shut.

'May not?' Burke enquired.

'*May* not. It all depends.'

'You haven't spoken to the CPS about this?'

'Of course not.'

'Then yes,' Burke said, 'we'd like to make a statement.'

Heck looked at McDougall. 'Before we actually write anything down, Wade . . . what are we going to be talking about?'

'We didn't *make* those films,' McDougall said sullenly. 'We didn't kill anyone.'

Heck leaned forward. 'Suppose I believe you . . . who *did* make them?'

'I can only tell you who sold them.'

'That'll do for starters.'

'One bloke . . . don't know his name. Always the same fella, though. Always comes to the same place in the same green van.'

'What place?'

'A lorry park down in Newham.'

'You sound like you have personal experience of this?' Reed said.

The prisoner nodded. 'It's me and Alfie who do the buying. Not with our own money, obviously.'

'You and Alfie pay the money and take possession of the merchandise?' Heck said.

'Yeah. We can look after ourselves, me and Alf, so . . . in case it ever cuts up, Margot sends *us*. After she's set the deal up . . . on the phone, or whatever. We get paid extra for that, though . . . so it's always worth it. And nothing ever happens. Just straight business.'

'Tell us about the bloke?' Heck said.

McDougall frowned. 'Foreigner. East European, I'd say.'

'How old?'

'Late thirties.'

'White?'

'Like I say . . . European, but eastern, I think. Darkish skin. Spoke with an accent.'

'Good English?' Reed asked.

'Enough to get by.'

'Hair?' Heck said.

'Black. Short.'

'Big fella?'

'Average height, but massive across the shoulders. That's all I ever really see. It's dark, because the exchange is usually at midnight. We park behind a row of oil drums about fifty yards away. We always know when to walk over, 'cause he gets out his van and waits.'

'And this van's a green transit?' Reed said.

McDougall nodded.

'Registration number?' Heck asked.

'No clue.'

'And this bloke always comes on his own?'

'Never seen anyone else with him.'

'OK . . . how does it go down?'

McDougall shrugged. 'We hand the cash over, he gives us a bag of films.'

'How much money are we talking?' Reed asked.

'Me and Alfie never know. It always comes to us in sealed brown paper.'

'And he just takes this packet, gives you the mucky movies and drives off?' Heck said. 'Without checking it first? He must be very trusting?'

'Why not? We've been doing this a while.'

'Is this guy ever armed? I mean with a firearm.'

McDougall gave it some thought. 'I never saw that, but I wouldn't be surprised. That sort of bloke, if you know what I mean. I once overheard Lance and Margot talking. Sounds like part of the original deal was that none of these movies ever show up online . . . and if they do, there'll be trouble.'

'As in . . . trouble for Lance and Margot?' Heck asked.

McDougall half-smiled. 'As in . . . this guy will kill them both. Least, that was the impression I got.'

Heck sat back, thinking that it all rang eerily true.

The Friths had spent their professional lives in the adult movie market. They'd probably made lots of connections in that time, but ultimately that was all they'd ever really done – produce and sell mainstream pornography. Of course, in the age of free video-sharing websites, there was less and less money to be made in that field, unless you were prepared to venture ever further into the extreme. And during one such foray, most likely on the Dark Web, they'd made contact with a whole other universe.

On one hand, it was frustrating because it meant that Heck still wasn't as close to this organisation as he'd hoped, but on the other, Wade McDougall was the best lead he'd had.

'How often did you meet this guy?' Reed asked.

McDougall pondered. 'No set time. Just when Margot told us. She was the one who made all the arrangements.'

'And it's always at this lorry park in Newham?' Heck said. 'Around midnight?'

'Not around . . . bang on. If we're late, he won't wait.'

'OK . . . and when were you next due to meet him?'

'That's the funny thing . . .' McDougall eyed them warily. 'Tonight.'

'Ma'am . . . the way I see it,' Heck said, 'we've got to act on this fast.'

They were back in the Charge Office at Finchley Road, he and Reed in conflab with Gwen and Gemma, the former of whom had been summoned out of her interview with Lance Frith, the latter who'd just arrived from the hospital and was able to report that Quinnell was doing well.

Aside from the Custody Sergeant and his assistant, there was no one else around. All the prisoners taken at Deercot Road, including Margot Frith, were now in their respective cells, conferring with their solicitors or waiting for them to arrive.

'We can be the ones who meet this guy,' Heck said, 'but if we don't do it tonight, the Friths' legal reps will find a way to pass the message on and the whole thing'll get called off. This bastard with the pen drives disappears, and that's it. We've got nothing.'

'We might already have nothing,' Gwen said, tapping her pen irritably on the charge desk. 'Both the Friths have consulted with their brief. He could already have made a phone call.'

'I can't believe he'd be stupid enough to use his own phone,' Gemma said.

'He could have brought a spare along for this very purpose.'

'That's true, ma'am,' Reed said, 'but Heck's right. If we don't take the opportunity to meet this green van at midnight tonight, word will get out somehow, and this guy will never show up again.' He shrugged. 'If he doesn't show tonight . . . well, there's nothing we can do about that, but if he does, we're quids in.'

Gwen clucked with dissatisfaction. 'My problem is that undercover ops like this need proper planning.'

Reed glanced at his watch. 'It's nearly ten-thirty. No time for that.'

She regarded the two men carefully. 'Who goes?'

'*We* will,' Heck said.

'Just the two of you?'

'Well . . . Gary can hardly assist, Gail's not here any more and no one else is available.'

Gwen looked so unhappy with the plan that it felt as if she was about to kibosh it.

'Ma'am . . .' Heck urged her, 'this may be a once in a lifetime opportunity.'

'All right, all right . . . but I don't like it. Not the two of you on your own. So . . . get back to Staples Corner first and draw yourself a pistol each. I'll arrange to have a Trojan unit in close support as well.'

'Ma'am,' Heck groaned, 'going back to Staples Corner now will add another—'.

'Don't argue with me, Heck. Just do as you're damn well told, OK?'

He nodded.

'We'll get some local plod on the scene too,' she said.

'So long as they keep well back . . . we don't want to blow it now.'

'*Heck!*' Gwen's eyes flashed with impatience. 'I know you're convinced you're the only copper in the UK who knows what he's doing. But try and have a little faith, eh?'

Chapter 29

As part of his co-operative approach, Wade McDougall agreed that Heck and Reed could take his car, a distinctive beige BMW Sedan, to the meeting at Newham. This was the vehicle the Green Van Man was used to seeing and, with luck, it would lull him into a momentary false sense of security – sufficient at least for them to grab him.

The main problem, though, was time.

It was 10:35 p.m. when they left Finchley Road. The ten-minute drive back to Staples Corner wasn't much of a problem, but drawing firearms from the SCU armoury was never a quick and easy process, not least because the unit's official armourer, a retired and cantankerous ex-firearms sergeant called Joe Mackeson, only worked nine-till-five, and now had to be called in specially. He only lived around the corner in Dollis Hill and was already on site when the two detectives arrived, but as he issued them each with the requisite Glock 17 and shoulder holster, plus two fifteen-round magazines apiece, he still managed to take his time and to complain endlessly about being dragged from his late-night comedy shows.

They scampered upstairs to their lockers, donned their

covert Kevlar vests, and raced back down to the car park. Here, Reed watched in silence as Heck opened the boot of his Megane, dumped his official-issue shoulder strap and replaced it with a different make and design, this one with a clamshell-style inverted holster, so that when he clipped his Glock into it, it hung upside down.

'Is that a fast-draw holster?' the DI asked, incredulous.

Heck shrugged as he pulled a black anorak over his T-shirt and gun-harness and zipped it up. 'Suppose you could call it that.'

'Didn't know those things were even legal.'

'It's not in regs, that's for sure. But it works.'

'Where'd you get the idea? Some old sweat who was around in the good old days?'

'Uh-uh.' Heck climbed into the car. 'Steve McQueen in *Bullitt*.'

It was now 10:45 p.m., so they made a blue-light run down to Putney, where they retrieved McDougall's Sedan and headed northwest, joining the North Circular at Neasden.

This was not an officially registered police vehicle, so Heck couldn't simply stick his detachable beacon on the roof. Nevertheless, it was midweek, and the hour was late, which meant that traffic on the North Circular was conveniently light.

'You really think a whole raft of our targets could have been snatched by these people?' Reed wondered.

Heck shrugged as he drove. 'I don't know, sir. It's a theory. One minute I think it's viable, the next it seems far-fetched. I've no clue how they're doing it, if they are. But aside from your score, no one's made any ground at all, which is weird. Gwen's more sold on it than Gemma. Gemma thinks it too much of a coincidence . . . I mean, that we and someone else are both after the same group at the same time.'

'It would be more of a coincidence if there was no common denominator,' Reed replied.

Heck threw a querying glance at him.

'They're top of everyone's shit-list, aren't they?' the DI said. 'If *we* want to take them down for that reason alone, why shouldn't someone else feel the same way?'

Heck pondered this. It made a kind of sense, though if this was vigilante action, it would take an extraordinarily organised firm to pull it off. Plus, that hardly tied in with the production of murder videos as a form of extremist pornography.

'Whatever,' he said, 'thanks for your support back there, sir.'

'I think you'd have swung it anyway, Heck. You can be a pretty persuasive guy. But the thanks are appreciated. Especially as you can't stand the sight of me.'

'Never said that, have I?'

'You don't need to. I've got eyes and ears.'

Heck mulled it over. 'It's not the case that I "can't stand the sight of you", sir.'

'Perhaps if you called me "Jack" instead of "Sir", that would help.'

'Never thought there'd be a day when a senior copper begged an underling to call him by his first name.'

'I'm not begging you. But I can't force you either, so it's your shout.'

'I'll stick with "sir", if you don't mind.'

'Whatever.'

'Said I didn't hate you,' Heck explained. 'Didn't say I liked you.'

Reed nodded. 'Always best to be straight with people.'

They made it to the spot McDougall described to them at twenty-to-midnight.

It was a derelict lorry park located next to a flyover of the North Circular Road. The lorry park itself, which was accessible by a flimsy wire-mesh gate hanging from corroded hinges, was largely empty, a couple of rusting hulks at one end of it, the rest just cinders and weeds. The row of oil drums where McDougall told them he always parked was visible on the west side, in front of an overgrown embankment, along the top of which ran an elevated section of the Hammersmith & City line. To the east, underneath the flyover, it was too dark to see anything of consequence, though McDougall had told them it was a rubbish-strewn wasteland: relics of cardboard city littered here and there, more dumped vehicles, abandoned fridges, shopping trolleys and the like.

They made a quick recce, just to ensure they were in the correct spot, and then headed back onto the road network, hooking up with the Trojan in a small terraced street about five minutes' drive away. It was an unmarked troop-carrier, manned by four plain-clothes shots and their inspector, a guy called Renshaw – a short, compact Cumbrian, with hard-bitten features and a jutting white beard.

'This guy might not be carrying,' Heck said, 'we simply don't know, but just in case, I could do with you and your lads finding optimum clean-shot positions around the lorry park. You've got night-vision scopes, yeah?'

Renshaw's expression implied contempt for such a question.

'You've been emailed all the details?' Heck added. 'But just to remind you . . . the target vehicle is a green transit van. As far as we're aware, there'll only be one person inside. He will park on the east side of the plot and get out of the vehicle to meet us. Apparently, this is his unchanging MO. He's only expecting two customers – that's us two. Hopefully, in the shadow of the flyover, he won't be able to see us properly until we're right on top of him.'

'What if he puts a light on you?' Renshaw asked.

'Theoretically, he won't. He won't want to attract any attention to what he's doing. That's why he always comes at midnight, so it's dark whether summer or winter. In addition, we're told that he's in a kind of comfort zone. He's done this so many times now that he doesn't expect anything to change. That means the two parties always approach each other in the same way. We, for example, will park alongside the oil drums on the west side. We'll be in the same car that this guy's contacts always use. Soon as he's ready for us, we walk over . . .'

'And you don't know whether he's carrying, or not?' Renshaw interrupted.

'No,' Heck admitted. 'We just need to be prepared for anything. As soon as we meet him, we give him this . . .' He produced a bundle wrapped in brown paper and tied with string, 'which he'll think is cash, though on this occasion it contains nothing but newspaper strips. Hopefully, we'll get close enough with it before he notices that we're not the usual guys. That's also when we make the arrest. You'll know because you'll hear us shouting.' Heck felt absurdly apologetic given that he and Reed would be in the greater danger. 'I know it's a bit thrown-together, sir, and I know it's risky . . . but we're acting on intel we've literally only just received. There's nothing else we can do.'

Renshaw shrugged. 'Don't beat yourself up too much. Dig-outs rarely come off all sweet and clean. Be a fucking drag if they did.'

'One other thing,' Heck said. 'We need this fella alive. If you have to slot him, you have to slot him . . . but please make sure you really *have* to, yeah?'

'Don't worry. We know no other way.'

It didn't sound convincing, but Heck and Reed had no time to discuss it with him.

They left the firearms team to make their own recce and deploy as they saw fit and drove back to the lorry park, finally arriving alongside the row of oil drums at four minutes to midnight. Heck parked and applied the handbrake.

They waited.

A gust rustled across the open expanse, whipping up shreds of litter. With a crashing and banging, an Underground train passed along the embankment behind them, its array of reflected light dancing over the cindery emptiness.

Another silence followed. Reed glanced at his watch.

For the first time since meeting him, Heck thought that the DI seemed tense. His posture was taut, his shoulders rigid. No one was ever cosy before a potentially dangerous arrest like this, but one aspect of Jack Reed that even Heck had found appealing was his air of relaxed competence. This was a cop who normally gave the impression that nothing fazed him; that he knew what he was doing at any given time and was always comfortable.

'Where do you think Renshaw's men are?' Reed wondered.

He leaned forward, peering through the windscreen and across the lorry park, scanning the vast, black bulk of the flyover as it soared horizontally over the eastern sky.

'Well, they're not going to be up there,' Heck replied. 'First of all, if the target does what he always does, it means he'll be standing leeward of the van, so they wouldn't be able to see him. Secondly, after stressing that we don't want this guy slotting unless it's absolutely vital, this should be a close-contact op. Renshaw's only got four men, so he's not going to stick any of them up there, where they'll be well out of it.'

Reed sat back again, as though content to be schooled, which seemed at odds with the tall, fearless man who had faced down the Black Chapel dressed only as a country vicar. One difference this time, of course, was the presence of firearms.

'This your first time across the pavement?' Heck asked him.

'First time I've ever carried on duty, yeah.'

'Not much call for it down at Critical Incident?'

'Well . . .' Reed mused. 'I've locked up a few murderers in my time. A few rapists. None of them were armed when we nicked them.'

Heck was genuinely surprised. 'First time I saw you, I had you down as ex-military. Former army officer, or something.'

'Me? Some chance. My dad was a porter on Southampton docks.' Reed looked oddly amused. 'That take a bit of wind out of your sails, does it? You being a class warrior and all.'

'I'm no class warrior.' Heck scanned the lorry park. 'With me it's purely personal. But you *do* have a rather fine command of the Queen's English.'

'Suppose you can blame Oxford for that.'

Oxford would explain plenty, Heck thought. You had to admire a guy who'd made it to the Dreaming Spires from a dockland background, but it doubtless had opened all kinds of doors for him. Probably got him fast-tracked through the ranks the moment he joined the job. In that regard, it seemed weird that he wasn't already spoken for romantically, perhaps with some posh lady from the Home Counties. Or maybe he *was* spoken for and, where Gemma was concerned, he was contemplating playing away.

'Family man, are you?' Heck asked.

'Was,' Reed replied. 'Didn't last.'

Which wasn't music to Heck's ears either, for obvious reasons.

'Job?' Heck asked. 'Usually is.'

'Not really . . . my wife died.'

It was a simple but gut-punching comment, which only struck Heck belatedly. He glanced awkwardly around. 'Sorry to hear that.'

Reed gazed through the window. 'Road accident. And we'd

only been married two years. Hadn't managed to have any kids at that point, thank God.'

'Me and my big mouth, eh?'

'Shouldn't dislike me any the less for that, Heck. I hear you've had a rough time, too . . .'

There was a sudden *clatter* of metal from out in the darkness.

Almost by instinct, Reed went for his gun.

'Whoa . . . easy.' Heck grabbed his arm. 'Probably just one of the shots. They like to think they move around like panthers. But, take it from me, they don't.'

'Fuck,' Reed breathed aloud.

Again, they scanned the encircling night.

'Remember . . . our guy's coming in a vehicle,' Heck said. 'And if he suspected anything, he wouldn't be coming at all.'

Several seconds of quiet passed, broken only by further gusts of wind sighing through the embankment foliage behind them. It was now midnight, but there was still no sign of the guy.

'You a bit of a veteran when it comes to this sort of thing?' Reed finally said.

'Wouldn't say I'm a veteran,' Heck replied. 'Done it once or twice. Can't say I'm a fan.'

'Even though you've got Steve McQueen's gun in your armpit?'

Briefly, there was humour in Reed's voice. He was trying to make light of it. For his own sake mainly.

'The way I see it,' Heck said, 'if I've got to protect myself by using lethal force, I might as well be able to do it properly. But remember . . .' he patted his concealed weapon, 'when you've got this in your hand, never think of it as anything less than a portable life sentence. If you absolutely *must* slot someone, be two hundred per cent certain it's the right bloke.'

'Well . . . they always said on Level Two that the most important thing was watching your backgrounds.'

'Yeah, except that doesn't mean much on nights like this.'

They peered into the opaque shadows beneath the flyover. They'd been here several minutes now, and their eyes still hadn't adjusted to an extent where even the whole of the lorry park was distinguishable, let alone those deep, hidden reaches under the road. En route, Reed had phoned East Ham Central, to ascertain the likelihood that vagrants, drug users and other homeless might be camping there but had been advised that at present the site was clear of occupation. That was good to know, but in this darkness you could never be absolutely sure.

The DI glanced at his watch again. It was two minutes past.

Green Van Man was officially late and getting later.

'You know, like we said . . . it's entirely possible this pigeon may already have flown.'

'Yep,' Heck agreed.

'You said yourself that the Friths' solicitor could have tipped him off by now.'

'Could have,' Heck admitted. 'It's a possibility, but whatever happens here tonight, Lance and Margot are going down.'

'Not necessarily for a long stretch.'

'Aiding and abetting murder? That's not totally unlikely, is it?'

Reed considered. 'The Friths are providing a willing market for these murder videos, I suppose. So, you could argue they're procuring the commission of the crimes. There may be a case to be made there, so no, it's not totally unlikely. You saying you think they may attempt to cut a deal too?'

'Wade McDougall did,' Heck replied. 'And he's a more practised villain than the Friths. Probably got better instincts.

The other thing is . . . McDougall's using his own solicitor, not the same one as the Friths. So, they don't necessarily know he's talked yet. From their point of view, the worst thing that can happen tonight is miladdo turns up to make his sale, there's no one here to buy and away he goes again. No one's any the worse off. That gives them time to think this thing through, to maybe realise they're better off serving the bastard up rather than giving him a chance to escape. So, yes, to answer your original question, there is a possibility they've warned him already, but I reckon it's thin . . .'

His words petered out. He raised a finger.

Two parallel beams of light were cutting sideways across the desolation beneath the flyover, picking out abandoned wrecks, burned tyres and other scattered rubbish. As they watched, a transit van, from which the lights emanated, turned into the lorry park through its open gate. It wallowed sluggishly across the cindery surface to the far side, before grinding to a halt. Its engine fell silent and the headlights went off.

Heck reached under his anorak to turn his radio down, and whispered, 'Game on.'

Chapter 30

They had about fifty yards of open ground to cover, and did so slowly, in a determined effort to look as relaxed as possible, all the time maintaining ten to fifteen yards between themselves as they advanced. You didn't need any firearms training to know that a couple of bodies standing close together made a much easier target than a couple standing wide apart.

The only problem was . . . to the eye of experience, that in itself might seem unusual.

All Heck could see of the guy was his dark outline against the pale, boxy shape of his vehicle. He was shorter than Heck had imagined, no more than five-seven or -eight, but solidly built, his neck so thick that it was barely discernible, his head large and flat across the top – it looked like an anvil.

Increasingly as they approached, Heck felt uneasy. Surreptitiously, he lowered the zip of his anorak. The figure by the van waited motionless, watching them.

At which point he'd wise up was anyone's guess. If it had been raining, they could have pulled their hoods up and probably got away with it. But to have done that on a dry August evening would have been too suspicious.

The man adjusted his position, leaning forward slightly.

Was he scrutinising them more carefully?

Heck's hand stole slowly towards his left armpit.

And then, with the repeating crash of steel riding steel, another tube train rumbled along the elevated line behind them, its lightshow glaring across the lorry park.

The green van came fully into view, as did the short, stocky, white-faced figure of its driver. He wore blue jeans and a grey, zip-up hoodie top. His hands were planted in its front pockets, a white plastic bag suspended from his right wrist, where he'd looped it.

The question was, how much of the two cops did the lightshow reveal?

Probably not a lot. They'd be framed against the passing train, nothing more than silhouettes. But even so, that would be enough to show that one of them wasn't six-foot-five.

At a distance, six-foot-three Jack Reed might pass for that.

But not this close, less than twenty yards away.

The waiting figure adjusted position again. It was a sharper movement than previously.

'Hit the deck!' Heck shouted, diving to the floor.

Reed did the same, and just in time – as the waiting man opened fire with a concealed weapon in his front pocket. Two blinding flashes split the night.

Heck rolled sideways, his Glock already drawn. 'Police officers . . . drop your weapon!'

When he came to a halt, he took aim with both hands.

However, Green Van Man had already leapt back into the driving cab. As he did, a police-issue MP5 fired a single round from somewhere close by, the heavy slug visibly denting the vehicle's side, but not punching through.

'Damn thing's armoured!' Heck shouted. 'I don't believe . . . *Sir, you all right?*'

'I'm OK!' came Reed's voice, though he sounded dazed.

'Stay flat . . . the shots are on it!'

Another MP5 *boomed*. This bullet struck the van's driver side window, which spiderwebbed, but again was not smashed through.

'Jesus wept!' Heck exclaimed. 'That's military grade!'

With a cough, the van's engine growled to life and it lurched forward.

Heck had no choice but to open fire on its wheels, putting three rounds into the front offside and three into the rear offside.

The vehicle jolted downward as both tyres exploded, but continued barrelling forward, its undercarriage grinding along the ground. It limped forty yards or so, veering right, as more heavy gunfire from unseen positions slammed into it. However, its reinforced hull resisted, and the driver was still giving it full throttle, the wounded machine chewing its way through the perimeter mesh fence and clattering out of sight into the shadows beneath the flyover, where, by the sounds of it, it smashed through various obstacles.

Heck rose to his knees, dragging the chequer-banded baseball cap from his back pocket and jamming it onto his head. Not too far to the side of him, Reed did the same.

Beyond him, two firearms officers ran in an arc across the north side of the lorry park. They too wore hi-vis caps but carried MP5s at chest-level. Heck looked south and saw another officer coming diagonally towards him. In all cases, torches had been attached to their barrels, issuing intense beams. From a distance and a static position, their night-vision scopes would be adequate, but at close quarters, when moving through a darkened landscape this was the only real option; you couldn't scamper around while watching the world through a rifle sight. The downside, of course, was that it made you into a clear target.

From somewhere beneath the flyover, there was an echoing

impact, and the throb of the van's engine cut out. Driving without headlights, it had finally hit something that wouldn't yield.

The firearms officer from the south now reached the two detectives. He was a young, black cop, with a slim build and a military bearing. He yabbered into his radio, presumably calling in additional units, but broke off to speak with them.

'Either of you two hit?'

'Negative,' Heck replied.

'Good . . . stay back. Leave this to us, yeah?'

'Sounds like he's had a smash,' Heck replied. 'Probably on foot now, headed towards the other side of the overpass.'

'We've got the other side covered,' the shot answered, advancing into the shadows, torchlight blazing ahead of him.

Heck scrambled over to Reed, who was still on one knee, his Glock drawn but dressed down. The DI was breathing hard, sweat sparkling on his forehead, but he looked looser-limbed, less tense. It was the same for Heck; it always had been. You might be nervous to start with, but the instant you made contact with the enemy, all fear left you, the adrenaline pumped and it was arse-kicking time.

'Bloody thing's like a tank,' Reed muttered.

'Agreed. Which means there's even more going on here than we thought.'

Heck looked back across the lorry park, but of the firearms men there was now no sign, which meant that they had all gone forward. If, as the young black cop had mentioned, there were units on the far side of the flyover too, that likely meant the target was already contained.

Keeping low, guns in hand, the detectives ventured to the edge of the flyover.

Ahead of them, blobs of light moved erratically as the shots scrambled and slithered forward, presumably hemming the bastard in. With luck, he only had that pistol, so he was more than outgunned.

Reed glanced at Heck. 'We're not letting these heroes grab all the kudos.'

Heck shrugged. 'Whatever you say, sir.'

Reed jumped up and gambolled forward across the flattened section of fence. Beyond there, the firm ground of the lorry park gave way to a mulch of filth and trash. There was also that wreckage they'd glimpsed; a virtual jungle of abandoned vehicles and tossed-away property. They'd no sooner navigated around the gutted shell of a Mini Cooper than they were sidling through thickets of rotted furniture and rusted appliances.

Just then a thunderous chatter of automatic fire echoed ear-splittingly in the cavernous space.

Heck dropped to the floor, Reed following.

The firing broke off.

'That one of ours?' the DI asked, breathless.

'Unlikely,' Heck whispered. 'Our lads wouldn't fire in protracted bursts like that!'

He holstered his Glock and slid forward through the darkness on his belly, using only his elbows. When he reached a tall, angular object – something black as char and stinking of grease, an old oven no doubt – he rose and peeked over the top.

All the lights had gone out, presumably switched off by the shots, who'd only now realised what they were up against. The automatic fire recommenced, continuing uninterrupted for what seemed like a full minute. Heck crouched lower but could pinpoint the source of it: a flickering dab of flame about forty yards ahead and twenty to his left. It moved back, forth and around, as if the gunman kept changing position.

Abruptly, the shooting stopped again, its echoes resounding for a moment or two.

This could only be because he needed to reload. Which was worrying; he'd just pissed away an entire magazine, so how many spares did he have?

Even more worrying was the lack of response fire.

Where was the firearms team?

Heck strained his eyes as he scanned the blackness.

But nothing moved or sounded. There was no explosion of return fire; there wasn't even a crackle of radio static.

'Fuck's going on?' Reed whispered, crouching alongside him.

Heck shook his head. He circled the oven, dropping to all fours and shuffling forward. Reed brought up the rear, and a few seconds later they paused behind an old sofa, listening.

'Think they might have withdrawn?' Reed wondered.

'Would make sense,' Heck replied.

At which point an MP5 *boomed* not twenty yards to their left.

In the brief glare, Heck saw one of the firearms cops standing upright, carbine at his shoulder, eye at his night scope. He fired a second round, but a fusillade of automatic fire responded, this time from a different position. The volley sprayed in a wide, turning arc, cutting across the firearms guy mid-section, dropping him to the dirt with an agonised gargle. Before either Heck or Reed could move towards him, several slugs punched through the sofa, tufts of spongy stuffing bursting out.

Heck lurched to the right, moving at a crouch again, grabbing Reed by the collar and hauling him along. They shuffled down a weed-filled avenue formed between heaped plastic sacks and piles of string-tied magazines. Green Van Man, who might have had night vision himself, swivelled after them, continually firing, hammering everything he hit into fragments. They went to ground again, and only just in time, bullets whining overhead.

Abruptly, the firing ceased, the protracted, echoing roar taking an age to die away.

Nothingness followed, during which they were deaf and blind. They had no clue where the gunman was, whether he'd moved position again in his quest to find them, or whether he'd seized his chance to do a runner.

But then Heck heard someone approaching from the front.

He gestured at Reed to keep still and tensed where he lay. Just ahead, around the corner of another abandoned, lopsided vehicle, a hunkered shape scuttled into view. Whoever this was, he hadn't seen the detectives, and as he crawled past, Heck reached up, snatched him by the collar of his Kevlar vest and yanked him down. With an angry grunt, the newcomer, who was all wiry muscle, rammed a knee into Heck's groin and smashed a forearm down across his throat, pressing him back into the weeds and stones.

'Fuck's sake,' Heck gasped, noting the white beard and chequer-banded baseball cap.

The eyes in the sweat-drenched face widened and the grip slackened.

'Fuck are you playing at?' Renshaw hissed. 'I could've killed you.'

'Yeah?' Heck whispered; only then did Renshaw realise that Heck's Glock was jammed muzzle-on against his genitals.

'Fucking get off me!' The firearms officer tore loose and got to his knees.

'One of your boys got slotted,' Heck said.

Renshaw whipped back round to him. 'Who? Where?'

'Don't know who. Somewhere to our left . . .'

'How badly?'

'Don't know.' Heck kneeled up. 'About thirty or forty yards that way.'

'Could be Andy Gillman. Fuck's sake . . . I asked you how badly?'

Heck pulled him nose-to-nose. 'I don't fucking know . . . all right?'

'They're kitted out with the latest body-plate. They should be—'

'All I can tell you is he definitely got hurt. We heard him squawk.'

Renshaw looked bewildered and frightened, all trace of his earlier confidence long dissipated.

'What's going on, Renshaw?' Reed hissed. 'I thought you guys were the experts.'

That seemed to bring Renshaw to. 'Hey, dipshit! You didn't tell us we'd be facing firepower like this.'

'We didn't know,' Heck said. 'But I *did* warn you that we didn't know . . .'

Metal *clunked* some twenty or thirty yards to their right. Renshaw risked standing, and raised his MP5 to the firing position, but only so he could look through his night scope. Heck and Reed crab-crawled forward until they were flush against the lopsided vehicle, and then rose up too, flattening themselves on its bodywork and edging around the corner, screening themselves from the shooter's last position.

'No sign of the fucker,' Renshaw said, sliding around to join them.

'I appreciate that you're outgunned,' Reed whispered. 'But what counteractions did you initiate once you realised that?'

'Soon as we came under heavy fire, I ordered the lads to pull back,' Renshaw said. 'Andy was the only one who didn't copy. Mustn't have heard 'cause of the racket. I've called in additional units.' He glanced at the luminous dial of his watch. 'Five minutes tops. Division are already closing the adjoining roads. We'll contain this bastard, don't worry. I summoned a casevac too. Terry Chowdry got hit. Both his fucking legs, poor sod.'

'So, you're actually *two* men down?' Reed said.

Renshaw's face twisted into a snarl. 'Chowdry's alive, in case you were worried for him.'

'But he's out of the fight?'

'Course he fucking is.'

'Where is he now?' Heck asked.

'Laying low over that way somewhere.'

Renshaw gestured vaguely, as though unsure of the actual direction, which, in truth, they all now were, having been turned around so many times. Their vision had attuned – some moonlight penetrated under the bridge, but all this really did was create a wasteland of jumbled, indistinct shapes.

'Where'd you say Gillman was?' Renshaw asked.

'Round the other side of this thing,' Heck tapped the wreck they were sheltering behind, 'and down that alley through the trash.'

Renshaw nodded and moved to the corner.

Heck went with him. 'From where we are now, I'd say two o'clock. But, sir . . . if support units are en route, we're better sitting tight.'

Renshaw's features were saturnine in the dimness, but his eyes glinted. 'If it was one of your lads, what would *you* do?'

There was no rational objection Heck could make to that.

Renshaw slid around the corner. They leaned out to watch his progress. The alley they'd come down was only faintly illuminated but looked to be clear.

'You two get your arses out of here,' Renshaw whispered back. 'Don't go to your car. Get out of the lorry park. RV on the same road where we hooked up earlier. Copy?'

Heck looked at Reed. They both nodded.

Renshaw turned back to the alley – only to find that the outline of a man had now risen into view from behind the rubbish bags at its far end. He stood to about five-foot-seven, and was of stocky build, with a bull neck and a flat, anvil-shaped head.

He was also levelling a firearm.

Renshaw raised his own weapon, shouting that they were police officers – but the blinding blast of automatic fire hurled him backward, slamming him against the vehicle, right at the corner alongside which Heck and Reed stood goggle-eyed, his blood spattering up its battered green bodywork.

Green.

Incredibly, even in that whirlwind moment, there was time for Heck to realise that they'd unwittingly come up against the very vehicle they'd been chasing.

Vaguely aware of Renshaw flopping lifelessly down, he and Reed scrambled back to the other side of it, unsure whether or not the gunman had seen them. There was even more rubbish here; no immediate flight was possible without clattering over heaps of twisted metal and creating a fearsome racket. Instead, they had to lurch down the length of the van until they reached its front end, which had mashed full on with an immense concrete stanchion.

The cab hadn't been completely crushed, but the roof had concertinaed down, the reinforced windshield had been bashed in and the driver's door hung from a single warped hinge.

They halted, breathing hard, listening.

From the other side, they heard the gunman kicking his way through the detritus. He was coming.

Heck pointed. On the immediate right of the vehicle's shattered front, if they slid between the stanchion and an upended refrigerator, it looked as if open space beckoned.

Reed went first, turning sideways to negotiate the gap. As Heck waited, he glanced back to the far end of the van. No figure had appeared there yet, but a heavy tread drew closer. As he turned back, ready to push through after Reed, his eyes fell on something else: a ragged old rucksack lying in the driver's side footwell.

It was nothing, an old canvas thing with shoulder straps, fastened with two buckles – but it had to contain something belonging to the man who'd caused this carnage. And if Heck was about to flee from here and continue the enquiry another day, it only made sense for the rucksack to flee with him.

He reached in and yanked it out of the van. It was heavier than he'd expected, but he jammed it under his arm as he slid through the gap between the stanchion and the fridge. As he did, the shooter appeared at the far end of the vehicle and opened up.

The fridge took the brunt, flying apart in a rain of shrapnel. But Heck was already past it, slinging the rucksack over his shoulder as he ran hell for leather into the darkness.

Chapter 31

Even in circumstances like these, Heck was loath to peg blind shots behind him. Renshaw had said he'd pulled his remaining men back, but he hadn't said where to – which meant they could still be within range. Not that there was time to ponder this. The submachine gun continued to chatter as they fled, hails of lead ripping through the objects they ducked and dodged around, a wheelie bin bursting apart, a stack of tyres shredded like paper.

Green Van Man clearly didn't have a night-sight himself; he was taking pot-luck as he pursued them, raking the darkness with bursts of fire, only stopping to reload, which he did quickly and efficiently.

'How many fucking clips does that nutcase have?' Reed stammered.

Heck was too busy trying not to lose his footing to respond.

'And what's the fucking point?' The DI turned to shout over his shoulder. 'You mad, mate? There's coppers closing in from all over London! You should get away while you can!'

The response was another protracted fusillade, the stroboscopic muzzle flash only fifty yards behind, slugs whipping past.

'He wants this rucksack,' Heck panted, as they pelted across firmer ground. 'It can only be *this*!'

If it was true that they possessed something so valuable to the maniac, that was all the more reason not to relinquish it, of course. Either way, Reed barely heard; he was too distracted by a twinkling line of streetlights ahead of them – they'd run southward down the length of the flyover, but were now veering east, looking to emerge on the other side.

Their stalker ceased firing, but maybe that was to ascertain their position. And in short order, he managed this, zeroing in as they raced out from beneath the overhanging concrete into brighter moonlight, his weapon opening up again. They separated, running in zigzags across flat cement, myriad chunks of which catapulted loose as it was peppered with gunfire.

Seeing that they were in some kind of empty compound encircled by high mesh, Heck veered left towards what looked like a single gate, on the other side of which loomed a boarded-up church. In contrast, Reed spun around, dropped to one knee, took aim with both hands and fired three shots into the shadows.

The submachine gun was abruptly silenced.

Heck ran on. As he reached the gate, he leapt, slamming it with the flat of his foot. The impact was massive, jarring his ankle and knee, but the bolt was corroded, and it snapped, the gate swinging open.

'Jack!' he shouted, spinning back, mopping the sweat from his eyes.

Reed had risen slowly to his feet, weapon dressed down, but instead of running was scanning the shadows, certain he'd scored a hit.

'Jack!' Heck hollered. 'Over here!'

Reed turned and walked slowly, only belatedly breaking into a trot. 'Think I might've—'

'No!' Heck interrupted him. 'You haven't!'

'Seriously, Heck . . .'

Reed was ten yards away when a strobe-like flame bloomed again – just to the left of where it had been previously. The DI jolted around three-sixty degrees, before dropping to the ground.

The interior of Heck's mouth went dry. Fresh sweat broke on his already sodden brow. Then something happened that he didn't expect.

The firing ceased, and Green Van Man emerged from the shadows, weapon by his side.

Clearly, he hadn't seen Heck. It wasn't as dark out here as under the North Circular, but it was painted in shades of grey, and Heck realised that he was probably camouflaged by the wall of the derelict church behind him. If that wasn't enough, the bastard was still a good seventy yards off – that would make it difficult for anyone to see clearly. Hence his wary advance.

But this wasn't the best time for Reed to start moving.

He turned to look at Heck, his face a mask of sweat, his eyes straining orbs of pain. But his teeth were set in a determined clench.

'My leg,' he whispered. 'It's my left leg . . .'

'Stay where you are,' Heck hissed. 'Play dead.'

Reed did so, and as Green Van Man was still sixty or so yards away, he possibly hadn't yet seen the casualty move. But Heck couldn't take that chance.

He backed from the open gate and turned to the alley situated between the fence and the church wall. When he ran that way, he did so at top speed, at the same time drawing his Glock and firing repeatedly. He didn't have a chance of hitting the guy, of course; the point was to draw attention away from Reed.

Which it did.

Heck only saw it peripherally, but the guy dropped to one knee, swivelling from the waist as he opened up again, his stream of lead chopping the fence down one section after another as Heck dashed past it.

'You want this, you bastard!' Heck shouted, holding the rucksack aloft. 'Come and get it!'

When he reached the corner of the church, he halted and looked back.

The gunman had stopped firing and now was running, reloading on the hoof. Instead of heading towards the gate, a route that would have taken him past Reed, he crossed the compound diagonally, intent on penetrating the fence at the point where he'd shot it down. Heck pegged another wild shot at the gunman, causing him to duck, and then dashed around the corner of the church.

Another narrow passage led him forty yards, before he blundered out into open space.

The row of streetlights they'd spotted earlier still looked a considerable distance off, and clearly was on higher ground. Before that lay the vast spread of a demolition site. In the immediate foreground, it was all churned earth and muddy pools, with pieces of heavy plant dotted here and there: JCBs, diggers, bulldozers. Past those, Heck saw houses, though they were little more than empty shells, their roofs just rotted timber skeletons.

He hurried forward anyway, but when feet came clumping down the alley behind, swerved left, slogging along now rather than running, his trainers heavy with clay, half tripping through trenches carved by caterpillar tracks. The cause of these, a particularly large bulldozer, sat just ahead on the right. Heck swung towards it, looking for shelter, automatic fire blasting the ground around his feet, kicking up massive divots.

The night was now filled with police sirens, and yet the gunman was still pressing his attack.

Whatever Heck carried in that rucksack had to be pure gold. He slung it over his shoulder as he slid to a halt behind the bulldozer. He knew he'd only have a moment's respite. It was tempting to draw his Glock, level it two-handed and simply back away. The dozer filled his vision, but as he retreated from it, it would reduce in size, and the gunman would appear either to the left or right. Heck, the readier of the two, would then pump his trigger and keep on pumping until the bastard was down.

And yet, that bastard was also likely to come around the corner blazing.

A Glock 9mm against whatever this monstrous weapon was?

It was no contest.

Heck turned again, running for the nearest houses.

They were only about twenty yards off, and no more than relics, all that remained of some old, forgotten East End neighbourhood. But they had to offer hiding places.

From over his shoulder, he heard a clatter of feet on metal.

He risked another glance.

To his surprise, the maniac wasn't coming around the side of the dozer but had perched on top of its bonnet, eyes no doubt searching the gloom.

Heck drove himself on, trudging through quagmires.

But what lay ahead didn't look promising.

The houses were located in a man-made canyon, with high, industrial-age walls hemming it in to the north and south. At the eastern end, on a high parapet, he again saw that row of streetlights; they were at least fifty feet up – so high that they didn't cast much light into the shadow-filled ruins below, though it was enough to show that what remained of this old housing development was a cul-de-sac.

Heck slid to a stop, looking back one final time.

His pursuer was silhouetted against the London sky. His

weapon still hung by his side, as though he was done using it.

But there was no guarantee of that. It might simply be that the guy had lost track of his prey – so if Heck returned fire now, and missed, which was entirely possible over this distance and in this dimness, he'd be revealing his position again.

He ran on, ducking through the first open door he came to and entering a front room with bare boards underfoot and mildewed strips on the walls. Panting, he moved to the window – and had to narrow his eyes to focus on what he was seeing.

Because Green Van Man, it seemed, had now become Bulldozer Man.

He'd climbed into the cab and bent down, presumably to twist and manipulate the requisite wires under the dash.

With a gut-thumping rumble, the machine shuddered to life. The yellow beacon on its roof began spinning and diesel fumes blasted into the night. Its headlights came on, dazzling in their brilliance, as gears clanked and groaned, shifting it awkwardly back and forth, gradually bringing it around ninety degrees until facing the houses. With an immense roar, its caterpillar tracks commenced rolling, projecting it forward. Noisily and jerkily, but at surprising and increasing speed.

The driver played again with his gears and levers, adjusting the height and angle of the colossal steel blade, tilting it slightly backward, so that its razor teeth jutted forward.

Heck backed across the room, stunned. The madman hadn't lost the trail after all; he'd simply changed weapons to something more appropriate.

Heck ran again, fleeing clean through the house, exiting via an empty frame where the back door used to be and scrambling to the top of a mound of rubble, from where, even in the half-dark, he had a reasonable view of his surroundings. The few houses left here had been constructed in no obvious pattern. What had once been narrow access roads snaked between them, most now churned and broken and clogged with further mountains of bricks and girders.

Though it was even clearer from here that he was in a cul-de-sac, the towering walls of derelict factories to left and right, he knew that his only chance lay in pressing on, putting as many obstacles between himself and the dozer as possible. He scrambled down the other side of the mound and ran along an entry. But when he got through that, he saw that only one building remained. This looked more like a small industrial unit: three storeys high and flat-roofed, with a corrugated metal fence encircling it.

Behind him, the dozer came on, not even slowing as it reached the buildings, their ancient, decayed structures collapsing in front of it. Dust filled the air, masonry cascading as the mighty blade sliced through one obstruction after another. The mechanical beast rose and fell as it ploughed over and through the resulting debris, crushing everything beneath its tracks.

Heck retreated slowly, ejecting his spent magazine, inserting a fresh one and squinting along the barrel of his Glock. But only when the last wall came down, did he realise the true peril of his position. The dozer's blade was at half-mast and angled forward, shielding the front of the driving cab. He pinged shot after shot at the approaching mechanism, trying for its windshield and headlights, but every shell rebounded from the heavy, dirt-encrusted steel.

When he was six shots down and the bulldozer was thirty yards away, there was a grind and clank of gears, and it sped forward at a velocity he'd never known possible.

Heck turned and charged at the corrugated metal fence.

He struck it shoulder-first. It looked flimsy, but it only bowed and didn't collapse. With the bulldozer revving up behind, Heck had only seconds to work out that it was braced on the other side by a horizontal crossbar. He jammed his gun at the relevant point and fired three rapid shots.

The thin metal was smashed through and so was the timber joist.

When he threw himself at it this time, the whole thing fell flat.

Heck tumbled across it, jumped to his feet and, with the mechanical monster filling the entire world at his back, staggered on through the yawning doorway to the old workshop.

The dozer ploughed in after him, its massive blade tilting upward to pummel the brickwork above the door, which fell en masse, the caterpillar tracks carrying it up and over the resulting landslide of wreckage.

Heck backed away as dust engulfed him, his breath wheezing, sweat soaking his aching body. When he entered what had to be the last room and came up against a heavy, square pillar, all he could do was slide around it and continue to retreat, but he knew there'd be no further escape – this workshop had been located at the rear end of the gully. Nothing lay behind it but soil and rock.

When he came to the back of the premises, a bare wall barred further progress.

He flattened himself against it, coughing, his attention fixed on the vast, shadowy goliath as it thundered its way forward into sight, engine roars reverberating, rubble raining on all sides. Almost nonchalantly, its blade struck the pillar, which fractured midway and fell aside as the dozer bullocked past.

With a grinding of chains and cylinders, it adjusted its blade to the vertical, so that its serrated steel teeth were directly in line with Heck's chest. He dropped into a ball and wrapped his arms around his head. The driver lowered his blade, intent on squishing him. Heck screwed his eyes shut . . .

And so didn't see what happened when the ceiling fell in. The pillar so casually flattened had been supporting everything above, which now came down in an all-consuming deluge of bricks, steel and timber.

Even over the engine howl, the earthquake-like cacophony grabbed Heck's attention.

He glanced up, and as the avalanche broke through, scuttled forward under the dozer's blade. There was only two or three feet of clearance, but it was enough.

The guy in the driving cab wasn't so lucky. He too had heard the explosion overhead, but though he brought the vehicle to an immediate halt, he had no time to do anything else – before several tonnes of debris struck the roof of his cab.

Almost five minutes had passed after the fog of dust settled before Heck was able to kick his way out from beneath the dozer's blade. He flat-footed bricks away but had to corkscrew completely around in the small, almost airless space he'd found for himself and grapple manfully with several fallen joists, before he could twist them loose and push them back.

Coated in dust, still coughing hard, he clambered wearily out, dragging the rucksack after him. He straightened up and spent another minute leaning against the now silent machine, which sat crumpled and half-buried beneath a massif of bricks and beams. The blade itself, though tilted at an angle, looked to contain at least a quarter of a tonne of rubble.

The dozer's cab was completely submerged, not just under bricks and masonry but huge slabs of roofing stone. Of the driver, Heck saw only a left arm, broken and bloody, and jammed outward at a grisly angle.

A buzzing sound drew his attention to his pocket. He took his phone out, and saw that he'd missed about twenty calls, all from Gemma. This one, he answered.

'Thank God!' she exclaimed, sounding genuinely relieved. 'Gwen's on her way down there right now.'

'I'll be waiting for her, ma'am.'

'You all right?'

'Think so. Jack's OK too. Or he was when I last saw him. He's going to need an ambulance, though. In fact, we're going to need several ambulances.'

'So . . . what happened? All we heard was there'd been shots fired.'

'There were, yeah.'

'What about the man in the van?'

'He may be useful to us . . .' Heck unbuckled the dust-caked rucksack and found that it was crammed with what looked like documents and photographs. He glanced into the cab. 'But he isn't going to be answering any questions.'

Chapter 32

Heck went straight to East Ham police station for a hot
debrief with Gwen Straker, during the course of which the
chief super put on a brave face at the sight of her battered,
bedraggled detective and adopted a 'purely business' approach.
She advised him that the firearms chief, Renshaw, had been
pronounced dead at the scene, while three other officers, Jack
Reed included, were being treated for gunshot wounds. She
then elicited the facts as he knew them. After that, she left
for the hospital where the casualties were being treated,
leaving Heck with the East Ham duty officer, now acting as
Post Incident Manager.

Professional Standards duly arrived, and the whole Post
Incident Procedure kicked in properly, Heck handing his
weapon over for forensic examination – the 'fast draw' holster
raising one or two eyebrows, but no particularly hostile
comments – and then, after being seen by the FMO, producing
his initial personal statement. As none of the shots he'd fired
were deemed to have injured any person, much less killed
them, no requirement was made for him to hand over his
clothes, and he was ordered to go home and grab some
much-needed sleep.

Heck headed off, but en route, diverted back to Staples Corner, where he intended to log the rucksack and the paperwork it contained into evidence. However, by the time he reached the SCU base, it was already after three in the morning. It felt pointless heading home to Fulham now, when he'd only have to come back here in a few hours' time. They had a rec room attached to the canteen, where there were one or two comfortable armchairs, but, despite being physically exhausted, he knew that sleep wouldn't come easily.

The Serial Crimes Unit was deserted and lay in half-darkness as he wandered around it.

Which was all to the good.

He didn't bother turning the lights on as he rummaged around in the supplies room, finally extricating a forensics examination sheet and a fresh pair of disposable gloves. When he ascended to the MIR, the lights up there had been turned low and it was only manned by a couple of sleepy-looking support staff, but that was two too many, plus the room was in its inevitable state of mid-investigation disorder. Instead of setting up in there and no doubt having to deal with bored questions which he couldn't be bothered answering, he mooched around some of the other offices, and finding that Gemma's was the one with the cleanest desk, he opted for that. Clearing away her PC and keyboard, he gloved up and spread the forensics sheet on the desktop. Inserting each sheet of paperwork from the rucksack into a separate plastic envelope, he laid them out in orderly rows before switching on Gemma's anglepoise lamp and standing back to assess them.

He was clearly more tired than he'd thought, because he couldn't initially make head nor tail of what he was seeing: to his bleary, achy eyes, it was nothing more than a mass of what looked like personal documentation, along with both black-and-white and colour photographs – all that, and a single blue pen drive with a crimson stripe at the point where its lid detached, which had been lying at the very bottom of the rucksack.

But then, after he'd peeled off his anorak, got himself a cup of coffee and looked more closely, certain names began registering, and it became apparent that a number of the photos were blow-ups of official police mugshots.

When he leaned down to examine each separate sheet in close detail, an astonishing tale unfolded, one he'd already suspected awaited them somewhere down the line, but which, when presented like this, in words and pictures, had an enormous impact on him.

He'd gradually been succumbing to bone-deep fatigue, but the intelligence arrayed in front of him had a sharp reviving effect, so much so that he was able to peruse it for at least another couple of hours. But it was only when he plugged the pen drive into Gemma's office laptop and watched the three films uploaded there, that he came fully awake.

'Heck!' Gemma exclaimed wearily. 'What are you doing?'

Heck jerked awake, to find her standing in the doorway to her office, her raincoat draped over one arm, her handbag over the other, sunlight streaming in behind her. He sat up awkwardly, painfully, his bruises from the previous night stiffening. He rubbed at his forehead, which throbbed through lack of proper sleep.

'Sorry, ma'am.' Spotting the clock on the wall, he saw that it was just before seven. 'Didn't seem to be much point in going home last night.'

She bustled in, closing the door behind her. Then she noticed his grubby clothes, his dirty hands and face, his mussed hair; her nostrils wrinkled at his rank, sweaty aroma.

'Couldn't you even have had a shower before you slept in my chair?'

She picked his filthy anorak off the floor and tossed it on top of the filing cabinets.

'I'm afraid not.' He stood up, arched his back and pointed at the table. 'I needed to get stuck into this lot.'

'And what is *that*?' She hadn't noticed the spread of paperwork yet; she was busy looking at something else. 'Why are you wearing a non-issue gun harness?'

'Oh . . .' Heck felt at his armpit; he'd forgotten that he was still wearing the holster. 'It's an American rig. I got it off the internet.'

'Please don't tell me you were wearing that last night?'

'I didn't shoot anyone . . . so it doesn't matter.'

She shook her head as if *this* was too much to process. 'How many rounds did you discharge?'

'A clip and a half.'

'Good God. I take it you're able to account for each one?'

'I gave a full statement to that effect, but I didn't shoot anyone, OK?' He unfastened the harness, wrapped the empty holster in the strap and laid it on the filing cabinets. 'I kind of wish I had done. It would have saved *me* a lot of grief, if no one else.'

Gemma looked at her desk. 'Is this the paperwork you retrieved from Green Van Man?'

He nodded.

'Just to be clear . . . you didn't remove this from the crime scene afterwards?'

'No way. It was in mid-action. I had no choice because there was no guarantee we were going to collar this fella. If he'd got away and he'd taken this with him, we'd be sitting on a big pile of nothing right now.'

'And you're already working on it? Even though you haven't yet been cleared to resume operational duty?'

'So, clear me. You're my commanding officer. If it bothers

you, get in touch with Professional Standards. They seemed happy enough last night.'

She gazed at him for long, non-comprehending moments, wondering how it was that Heck always seemed able to bounce back from potentially devastating experiences on duty with seemingly no ill effects, and secretly suspecting that in actual fact he was just very good at concealing them. It wasn't as if the same viewpoint hadn't been expressed by several other senior officers, including Joe Wullerton.

'Like I say,' he added, 'the bastard in the bulldozer killed himself – I didn't do it. So yes, there'll be other things to deal with, but it's all purely technical.' He scrubbed a grimy hand through his matted hair. 'And frankly, this stuff is more important anyway. In fact, on first viewing, it quickly becomes apparent why that maniac fought to the death to keep it.'

She glanced at the paperwork again, but more, he thought, because she seemed to lack the energy to spar with him. It struck him that Gemma was in a worn-out state too, wearing the same clothes she'd been in the day before, her blonde locks a mess, make-up faded, cheeks sallow. Almost certainly, she'd spent the whole night at Finchley Road, dealing with the prisoners left over from the cinema raid.

'Just wait.' She opened her office door and shouted: 'Anyone going down to the canteen?'

There was no reply, though clearly there were staff around. Heck could hear phones ringing, muffled conversations.

'Bloody great,' she said.

He moved to the door. 'I'll go?'

'Forget it.' She pointed at a chair in the corner; not *her* chair, he noticed. 'You grab another two or three minutes. You look like you need them. Coffee and a bacon barm?'

He couldn't resist smiling. 'That'd be wonderful.'

She left him in the doorway. Torpor crept up on him again. He found himself leaning against the jamb.

'Well, well . . . sounds like you had another adventure last night,' a voice said.

Heck opened his eyes and saw Gail in the corridor, stripping her jacket off.

'Just be glad you weren't there,' he replied.

She eyed him with a cool air. 'I hear Jack Reed got shot in the leg?'

'Yeah. Two rounds. Shattered knee, shattered tibia. Lost pints of blood. If he hadn't used his own belt as a tourniquet, he'd likely have died at the scene.'

Her expression turned neutral. On one hand, it probably struck her that merely having been present at such an event would be stressful for anyone, but on the other, she no doubt reminded herself that this was Heck, who mostly got what he deserved.

'And is Her Ladyship furious with you?' she asked.

'Well . . . she's buying me breakfast.'

'Quite a price to pay to win *that* degree of affection.'

'We'll see how affectionate she is when she comes back up and I lay my latest theory on her.'

'Anything you care to share?'

'Not yet . . . sorry.'

She looked peeved again. 'Why be sorry? It's not like I'm part of it any more.'

'Gail . . .'

'Don't say anything, Heck. Just go and solve the case and be everyone's hero for quarter of an hour . . . before you give her another reason to fall the hell out with you. And if you hear anyone choking to death on the dust between the filing cabinets, don't worry . . . it's only me.'

'Gail!'

But she'd already gone, vanishing into the MIR.

Gemma returned five minutes later, carrying food and drink. She handed Heck his bacon roll, he thanked her and munched ravenously into it. She also ate, leaning back against the door.

'Anything new on the perp?' Heck finally asked, mouth half-full.

'Nothing on him to indicate who he was,' Gemma replied. 'No facial recognition was possible either . . . seeing as he hasn't got a face. We've fingerprinted and DNA-checked him, but there's nothing in the database. We've circulated his details to Interpol, but they haven't got back to us yet.' She took a swig of coffee. 'The gun, by the way, was an FN SCAR assault rifle. Belgian-made, almost never seen off the battlefield.' She gave him an appraising look. 'You're really lucky to be alive.'

'I'd say someone up there likes me, but I've not given Him much cause of late. It's probably because I was close to Jack. Jack's the sort the gods protect.'

'Yeah, well . . .' She scrunched her crumb-filled wrapper into her empty beaker and lobbed them both into the bin. 'It's only because of *you* that Jack's alive.'

'Or because it was too dark for Green Van Man to take proper aim.'

'Jack said you deliberately decoyed the gunman away after he got wounded . . . purposely drew his attention to yourself.'

Heck shrugged as if it didn't matter. 'Reed's a better bloke than I thought he was. But even if he wasn't, one dead copper's always one too many.'

She moved away, tucking the tails of her blouse into her skirt. Producing a mirror and a brush from a drawer, she set up on one of the filing cabinets and tried to do something with her hair.

'Where's Gwen, anyway?' Heck asked.

'She's been with Joe Wullerton since the early hours. He's then going on to NPCC, who'll have reps at this morning's meeting of COBRA at Downing Street.'

'COBRA?'

'Of course.' She eyed him through the mirror. 'Last night's craziness was terror-related, wasn't it?'

This was something they'd agreed the previous night, almost as soon as the dust had settled. Because whatever the real organisation was they'd stumbled onto here, it might not take long for the rest of it, firstly, to note that one of its drivers was missing, and secondly, to link it with the shooting incident that everyone was now talking about – which might lead to a wholesale dismantling of whatever operation was in progress. The only option had been to put out a different but plausible cover story.

'She's also got a last-minute meeting with a certain Superintendent Brakespeare from Operation Trident,' Gemma said.

'Trident?'

'Concerning this nutty gang kid, Spencer Taylor. The one who did the shooting over in Tottenham earlier this month.'

'And?'

'Taylor still hasn't been found. Seems we are now the official go-to people when wanted felons drop out of sight. If only they knew the truth, eh?'

'I hope she told Brakespeare to take a running jump.'

'Most likely, she didn't.' Gemma came back to the desk. 'You know why . . . because right at this moment, Mark, we need friends rather than enemies. Anyway, enough chit-chat. Talk to me.'

Heck did. Outlining his latest thesis for the next half-hour, along with all the reasoning and calculation that had led him to it. Gemma listened in a state of growing incredulity – for once making no interruptions. But it was only when he opened the laptop and played back the first of the three videos that were stored there that she halted proceedings, taking out her phone and making a call.

'Gwen . . . it's me,' she said. 'Just wondering how you're doing and where you're up to? OK . . . excellent. Can you come straight to my office? There's something you could do with hearing. Yeah . . . it's Mark Heckenburg. He has a new theory, well it's an extension of his old one really. Yes. Yeah . . . look . . . I think you should get up here ASAP and hear it for yourself. Yeah . . . OK.'

She cut the call and looked at Heck. 'She'll be here any time.'

Gwen Straker, who'd been in the process of entering the car park when Gemma called, arrived five minutes later. Like Gemma, she too had clearly been up all night, looking uncharacteristically ruffled and saggy-cheeked.

'The official story about Newham is that it's terror-related,' she confirmed, dumping her bag and peeling off her raincoat. 'The whole of that area's been sealed off, and Joe's had NPCC impose the highest level of classification. At present, no one outside Sledgehammer and NPCC knows exactly what happened. How long that'll last is anyone's guess. Counter-Terrorism have an inclination, but they're not asking any questions yet.'

'Won't the casualties and their relatives ask questions?' Heck wondered.

'Everything the wounded officers' relatives have been told is "need to know". With the exception of Jack Reed, the injured lads themselves don't know a great deal. The deceased officer . . . Inspector Jake Renshaw, has no family apart from a daughter in New Zealand, who won't be here for a couple of days.' Gwen finished by eyeballing Heck long and hard. 'That's a lot of favours I'm calling in, Mark . . . I sincerely hope this new lead you've allegedly got is workable.'

He shrugged. 'Ma'am . . . in criminal investigation, we can only follow the evidence.'

'Don't lecture me, just give me the good stuff.'

'And, personally . . .' he swept his hand over the table, 'I've never been handed a wad of evidence quite like this. In case you were wondering, Green Van Man was carting this around in a rucksack. When I snatched it off him, that's when he came after us. Me and Reed, I mean . . . instead of making a run for it. When I realised this mattered to him, I decided that there was no way in hell he was getting it back.'

Gwen pulled on a pair of disposable gloves and leaned down to examine the paperwork. The bulk of it comprised individual typed sheets. In each case, there was a name at the top in capitals and a mugshot in the top right corner. She recognised several of those names and faces immediately. One sheet belonged to Eddie Creeley, for example, another to Leonard Spate, another to Christopher Brenner, another to Terry Godley.

'You'll note that there's personal info on each of these sheets,' Heck said.

Gwen nodded, observing that in each case, as well as the mugshot and name, there was a physical description, including hair colour, distinguishing marks, even body shape and esti-mated weight. There was also, on the bottom, a time and date, and underneath that, a postcode.

'You were on the money about where most of our suspects have gone,' she said.

Heck shrugged. 'No surprise to me.'

She gave him a half-irritated glance.

'You don't need to count them,' he said. 'Of the twenty names on our Most Wanted list, fourteen are here. In all cases, the places where they were picked up correspond roughly with the geographic locations we were investigating.'

She glanced round at him. 'What do you mean . . . picked up?'

'Ma'am, I think these postcodes represent the locations where our fugitives were collected by Green Van Man.

Voluntarily, of course. They probably thought they were being spirited off to some safe haven overseas. But, in reality, he was delivering them to a nastier fate.'

She pondered this.

'There are thirty-eight personal info sheets here in total,' Heck said. 'As I say, fourteen of the names featured on them were on our list. But a quick skim through will show that the rest of them were bad eggs too. Look at this one . . . Byron Jervis, remember him?'

'The name's familiar.'

'Murdered a little girl he'd abducted from a back garden in Blackpool.'

'I remember him now,' she said. 'That was several years ago, though.'

'These files date back about six months,' Heck said, 'but all these guys are fugitives who've been on the run for a while.' He picked another up. 'Gavin Fortescue wasn't on our list either, but he battered to death a mentally ill man after luring him out onto some wasteland in South Yorkshire.'

'Yes, I remember.' Gwen shook her head. 'It's not like these fellas are any actual loss, is it?'

'No, it isn't, ma'am,' Heck agreed. 'And I'll state for the record that I've no interest in their welfare. The fact that the majority of their violent deaths are probably recorded on the various pen drives we took from that cinema in Putney doesn't upset me in the least. But we have a specialist police unit to preserve.'

She nodded thoughtfully.

'I'd draw your attention to something else,' he said. 'And this is the bit where DSU Piper rang to make sure you were coming in. Because, if you think these revelations have been tough to swallow . . . wait till you hear this one.' He picked up a bunch of grainy black-and-white photographs. 'See anything familiar?'

Gwen assessed the first image. It had clearly been taken at night, with a night-vision camera. It depicted a man leaning in through the open window of a vehicle, with a large envelope in hand. He had a mat of flaxen-blond hair, and lean, hawkish features comprising a narrow jaw, high cheekbones and a hooked nose.

'I . . . isn't that Ray Marciano?' Gwen said.

'Correct,' Heck replied. 'You knew him?'

'Not well. But I worked with him a couple of times.'

'Formerly a DI with the Flying Squad,' Heck said. 'Famous for his white-blond hair. Oddly enough, one of our vanished villains, John Stroud up in Shropshire, was seen by a witness talking to an unidentified blond-haired guy shortly before he disappeared.'

'Ray Marciano,' Gwen said slowly, clearly unable to process it.

'Highly decorated officer,' Gemma reminded her.

'And yet, despite that,' Heck said, 'he resigned last February . . . just around the time our wanted-persons files date back to. Went to work for a noted defence lawyer.'

'Heck . . .' Gwen's face was suddenly like stone, 'what exactly am I looking at here?'

'You can see that this is a kind of clandestine meeting?'

'No . . . all I can see is Ray Marciano at a vehicle window.'

'OK, look at this one.' Heck offered her another pic, in which Marciano was handing the envelope through the window, putting it into the grasp of an unseen person.

'And this one.' The next pic showed the envelope being opened, presumably by whoever in the vehicle had received it, and a document in the process of being extricated.

'Lo and behold,' Heck said, offering her the final pic from the series, a close-up of the document itself, which displayed a recognisable name and face, 'it's one of our twenty Most Wanted. This one is Henry Alfonso from Canning Town. You may recollect, ma'am, he robbed houses all over North London by breaking in late at night, wearing a ski mask and wielding a butcher's knife. Of course, if he ever found a woman living there alone, he raped her. You've got to give Ray Marciano credit . . . he only chose the cream of the crop.'

'Stop right there!' Gwen said. 'This means nothing. This series of photographs could have been cobbled together any time. They might be completely unconnected to each other.'

'They could, ma'am,' he agreed. 'But they're not actually photographs. They're image-grabs.' He indicated the pen drive. 'From some of the footage on here. It contains three short films in total . . . on each occasion, it's a different late-night meeting between Green Van Man and Ray Marciano. And on each occasion Ray gives our pal an unmarked envelope. A bit like these . . .' He pointed to three brown paper envelopes sitting in separate plastic folders.

'Those are some of the original envelopes?' Gwen asked.

'They were in the rucksack with everything else,' Heck said. 'Anyway, no words are exchanged during these secretly filmed meetings . . .'

'How do we know they were secretly filmed?'

'Watch them, ma'am. The camera, which was probably Green Van Man's phone, is covertly placed on the back of the seat behind him. He only takes it down to get clean shots of the envelopes and their contents after Ray has gone. Needless to say, in each case, the envelope contains another of these wanted-persons sheets.'

Neither of the two women spoke.

'It's unpalatable, I know,' he said, 'but to me it's proof that Ray Marciano is involved in this. Most likely, he tracks the targets down. He's the ace investigator, after all. He then makes some kind of arrangement with them – as I say, they think they're off to safety, probably at some considerable expense – and then Ray informs Green Van Man where and when he can pick them up. They get into the van, which is armoured like a bloody tank. Once they're in, there's probably no way out.'

There was a prolonged silence while Gwen pondered everything she'd been told.

'You're seriously suggesting that Ray Marciano—'

'We should also consider that Morgan Robbins could be involved,' Heck interrupted.

This time Gwen looked genuinely, seriously shocked. 'Morgan Robbins the solicitor!'

'Ray works for him.' Heck pointed to another of the photos. This one had been taken during daytime hours, on a busy street. It showed Marciano deep in conversation with Robbins himself, a tall, regal-looking chap with a shock of white hair and huge white eyebrows, wearing a stylish suit.

Gwen shook her head. 'Like you said . . . they work together. Green Van Man could simply have taken this picture near the entrance to Robbins's office just to try and implicate him.'

'The third video on the pen drive was taken in a London pub somewhere,' Heck said. 'It's only half a minute long, but it shows Ray Marciano and Morgan Robbins on the other side of the table.'

'You can't tell what they're saying,' Gemma chipped in. 'The sound quality's poor, but at least it proves that both of those guys together were at a meeting with Green Van Man.'

But the SIO still looked unimpressed.

'Ma'am,' Heck said, 'we can check this easily enough. We just need to do some forensic work on these documents. I'd like to guess that they perfectly match whole batches of stationery that are sitting on the shelves in Morgan Robbins's office right now. I bet they've been handled by all kinds of his people – probably innocently in most cases – but there're bound to be fingerprints. We might even get DNA from the envelopes . . .'

'Heck, stop!' Gwen raised a hand. 'There is way too much *betting* going on here.'

'It's not like it doesn't add up,' Gemma said. 'Morgan Robbins was a prosecutor for years and years. He dealt with some of the worst of the worst. He probably lost plenty of important cases that left him deeply frustrated.'

'And that's given him an abiding hatred of criminals?' Gwen sounded more than a little sceptical. 'If so, how come he's now a defender?'

'We all get pigged off with the system, ma'am,' Heck said. 'Perhaps he decided one day that it wasn't worth worrying about any more and that he'd take the big money instead. That decision would have been made easier if at the same time he'd found another way to punish these villains . . .'

'For heaven's sake, Heck!' Gwen exploded. 'Think about what you're saying . . . that Morgan Robbins and Ray Marciano have formed some kind of vigilante ring, kidnapping and killing wanted criminals? And that Green Van Man is their partner? If that's the case, why has Green Van Man taken these pictures and videos? Why was he carrying them round with him? Like you said, it's a treasure trove of evidence. If he got pulled over for a simple traffic stop, the whole operation could have gone down the plughole.'

Heck mused. 'All I can think is that he kept it as a kind of insurance.'

'You mean against prosecution?' Gwen snorted with contempt. 'If he gets pinched, he offers us all this? If that was his plan, it wouldn't make much sense for him to then resist us with deadly force.'

'When I say insurance . . . I mean against his own people. Consider the possibility, ma'am, that these filmed gladiatorial combats were never intended for public consumption.

Remember Green Van Man's threat to kill the Friths if they put the movies online? Isn't online the obvious place to display your wares if you want to make real money? The Dark Web would be perfect for this.'

Gwen regarded him dubiously but continued to listen.

'Clearly, this was *never* intended to be a form of underground entertainment.'

'But he *was* selling them,' Gemma said, one of her own doubts finally surfacing.

'Yes,' Heck agreed. 'Because he'd broken ranks.'

'Trying to make some money on the side, you mean?' Gwen said.

'Yeah,' Heck replied, 'and keeping all this documentation was a shield against punishment if his bosses ever found out.'

'You mean he'd just threaten to drop them in it?'

'Yeah, but only if he had to. He was on a good number, selling to the Friths – but he didn't want it to go further than that, to reduce the chance of word getting back.'

Gwen kneaded her forehead. 'So much of this is pure conjecture.'

'With respect, ma'am, I disagree,' Heck said. 'Look what we've got. Photographs and descriptions of the targets. If they correspond with the deaths captured on film . . .'

'Which we haven't confirmed yet, because we haven't had a chance to peruse all the contents of the pen drives seized from the Friths,' Gemma said, 'but the chances are that they will.'

'We've even got the postcodes where they were picked up,' Heck added.

'Ah, yes . . . where Ray Marciano set them up like ducks in a row.' Gwen's face clouded with doubt again. 'After he'd tracked them all down. Seriously, Heck . . . Ray Marciano may have been a good detective with lots of contacts, but are you trying to tell me that, completely alone, he managed to get somewhere the whole of Operation Sledgehammer couldn't?'

'Ma'am, we've been on the case less than three weeks. Ray went to go and work for Morgan Robbins six months ago. He could have been doing the spadework a lot longer than that. Either way, he's had a bit of a head start.'

She sighed long and hard, before something else on the desk caught her attention. It was a set of three photos that Heck hadn't bothered to show her.

'What's this supposed to be?' she asked.

Each image took a slightly different angle on a large, Gothic structure. A building of sorts, though at first glance it was all turrets and pinnacles, much of it clad in scaffolding.

'That . . . I have no idea,' Heck admitted.

The images had been taken on super-zoom and displayed only the building's arcane architectural features, catching none of the encircling landscape, so there was no real context or reference.

'I suppose it must be relevant,' he said. 'It may even be where the fights are taking place. We'll need to pin down exactly what and where it is, though initially I'd suggest we have bigger fish to fry.'

'Well, you're right about that, at least . . .' Gwen stood with hands on hips. 'Look . . . I appreciate the work you've put in here. And yes, I *do* think that all this bears further investigation. But . . . I'm afraid it's way out of our league.'

Heck glanced at Gemma, who returned his gaze blankly, as if she was thinking the same.

'Come again?' he said.

'It's the Morgan Robbins factor that worries me most,' Gwen said.

'I admit there's no smoking gun where he's concerned . . .'

'Pictures of him talking to Ray Marciano are worthless, Heck.'

'What about the video taken in the pub?'

'That's intriguing, but Robbins could argue that was legit too . . . especially with no Green Van Man around to refute it.'

'Ma'am!' Heck pleaded. 'Why would Ray Marciano be doing all this on his own? It's a hell of a lot of legwork for him.'

Gemma interjected again, 'You were right, Heck, when you said that it's probably costing these crims a lot of money . . . but maybe that's the whole thing? They thought they were buying safe passage out of the country, but in reality, Ray and Green Van Man were pocketing the cash and then killing them. I can buy that easily, but that doesn't prove that Morgan Robbins is involved.'

'They're not just killing them,' Heck said. 'Why go to all the trouble of setting up this gladiatorial thing? Is it even possible that two men alone could do that? It feels bigger to me.'

'I agree,' Gwen said, rather to his surprise. 'And Ray works for Morgan Robbins, and we've got the video of them meeting Green Van Man, and we may well lift some DNA profiles from all this stuff which will implicate staff at his office, and sometimes two and two do indeed make four. But think about it, Heck . . . if we seriously suspect that Morgan Robbins, who heads one of the most prestigious law firms in London, is organising the abduction and murder by glad-iatorial combat of numerous wanted criminals, we'd better be one hundred per cent sure of our facts before we move on it. And . . .' she gestured at the desktop, 'in that regard, this is nothing like enough.'

'No arguments there,' he said. 'We need to do a lot more digging.'

'Someone does,' she replied. 'As I say . . . not *us*.'

He regarded her solemnly.

'Don't look so worried,' she said. 'I'll admit to being sceptical about some of this, but there's enough here for me to take to NPCC.'

'NPCC. Ma'am, you're not serious?'

'Heck . . . *we* can't deal with it, OK? Operation Sledgehammer has been badly sidetracked as it is.'

'But this *is* part of Sledgehammer.'

'Only inasmuch as it's led us to several of the fugitives,' she said. 'Or to what we think was the fate of several of the fugitives . . .'

'*Fourteen*, ma'am,' he argued. 'Hardly several.'

'Even if that proves to be the case, we'd still have several outstanding. And it's *our* job to catch them.'

She moved to the door as if that was all that needed to be said.

'So, what happens when you go to NPCC?' Heck asked. 'Won't they just authorise the formation of a completely new task force?'

'Hopefully.' Gwen tried to smile. 'Look, you've done a good job, Heck. Our contribution won't go unmentioned.'

'I'm more worried about how long all this is going to take. I mean, the top floor don't exactly rush about, do they!'

'I'm well aware that we need to expedite this thing.'

'If we don't, we risk losing everything we've fucking got.'

'*All right!*' Gwen's expression hardened. '*Mind your bloody tone, Sergeant!* I know exactly how urgent this is, because *I'm* the one who's told the world a bare-faced lie that last night was a terrorist incident. *I'm* the one who's going to cop it first if this thing goes belly-up.' She glanced from Heck to Gemma, then back to Heck. 'I'll ring Joe now and try for another meeting with NPCC today. Assuming that's OK with *you*?'

His mouth twisted shut with frustration, but he said nothing else.

She left the office, banging the door behind her.

'You know,' Gemma said, 'most detectives would be happy *not* to get involved in a case where the main suspects are part of the country's "Magic Circle" of legal eagles. This has got the air of being more than a minor ball-acher.'

He slumped back into the chair. 'I thought you were onside.'

'It's not about being onside. Gwen's right. We can't push things any further on our own.'

'Especially if we don't try.'

'She's trying now. Hey . . . do *you* want to be the one to face that bunch of bureaucrats on the top floor? I wonder how far you'd get.'

Heck couldn't help sulking, but everything Gemma said was correct. This vigilante business, and now the potential involvement of a very big fish like Morgan Robbins, was likely to swamp Operation Sledgehammer. The two cases were connected, but one was threatening to become so much more massive than the other that it was already destabilising the enquiry. Not that this made him feel better.

'And I want to thank you again,' Gemma added, 'for what you did for Jack Reed.'

'You've already thanked me for that. Why do it twice?'

'Because you've been on your game this last day or so. And, sometimes . . . well, maybe you don't get enough slaps on the back.'

'Ouch.' He rubbed his left shoulder. 'That was some slap.'

'All right . . . as you're determined not to let me be nice to you . . .' Brusquely, she handed him a pile of forms bound with elastic bands, 'take these, please.'

'OK, I'm sorry, I'm sorry . . .' He held up a hand for peace. 'I just . . . I . . .'

He was too dog-tired even to articulate himself, he realised, or to rein it in when he ought to. *You can't keep doing this,* he told himself. *Getting pissed off with her won't help. What do you expect: hugs and kisses for doing your damn job?*

'It's just that . . .' he made a hapless gesture, 'the only thing I've got to offer is . . . *this.* Going with leads and making scores, I mean.'

She regarded him stonily.

'I want to get a result here,' he said. 'For all the reasons you already know. I *must* get a result. But . . . given what it's taking to do that . . .' he couldn't resist a chuckle, 'I'm not getting much back, am I?' He shook his head. 'Seriously, ma'am . . . I'm sorry.'

'Does this not illustrate to you, Mark,' she said, 'how truly ill-advised it is to allow one's love life and one's working life to become entangled, especially in this job?'

He couldn't answer.

'What did we say only yesterday about professionalism?'

This time he didn't bother answering; the question was rhetorical.

'Look, you've not exactly been an exemplary officer during the *whole* of this case,' she said, 'but you were hot stuff when it mattered, and as such, you've brought a significant part of it to a kind of conclusion. And once again, whether you accept it or not, thank you for saving Jack Reed's life. And as I said,' she indicated the elastic-banded documents, 'these are now your responsibility.'

Heck looked down and saw that they were photocopied notes relating to the pursuit of prostitute-strangler, Malcolm Kaye, in Liverpool.

After everything else, this felt like the ultimate kick in the nuts.

'I'm being reassigned?'

'Only in a couple of days. I'm clearing you to resume duty, as you requested, but you've been involved in a police shooting incident, so, even if it's only technical in your case, you *will* be needed for further post-incident enquiries. As such, stay put at the office and familiarise yourself with the Merseyside enquiry. As soon as everything's sorted here, you can high-tail it up there and assist Charlie Finnegan. You won't need me to point out that Malcolm Kaye's name is not in the paperwork we got from Green Van Man . . . so there's no reason to assume that he's not still at liberty.'

'There's definitely no one else who can go?'

'No. I'm sorry, Heck, but I've got to juggle the few resources available.'

'Gemma . . . we can cross fourteen names off that Most Wanted list. With Reed's pinch, there're only five left. That frees up a lot of people.'

'Like Gwen said, we've yet to establish the facts surrounding those fourteen names. And when we do, everyone who gets freed up will be reassigned just as you've been. One by one, we'll be able to strengthen each enquiry. Do you really have a problem with that?'

'My only problem is that if we're intent on dragging the top floor into this, nothing's going to happen quickly enough. You know that as well as I do.'

'Heck, there are procedures, OK? I know that's an alien concept for you, but when you're dealing with someone like Morgan Robbins, who knows more legal tricks and turns than the whole of the Met put together, you don't go stamping all over it with your size elevens.'

Realising there was no point arguing further, he trudged to the door.

'Take the rest of the day off,' she said. 'You've earned some sack time, if nothing else. Report back here tomorrow. You can work a nine-till-five.'

He made no reply as he opened the door.

'Look . . . it may be that NPCC decide to bring us back

in at some level. They may even decide we should take point on it, but until then we've got other stuff to deal with.'

'I hear all that, but . . .' he held up his photocopies, 'this feels like a punishment?'

'Don't be a child, Heck. It doesn't suit you.'

'The Liverpool enquiry's getting nowhere.'

'Maybe that's why I'm sending *you*.'

'And Charlie Finnegan's the biggest slimeball in the whole of National Crime Group.'

'Perhaps you can teach him the error of his ways by demonstrating the error of yours.'

She met his gaze boldly, daring him to respond further.

He didn't bother. Yet again, the die was cast.

Heck left the building, fully intending to head back to his flat in Fulham, to get some sleep. But by the time he'd got there, having first collected his Megane, a new idea had started niggling away at him . . . which, given that he wasn't officially back on duty until tomorrow morning, he had time to explore.

But only if he moved extra quickly.

Chapter 33

Heck was home long enough to grab a shower and a shave and to don some clean clothes. After that, he threw some trainers and a fresh set of scruffs into his grab-bag – just in case – chucked the bag into the boot of his Megane and hit the road again, heading back to the North Circular, which he joined at approximately 11:00 a.m.

By the time he'd arrived in Newham, it was just past noon, though from here on his progress slowed. The streets surrounding the lorry park were all closed. He couldn't even use the slip road to exit the North Circular at that point, as it was bollarded off with cones and *Police Incident* notices, so he pressed on south for another mile before diverting and having to negotiate his way back through residential estates. That way too, he encountered problems, several side streets adjoining the lorry park sealed with incident tape and guarded by constables or bottled up with press vans.

He made use of his warrant card, but though that got him through the outer cordon, he was restricted to travelling on foot the rest of the way. Walking down the ramp into the lorry park itself, having to show his ID at yet another checkpoint, he was struck by how different the place felt in daylight, with significant numbers of police personnel on site. The majority of the lorry park had been fenced off with yet more incident tape, though a small area on the railway side had been turned into an officially designated investigation team parking area, much of which was already occupied by divisional cars, CSI vans and photographic units.

Heck had only just arrived there when he had to step aside to allow a hearse to pull out. There was no fanfare or ceremony, though one or two of the watching uniforms had removed their helmets. The only assumption could be that these were the last mortal remains of Inspector Jake Renshaw. Heck watched the car glide past with the usual indifference he tried to affect when it came to cop killings. You really couldn't afford to let it get to you, though that was always easier said than done.

As he stood there, his phone buzzed in his pocket, indicating that he'd received an email. When he checked, it was from Gemma:

Professional standards remind you that a full statement is still required. You may want to confer with Jack to get the facts right on that, under their supervision of course. Neither of you fired a fatal shot, so it's only a formality. But it's got to happen. As supervisory officer on the scene, Jack has already claimed full responsibility for taking you forward into an unofficial support role with the firearms team. Joe Wullerton wants to see you too. No need to panic on that. Just checking you've taken the requisite legal advice. He also intends to send you for counselling, but you can fit that round your regular duties.

Heck wasn't surprised that Reed was ready to take the rap. It was the kind of holier-than-thou crap he specialised in pulling. There was no denying that it helped, though; it would certainly mean that Heck would have less difficult questions to answer than otherwise.

With the undertakers' vehicle clear, he flashed his warrant card and was passed under the next cordon. As he walked across the lorry park towards the flyover, he saw that most of the area underneath it was now screened off. Access to that zone was only possible through a forensics tent, at the front of which a burly bobby made Heck sign the official crime scene log. Inside, he took a clean Tyvek suit from its cellophane wrap, climbed into it and pulled on a pair of disposable gloves and shoes.

From here, Heck entered the area under the flyover via a path laid with raised forensic boards. It led through various taped-off areas in which glaring arc-lights, low conversation and repeated camera flashes revealed that plenty of evidence-gathering was still in progress. In fact, there were so many live crime scenes here now that the pathway divided several times, and temporary signposts had been erected – which was useful as, in daylight, Heck couldn't easily find his way back to the green van.

When he got there, as it was the actual scene of a police murder, it was doubly cordoned off and surrounded by evidence flags, each one marking a spent bullet casing.

The van itself, its nearside tyres hanging in rags from where Heck had shot them, was still front-on to the immense concrete pillar. It was in a filthy state, covered in dents where repeated gunfire had hit it – though, noticeably, none of the slugs had penetrated – and spattered up its nearside flank with gobbets of drying blood.

Only one CSI was currently present, a young Indian woman, also clad neck-to-foot in Tyvek. She hadn't initially noticed Heck and was standing inside the inner cordon, carefully photographing items laid out along the top of a white plastic trestle table.

'Looks like an ordinary van from the outside, doesn't it?' Heck said conversationally.

The CSI looked around. Her name tag said that she was Sumitra Bharti and advised that she was the Crime Scene Manager.

'But check it inside, and I suspect you'd be surprised,' he added. 'Anyone riding in this thing's on a one-way trip.'

'And who might you be?' she asked.

'Oh, sorry . . . DS Heckenburg.' He showed his warrant card. 'Serial Crimes Unit. Currently with Operation Sledgehammer.'

'Oh . . .' She evidently recognised his name. 'You were one of the officers who . . .?'

'Yes, I'm afraid I was.'

'I'm surprised you're back here so soon. Sounded like a bad night in Raqqa.'

'I've not known many worse,' he admitted, still fixated on the erratic spatters of blood. 'I didn't know Inspector Renshaw very well, but . . . he was going back to help one of his injured lads when he got shot. He didn't need to do that. I mean, I think he probably made mistakes in his deployment, but you couldn't knock his concern.'

'If you were involved in this incident . . .' Bharti said cautiously, 'shouldn't you be at home?'

'Not these days. We don't automatically get suspended any more.'

'But I don't think you should be here, should you?'

He turned to face her. 'That's a matter of opinion, to be honest.' Heck was on dodgy ground, and he knew it, but it wasn't as if he was being investigated himself, and until a new task force was put together – which they simply didn't

347

have time to wait for – this was still his case. 'I've got some-thing to check that's been bugging me all night . . .'

She still seemed uncertain. 'How can I help?'

'Have you examined this vehicle internally yet?'

'Only to give it a cursory once-over. We've only just moved the officer's body.'

He nodded. 'I understand.'

'We've not been in with the hoovers and tweezers yet.'

'No, but when you glanced in there, did you see anything unusual?'

'You mean apart from the fact it's like a mobile five-star prison? It's heavily armoured, which you're obviously already aware of. There's no way to open the rear compartment from the inside, but it's very comfortable. Insulated, so it's probably warm in winter. Carpeted.'

'Carpeted?'

'Richly. There's even a comfy chair.'

That settled it, Heck thought. This van was how they'd been transporting the poor bastards after they'd lured them inside with false promises. He stood with hands on hips, regarding the wreck.

'So . . . is that it?' Bharti wondered.

'Not quite. I realise you haven't done a full internal yet, but . . . there isn't a satellite-navigation system, by any chance?'

'That, I *can* help you with.' She turned to the forensics table. 'It's over here. It was probably fitted to the inside of the windscreen. Fell out of the van when the windscreen was dislodged on impact with the pillar.'

Heck felt pinpricks of excitement as he gazed down at the small device; it was dusty but undamaged, its disconnected power-cable hanging over the table's edge like a tail.

'Does it still work?' he asked.

'I honestly don't know.'

'Can we try?' He dug his pocketbook out. 'There're a couple of things I'd really like to check.'

'DS . . . Heckenburg?'

'Yeah?'

'This feels a bit irregular to me.'

He glanced across the tape at her. She was watching him worriedly.

'It's nothing to be concerned about,' he assured her. 'This may be an important lead, but likewise it may go nowhere. But the sooner we know, the better.'

'Well . . .' She still seemed uneasy but turned, took a pencil from her pocket and, using the blunt end, depressed the satnav's power switch. It immediately came to life.

'All I need is recent destinations,' Heck said.

She tapped a couple of times on the touchscreen and a list of postcodes emerged. Even craning his neck, Heck wasn't in a position where he could see them properly.

'Can you read them out?' he said, checking his pocketbook and the list of postcodes he'd copied from the wanted-persons documents.

Bharti began to read, working her way down. The first one he didn't recognise, but he made a note of it anyway. However, the next three were all familiar, corresponding with the top three already written in his pocketbook. They were the locations where Eddie Creeley, Leonard Spate and Ronald Ricketson had allegedly been abducted, in Humberside, Cumbria and North Wales respectively.

Despite himself, Heck leaned forward to try and see more.

'Sorry, Sergeant . . . but you need to stay on that side of the tape.'

'I will, I promise . . . but we need more. Can you scroll down a bit?'

She did so, reading out additional postcodes, the next two

of which related to the abductions of Terry Godley and Christopher Brenner.

'Any more?' he asked.

'I'm not sure how much juice there is left,' she said, but she did as he asked.

Another three postcodes appeared. Again, the first of these was not on his list. Heck wrote it down anyway. But the next one married up with the paperwork on wife and mother poisoner, Jerry Brixham, and the next with underworld contract killer, Peter Freeman, both of whom had also been on the Most Wanted list.

This was falling into place more neatly than Heck could have imagined. He could just picture Ray Marciano handing over those documents, which he'd prepared himself, having located and made contact with the fugitives, and then Green Van Man collecting the unwitting victims from specified locations, using postcodes and his trusty satnav.

'The battery icon's now on red,' Bharti said, interrupting his thoughts. 'I'd say this thing's about to die.'

'That's OK . . . thanks very much for this.'

Heck backed away from the tape and glanced down his list. He wasn't sure exactly how much he'd learned here. All it had really done, in truth, was confirm his theory that Green Van Man had visited the locations on the paperwork, in each case – *presumably* – to collect his unsuspecting cargo. Also 'presumably', when the CSIs got inside the van properly, especially into the back of it, they ought to be able to uncover minute traces of everyone who'd travelled. That would be the final proof.

But, of course, that would take time, which was in short supply.

He analysed his list again.

It wasn't impossible that the postcodes he didn't recognise could be equally useful. The area code on the top one looked like a London address; there was nothing hugely suspicious about that. Anyone living in London and driving around on a day-to-day basis would probably need use of a satnav. But the second one, he was less familiar with. He quickly dug his iPhone out and tapped it in.

It referred to a location in Cornwall.

Heck felt another prickle of interest.

As far as he knew, no one on the Most Wanted list had any connection with Cornwall. And that had to be good news, because from the beginning this had never simply been an exercise in seeking to marry up locations on the satnav with names in his pocketbook . . . but in looking out for possible locations where Green Van Man might have taken those names to.

'You suddenly seem energised,' Sumitra Bharti said.

Heck tucked his phone and pocketbook away. 'You've given me a new lead, that's why.'

'That's what we're here for.'

'Are there still items inside the vehicle . . . I mean, of evidential value?'

'As I say, we haven't swept the interior yet. We only got the satnav because it was thrown out during the crash.'

'You've looked, though?'

'Sure . . . there're a few bits and pieces in the cab.'

'Such as?'

'Most of it's probably trash. Paper cups, a hamburger carton, that kind of thing. There's a pistol, of course . . . which you probably know about. Some bullet casings. A bit of paperwork.'

'How long will it take to assess all that stuff?'

'It'll be later on today. Once we've logged and photographed everything, we'll email the images to your exhibits officer. Probably by this evening. We'll be working through the night, so certainly before tomorrow.'

Heck chewed his lip. 'Can you do me a favour, Sumitra . . . can you copy me in on every image you send? I mean, *me* personally?'

'That's not normal procedure.'

'Maybe not, but there's no reason why you can't, is there? I'm part of the enquiry.'

'I suppose not.'

'It's just that I'm likely to be away from the office for a few hours, and I'd like to keep abreast of everything while I'm on the road.'

'I'll have to record that I'm doing that, of course.'

'Of course.' Heck gave her his email address and thanked her profusely as she noted it.

As he made his way back along the boardwalk, he had a spring in his stride, though he wasn't entirely sure why. These weren't leaps and bounds forward. But a new line of enquiry was always to be welcomed, especially when time was as short as this.

He thought about Gemma's last email.

Another chat with good old Professional Standards. Then some psych counselling.

Or, alternatively, a quick spin down to the most scenic corner of the UK?

It wasn't a real question, when you considered it – as much as a total no-brainer.

Chapter 34

Like most Brits, Heck mainly knew Cornwall as somewhere to go for a break.

It wasn't all idyllic and it had its fair share of crime, even murder, but a *lot* of it was idyllic; in truth, the whole of the West Country was famous for its pastoral ambience and picturesque villages where placid ways of life ambled on regardless of other events in the world. Even now, processing slowly into its heart via the clogged artery that was the M4, he was encircled by acres of verdant countryside, which, drenched gold in the August sun and dotted with harvesters and hay bales, seemed almost quintessentially English.

Not that this lessened the frustration of constant slowdowns and standing traffic.

At 6:30 p.m., sluggish from lack of sleep, he left the motorway south of Exeter, eventually stopping for a couple of cans of Red Bull at a café on the edge of Dartmoor.

Heck was vaguely aware, as he walked across the café car park, that all was suddenly quiet, that wild scenery loomed ahead and a colossal sky arched above, fast turning lilac as evening drew on, but briefly he had other priorities.

The two energy drinks had an adequately reviving effect, but even then he felt grotty.

He glanced around the small eatery. Everyone seemed friendly enough, but there were many times out and about on SCU business when he'd have given a lot for a familiar face, especially after being on the go for hours, after getting shot at and being chased by a bulldozer for Christ's sake, and especially after being told he'd done the hard stuff, so now it was time for someone else to waltz in and do the easy bit (and take the credit of course).

But that was the job all over. Heck had learned that soon after signing up, and he hadn't gone anywhere else, so he could hardly complain.

'I never complain,' he told himself as he traipsed back across the car park to his Megane.

Though that, of course, was a lie – as Gemma would attest.

'Darling Gemma . . . the stuff I do to be part of *your* world.'

On reflection, while driving out of Moretonhampstead, some 250 miles from his start point that lunchtime, even Heck couldn't believe just how much effort he was putting in here.

A minor road, the B3212, now lay ahead, cutting through the very middle of the expansive, grassy wilderness that was Dartmoor itself. Heck had consciously opted for this lesser-known route because he'd hoped there'd be fewer vehicles on it than on the A30 to Launceston, but this was hill-farming country, its various hamlets connected only by the narrowest, most meandering lanes, and a couple of times he had to negotiate tractors and flocks of sheep.

All the way, he pondered St Ronan on Cornwall's north coast, a minor village located midway between Port Isaac and Tintagel Head. This, it seemed, was the location of the postcode he was tracking towards.

Specifically, it belonged to Abbot's Walk, St Ronan's seafront road. Having checked the details before setting out, it was no more than a fishing village, with only a minimal tourist industry. Its population was roughly six hundred, which was low even by Cornish standards. When he'd made a search on SCUA (real name 'SCU Advisory'), the name didn't crop up at all, which indicated that, not only was it not the subject of any serious ongoing criminal investigation, it most likely never had been.

Hoping to God that he wasn't on a wild goose chase, Heck drove on, crossing the border between Devon and Cornwall just before 7:30 p.m., a green wilderness now unfolding on all sides of him, its distant horizons topped with tors or the sentinel relics of tin mines. He followed the A395 as far as he could, and, from here, a network of empty lanes ascended to a ridge where a weathered Celtic cross stood by the roadside, before descending again, bringing him finally to a dramatic coastal vista, the sheer cliffs of countless headlands plunging precipitously into foaming, cerulean seas.

He reached St Ronan earlier than he'd anticipated, shortly after 8 p.m.

The village was every bit as quaint as he'd expected, mainly comprising whitewashed cottages with pantiled roofs and flower-filled window baskets and built higgledy-piggledy down its own coombe to the water's edge, where a stone quay curved outward like a bow, entrapping a small harbour filled with leisure craft.

From the moment Heck arrived, the restful atmosphere might have made him feel that his worst fears were true and that Green Van Man had loved this place simply for what it was – if it hadn't been for the island. He caught sight of this as soon as he crested the top of the coombe, and it almost caused him to crash. He actually had to pull his

355

Megane up by the verge so that he could climb out and have a proper look.

Directly northwest of the village, perhaps half a mile offshore, there was a hummock of land. It boasted a horseshoe of diminutive buildings around a small harbour of its own, but further inland it was dominated by a much more massive structure, possibly an old baronial hall of some sort. It may even have dated from medieval times, as its highest point was a central, flat-topped tower with what looked like genuine battlements.

There might have been some doubt in Heck's mind that he was looking at the same Gothic building that featured in those unexplained photos taken from Green Van Man's rucksack – were it not for the scaffolding, which even from this distance, clad considerable portions of the edifice.

His destination, Abbot's Walk, was a small promenade of nautically themed shops and pubs running along the seafront. When Heck got down there, it was dotted with strolling couples enjoying a balmy summer evening, but perhaps inevitably, there was no parking available.

He finally located a space in a small car park at the rear of an ivy-clad, sea-facing hostelry called the Rope & Anchor.

Heck parked, grabbed his bag and walked down a passage back to Abbot's Walk, crossed the road to the seafront fence and gazed again at the object of his interest. It was mid-evening now, and the sun had sunk towards the horizon, turning the sky ember-orange and the sea salmon-pink. The building on the island was fast losing definition, but there was enough daylight left for him to see it in more detail, especially when he popped a couple of coins into a local authority telescope standing on a plinth on the promenade.

Medieval in origin perhaps, but large parts of it had been

extended and rebuilt many times since then. With the advantage of the telescope, it actually looked to be comprised of several buildings, which clearly had been constructed at various periods and in different styles. The foremost of these, and seemingly the most modernised, was a towering Victorian entrance hall. It was built from dark stone, but glass occupied most of its windows, and television aerials nestled among its gargoyles and pinnacles. Behind that and much more impressive, mainly because of its height, was the immense battlemented structure that Heck had seen from the top end of the village. This part definitely looked medieval; it was more like a castle's keep than the wing of a country house, though it was difficult to be absolutely sure as so much of it was covered in scaffolding. Many of the other buildings were similarly clad, which suggested that full-scale refurbishments were in progress.

Heck slipped his phone out, zoomed in and snapped three or four pictures – at which point someone addressed him. 'Excuse me . . .?'

Heck turned and saw an elderly woman, thin and rather prim-looking, with short, dyed-blonde hair and steel-rimmed glasses. She wore a buttoned-up blouse and a knee-length, tartan skirt. She had a local accent, but it was only slight; there was a hint of education and breeding about her, and also an air of disapproval.

'I'm afraid we'll have to charge you for that parking space you've taken. I know there isn't a sign, but it's really only for use of customers.'

'Oh, you're from the Rope & Anchor?' Heck said. 'Do you have a room?'

'A room?' The question seemed to take her by surprise.

'Yeah, apologies for not booking in advance, but if you've got a spare room, I'll take it.'

She eyed him again, curious rather than hostile. He'd left

his jacket in the car, but after the long drive, his shirt was creased, his collar unbuttoned and his tie-knot loose. He couldn't have looked much like a holidaymaker.

'We *do* have a spare room,' she said. 'But it's in the attic . . . and it's not one we let out very often. The more comfortable rooms are fully booked at this time of year.'

'It's fine.' Heck slipped his phone back into his hip pocket. 'The room in the attic will do.'

'You haven't even seen it yet.'

'It doesn't matter.' He gave her his most easy-going smile. 'It'll do.'

She shook her head at the enigma of non-Cornish folk and turned. 'Come this way.'

He walked across the road alongside her.

'What's the building over there on the island?' he asked as they reached the front door of the pub.

'That's Trevallick Hall. It's very historic, but it's been neglected for quite a few years now. Still, we're hoping that's all about to change. If you'd like to come in, we'll do the necessaries.'

'Sure.'

Inside, the place was agreeable enough; wood-panelled, with low ceilings, uneven floors, and walls clad with seafaring accessories like crab nets, cutlasses and spyglasses.

Reception was a small counter in the hall, where Heck waited for his credit card to be processed, and as he did, glanced left into the main bar. Heavy beams, like ship's timbers, crossed its ceiling, hung with tankards, and there was a huge granite fireplace. A TV on a shelf was running a newsreel about the latest 'terror attack' in London, its screen displaying the Newham flyover and its blockaded undercroft, but the pretty, red-headed barmaid, probably having heard the same 'latest' all day, ignored it and gossiped with several locals perched along the counter. There was one other customer in there, slumped behind his newspaper in a wing-backed, red leather armchair.

'So, are you down here for a break, Mr Heckenburg?' the landlady, whose name was Mrs Nance, asked. 'Or is it business?'

'Hopefully a bit of both,' Heck replied. 'Guess we'll have to see.'

'Just the one night, is it?'

'At present, but if I need to stay here longer . . .?'

'The room will be available. As I say, no one has booked it.'

A shout of laughter drew Heck's attention to a room on the right, to which the door stood only ajar. This afforded him a partial view of several rugged-looking guys in scuffed boots and grey overalls. They lounged on benches and drank beer as a couple of their number moved around a snooker table with cues in hand.

'There you go.' Mrs Nance handed him his receipt and a key with a wooden tab. 'It's number nineteen. Straight up the stairs. The very top floor.'

Under normal circumstances, the room would probably have been unacceptable.

It was located under the eaves, as its slanted ceiling attested, and if that bespoke a certain olde-worlde charm, this was undermined by the low-quality furnishings, which included a narrow, single bed, a free-standing wardrobe riddled with woodworm, and a rickety writing table with an uncomfortable, stiff-backed chair. The carpet was old and threadbare, and there was no en suite. But it was clean and tidy, and the bed looked freshly made. Better still, the window, which was arched and recessed, gave him good vantage of Trevallick Hall.

He quickly texted Gemma, attaching the pictures he'd taken, and adding the message:

Look familiar? Call me when you get the chance.

After that, he got into jeans, a polo shirt and a pair of trainers and went back down to the bar. By now, only a couple of the locals remained. The chap with the newspaper had gone, but there was loud laughter from the workmen in the snooker room.

Heck ordered himself a beer and took a leaflet relating to Trevallick Hall from a 'local interest' rack. He settled in the red leather armchair to read but found the info sparse.

Trevallick Hall is a stately home occupying its own island, located approximately half a mile off the North Cornish coast, but considered to be within the parish council of St Ronan. The current building, which comprises remnants of several earlier buildings constructed on the same site, including a grand Regency dining room, a timber-framed Tudor banquet hall and a 116ft-tall battlemented tower dating to the 14th century, was acquired in 1849 by James Fowler-Horton, 8th Earl of Galloway, which is in the Scottish peerage. Work on the Hall as it stands today was completed in 1855. The Fowler-Horton family resided there until 1965, at which point it was sold to Cornwall County Council for use as a conference centre and wedding venue . . .

He was distracted from this when his phone buzzed the arrival of an email.

He expected it to be from Gemma, but in fact it signalled a sender he wasn't familiar with. He opened it anyway.

1/9. As promised. Sumitra.

When he opened the attachment, the image displayed a pistol lying on the green van's passenger seat. It looked like a Beretta M9, but that was no more than he'd expected.

'Finished with that, sir?' a voice asked.

The barmaid had appeared at his side with a cloth in hand and was ready to remove his empty pint glass.

'Yes, thanks.' He pocketed the phone.

'Can I get you another?'

'Same again would be great, thanks.'

'Not be a sec.' She removed the glass and the leaflet and commenced mopping his table down. 'Interested in local history, are we?'

'Not generally. But I was a bit intrigued. Mrs Nance said something about Trevallick Hall looking forward to better times.'

'We all hope so. The local authority made a right mess of managing it over the last few years. Tried it as a restaurant and function room for weddings and that. But it's a boat-ride to get there, so it never did well. Plus, parts of the building are very old and have deteriorated. Bit of a money pit, as I understand. Anyway, they stopped using it, boarded it up, forgot about it . . . been empty for decades.'

'But, now . . .?' he prompted.

'Now it's been bought again. That very rich foreign lady who was in the news a lot earlier this year. Turkish, or something . . . or Armenian. Would that be right?'

'Not . . .' At first, Heck could hardly say it. 'Not Milena Misanyan?'

'That's her, yeah. Got lots of interests in the UK now, apparently. She's turning it into a hotel and casino, I believe. Luxury rooms, swimming pool, nightclub. Regular boat service to and from the mainland. We've all got our fingers crossed. Do the town a power of good.'

As the barmaid moved away, Heck sat stiffly, flesh tingling.

He didn't exactly feel vindicated in having come down to St Ronan, but there was clearly no way that he wasn't onto something here. The package of evidence he'd retrieved from Green Van Man had contained several shots of Trevallick Hall, along with photos of Ray Marciano, who worked for Morgan Robbins, the solicitor, and of Morgan Robbins himself, who'd worked for Milena Misanyan.

Somehow, he'd squared the circle, though what kind of circle was it?

On impulse, he looked the woman up on Wikipedia. Initially, it told a straightforward rags-to-riches tale. Misanyan, an Armenian billionaire and investor, who, according to *Forbes*, had a net worth of $6.6 billion, was one of the richest women in the world, but had emerged from humble beginnings. Born in a dirt-poor neighbourhood of Yerevan, where her father was a widowed rubbish-collector, she finished school early so that she could provide for her two younger sisters by working as a waitress. With the arrival of *perestroika*, and private enterprise tacitly encouraged in Armenia, she and her sisters began selling cheap, imported light bulbs from street corners, which, unlikely as it might seem, made them considerable amounts of money. After Armenia gained its independence in 1991, she moved to Russia, where she invested in farming, construction and bodyguard recruitment, the latter of which led her into arms dealing (particularly on the black market, according to rumours – the former Soviet countries hosting a wide range of burgeoning crime syndicates who wanted the latest hardware). By the mid-1990s, she was involved in real estate and the trading of oil and oil products, at which point there was no looking back for Milena Misanyan.

Heck pressed on down to a section titled: *Scandals*

Unsurprisingly, Misanyan's rise to power had not been without controversy; she was several times accused of bribing government officials in the deal that landed her a controlling interest in one of Russia's biggest oil companies and was again suspected of utilising her organised crime connections when it came to acquiring ownership of other industrial giants. Of course, such was the political and economic chaos in the former Soviet Bloc at that time that none of this was properly investigated or accounted for, and by the age of 30, Milena Misanyan was officially a tycoon, with powerful financial and political allies, not just in Russia and Armenia, but all across Eastern Europe.

From what Heck could see, this was pretty standard stuff when it came to the rise of business moguls in the wake of the Soviet Union's collapse – it didn't really mean anything in terms of the current enquiry. Nevertheless, he read on, now reaching a section headed: *Charitable Works*
Noting that his newly drawn beer awaited him on the bar, he stood up and ambled over there, still reading.

Misanyan is believed to have donated millions to charitable works across Armenia, particularly in her home city of Yerevan, where she has set up several foundations dedicated to assisting, supporting and providing refuge for the survivors of criminal and sexual abuse. Misanyan rarely discusses it in public, but she is considered to be strongly sympathetic to female victims of male violence thanks to the events of 1990, when, as punishment for her refusal to allow a local street-gang to buy into her business, her two younger sisters, Anna and Maria, were raped and murdered and put on display

on purpose-built frames erected at the city dump.
Though she has never said so, this terrible incident is
believed to be one of the main reasons that Milena
Misanyan left Armenia for Russia . . .

'They're working on it now,' a voice said. 'The hall, I mean.'
Heck glanced up. 'Sorry?'

The barmaid smiled brightly. 'It's in the middle of being renovated, as I understand. Long job. Started about a year ago. Ms Misanyan's spending a fortune on it, but I'm sure it'll be worth it.' She nodded at the open doors to the vestibule, and beyond those, the single door to the snooker room. 'That's some of her workers in there, now.'

Heck regarded the men in grey overalls with greater interest. Again, the door was only partly open, so he didn't have a clear view, but those he saw had noticeably darker skin than you might normally get in Cornwall. He listened to them; though he could never have identified Armenian, they evidently weren't chattering in English.

He leaned on the bar to sip his beer. 'And currently they're on shore leave?'

'Sort of,' the barmaid said. 'Come in here most evenings. Bit of a rough-looking bunch, I admit. But they're well behaved. That's about as loud as they get.'

'Does Ms Misanyan ever come here?'

'I've never seen her, but the first thing they built on the island was a helipad. On the roof of the tower, or so I'm told. So, I suppose she goes direct.'

Heck pondered this. As he did, the phone again buzzed in his pocket. When he checked, it was another email from Sumitra Bharti:

2/9

He opened it and this time the attachment made him straighten up.

It depicted a single document apparently lying in the van's passenger-side footwell, but from the layout, which wasn't completely distinctive on the screen of his phone, it looked like another of those wanted-persons sheets.

Apologising to the barmaid, Heck moved to a chair by one of the pub's front windows, sat down and expanded the image as much as he was able.

When it lost definition too quickly for him to read it, he dashed back upstairs to his room, to boot his laptop up and look at it on a bigger screen.

It was indeed one of the wanted-persons sheets, laid out exactly like all the others. The mugshot portrayed a young-looking black guy. The name read: *SPENCER TAYLOR.*

Heck scanned down it, pulling out his pocketbook and flipping it open. The postcode where Taylor had presumably been collected married up with the London code in Green Van Man's satnav. But more important than any of this was the time and date of Taylor's rendezvous.

Heck moved back to the window, gazing at distant Trevallick Hall, now a dark outline spangled with points of light. As he stood there, his phone rang.

When he checked, the call was from Gemma.

'Ma'am?' he said, answering.

'What exactly is going on?' she said. 'And where are you?'

'Have you got a couple of minutes?'

'As long as it's worth my while.'

He told her everything that had happened since he'd left her office that morning, and everything he'd discovered. For once in his life, he left absolutely nothing out.

'Heck,' she eventually said, sounding tired rather than angry, 'what did you not understand about my telling you that you're grounded at Staples Corner for the foreseeable?'

'I understood everything, ma'am.'

'You did? OK . . . now think very carefully from this point on, because you've just admitted to a serious disciplinary offence.'

'Incorrect, ma'am,' he replied. 'If you're accusing me of disobeying a direct order, I haven't done anything of the sort. I can still get back to London tomorrow in time to sign on at 9 a.m. On top of that, I'm not even on duty at present, so actually you've no right to upbraid me about anything at all.'

'If you're not on duty, Heck, what're you doing following this lead?'

'That's what I do.' He slumped onto the bed.

'*Heck!*'

'I've said I'll get back to London as soon as. Look, Gemma . . . all I'm doing here is what I get paid for. Solving crime. In fact, I'm doing what you specifically authorised me to do. I'm following my nose. Am I not your rogue angel? Do I have a roving commission, or don't I?'

'Heck . . .'

He shut up, giving her the chance to jump in, to cut him down with some withering, acid-tongued response. But she didn't. Because, as he'd suspected, she couldn't. Though he'd doubtless infuriated her by playing truant once again, it was inarguably in a good cause. He'd found the next lead, and it was a strong one.

'Tell me a bit more,' she finally said.

'This offshore island,' he explained, 'has an old stately home on it. Gone to rack and ruin over the years, but apparently it's recently been bought and is now being renovated by Milena Misanyan.'

'She's turning it into a hotel, you say?'

'Yeah, in the long term. The main thing is that this is where Green Van Man's been bringing all the prisoners . . .'

'Green Van Man had a name, by the way.'

'Yeah?'

'We've heard back from Interpol. He's got a record in East Europe as long as your arm. He was Narek Sarafian. A known Armenian gangster. Into everything, apparently.'

'That would figure,' Heck said. 'There's a bunch of his countrymen downstairs. Milena Misanyan clearly recruits from close to home. Look, Gemma, the point is . . . *this* is the place.'

She paused to think. 'Is there any sign of activity on the island now?'

'It's too far away to see for sure, and too dark. I could do with getting out there . . .'

'Negative, Heck! Do you understand me? *Negative!* Gwen and Joe are with NPCC as we speak, and the signs are good. Do you want to blow the whole thing now? This firm may be missing a van and a van driver, which could put them on edge, but if you start a ruckus down there, they'll know there's something wrong for sure. Like you said yourself, they'll disappear, and we'll get no one of consequence.'

He shook his head. 'The problem is that we're out of time.'

'NPCC are well aware that we're on a ticking clock . . .'

'No, when I say we're out of time, I mean we are *out of time*. Gemma, I'm going to send you an attachment in a couple of minutes. It's another wanted-persons file . . . the subject on this occasion is one Spencer Taylor.'

'Spencer . . .?' Gemma sounded bemused. 'Aren't we supposed to be looking out for him?'

'Yes. It's the trigger-happy idiot from Tottenham and it looks like he'll soon be a new addition to our list. Narek Sarafian had a file on him too. CSI found it on the floor of the driver's cab. I suspect our pal didn't have time to insert this one into his evidence bag, and I know why . . . because it's very recent. The time of Taylor's abduction was 5 a.m. on August 23.'

'Crack of dawn yesterday,' she said dully.

'Correct. Now, I don't know how quickly these fights-to-the-death occur, but it's not necessarily as soon as the victim is brought down here.'

'You're saying you think Taylor might still be alive?'

'It's possible, isn't it? If these fights are for the benefit of Milena Misanyan, they'll happen at her convenience, won't they? I mean, she's an international businesswoman, she'll likely have a busy schedule.'

'Heck . . . how could she possibly know someone like Spencer Taylor?'

'Gemma, it's not *who* these guys are. It's *what* they are. Vicious criminals. Real toerags.'

'Yes, we all hate them. But this is something else again . . .'

'Have you read Misanyan's CV?' he asked. 'She's been verging on serious illegality all her adult life, but it's not just that . . . her two sisters were horrifically murdered and displayed on some kind of framework afterwards. Surely that's going to drive you a little bit crazy?'

'And why would she come to the UK to get revenge?'

'Who says it's just here? Maybe it's a full-time hobby for her. Look, ma'am . . . I know all this sounds unlikely, but this is where the evidence has led us. And if there's even a chance this idiot kid, Taylor, hasn't been in the arena yet, we might not just have an opportunity to save him, but to grab ourselves a living witness. I know he's a murdering little scrote, but surely we've got plenty of reason to get this thing moving?'

'I've already told you, Gwen's down at the Yard now . . .'

'Can't you interrupt them? This is serious. Look, I'm down here holding the fort, but as you say, I can't do much on my own . . .'

'Just hang tight a little longer,' Gemma interjected.

She now sounded *more* than tired, which initially puzzled him given the news he was bringing her. But while he was only working one case, intense though it was proving, she was literally overloaded with them. She still had the fallout from the cinema arrests to deal with, while the Newham shootings had created a furore that could even be heard down here.

'I'll send Gwen an urgent message,' she said.

'No disrespect . . .' Heck tried not to let his disappointment sound in his voice. 'But when you've done that, can you also mobilise Devon and Cornwall? Preferably their Major Crime Branch and Armed Response Unit. We'll need boats too, and choppers.'

'You know, you're asking an awful lot here, considering there's no other detective with you to corroborate any of this.'

'Don't take my word for it, ma'am. Check the attachment I'm about to send you.'

He cut the call and forwarded the image sent by Sumitra Bharti. At which point there was a knock at his bedroom door.

'Yeah?' he shouted.

'Erm . . . Mr Heckenburg, sorry . . . it's Ted Nance.' The muffled voice was strongly Cornish, much more so than Mrs Nance's had been. 'Sorry, but we've got a bit of a problem.'

Heck closed his laptop and slid it under the bed, before opening the door.

The man on the other side was wearing a chequered shirt and a cardigan and tie made of some curious fuzzy material. He had a moustache and a mop of greying hair and wore thick-rimmed tortoiseshell glasses.

'I'm sorry to bother you, sir . . . you're the gent who arrived in the Megane earlier?'

'Yeah.'

'I'm afraid it's been damaged.'

'What . . . on the car park?'

'I'm afraid so. I'm very sorry.'

'You don't mean it's been broken into?'

'I'm not quite sure.'

'Bloody great.' Heck closed the bedroom door, locked it and hurried down the stairs, Nance coming in pursuit.

'We've got a camera out back, sir,' the landlord said. 'So, I'm sure if we have a look . . .'

'Yeah, fine,' Heck said over his shoulder. 'Let me just check the damage.'

As he walked through Reception towards the back door, he knew that, if his Megane *had* been broken into, it couldn't be a coincidence. How often did motors get screwed in this neighbourhood, if ever? This was a further indication that he was onto something, but, bewilderingly, it also suggested that someone was onto him.

First, though, the car.

It was where he'd left it, at the far end of the small car park, a blue plastic dumpster on one side of it, a parked white van on the other. The car park lighting was not good; in fact, the lamp nearest to his Megane wasn't working. But even so, there was no visible damage as he approached, and the alarm was not signalling. Which confused him.

'What's actually happened?' he said, again over his shoulder.

'If you check near the front,' Nance replied, bringing up the rear.

Heck sidled between the van and his Megane, still not observing so much as a scratch. 'You say at the front?'

'That's right, sir.'

Not a break-in, then; more like legit damage. Though how the car could have been pranged at the front when it was parked nose to the wall, he couldn't fathom . . .

A figure stepped into his path.

Heck halted.

It was one of the Armenian workmen. He was middle-aged, short and squat, but powerfully built. With his hair thinning on top, his pug nose, jug ears and odd, protruding face, he had a rodent-like aspect, currently split by a crescent grin.

Before Heck could react, he sensed someone else at his back. He tried to spin around, but the impact on the rear of his skull was massive, jolting his head, stunning his senses. As Heck slumped to his knees, Rodent scuttled forward to prevent him falling full-length. He was vaguely aware of hurried, whispering voices. An object dropped down alongside him – a bulging sock, with sand spilling out of it. A classic underworld blackjack, it could deliver tremendous impact but had enough yield in it to reduce the risk of causing serious damage.

Someone took Heck's legs, and between them, his assailants carried him to the rear of the white van.

'Quickly,' a voice hissed.

It sounded like Nance, but the accent was no longer Cornish.

The next thing Heck knew, they were twisting him onto his back and feeding him into the darkness of the interior, where other hands took hold of him. He caught one glimpse of his second abductor, presumably the one who'd struck him, seeing a much younger face, with hair shaved at the sides but smoothed across the top of his head in an oily, black flat-top.

Then he was inside the vehicle. It was dark and smelled of salt water. Someone else climbed inside and the door banged shut, closing out what little light there'd been. Not that they seemed to need it; as Heck lay flat on the corrugated metal floor, his wrists and ankles were firmly and expertly bound with some tight twine, which had the potential to slice flesh if he wriggled about too much. In truth, he didn't wriggle at all; he was too groggy. Though, as the van's engine throbbed to life, and he felt the vehicle reverse out of its parking bay, awareness was ebbing back. Someone seated alongside him chuckled.

'I'm not very flattered you didn't recognise me.'

That voice again . . . Ted Nance. Except that Nance now spoke with a light Cockney accent, which wasn't a giveaway in itself, but again, all the pieces were steadily falling together.

'Ray Marciano, I presume?' Heck said.

'Yay,' the voice replied. 'You got there in the end.'

Chapter 35

There was no conversation as the van jolted along. The pencil-thin gleam of light around the edges of the rear doors revealed nothing, either inside or out. A short time after departing the Rope & Anchor, it slithered to a halt, and Heck, who was now fully conscious, fancied he could hear waves in close proximity.

The doors opened, and though it wasn't exactly light out there – the nearest lamps were several hundred yards away, just about delineating the seafront road and the shops and bars – it was sufficient to reveal that he'd been driven to the end of the stone quay. That was perfect for them, of course. He was too far from shore for any villagers to hear him should he shout out, especially over the breaking of the surf, and at this late hour they were beyond the reach of prying eyes.

A couple more men in grey overalls were waiting there. Ray Marciano, divested of his 'Cornish innkeeper' disguise, exposing his more familiar blond hair and lean, sharp, shaven features, jumped out, as did the other two henchmen who'd ridden with him and Heck in the back.

'Bring him,' Marciano said.

Heck saw no point in resisting; he couldn't anyway, as he'd been bound expertly. Help was on its way, he hoped, but when it would arrive was anyone's guess. All he could try to do now was buy time for himself . . . but in as subtle a way as possible.

They hauled him out and stood him upright. The back of his head throbbed, and he was still dazed from the blow, but not so much that he didn't see the motorboat bobbing and tilting on the waters alongside them, a single plank gangway leading down to it.

'Can you hop?' Marciano asked. 'Or do we carry you?'

'I can hop,' Heck confirmed.

'Good . . . but don't be thinking about jumping in. The lads who've tied you know what they're doing, so you won't be able to wriggle out of it . . . and no one's coming in after you.'

'I've come this far, I might as well go the whole hog,' Heck replied.

Marciano smiled at that, amused by Heck's air of affected nonchalance. He turned and signalled to Flat-Top and Rodent.

The pair of them came forward, took one elbow each and steered Heck to the head of the gangway. It was so narrow that they weren't able to walk down it one to either side, but Flat-Top went first, sauntering ahead, while Rodent brought up the rear, a firm hand clamped to Heck's right shoulder.

There was only a single light in the boat, a lamp on a hook suspended over the outboard motor, and it illuminated little – though this was to Heck's advantage. He couldn't throw himself into the drink, but that didn't stop him throwing something else. Lying in the pitch-dark of the van's interior, and with his hands tied in front of him rather than at his back, he'd been able to filch both his phone and his pocketbook from out of his jeans. Making a call would have been impossible, as the light from his iPhone facia would have alerted his captors, so instead he'd had to content himself with covertly tugging his polo shirt from his belt, and concealing them both underneath it, and now, as he made his awkward way down the gangplank, releasing them.

Thanks to the near non-existent light and the roll and splash of the waves, they vanished into the water without anyone noticing. This, as it turned out, was a timely move. The instant he alighted in the boat, Marciano shouted down that they should search him. They did so, and finding nothing, bade him sit on one of the rowing benches.

'Cutting my blood supply here,' Heck complained, as one by one, they climbed down alongside him.

Flat-Top snickered to himself, as if this was going to be the least of their captive's problems. Marciano, who took his place on the facing bench, regarded Heck with equal amusement.

The boat chugged slowly away from its mooring, describing a slow, graceful arc across the choppy water before the ex-cop finally spoke.

'So was it the Cornish accent that fooled you?' he asked.

Heck frowned. 'Was that supposed to be Cornish?'

'OK, the fake tash then? The daft specs? The wig? It all had to be improvised at the last minute, of course, me not expecting you an' all.'

Heck shrugged. 'Never knew what you looked like anyway. Never bothered looking you up.'

'Aww.' Marciano sounded genuinely disappointed. 'So, you wouldn't have known me even if I'd lowered my newspaper back there in the hotel bar, eh?'

Heck shrugged again. 'Sorry.'

'Well . . . I recognised *you* straight away. Especially when I heard your name. There can't be many Heckenburgs knocking around, can there? A bit unexpected, mind. I mean, I had a bad feeling that someone would show up . . . but not the second-best detective in Britain.'

'Don't flatter yourself, pal. You weren't the first best even in London.'

'Well . . . I will admit I've never been as much of a headline-grabber as you.'

'Yeah, I wonder why.'

'Which is all the more reason I'm surprised and disappointed to see you here now.'

Heck regarded him blankly. 'If you're disappointed with your own security arrangements, you should be. But don't be surprised by how crap they are. I wasn't.'

Marciano chuckled. 'You can keep this bravado thing going, if you want to. But I'm the one sailing towards a happy future, and you're the one tied up in fishing line.'

Heck snorted. 'Anyone can hire a bunch of muckers to do their dirty work. I'm sure this set of gorillas can be relied on to beat the living shit out of someone if that's all that's required. Even so, Ray, if this is the best you've got, I'm unimpressed.'

'You know what I'm unimpressed by?' Marciano's mocking smile hardened. 'You pretending that you're a badass. Because, compared to these guys, you're not. You're really in deep shit, here, Heckenburg, and you know you are. So, what you need to do at this moment is shut your mouth and listen.'

He paused as if to think, the dark sea surging past with an ever heavier swell, the boat rising and falling as the island loomed closer.

'When I say I'm disappointed, Heck . . . I can call you "Heck", yeah? That's your nickname, isn't it?'

'Only where my mates are concerned.'

'Good . . . I'm in august company. But when I say I'm

disappointed, Heck, I mean I'm disappointed in *you*. I've followed your adventures over the years, and you're either a genius or a madman. I mean, they say the dividing line between the two is thin. So . . . maybe you're both. But one thing's always been apparent. You're resolute. You hunt these bastards down and you put them where they need to be . . . and sometimes that's the grave.'

'That's the job,' Heck replied. 'It's not because I get off on it.'

'I understand that. I'm not a sadist, myself.'

'Unless it pays, eh?'

'No way.' Marciano seemed entirely serious. 'It's not in my nature to be cruel. I believe that most crims deserve a second chance. They go down, bit of time in the clink, slapped wrist or two . . . then they come out again, and they're either sadder and wiser men, or they haven't learned anything and a week later they're back inside. But, you know . . . that's the life they chose. Costs society a bit of money, but it's better than them being out on the streets. But that's *most* crims, Heck . . . not all.' He paused again, for effect. 'You know as well as I do . . . there are some renegades who are way fucking beyond that. Whose crimes are so reprehensible that they won't even take a chance in court, they just do a runner, haven't got the guts to face their fellow men.'

'And so you decided to be their judge, jury *and* executioner.'

'I'm not the executioner. I just do what I always did.'

'You track 'em down, yeah?'

'Just like *you* do, Heck.'

'I deliver them to justice.'

'So do I!' Marciano laughed again, but it was a hard, flat sound, devoid of humour. 'Christ, fifty years ago, these wretches would have been hanged and no one would've batted an eyelid. You think if the Moors Murderers had been convicted before 1965, the death penalty would have been abolished? It would have lasted another decade, at least.'

'Even if it had,' Heck said, 'all those facing it would still have been given a trial first.'

'*We* give them a trial.'

'Trial by battle, Ray? Some might call that a dated concept.'

'Some would call brotherly love a dated concept. Doesn't mean it lacks virtue.'

'Do you actually believe this bull?' Heck asked him. 'Or these days, do you only believe what you get paid to believe?'

Marciano sighed, as if the prisoner was a lost cause.

'Seriously, Ray,' Heck said. 'You're not running this show. You don't own Fantasy Island, over there. So, you're getting paid to do this, and paid pretty well I'm guessing . . . you didn't pack the job in for monkey nuts, did you?'

'And you're trying to catch these worthless specimens purely because you want to save your career,' Marciano scoffed. 'Operation Sledgehammer? What a farce! I doubt it would have entered any of your heads to go looking for these long-vanished arseholes if National Crime Group hadn't been in trouble. So, don't give me dogshit dressed up as principles, Heck . . .'

They were interrupted by a grunt from one of the Armenians.

The island was almost upon them. Waves crashed invisibly, only faint hints of white to indicate where surf burst on its seafront walls. The floodlit end of a timber jetty drew near, and beyond that, higher up, the lights of Trevallick Hall twinkled through skeletal frameworks of scaffolding.

Heck watched as they slid into place alongside the dock. As they sat there, swaying, a rope was thrown down and a set of ladders lowered. Rodent edged past to take charge of the ladders, but before he did, he snapped open a glinting blade, bent down and sawed through the bonds on Heck's ankles. At the same time, Marciano drew a Beretta from the pocket of the black waterproof he'd pulled over his 'Ted Nance' shirt and tie and cocked it.

'Nothing stupid, Heck,' he advised. 'Let's not spoil things now.'

Heck said nothing as they manhandled him up onto the jetty and led him forward through a narrow, single-storey building with a flat roof and open doors at either end of it. It was almost like a customs point, with a couple more of the men in grey overalls lounging on stools, smoking. They regarded Heck with only passing interest as he was escorted through by Marciano, Flat-Top and Rodent. From here, they marched uphill via a rutted lane lined on either side by thatched-roof cottages. Possibly, these had once been residences for staff at the hall, but now they were boarded up.

'Planning something special for this place, is she . . . your boss?' Heck said.

'That's the general idea,' Marciano replied.

'Crime that she has to. Only in Britain could somewhere like this be left to rack and ruin.'

'It was only ever a luxury, this place, mate . . . a folly. People living like kings on money they never earned. No wonder they all lost everything eventually. Even Milena's only acquired this place on the basis that it'll soon pay for itself.'

'And in the meantime, it gets used for other stuff, yeah?'

'You'd be amazed by the variety of uses you can put to big old houses that no one wants.'

They stopped talking as they ascended a steep flight of steps. When Heck glanced back, it was too dark to see the jetty or the boat that had brought him here. The lights of the Cornish shore looked much further away than he'd expected.

They reached the top of the steps, and a paved path led

ahead of them, straight as an arrow between smoothly mown lawns. It ran perhaps a hundred yards to the open front doors of the Victorian entrance building. On either side of these flames flickered in hanging braziers, casting dancing shadows over the great granite frontage and across the single figure awaiting them there.

'The thing is,' Heck said, as they processed forward, 'if you're planning to practise this new novelty version of brotherly love on . . . well, *me*, you'll be opening the door to a whole universe of trouble.'

'I agree,' Marciano said, 'but I'm not in charge here.'

'You're making a mistake, Ray.'

'Your mistake was coming to Cornwall without any backup.'

'Doesn't that tell you something?'

'Yep. Tells me that we've got time.'

The waiting figure was only thirty yards off. Quite clearly, it was female.

'You don't feel any concern for a former colleague?' Heck asked.

'You never get on in this world by looking back, Heck,' Marciano said. 'You can only go forward. So, there's no such thing as a *former* colleague . . . nothing that matters, anyway.'

'That's pretty profound, Ray. I'd say write it down, so they can carve it on your gravestone. Except that people who die in prison usually get buried in unmarked graves.'

'Rather an unmarked grave than wet cement, Heck.'

And on that note, they arrived in front of the figure in the doorway. She wasn't just female, she was a mightily impressive female. Heck had no doubt that they were finally in the presence of Milena Misanyan.

Chapter 36

She was taller than the average woman, perhaps just under six feet, but of statuesque proportions, an outline enhanced by her thigh-length boots, tight white trousers and white, waist-length summer jacket. She wore white silk gloves and a yellow head scarf wound under the chin and around the neck, which lent her an air of the exotic. This was especially true when Heck drew close and saw her face-to-face.

Milena Misanyan was somewhere in her early fifties but, as he'd seen in that photo on the cover of *Time*, she possessed an ageless eastern beauty.

'The gent I telephoned you about from the hotel, ma'am,' Marciano said without preamble. 'Detective Sergeant Mark Heckenburg, from the Serial Crimes Unit at Scotland Yard . . . oh, ex of Scotland Yard.' He glanced at Heck. 'They've swept you all out of the way into a stable block somewhere now, haven't they? They'll be serving straw in your canteen next. If you've still got one.'

Heck shrugged. 'They do their best . . . but they can't keep good people down.'

'And are *you* a good person, Sergeant?' Milena Misanyan asked. Her voice was husky and carried an attractive trace of accent. But there was a chill about this woman. It wasn't just her imperious air, it was the ice in those lovely eyes, the implacable nature she exuded.

So Heck responded to her brazen question with one of his own. 'Are you an *evil* person, Miss?'

She seemed mildly amused, her ruby mouth curving into a half-smile, though the amusement didn't reach her eyes. 'Well . . . I suppose there are degrees of evil, just as there are degrees of good. Less commonly discussed are those degrees of provocation that might drive an individual from one side of the spectrum to the other . . .'

'Save it,' Heck interrupted. 'I didn't come all the way down to Cornwall for a sermon.'

She cocked her head to one side, regarding him with a new level of interest. 'No doubt you're the sort of man who believes that women should be seen and not heard, Sergeant.'

'No, I'm the sort of man who doesn't need to listen to the same speech twice.' Heck nodded at Marciano. 'He's already given it to me.'

Marciano snickered. 'He's in character so far. I've never worked with Heckenburg, but I heard he's annoyed the crap out of every fucker he's ever served under.'

'People generally don't like being shown how to do their job properly,' Heck replied.

'Conceited bugger too. Like you can't tell.'

'I'm intrigued,' Milena Misanyan said, 'that you're here in Cornwall with no support.'

Heck shrugged. 'Perhaps that's because I'm not actually here on company business.'

'Indeed?'

'Perhaps it's because I'm aware of the operation you've got going on here, and I fancy a part of it.' He nodded at Marciano again. 'Like miladdo here.'

382

'Interesting. You want to work for me, but you don't want to hear my point of view.'

'I know what happened to your family,' Heck said apologetically. 'It stinks. My brother died a horrible death too . . . blamed for a series of violent burglaries he never committed. He died in prison. Committed suicide after being raped God knows how many times, while the real scumbag walked free. Trust me, my hatred for criminals is also very personal.'

She looked at him long and hard. 'What do you think?' she asked Marciano.

The ex-cop seemed unsure. 'I heard about his brother. That's bona fide. And by reputation, he's a real wildcard . . . the kind you'd think capable of anything.'

'Capable of anything. How fascinating.'

'When we were on the way over here, he expressed a bit of interest in how much I earn from this. But I wouldn't say that interest was effusive. Mainly, he's acted like he disapproves of us . . .'

'I believe in saving the real conversation for the engineer,' Heck cut in, 'not his rubbing rag.'

'So is it true, Sergeant?' Misanyan wondered. 'You're genuinely looking for a new job?'

'If the money's right. Blondie here wouldn't give anything away.'

'And is it mainly about money with you?'

'Would you dislike me if it was?' Heck said. 'A lady like your good self . . . who's spent her life amassing a fortune that most of us can only dream about.'

'You think that's all I am?'

'I don't much care about the rest of it.'

'You should.'

She turned on her heel and walked through the entrance door. Marciano nudged Heck with the Beretta, indicating

383

that he should follow. Heck did so, Marciano alongside him, the two overalled escorts just behind. They strode through several tall rooms, which no doubt once had been grand; Heck caught glimpses of painted ceilings and frescoed walls, but much was now covered in scaffolding or dust sheets, or just plain old dust.

'You know all about the street vermin who murdered my beautiful sisters,' Misanyan said. 'That much is in the public domain. But what you probably don't know is what happened to those wretched creatures afterwards. I assume, Sergeant, that as you dream about taking revenge yourself, you won't mind hearing this?'

She glanced sidelong at him. Heck shrugged as he walked.

'I captured all six eventually. It was several years later, but I'd never forgotten who they were. I had them bricked up. Separately, of course. Built them into living pillars. We provided food and water through narrow plastic tubes. One of them lived that way for almost a year. Would you be capable of exacting such punishment?'

'I don't know,' he said. 'I never got the chance to find out.'

'Alas, it still wasn't enough. When I finally had those pillars demolished, steamrollered to dust and pulp, I was left with a deep, burning anger that would not go away.'

They passed outside again, through a glazed annexe, into what might once have been a small garden but now was heaped with building rubble.

Misanyan stopped and turned to face him again.

Heck shrugged. 'Just because I can suppress that feeling doesn't mean I don't get it.'

She glanced at Marciano. 'Is this even vaguely conceivable? Is Sergeant Heckenburg being honest with us?'

'I'm not so sure,' Marciano replied. 'He gave me some stick on the way over here.'

'I've already said,' Heck retorted. 'I don't have to like what you're doing to be OK with it . . . so long as the paycheque's good.'

'He's certainly been at the sharp end,' Marciano added. 'Seen a lot of shit, which might have pushed him towards our corner. But that'll be difficult to judge until it comes down to it. The fact he's alone is no guarantee. He's well known for going rogue while he's on the job. He could easily be working the case right now. He may not have sent the message back yet, or maybe he has and he's playing for time.'

She sighed. 'You see, even if I believed you, Sergeant, there'd be so much we'd need to discuss. Such as how you think you could actually assist us. We already have everything we need. On the disposal front, my men are as professional as they come. When it comes to the hunt itself, I couldn't do any better.'

Heck glanced at Marciano. 'Why don't you put him and me in a room together? We'll see whether you think you need to hire someone else ten minutes later.'

Marciano laughed.

Misanyan ignored the comment. 'There are also some questions that *must* be answered even if we decide you're a friend and not a foe. Such as how you located us in the first place. How you discovered what we are doing here.'

Heck shook his head. 'My lips are sealed till I get some kind of deal.'

Rodent, standing behind, drove a fist into his right kidney. Heck cringed at the intense pain but kept his feet.

'No more of that,' Misanyan said. 'I really doubt it would achieve anything. In fact, cut Sergeant Heckenburg loose. There's nowhere for him to run to anyway.'

Flat-Top opened a lock-knife and severed Heck's remaining bonds. Heck rubbed at the welts on his wrists. Still nauseated by the blow to his side, it was a relief to at least feel the blood flowing back into his hands.

'You need to understand, Sergeant,' Misanyan said, 'whatever's going on in that head of yours, whatever people are planning – even if they're on their way to this place right now – I have the means to leave directly.'

Heck remembered hearing that the first thing they'd constructed on the uppermost roof of Trevallick Hall was a helipad.

'Even if the worst happens,' she added, 'I can be over international waters within a very few minutes, where a range of luxury transportation is available to me. All, of course, registered in countries whose interests, shall we say, align with my own. Though I've recently made my home in the United Kingdom, nothing lost here will be irreplaceable.'

'But I'm guessing you'd rather not lose it,' Heck wheezed.

'Of course I'd rather not.'

'We're telling you this, Heck,' Marciano cut in, 'just so you know that you aren't going to win.'

'Unless I sign on,' Heck corrected him. 'And find myself working for a law enforcement system that isn't skint and which allows me to bring these shitheads in to someone who really knows how to deal with them. Oh . . . and allows me to earn some proper money in the process. I'd call *that* a win.'

'I dearly wish I could believe you,' Misanyan said. 'But I'm afraid it's too big a risk.'

'And probably for minimal gain,' Marciano added. 'You're too ill-disciplined, Heck. No one could trust you for long.'

'Yeah, if only I was the solid, steadfast type that you proved to be, eh?'

'The job's taken, pal.'

'Only as long as *you're* breathing.'

'I wouldn't keep pressing that button too hard,' Marciano said. 'You're really not in a position to be chucking your weight around.'

'And you still have some answers to provide,' Misanyan said. 'Follow me, please.'

They moved on, Heck with hands free but walking at gunpoint. They passed under a stone arch and into a building which, from the chill and damp of it, was the medieval part of Trevallick Hall, the keep, though even this was undergoing renovation. After descending a narrow stair, they took a stone corridor, passing numerous open doors, beyond which lay stacks of bricks and wooden boards, heaps of cable, light fittings, electrical tools.

'We have a certain driver in our employment who seems to have gone absent without leave,' Misanyan said, as they strode. 'With one of our vehicles, no less.'

'Have you reported it as theft?' Heck replied.

'Not yet. He is not the most reliable man at the best of times. He never really took to life in the UK, or to the restraint and loyalty I require. He came to us from a criminal background, rather than the Armenian military, which is where we normally recruit . . . and we have long suspected that he's looking for an opportunity to go back there. We wouldn't be happy about that, as you can imagine.'

That explained quite a bit, Heck thought. The gun-toting Narek Sarafian had been selling snuff-type movies now augmented with some exceedingly rare gladiatorial footage which he'd stolen from here, to build himself a lump sum that he could use to buy his way back into the Armenian mob. That paperwork they'd found in the van was his shield. The moment he got loose, he'd likely have emailed the threat back to his former boss, along with the necessary photographic evidence.

'It's not impossible that he's done a runner, as the English say,' Misanyan added. 'But then . . . rather worryingly, we hear about this mysterious shooting incident in East London.'

Heck was briefly distracted. They'd descended a second

flight of steps and turned left along another bare passage, at the end of which a narrow archway admitted them into the upper section of a vast, cavernous space, where it looked as if two or three levels of basement had been removed. Here, they proceeded out onto a gantry made of planks and scaffolding. It felt solid, but nevertheless had an air of the temporary, shuddering and creaking as they halted in the middle of it.

All kinds of arc and spotlights were suspended from the stone arches overhead, while there were several on the gantry itself, fitted to a waist-high barrier on the right-hand side. A small camera stood there too; a simple thing, something you could buy from any high street store. But with a tripod attachment, it was positioned against the barrier and angled downward. Heck knew what he was going to see down there even before he looked.

The arena: a roughly circular fighting pit, some sixty feet in diameter, completely enclosed by a single encircling wall of corrugated steel, which was about ten feet in height, its upper parapet maybe fifteen feet below the gantry. The floor of the arena also looked to have been made from steel and was a dull blue/grey in texture, but even so it was possible to pick out the dabbles of dried blood covering it from one side to the next. There were two doors that Heck could identify, at opposite ends. Because all the lighting was trained into the pit itself, everything beyond the encircling wall lay in shadow, so it was difficult to see what these doors connected to. But when he leaned over the barrier to look properly, the one on his right had a small wrought-iron table positioned alongside it. Even though he was a good twenty feet above, Heck could clearly see that various home-made weapons had been left on the table: a section of crudely sawn-off lead piping, perhaps three feet in length; a darkly stained meat cleaver; a claw hammer; a well-used baseball bat, its hilt bound with gorilla tape.

'Nothing to say?' Misanyan wondered, drawing him back to their previous conversation.

'Shooting incident?' Heck feigned puzzlement. 'You mean that terrorist thing at Newham?'

The woman regarded him blankly. 'But is it a terrorist thing? There has been very little information leaked to the press so far. And you see, it's only since then that we've failed to hear from our errant driver.'

'You're saying you think it was him? Is he armed? Why would he have got into a shoot-out with the police?'

She scrutinised him carefully.

'Coincidences sometimes happen,' Marciano put in. 'We could conceivably buy it, if it was proved to us that another bunch of home-grown jihadis had gone all out for their moment of glory, and that maybe our pal, Henrikh, decided to run off and start his new life at exactly the same time. But what doesn't happen is that no one talks about it.'

'Talks?' Heck purposely didn't respond to the name, 'Henrikh', which he knew to be incorrect. That was clearly an attempt to trip him up. He shrugged. 'You been on the dope, Ray? You are aware we're in a state of ultra-high security at present?'

'Which means jack shit to people like me, Heck. I may be out of the job now, but I've got more contacts in the Met than Jimmy Savile had warts on his genitals. Nothing happens in London without me knowing someone who'll happily tell all. Until now. For some reason, this particular so-called terrorist incident has had the Seal of Satan put on it.'

'And would an incident involving your man . . . Henrikh, be subject to the same secrecy? You said he's just a driver.'

'That all depends on what he got himself into, doesn't it?'

'We don't like losing people and possessions, Sergeant,' Misanyan said. 'But what we *really* don't like is not knowing how and why. Mr Marciano particularly doesn't . . . to such a degree that, when he found out that none of his old contacts in the police could tell him anything at all about Wednesday night's incident, he came rushing down here to Cornwall to speak to me in person.'

'And who should turn up here?' Marciano said. 'Well, how about *you* . . . offering a cock-and-bull story that you want to join us and providing no intel at all about how you found your way to us.'

Heck shrugged. 'You want that intel, I told you what you need to do.'

Again, Milena Misanyan regarded him for a long time. Her inscrutability was clearly her strength. With such a flawless poker face, he could easily understand how effective she was in the boardroom. In contrast, Marciano was turning twitchy. He muttered something to Rodent, who showed a grin full of broken, yellow teeth.

'You said you didn't come here to listen to a speech, Sergeant,' Misanyan said. 'Rude though you were, I have some sympathy with that viewpoint. The power of words has its limits. I am a firm believer that visuals are always more potent.'

She pointed into the arena. As Heck watched and waited, Marciano slid up behind him.

'You really came here looking for a fight, Heckenburg?' he whispered. 'Well . . . I think we can do a lot better than putting me and you in a room together. So, just keep watching . . . and be very careful you don't get what you wish for.'

Somewhere below, there was a metallic *clunk*.

The arena was still empty, but Rodent was now at the camera, peering through its lens, making last-minute adjustments, before commencing to film.

Another *clunk* followed, louder this time.

Heck looked again as the door on the right side of the arena opened by use of some automated device. Nothing happened initially, but then a figure nervously emerged from it. It was a black guy, lean and well-muscled, but clearly young. He wore only a pair of badly stained undershorts, his gaze darting wildly around.

'Hey, man . . . the fuck!' he shouted hoarsely. 'Where the fuck am I?'

He directed the question upward, but he didn't actually focus on the viewing gallery.

'He can't see us, in case you were wondering,' Marciano said. 'The lights are too bright.'

'Of course,' Heck replied. 'Wouldn't want him to recognise us and come looking to get even if he ever escapes, eh?'

'No one ever escapes.'

'Hey, man . . . hey, what the fuck, yeah! Come on, man . . . enough games. I've been in that room fucking ages.'

The *clunk* of the other door abruptly silenced him.

The kid, who simply had to be Spencer Taylor, turned sharply, standing ramrod-straight but visibly shivering as his two opponents idled into view. Just like the ones Heck had seen on the video footage, they were broad, muscular specimens, clad in tight black clothing, heavy-duty Kevlar and ballistics helmets. One wielded a machete in one hand, and a chain with a heavy padlock in the other. The second one carried a pickaxe handle with what looked like nine-inch nails hammered through it.

'Don't fucking do it, man!' Taylor shouted, his voice rising a full octave.

He pointed a shaking finger at them, but, rather irrationally, paced away from the weapons table even though he hadn't yet armed himself.

'A few of them do that,' Marciano commented. 'It's like

they think it's a joke or a game . . . you know, as if there's another door that might get them out of there if they could only find it. They soon realise the truth.'

Taylor realised the truth when the opposing pair split up, the one with the chain and machete circling around the edge of the arena towards him, the other walking directly across.

The kid backed away, still pointing.

'Back off, yeah! Man, I'm warning you!' His voice was now a falsetto shriek. '*Get the fuck away from me!*'

Only when he had no choice – because so often, Heck realised, the human brain won't grasp an awful truth until it absolutely must – he ran back to his own supply of weapons, selecting the heavy length of lead piping and throwing it to his shoulder.

He lurched to his right, the twosome pivoting around, tracking him, drawing closer.

'Get back . . . *the fuck!*'

He made wild swings at nothing as he retreated, but soon reached the opposite side of the arena. Again, his opponents closed in.

'So, how do we get them here?' Heck asked, still hoping to sound like a man pitching for a job.

'Surely you worked that out from the van?' Marciano said.

Another test, Heck realised.

'What van?'

'You can tell him,' Misanyan put in. 'He's here now. He isn't going anywhere else.'

'Isoflurane,' Marciano said. 'Combined with nitrous oxide, it forms an anaesthetic gas. The scrotes think they're being taken to safety. It's even cosy in there. We've got a rug, an armchair.'

'So, they settle down . . . and you gas them?'

'Well, the van's a sealed unit. It's got to be, to make them feel safe. Once they're in, there's a ventilation system to provide airflow. Our driver hits a couple of buttons, and out they go for several hours. Makes it easy to load them into the boat when it arrives at the end of St Ronan's quay. It's usually late at night, so there's no one looking anyway. Several of them have come armed, but letting them keep their guns is a good thing – lulls them into a false sense of security. And it's hardly a problem if they're out cold at the other end.'

'Sounds incredibly simple,' Heck said.

'The best plans always are.'

Down below, there was a whirlwind of contact, Taylor, to his opponents' surprise, going on the offensive first, running at them, screaming, laying heavy blows on their pads before darting away again. At this early stage, his youthful agility aided him.

'Whose idea was all this?' Heck asked.

Marciano chuckled. 'Nothing happens anywhere in Milena's empire unless it's her will.'

Heck glanced at the woman. 'It's an appropriate punishment,' he said. 'But I can't see there's much earning potential.'

'Hobbies rarely offer that, Sergeant,' she replied, though now she was barely listening.

She watched the fight intently, a gleam in her eye. Her full lips seemed redder, moister.

Heck wondered if it was possible that she'd licked them in anticipation.

Down below, Taylor shrieked again as he lunged at his oppressors, scampering away immediately afterwards, but sliding on his sweaty bare feet, landing hard and rolling. They lurched after him, but he jumped up and managed to stagger out of reach. He was panting dramatically, his shoulders heaving, his body gleaming and wet.

'This always the way it is?' Heck asked Marciano.

'You sound disgusted, Heck. Thought you wanted in.'

'It's a tough deal, when you see it in the flesh.'

'At least we give them a fighting chance. Which, you know as well as I do, is more than they deserve.'

There was another bout of contact, and again Taylor did better than many might have expected, mainly because he was nimble on his toes. It brought cackles of laughter and shouts of approval from somewhere overhead.

Heck glanced up and saw several windows in high sections of the arched stone ceiling. They were filled with heads, as the rest of Misanyan's Armenian thugs watched the action, slapping each other and bantering as the battle unfolded, wads of money changing hands between them.

'Everyone seems to be enjoying themselves,' he said.

'Keeps the staff happy, as they say,' Marciano replied. 'The lads even have their own scorecards. Whoever disposes of his opponent the quickest and most efficiently gets most points . . . that sort of thing.'

'And does this happen in other parts of the Misanyan empire?'

'I have many homes, Sergeant,' the woman answered, as she walked along the gantry to keep track of the fight below. 'And I seek many home comforts.'

He watched her, fascinated. She'd flushed in the cheek; her mouth was definitely wetter. She moved quickly, lithely, eagerly. It was verging on the sexual – now he understood why the recordings made of these gladiatorial events were not for dissemination online. They were Milena Misanyan's property. And hers alone.

He turned to Marciano, and said quietly: 'You realise she's round the bend?'

'Just watch the fight.'

Down below, Taylor's screams of rage and fear took on a new level of intensity. In his frantic dashing about, he'd landed awkwardly and twisted an ankle. He now had to limp in his efforts to escape. His opponents, meanwhile, stalked casually. Heck sensed that the entertainment was approaching its climax.

'Isn't much of a fight,' he said.

Misanyan turned and looked at him from beyond one of the spotlights. Half in shadow, her eyes gleamed eerily. 'Maybe *yours* will be better.'

'Yep.' Heck nodded, deciding that now was as good a time as any. 'Let's find out, eh?'

Marciano tensed, having read a change in their captive's body language. But probably the last thing even he expected was for Heck to leap up onto the low barrier, grab hold of a cable, yank it loose from its bracket . . . and jump.

Chapter 37

With a clattering and banging, the cable tugged free along the parapet, three of the arc lights extinguishing amid showers of sparks. Heck had half hoped to abseil down to the arena, but in fact he fell the first sixteen feet, at which point his line pulled taut, and he slammed knees-first against the corrugated steel. The cable clearly wasn't going to give any more, but there was sufficient of it for him to scramble down another six or seven feet, before dropping the final three and landing in a crouch.

Despite the shouting overhead, the three combatants were still occupied with each other, Spencer Taylor giving as good as he was getting, swinging wildly with his length of pipe, the armoured killers circling him warily. They'd moved away towards the door on the left, allowing Heck to scamper to the metal table where the spare weapons were, and grab the first thing that came to hand: the claw hammer. Thus far, the figures on the viewing gallery had been slow to react. But now there was a gunshot, a single slug ricocheting from the floor close alongside him.

This drew Taylor's attention. He glanced around, registering Heck's approach with bewilderment, his harrowed face beaded with sweat. His opponents, their ears muffled by their helmets, were slower on the uptake, but now they too realised that something was amiss. They retreated from him to look around, but the guy with the pickaxe handle wasn't quick enough. Heck swung the claw hammer into his lower right side, catching him around the edge of his padding. The impact was massive, the brunt of it on the guy's right kidney. He flopped down into a heap.

Heck leapt over him to face the other one, shouting at Taylor: 'I'm a cop! Use the door these bastards came through! Do it now!'

But Taylor was too dumbfounded to respond, the remaining opponent, the one armed with a razor-edged machete and heavy, rust-caked padlock grasping the situation more quickly. He came at Heck, arms windmilling. Heck jumped backward, only just avoiding injury, but now Taylor re-engaged, aiming at the machete man with the lead pipe. He hit the side of the guy's helmet with a full roundhouse swing, packing such force that the pipe broke, the helmet visibly warping out of shape, its visor catapulting off, exposing a face twisted by concussion. The guy's machete dropped to the floor, his chain-and-lock swinging harmless. Heck threw a full-on punch, smacking him on the nose. The dazed gladiator landed on his back, arms outspread, blood exploding from his nostrils.

'Quickly!' Heck grabbed the kid and shoved him towards the door.

He didn't risk glancing up, though he didn't doubt that the spectators would be taking aim again – and, on cue, gunfire cracked. With a deafening double *PTCHUNG!* two bullets caromed from the floor close by.

'Go, *go!*' Heck pushed the kid in front of him.

Taylor slotted through the half-open door, Heck following. Another two shots rang out, but they were already in the connecting passage.

This lower level of the keep was even more functional than those others Heck had seen, all steel and exposed rivets, lit by bare bulbs hooked along the ceiling with unlagged wiring. Both the arena and these adjacent passages had the air of temporary installations; no doubt, they'd all need to be removed again as the hotel approached completion.

When another basic steel door came in sight, standing ajar, Taylor slid to a halt, his lean, black body running with sweat. He gazed at Heck, bug-eyed. Heck barged past him, throwing his shoulder at the heavy metal. It shifted slowly, grating across an uneven floor. On the other side, two rows of benches faced each other across a long, narrow chamber. Pegs ran along either wall, from which items of body armour hung: more helmets, Kevlar vests, knee and shoulder pads. In the middle of the room, there was a wire basket in which various weaponry was waiting: baseball bats and blag handles, hammers, chains, riding crops.

There was also a man in there, seated on one of the benches.

He wore black leather trousers with pads on the knees; he'd just put on a pair of steel-toed boots and was in the process of pulling the laces tight. His upper torso was naked, swarthy, thickly muscled and covered with military-type tattoos. But he wasn't young. He had short, iron-grey hair and a lined, lived-in face.

Clearly, he was a reserve gladiator, just in case the victim ever proved too much for the twosome sent out originally.

But at present it was this third man who needed back-up.

Though he lunged across the room to the basket, Heck intercepted, swinging the claw hammer down, smashing it side-on to the back of the guy's head. He'd turned it sideways consciously, not wanting to punch a hole in the skull. But that was a mistake.

The guy hit the floor face-down but retained consciousness

sufficiently to roll away. Heck followed, grappling with him as he clambered back to his feet.

'Taylor, get the fuck out!' Heck shouted over his shoulder.

They shifted violently across the room. Taylor dodged around them, but he wasn't heading for the next door. Instead, he went for the basket, snatching out the first weapon that came to hand – a leather whip. It probably wasn't the ideal choice, but he gave it everything he'd got, laying stroke after stroke across the Armenian's exposed back, tiger-striping it with blood and rent tissue.

Grunting in pain, the Armenian tried to break away from Heck. In so doing, he caught a thundering uppercut. His head hinged backward, and Heck was able to tear his hammer-hand loose, before driving it down into the guy's jaw. Bone cracked, and the Armenian sagged to his knees, head lolling.

Heck pushed him aside and blundered on.

'Fu . . . fuck, man,' Taylor jabbered, staggering after him. 'What the fuck . . .?'

Heck reached the door without responding.

'I paid that blond bastard a hundred large . . . *for this!*' Taylor chuntered, only semi-coherent, speaking as much to himself as his rescuer. 'First time I met him, he spoke down a fucking pipe. Spooked the shit out of me. Thought he was a fucking ghost. But the next time, he showed himself. Gave me a postcode and everything . . . said there'd be a pick-up and that they'd take me to a port. He lied, man!'

Heck couldn't help thinking it funny that Taylor's main gripe was the rip-off factor, not the starring role they'd given him in a real-life battle against impossible odds.

'*He fucking lied!*'

'You're a bad lad, Spence,' Heck said, 'but I'm sorry to say that some are even worse than you.'

Beyond the room, they ascended a steep flight of steps

and entered another passage, this one made from stone again rather than metal; they were back in the older section of the keep. As they arrived here, they heard shouting and the rumble of running feet. It galvanised them into keeping moving, sending them scuttling through a high arch, at which point they felt a breeze on their faces and smelled the sea air.

Trying to trace the origin of this, Heck headed left.

They reached a junction – just as a figure came around it.

It was Flat-Top.

Heck's claw hammer pummelled his teeth to shards. There was no snickering laugh this time, as the hoodlum sank down, stupefied with pain, allowing Heck to grab him by his jug-handle ears and battering-ram his skull into the stone-work on their left.

They lumbered on, turning down a broad corridor clad in dust-sheeting. It terminated at a tall, narrow window with no glass in it and a bench underneath. Beyond that, Heck saw the night sky, but only through the upright poles of what had to be scaffolding. He climbed into the casement, a stiff, cool wind swirling round him.

They appeared to be at the rear of the keep, which, by the looks of it, had been constructed on the island's northern edge, because they were now looking out over the open sea, moonlight dancing on heaving, rolling waves. When Heck peered down through the scaffolding, it was a terrifying drop, a hundred feet or more to jagged rocks and exploding surf. He glanced upward. It was difficult to see how far the scaffolding ascended because, about fifteen feet above their heads, planking laid across horizontal bars provided a makeshift gantry for workmen – though that at least meant the gantry had to be accessible from other levels inside the building.

'Can you climb?' he asked Taylor.

'Fuck, man! Which way?'

'Take a guess, genius.'

The kid still looked nonplussed.

'We get up to that gantry, we can probably get back inside.'

'And how the fuck's that going to help us?'

Heck clamped the back of Taylor's neck and pulled him forward till they were chin-to-chin. 'Help's on its way, OK? Not that you bloody deserve it. But you're my responsibility now. So, I'm going to try to keep you alive . . . and that isn't going to happen if we end up in the sea. You seen those waves down there? Even if you can make it into the water without getting battered to shit on the rocks, you think you'll still have enough in the tank to swim around the island and then make it back to shore?'

There was a shriek of rage from somewhere behind; no doubt someone had just discovered Flat-Top. Taylor needed no second telling. Heck released him, and he climbed out through the casement, grabbing an overhead bar and hauling himself athletically upward.

Heck slid the hammer into the belt at his back, and followed, the pair of them ascending side-by-side. Of course, it wasn't easy. The scaffolding poles were spaced far apart and were cold and slippery. It was rickety too; though clamped to the keep wall, the skeletal structure shuddered and shook. Below them, an abyss yawned.

'Jesus!' Taylor squawked as both feet lost their purchase at the same time. He whimpered hysterically as he hung by two hands. Heck hooked an arm around his waist, allowing him to find his footing again.

'*Fuck . . . Oh, fuck . . .*' The kid's eyes were like moons in a face more strained and drawn than Heck had ever seen in a person under twenty years old.

'Just keep going. You're younger than me . . . probably fitter.'

Taylor climbed on, hand over hand, foot over foot. Heck matched him, and the next thing, they were clambering onto the gantry. Taylor lay full-length, fingers gripping the wood, his body shuddering. Heck crouched, breathing hard. On their left, lit by occasional suspended bulbs, the gantry ran alongside the building for sixty or seventy yards, before terminating at a hanging tarp. On their right, it was more promising, running thirty yards to the foot of an upright ladder.

Heck tapped Taylor's shoulder and indicated the way they should go.

'No way!' the kid moaned. 'If more cops are coming, why don't we just lay low and wait?'

'Because these nutjobs'll search *everywhere* . . . you know why? Because they've *got* to.'

Wearily, Taylor swayed to his feet.

They went single file along the gantry, until they reached the ladder. Heck looked up: it ascended another thirty feet, braced by a single steel pole at its back.

He tested it with both hands, and it felt secure. But this would be an even more nerve-racking climb than the scaffold, especially as at the top it disappeared through a square hatch in a ceiling made from sheets of opaque plastic.

'Follow me up, Spence,' Heck said.

'You serious, man . . . you think this'll hold?'

'It's designed for hairy-arsed brickies carrying hods. Course it'll hold.'

Heck commenced the climb, face upturned. As the ladder was narrow, he could only ascend with hands and feet close together, which felt clumsy and unnatural. In addition, the ladder shivered and rattled in the spiralling wind, which came straight off the Atlantic and was surprisingly cold.

He halted halfway up and glanced back down.

It was a dizzying sight: Taylor's face written with terror,

the vertical drop below him so sheer that it tilted all perspec-
tive. Heck hung there desperately, feeling as if he, the ladder,
and the keep of Trevallick Hall itself, were toppling.

'You all right?' he shouted, clinging on tight to stabilise
himself.

'Yeah, man, yeah . . . just go, yeah? *Go!*'

Heck continued up, trusting that the kid was too adrenalised to feel the bite of the wind. He was about ten feet below
the hatch when he heard voices above it. He froze, signalling
with his hand that Taylor should do the same. The voices
were foreign, presumably Armenian, and were accompanied
by several pairs of feet thundering by overhead. Heck hung
there with eyes clenched shut. Any second, it seemed that
one of them would simply glance down through the opening
and spot him. They were all likely armed by now, so he and
Taylor would be fish in a barrel.

But it didn't happen.

The footfalls dwindled, the voices fading.

Heck recommenced climbing. When he poked his head
through, he saw another timber walkway, this also running
alongside the keep's outer wall, though it was broader than
the one below. That had been two planks in breadth, whereas
this one was five. It had been laid over the top of the sheeting,
which extended further out by ten feet or so, and banged
and bellied in the breeze.

Heck heaved himself up and knelt on the planks. There
were apertures in the wall along this section – more windows
with the glass missing – each one spaced about ten yards
from the next. As the gantry walkway lay only a few inches
below each, and they were all a good seven feet in height,
it was simply a matter of choosing one and stepping through
it to get back inside. Heck waited until Taylor was alongside
him.

'How you doing?' he asked.

The kid hung his head, wheezing for breath. 'Yeah, man . . . I'm good. Cold though.'

Heck was in a similar position, his jeans and polo shirt damp with sweat, the chill cutting into him. He pivoted round to get his bearings.

The left-hand route was partially blocked by a cement mixer and several bags of cement powder, so they went right. As they did, Heck peered upward. Thirty feet above, a battlemented parapet was defined against the star-speckled sky and rendered even more visible by electric lighting suffused over the top.

He remembered being told about the helipad.

Was this it then? Were they almost at the hall's highest point?

Not that it mattered. The first aperture approached. He flattened himself against the wall, waiting until Taylor had fallen in behind him, and then risked a peek. It was an embrasure rather than a proper window, tall but very narrow – so much so that only one man could climb into it at a time – with a stone floor sloping sharply down to what looked like another sheer drop, this one inside the building. Heck sidled in, ventured a short way and found himself looking forty feet down a plunging stairwell.

He shuffled back and re-emerged onto the walkway, already in the process of telling Taylor that they needed to find another route – only to discover the kid in the grasp of a guy in overalls, who must have stepped out from one of the apertures behind them.

The guy wasn't especially big or brawny; like the one Heck had knocked out in the changing room, a head of ash-grey hair complemented his dark, leather-skinned features. But his teeth were locked, and he tightened his thick-sinewed right arm around Taylor's throat, gleefully squeezing the life out of him.

Taylor *glugged* like a man drowning as he rent at the locked forearm. But the hellish grip weakened when the assailant saw Heck appear.

Not having expected two of them, he tried to shout to whichever of his confederates were close by, only for Heck's right fist to fly into his left eye with crunching force. The guy's head jerked backward and blood spattered down his left cheek, but he clung on, using Taylor as a shield – in response to which, the kid rammed his elbows backward, both times finding rib-bones. The hold was broken, and the Armenian staggered away.

Heck slid past Taylor, advancing on their opponent – who continued to back off, though on reaching the cement mixer, he used it to stabilise himself, and a six-inch blade flicked open in his right hand. Despite his left eye streaming blood, his grimace of pain curved into a sickle grin.

'Spence, get out of here!' Heck shouted over his shoulder.

'The fuck, man! Which way?'

Heck risked a glance. Two more of them had appeared some distance to their rear.

'The sky's the limit, pal!' he shouted.

Taylor looked around, and seeing that they'd already reached the top of the ladder, leapt up and caught the bar over his head, swinging himself back onto the scaffolding.

The knifeman, meanwhile, came at Heck slowly, passing the blade from hand to hand. He looked confident, but his injured left eye had virtually closed. A vicious backhand slash, aimed at the belly, drove Heck into retreat – at which point his right heel connected with the cement bags and he stumbled down onto his haunches.

The knifeman came on faster.

But Heck jumped back up, his right hand full of cement powder, which he flung in the guy's face, primarily at his one good eye. With gasps of angry pain, the Armenian tottered to a halt. Heck launched a heavy foot into his groin and caught him under the chin with two fists clamped together, the *SMACK!* of which echoed even over the sea wind.

The guy hurtled sideways, landing full-length on the plastic sheeting, which, by a miracle, held. Heck ran past him, no longer sure which way he was going. A glance backward showed the newly arrived Armenians close behind. But when he looked to the front, several more were emerging from yet another of those unglazed apertures.

Heck stopped running and commenced climbing.

As he ascended through the framework, he looked down and saw, rather to his surprise, that no one was following. A couple of them were leaning out from the walkway, trying to bring their unconscious mate back to safety. Two others were engaged in frantic conversation, which he could make neither head nor tail of, though it seemed curious that they weren't at least staring up after him.

Either way, it was an advantage Heck had no hesitation in taking, clambering all the way to the top. When he got there, the first thing he saw as he stepped through a gap in the crenellations was that he was now on the roof of the keep, as he'd suspected, the highest point of Trevallick Hall. It was a flat, square area, perhaps ninety yards by ninety, surrounded completely by battlements, though such ancient fixtures were rendered anachronistic by the new layer of tarmac that covered the roof, and, in the very middle of it, the helipad, a wide-open area surrounded by floodlights, marked with a bright yellow letter H. Currently, on top of this sat an Augusta Westland Koala helicopter, headlights on full blast, rotor blades turning lazily.

But this caught Heck's attention only fleetingly. Because some forty yards to his right, Spencer Taylor knelt in what looked like abject defeat, his head drooped.

'Hey . . . *cop!*' a voice shouted.

Heck spun around, and the reason for Taylor's capitulation became obvious.

A squat figure approached. It was Rodent, now wielding an automatic weapon, the same type of FN SCAR battle rifle that Narek Sarafian had used. Clearly, he'd been awaiting them, first intercepting Taylor, who'd known better than to argue. Now the weapon was trained muzzle-first on Heck.

Wearily, he raised his hands.

Rodent didn't lower the rifle, but flicked it right, signalling that Heck should cross the roof and kneel alongside his compatriot.

As Heck went, his eyes roved their surroundings – and other things came to his attention. Immediately, he understood the lack of pursuit pressed by Milena Misanyan's men stationed below.

The woman herself, now wearing a long crimson overcoat, stood on the landward parapet, alongside Ray Marciano. They were conversing animatedly, their attention riveted on the mainland, which at this time of night should be all but indistinguishable, yet now was a scurrying mass of twinkling blue lights. Certain of these had even set off across the water.

Little wonder the twosome now came quickly back across the roof, though as they passed the helicopter, they separated, Misanyan climbing into the cockpit on the passenger side. An interior light came on briefly and Heck saw her settle alongside the pilot, who was already in harness. She fitted on a pair of headphones, while he manipulated the controls, and the blades swirled more vigorously. Marciano, meanwhile, diverted towards the prisoners. As he did, he reached under his jacket and drew out his Beretta.

'Jesus Christ,' Heck muttered, but it wasn't a blasphemy, it was a prayer that he could manage to make good use of the one chance he was likely to get here.

407

Rodent backed away until he was ten yards off. Marciano stopped alongside him.

'Sorry about this, Heck,' the ex-cop said. 'But my orders are that we finish what we started.'

'Uh-huh,' Heck nodded.

Side by side, Marciano and his man took aim, one weapon for each of the two prisoners.

And Heck took his chance, hurling the claw hammer he'd filched from behind his back. It spun through the air, a blur, travelling so fast that Marciano barely glimpsed it before it smacked him on the top right corner of his head, cavorting away as it dropped him into a crumpled heap.

Fleetingly stunned, Rodent turned his scrutiny first on his fallen ally and then on Heck, who had now jumped to his feet. In what seemed like slow motion, he brought his weapon around to lock it on the new target – and never saw Spencer Taylor come gambolling forward, dive and hit him in the midriff with his shoulder. Rodent rocked with the force of it, but didn't fall; he swivelled back round, raised his weapon and clubbed the back of Taylor's head.

As the kid sank down, Heck also crossed the space between them. Rodent saw him in his side-vision. He swung the SCAR like a bat, but Heck caught it in both hands and kicked the guy in his left knee. The Armenian grunted and tried to hop backward, the SCAR coming loose in his grip. As Heck tried to yank it away, Rodent clawed at his face, gouging the flesh, but Heck deflected the blow, slamming his left fist into the guy's jaw. The firearm went spinning away as Rodent staggered sideways, Heck following, bludgeoning him with a right and another left. Dazed though he was, the tough Armenian stayed upright. In fact, he barrelled forward, head lowered, wrapping his brawny arms around Heck's waist. Heck, briefly off-balance, smashed an elbow down into his spine, dropping him to his knees, and another into the back of his neck.

'*The fuck* . . .' the shrill voice of Spencer Taylor called somewhere to the right.

Heck had no time to look. He grappled with Rodent's hands, which had hooked onto the belt of his jeans, threw them off, and with another well-aimed kick, this time to the guy's right temple, knocked him out cold.

'*Fucking stop, man, yeah? D'you hear me?*'

Heck whirled, to see that Taylor had retrieved the SCAR and was advancing on the copter, which, from the down-blast of its spinning blades, was about to ascend.

'Spencer!' Heck shouted.

'*I said stop . . . you fucking hear!*'

The copter ascended.

'*You fucks!*' He hefted the SCAR to his shoulder. '*You're taking me out of here!*'

'Spencer!' Heck bellowed.

The craft was thirty feet above the helipad when the kid opened fire, a hail of high-velocity rounds hammering first into its underside, then cross-stitching the cockpit canopy.

'Shit!' Heck tottered to a halt. 'Oh . . . *shit!*'

Taylor fired relentlessly as the copter tried to loft itself away northward, fragmenting its rotor blades, splinters of which whirled in every direction. It rapidly lost power and balance. Heck could imagine the pilot slumped dead over his controls, Milena Misanyan rigid alongside him, screaming . . .

Before his eyes, the heavy craft tilted over until it lay sideways in mid-air – and then dropped abruptly from sight, turning end-over-end down the exterior wall of the keep, caroming off and through the scaffolding, bent and broken poles deluging alongside it. The final explosion on the rocks far below shook the venerable building to its foundations, a great mushroom of smoke and flame erupting upward past the top of the battlements, the searing heat and light of it swamping the entire roof. Heck stood helpless, his sweat briefly drying, his hair stiffening.

A few yards away, Taylor's head slumped backward, his confused gaze lingering on what was nothing more now than a roiling pillar of smoke. The SCAR hung limply by his side.

A second passed before Heck moved warily towards him.

'Spence,' he said, 'put that bloody thing down, eh? Before anyone else gets hurt.'

'*The fuck!*' Taylor shouted, jolted out of his trance. He spun around and trained the weapon on Heck. 'There're more of 'em, loads more . . . we know, we've seen 'em.'

'Hey, hey . . . whoa!' Heck raised his hands but couldn't help retreating – the kid limped towards him with a manic expression, the gun still levelled.

Heck pointed southward. 'Look at the mainland. That's the law and his big brother, pal. These guys have already seen it . . . what's left of them. They're probably getting into boats as we speak. But even then, they won't get far. So, it's over . . . yeah?'

'Nah, man. Nah . . . no way.' Taylor's finger locked on the trigger. 'You're a cop too . . .'

'I am, mate, yeah.'

'Then you're not my fucking mate! You say you're here to help, but really you're here to pinch me!'

'You saying I didn't help you, Spence?' Heck was aware of the south battlements approaching behind. At this rate, he'd pass clean through them. So, he halted, lowering his hands but keeping the palms upright, showing that they were empty. 'Spence . . . let's just cool it, yeah?'

'Stop telling me what to do! You fucking pig! You think you and your bluds are going to send me down?'

'What's the other option? You going to shoot it out with the whole of the Devon and Cornwall Police? How many rounds you got left?'

410

'Hey, man, don't be fucking changing the subject!'

'Spence, whatever you're accused of . . .'

'And don't be calling me Spence! It's not my fucking name, all right?'

'Spen*cer*! . . . whatever you're accused of, I'm sure we can sort it. That chopper that went down . . . you didn't do that, it just crashed. Pilot panicked and pressed the wrong button.' He shrugged. 'Simple as, yeah?'

But Taylor raised the SCAR to his shoulder and aimed it at Heck's face. 'You gotta get me off this island!'

'And how can I do that? You hear that sound?' Heck made as if to listen, and if Taylor had bothered doing the same, he'd have heard the distant but fast-approaching whirr of additional sets of rotor blades. 'You think that's the ghost of the one you just shot down?'

'Man, I didn't shoot it . . . you just said so!'

'All right, fine, listen . . .'

'Don't be telling me to listen!' Taylor's red-rimmed eyes strained in their sockets, sweat again beading his near-naked body. 'I'm the one giving the orders, you're the one following 'em! So shut your pig mouth, and just do what I tell . . .'

He never saw the clenched fist that rammed upward into his groin.

Taylor hadn't realised that he was standing directly along-side Ray Marciano's unconscious form, or that the ex-cop wasn't unconscious any more. The kid slumped to his knees, face written with unbelievable pain – and was completely unprepared for the expert karate chop aimed at his throat.

'Really, Heck?' Marciano clambered to his feet and extricated the SCAR from the gangbanger's unconscious hands. 'You came all this way to save a gobby little twat like that?'

Heck shook his head. 'I *was* wondering . . .'

Marciano kept the weapon levelled, as he made a couple of checks to ensure that it was still loaded. 'Thought he'd never shut up.'

A lump the size of a plum lowered on the top left corner of his forehead; it was so swollen that it pulled his long, sharp features out of shape, but he didn't seem especially angry.

'OK, Heck . . . well, I had my orders, as you know. But now . . . as the person who issued them isn't with us any more, perhaps there's a deal to be done, eh?'

Heck didn't reply.

'Better make it good, though.' Marciano winked. 'Otherwise, I can't let you walk away from here, knowing the stuff you do.'

'Ray, you must understand I'm not authorised . . .'

'And don't give me any fucking pap.'

'You seriously think I can make all this disappear?'

Marciano pondered their surroundings, as if only now the gravity of the situation was dawning on him. Acrid smoke drifted across the roof; bullet casings were scattered everywhere; Taylor and Rodent lay prone where they'd fallen. Sirens could be heard crossing the strait, while somewhere overhead at least one police helicopter was very close.

Marciano sighed. 'You a man of honour, Heck?'

'What do you mean?'

'How about . . . I give you Morgan Robbins, the one who actually made this happen, and you don't chase me so hard?'

'What're you talking about?'

'It's not like it'll be tough for you. None of you lot think I did anything really wrong.'

'Apart from taking money to see men killed.'

Marciano barked with laughter. 'Are you telling me you'd pack the job in if they reinstated the death penalty, Heck?

Can't see it, somehow . . . and hey, we might do just that once we've left Europe.'

'Ray . . . it's over, mate.'

The ex-cop sniffed, his smile wilting. 'Impossible situation to present you with, I suppose. Never mind.' Hefting the SCAR one-handed, he retreated towards the west-facing parapet, halting en route to scoop up the pistol he'd dropped and pocketing it.

'Where the hell do you think you're going?' Heck shouted.

'Where do you think?'

'You're going to jump? Don't be so bloody stupid!'

'Being stupid would be staying here . . . and spending the rest of my life in jail with all those scumbags I was responsible for sending there.'

'Ray, you'll rip yourself to pieces . . .'

'I seem to remember that you once jumped from a high point into deep water. You did OK out of it.'

'This isn't deep water . . . it's the shoreline. And that was nowhere near as high as this.'

'I've always taken chances, Heck . . .'

The thunderous roar of the local chopper now sounded directly overhead. A spotlight swept the roof. Marciano grinned broadly, before turning and running.

'Hey, *whoa!*' Heck called. 'What about Morgan Robbins?'

When the ex-cop reached the battlements, he halted and turned, laughing loudly, though briefly Heck could hear nothing but the tinny-voiced commandments issuing from the police loudhailer high overhead.

'Say again . . .' Heck shouted.

'Locker 342!' Marciano repeated. 'Liverpool Street. Look for "Spartacus".'

'Sparta . . .?'

413

'So long, Heck.'

And he'd gone, vanishing through the nearest embrasure.

Heck scrambled over there, but when he looked through the gap, saw only the blackness of night and a silver sparkle of moonlight on the rolling, sighing sea.

Chapter 38

September 6 was a Wednesday. It was cool and breezy that evening, and though the nights weren't really drawing in yet, by eight o'clock, dusk had settled on North London. A stiff breeze, faintly redolent of autumn, buffeted the leaves in the parks and along the avenues of residential streets.

Being midweek, of course, there wasn't a great deal of activity. It was the quietest night of the police officer's week, and if you were working late shifts, it might well provide an opportunity for you to catch up on paperwork, or to sit on some corner in your vehicle, relaxed but watchful, ear cocked to the eerie hiss of the radio.

Not so Heck. Not tonight.

When he arrived at the Duke of Albion, he was in dapper mode: best shirt and tie, brand new suit, face cleanly shaven. A firm believer in that 'uniform' thing, he was no stranger to this look, though today he'd probably gone to town a little more than usual.

He made quite a contrast with Gail Honeyford, who was sitting alone in the Duke's snug in jeans and T-shirt, her hair down and a scruffy sweatshirt tied around her shoulders.

She sipped from a bottle of lager as she pored, with pen in hand, over several forms.

'You reached the stage already where you're taking work home with you?' Heck said.

She seemed unsurprised by his arrival, clearly having watched him enter from the corner of her eye. 'What are you doing here, Heck?'

'Came to find you. Not a particularly good place to hide, the closest boozer to Staples Corner.'

'I'm not trying to hide,' she said. 'I've just got stuff to do.'

'Tonight?' He frowned with disapproval. 'Just up the road from here, there's an SCU do on. You got your priorities in a twist, or what?'

She sat back. 'I can't go. I'd feel like a total fraud.'

'A fraud? You more than played your part in Operation Sledgehammer.'

'Yeah . . .' She shot him a look. 'But I wasn't there for the best bit, was I!'

'To be fair . . . near enough no one was.'

'*You* were. And I should've been there with you. Instead, I was back in the office, filing.'

'Listen . . .' He plonked himself on a stool. 'Tonight's party is not just because we've accounted for most of our fugitives *and* locked up the Tottenham shooter, but to celebrate the charging of Morgan Robbins with conspiracy to murder before . . . and this is the important bit, *before* NPCC could even set up their new task force.'

'You here to console me, Heck, or rub my nose in it?'

'The point is *I* wasn't there for any of that. I wasn't the one who arrested Robbins. I didn't interview him, I didn't charge him . . . and I'm still going to the party.'

She snorted. 'I don't suppose even *you* can be expected to do everything. Especially when the brass want some of the glory for themselves. But I must've missed the bit where it was someone else who came up with the idea to check that locker at Liverpool Street.'

It was less easy to argue this point, he conceded.

Locker 342 at Liverpool Street Station had turned out to be a hidey-hole used by one of the late Milena Misanyan's London-based accountants. Inside it, there was only one item: an external hard drive, which, when opened, contained masses of illicit financial data relating to the billionaire's UK-based interests. What they'd in effect discovered was an electronic accounts book, which provided a comprehensive record of Misanyan's illegal activities in Britain – everything from bribing public officials to fraud, from insider trading to embezzlement, from cybercrime to money laundering. More important than this though, before any of Misanyan's affairs had been handed over to the City of London Police's Economic Crime Directorate, Operation Sledgehammer had taken personal charge of one particular electronic folder entitled 'Spartacus', which solely contained intel concerning payments relevant to the gladiatorial combats at Trevallick Hall.

If Heck hadn't seen it for himself, it would have staggered him.

The fugitives each paid a hundred grand for the privilege of being rescued. Fifty of that went into Ray Marciano's pocket (on top of his monthly salary from Morgan Robbins), twenty-five of it went to Narek Sarafian, the driver, and the remaining twenty-five to Milena Misanyan or, if she wasn't on the island at the time, one of her trusted reps. Not that she really needed it. It was little more than a minor recompense in her case, because each time there was a successful delivery, she paid Morgan Robbins the princely sum of £250,000.

For Misanyan it had been an expensive if depraved hobby, though with her fantastical net-wealth it hardly cost her anything in reality. Where Morgan Robbins was concerned, it was a different story. He might well have genuinely hated those incorrigible men he'd delivered to their deaths, but as Heck had suspected all along, ultimately it was still a case of him surrendering his principles and going for the big bucks.

In light of that, there was no question that it was Heck who'd brought a major case to a satisfactory conclusion. But only because Ray Marciano had taken a decision to give the info to him rather than to kill him. Heck still couldn't work that out.

Most likely, Marciano had opted for a scorched-earth policy, seeking to take down the entire UK-based Misanyan operation, to weaken it to the point where it couldn't pursue him. Of course, this was based on the assumption that he would survive jumping from the castle parapet – which was one reason at least why Heck wasn't yet convinced that the ex-cop was dead.

'Hello?' Gail said tetchily. '*Earth to Heck!*'

'What . . . oh yeah, sorry. Look, the important stuff was spoon-fed to me.'

'Yeah. Spoon-fed with a machine gun.'

'Gail . . . you need to grow up. You really wish you'd been there for *that*?'

'Hey, I'm not like you, Heck. I *do* care whether I live or die, but I didn't join SCU because it's a safe haven. And whether I like it or not, you and me were partners on this, so I *should've* been there.'

Heck sighed. He was no closer to understanding Gail Honeyford now than he had been the first time they'd worked together. But her desire to assert herself was not unusual for someone with high ambition, and he couldn't criticise her for that just because he had none.

'Look . . .' he said, 'have a drink, eh?'

'I've already got one.'

He lumbered to the bar and bought himself a pint of bitter. When he sat down again, they sipped in aimless silence.

'On reflection,' he eventually said, 'it doesn't surprise me that Gemma ended up sending you indoors.'

Gail's expression hardened. 'Oh, really?'

'She's been a bit screwed up recently. I mean, by her normal standards. She's looked tired, she's not been seeing stuff as clearly as she usually does.'

'Gee . . .' Gail chuckled without humour, 'I wonder why.'

'The reason doesn't matter. The point is . . . she gave you a gig that you weren't quite ready for. Soon as she saw you were in danger of going under, she pulled you.'

'She never pulls you, and you seem to be in danger of going under all the time.'

'She probably has higher hopes for you than for me.'

'Well . . .' Gail swilled more lager, 'that's unfortunate.'

Heck was puzzled. 'What do you mean?'

'You might as well be the first to know,' she said. 'I owe you that much at least. First thing tomorrow morning, I'm—'

He jabbed a finger. 'Don't you dare say you're putting in for a transfer.'

She watched him guardedly. 'Why shouldn't I?'

'Because . . . because this is the crème de la crème. Look, Gail, NCG's the serious end of the market, and SCU's the serious end of that.' He shook his head. 'It'll be seen as a massive step back if you decide you can't hack it.'

'It won't be about that.'

'No, but that's how it'll be seen. And you know that in your bones. You hung on in Surrey and fought your corner for years after that Ron Pavey business, because you knew what they'd all have said.'

Her belligerence diminished a little, as she recalled that Heck had been one of the few people on her side during that most difficult period of her career; in fact, he'd been a help, a *huge* help. 'Look, Mark . . . you're one of the good guys. I'm sorry for sounding off at you.'

'If sounding off is what it takes to keep you here, do it. It's at least partly *my* fault, anyway.'

'It's not your fault.'

'I should never have dragged you into my world. Not without prepping you properly . . .'

'Damn it, Heck! I'm not a rookie! I voluntarily did my bit up in Hull, even though I knew I'd likely catch it. *I'm* the one who slagged DI Warnock off, not you.'

'And now you want to leave?' He gave a crooked smile. 'Really? Even though you've had a good old taste of it . . .'

'All right, I don't want to leave.' She made a wild, frustrated gesture. 'This is everything I want in the job. I mean, apart from the getting stuck behind the filing cabinets bit . . .'

'I understand that, and Gemma does too. But you've gotta walk before you can run. Gail . . . come to the party tonight, eh? At least show your face for half an hour.'

'Just like that? Drive over there with you, so we can walk in arm in arm?'

'I wasn't meaning that.'

'I know you weren't.' She sat back. 'But be honest. Isn't it the case that you wouldn't mind Gemma seeing us doing that? Getting her a bit jealous.'

'I don't follow.' He felt genuinely puzzled.

She rolled her eyes. 'You're obviously still mad for her, Heck. Why don't you just go and get her?'

'Take a club, you mean? Drag her off by the hair to my man cave? I can't believe that you of all people are suggesting that . . .'

'I'm not, you big bloody ape!' She leaned forward. 'Just tell her how you feel. Lay it out once and for all.'

'I already have.' He made a hopeless gesture. 'She doesn't want me. And even if she did . . . she can't see any way to make it happen that would suit us both. Least, I think that's what she said. Mind, I don't think she's as keen on Jack Reed as I first thought.'

Gail waved her bottle dismissively. 'He cuts a dash, that's all.'

'I think he made a bit of an impression.'

'Look . . .' She shook her head, 'everything I've said about her notwithstanding, a woman like Gemma can take her pick. She's got the looks, the intellect, the personality . . . not to mention the power. She still gets hit on, of course. There must be a dozen blokes have asked her out since you and her broke up, all of whom she's sent off with a thick ear.'

'What are you trying to say?'

'They don't measure up, Heck. None of them. But then along comes Jack bloody Reed. Maybe he's a bit closer to her exacting standards. Maybe she's briefly taken aback and she wonders could this be the guy. But she's not exactly made a move on him, has she? How long's he been in SCU?'

'I dunno . . . four months.'

'OK . . .' She shrugged. 'Four months, and they're still at arm's length.'

'But when I asked her, she didn't deny there was interest there . . .'

'Of course she didn't deny it. Look . . . you say she's been acting screwy recently? That she's seemed tired, distracted. You don't know why? I mean, come on, Heck, you're the most intuitive detective I've ever worked with. Surely you can figure *this* out?'

'If you're trying to say that deep down she's got *real* feelings for me . . .'

'Well, what do you think?' She shook her head, amazed that he could be so slow. 'And it's a problem for her, isn't it? It's clearly been a problem for some time, but now she's getting tired of it, now she's trying to find a way to make it disappear. And then along comes Jack Reed, and he seems like a viable option. Except . . .'

Heck shrugged, nonplussed. 'Except . . .?'

'Lord help us.' Gail rolled her eyes. 'Except you can't force yourself to feel affection for someone if those emotions are already spoken for.'

Heck gazed at her with fascination, his mouth slowly turning dry.

'She doesn't just have feelings for you,' she continued. 'It goes way further than that. This is why she's been distracted, why she's been off her game. Because she's finally tried to face this thing off . . . and she can't.'

'Is it . . .?' He didn't quite know how to phrase the question. 'Is it because you're a woman that you know this . . .?'

'No, it's because I'm a normal person, and at least fifty per cent of my bandwidth is tuned to normal life. Unlike yours, which is entirely focused somewhere else.'

'You . . .' he shook his head, 'Gail, you couldn't be mistaken about this?'

'The only way you're going to know, Heck, is if you go to that party right now, and talk to Gemma . . .'

'But I've told you . . . it can't happen.'

She leaned forward and stuck a finger into his shoulder. '*You* have to find a way to make it happen.'

'Like how?'

'I don't know. If things are impossible as they are, change them. *You're* the one who's going to have to do it, Heck . . . and soon, because Gemma might realise she's made a mistake with Reed, but she's still going to keep pulling the other way.'

He sat rigid, pondering.

Gemma Piper had been Heck's first and only serious adult crush, he realised, and somewhere inside he knew she'd be his last. He needed to be with her.

Whatever it took.

That last bit was the difficult part. Yet, all of a sudden, from nowhere, an idea was germinating. In truth, it wasn't out of nowhere – it must've existed just below his consciousness for a long time. But only now, with the clarity of vision Gail had provided, did he decide that it was time to recognise the only truly important thing in his life.

He jumped up from the table so fast that Gail moved her chair back in surprise.

'You little belter.' He clutched her hand in both of his own. 'You bloody little belter.'

'Yeah, I hear that a lot. You've no idea how boring it gets.'

'It won't be seen as inappropriate if I kiss you on the head?'

'No, kiss me on the head. I need it.'

He did so, before backing away. She watched him in vague surprise, as if she hadn't expected her words of homespun wisdom to find their mark so quickly.

'You can still come,' he said. 'There's nothing to—'

'Shut up. Staying here.'

'Fair enough.' He backed off faster now, towards the door. 'But I'm going to shout your name from the rooftops tonight, Gail. I'm going to let everyone know that you were up to your eyebrows in that case. That you were every bit as important as I was.'

'Don't overdo it, Heck.'

'I'll tell them that not only have they got a brilliant young detective in Gail Honeyford, they've got a potential new DS . . . and that they should act on that ASAP.'

'Heck, I . . . *what?*'

But he was already out of the door.

Heck was halfway up the Edgware Road, when he got through on his hands-free.

'Yeah, Bob Hunter,' came a voice at the other end.

'Bob, it's Heck.'

'Well, well . . . it's the man of the moment.'

'Is that DI post still open?'

'Yeah, sure . . .' But Hunter sounded wary.

'And you guarantee you can swing me the requisite promotion? No bullshit, Bob, I need to know.'

'Already had it OK'd. Told you you had money in the bank. Heck, what's going on?'

'I'll get back to you later. Before the end of tonight, I promise.'

'I thought after your latest success you'd be pretty well cemented into SCU.'

'Nah . . .' Heck shook his head even as he drove. 'I don't think there's much future with SCU.' And he cut the call.

Long before he reached his destination, he pulled up beside an off-licence.

Inside, though he half-hesitated when it occurred to him that he might be tempting fate, he paid £36 for a bottle of Moët. When shopping in the Fulham minimart, this was more than he would have paid for a crate of beer, but one thing Heck rarely did was chuck his money away – not through choice, but because he had relatively little to chuck it away on. On impulse – and on this occasion, he *really* wondered if he was tempting fate – he also bought a cellophane-wrapped block of eight PVC champagne flutes.

'You won't get much in each of those with only one bottle,' the woman behind the counter said, trying to lure him into buying a second.

'It's OK,' Heck said. 'I'll either need two . . . or none.'

Chapter 39

The Ace of Diamonds was officially a London pub, but stood within a stone's throw of the countryside. Located just off Cockfosters Road, in the capital's outer ring of suburbia, Gwen Straker had chosen it for the party because it was reasonably close to Staples Corner – close, as within a thirty-minute drive. When Heck got there, it was just short of nine o'clock.

Even though this was a Wednesday, the car park was crammed with vehicles, so he drove to a secluded side lot and, after stowing the champagne in the passenger footwell, walked around to the front entrance. He entered a small lobby, with open glass doors on the left giving way to the main downstairs bar, which was only sparsely populated. To the right, meanwhile, an easel carried a *Private Function* notice on it, and an arrow directed him towards a carpeted stairway.

As he ascended, the sounds of a noisy upstairs party embraced him. The doors to the function room were wedged open, so thumping rock music emanated, along with the intense heat of numerous bodies milling jovially together in a confined space.

Heck loosened his tie before entering, his brow immediately turning damp.

It was a well-designed venue, long rather than wide, with pub-type tables and chairs along its entire length, but also boasting several lower tables inserted between pouffes and sofas. The buffet lay along a row of worktops to his left, and though much of it still nestled under silver foil, what he could see looked mouth-watering. The bar was located at the far end, though he could barely distinguish it, such was the thicket of customers clamouring for drinks.

Though he'd hoped to make an instant impression in his smart gear, Heck realised that it was already a lost cause. He stripped his jacket off, hung it in a side cloakroom, and loosened his tie further as he sidled into the crowd. He felt progressively stiffer and more uncomfortable – making a full-on approach to Gemma had seemed like a great idea a few minutes ago, but now that he was here, he was less sure; he wished he had Gail at his back to egg him on. Instead, he had to make do with Charlie Finnegan, who materialised in front of him, red-faced and sweaty, his normally greased-back hair hanging in damp strings. But he was in a good mood as he drained the last dregs of what looked like it might have been a large malt and ice, even going so far as to clap Heck on the shoulder.

'Yo, Charlie,' Heck said, having to raise his voice to be heard over the music.

Finnegan made a show of looking past him. 'No Gail Honeyford?'

'I'm afraid not.'

'More's the pity. Hottest chick we've seen here in a while . . . excluding the Lioness of course, but she hardly counts.'

'Did Gary make it?' Heck asked.

'Nah. Not up to it. His missus rang earlier. He's pissed off, but apparently he has to have a few more days without excitement, and strictly no alcohol.'

Heck nodded, unsurprised.

'Some good news, though, eh?' Finnegan said this as if Heck would already know what it was.

'What?' Heck said. 'Progress up in Liverpool?'

Finnegan waved that away as if it didn't matter. 'Down in Cornwall. You've heard what's happened?'

'No.'

'Ho-*ho*!' Finnegan clapped Heck's shoulder again. 'They've found bodies, mate.'

Fleetingly, Heck was distracted from his purpose here. 'You mean at Trevallick Hall?'

'Where else?'

'Ray Marciano?'

'Nah . . .' Finnegan shook his head. 'He's well gone, they reckon. Tide would've carried him away. Nah . . . these were inside, down in the basement. Well, in the foundations actually. Under about two feet of new cement. That was *your* idea, wasn't it?'

Heck nodded. 'It was something Ray Marciano said to me . . . about getting buried in wet cement. Only occurred to me afterwards that he might have meant it for real.'

'Big break, either way,' Finnegan said. 'If that hotel had gone up, been finished like . . . could have been decades before they were found. If they ever were.'

'How many?' Heck asked.

'Latest count, nineteen.'

Heck nodded, thinking hard.

Even though there was still no trace of Ray Marciano, this was terrific news. In terms of the actual murders, they didn't just have the video evidence now, which, though it required strong stomachs to view, was compelling, they also had the arena where the combats had taken place, and this had so far proved a happy hunting-ground for the forensics teams, who'd already uncovered numerous different DNA profiles, all of which had corresponded with known missing persons, including eleven from the Most Wanted list. If they'd now found bodies as well, the case was almost cut and dried.

'Gwen went down there earlier this evening,' Finnegan added. 'Gemma's going down first thing tomorrow. And that's not all. Late this afternoon, Trident started locking up members of the Toreadors. That little shit Spencer Taylor's been singing like a canary. Talk about everything coming together at the right time. They won't dare close us down now. Imagine how the press would react to that.'

'That's good, Charlie,' Heck nodded. 'That's all good.'

Finnegan pointed at the bar. 'What're you having?'

'Nothing for a minute. Thanks anyway.'

'Up to you, but you'd better get your skates on . . . we'll be buying our own soon.'

Heck nodded again, and Finnegan pushed his way past, calling for another treble Glenfiddich. 'In fact,' he shouted, 'make it a quadruple.'

Heck moved on, still looking for Gemma, but then was called over to one of the sofas, where Jack Reed was propped up on a pile of cushions, a pair of crutches alongside him and his left leg, encased in plaster, resting on the table in front of him, on top of another cushion. Even if he was on painkillers, it wasn't stopping him chugging beer from a bottle. He looked uncharacteristically scruffy, his jaw bristling, his hair unruly, wearing only a T-shirt and a pair of tracksuit pants from which the left leg had been scissored away. He guffawed loudly as he swapped saucy quips with two of the team's secretaries, who, with a marker pen each, appeared to be trying to cover his entire cast with elaborate artwork.

'Yeah, that's it,' he coaxed them. 'Bit higher, bit higher . . .' He glanced at Heck again. 'If it isn't my saviour. Take it you've heard?'

Heck nodded. 'It's good news, but I'd prefer it if we could find Ray Marciano.'

'Shit, don't worry about him.' Reed had clearly been here for some time. He was slurring his words. 'You don't think he's going to come after *you*?'

'No. If he'd wanted that, he could've done me on the roof. I'm just wondering where he's going to show up next.'

'Probably the deepest Amazon, or some such place. Where we can't get at him.'

'It'll need to be somewhere Milena Misanyan's people can't get at him as well,' Heck replied. 'But, somehow, I don't think any of that's going to faze our pal Ray.'

'Whatever,' Reed said. 'Fancy a ride back to Cornwall tomorrow? For a press conference, I mean. Probably only a small one. I'm not sure how much Gwen'll want to release yet. Obviously, with some of the stories that have got out, everyone's going to be there. There are news crews from Taiwan, Australia, Brazil . . .'

'I'd rather not do press conferences, sir.'

'You should. You're the star of the show, and I'm not even on duty. I'm only here tonight for the beer.'

'Did Gemma ask for me to do it?' Heck said.

'No, Heck . . . she asked *me*. But I told her what I've just told you. *You're* the man. So, you'll step in for me, yeah?'

'Hadn't we better check with Gemma first?'

'If you must.' Reed stuck his thumb over his shoulder. 'She's back there.'

Heck pushed on past, feeling the tension tighten in his chest.

Gemma was on a stool at the far end of the bar. She was sipping some kind of cocktail through a straw and picking at a dish of olives. Though she was alone and didn't seem to be enjoying the party, she'd patently made an effort for it. She was prettily made up, wearing white heels, a tight denim skirt and a sleeveless blouse, her blonde locks styled in a French plait.

It reminded him painfully of the first time he'd laid eyes on her, when they were both young detectives, and he'd seen her dancing to hard rock at an equally hot and crazy police party. She'd been wearing high heels and denim that night too, but denim cut-offs rather than a skirt, and rocking out wildly, her damp hair, much longer then, flying. He'd thought she had the best figure and best legs he'd ever seen. How he'd plucked up the courage to wait for her at the edge of the dance floor and press an ice-cold bottle of lager into her hands as soon as she stepped off it, he couldn't imagine – but somehow he had.

Incredibly, it was almost as difficult plucking up the courage now – and that was just to go and stand at the bar alongside her.

They made eye contact briefly, he asking if she needed a refill.

She popped another olive and shook her head.

'So,' he said, after his own beer was served. 'Bodies found, but none of them Ray Marciano.'

'He'll be there somewhere,' she replied.

'Hopefully.'

'Come on, Heck . . . two hundred feet into the sea, assuming he didn't hit the rocks? There's no chance he's made it.'

'And yet we've found no trace of him.'

'We will. Contrary to popular belief, the sea often gives up its dead. Anyway, at least we've charged Morgan Robbins.'

'True, ma'am, but which of the two would you have considered the more dangerous?'

She seemed unconcerned. 'If Ray *did* survive, he'll show up again, and then we'll have him. Speaking of no-shows, I see no sign of Gail Honeyford tonight.'

'She's not coming.'

'Still sulking, is she?'

'She's just not coming.'

'That's up to her. Just so you know . . .' Gemma dismounted her stool, 'I don't want tonight to be too much of a late one. I know it's a party and all, but me and you are on our way down to Cornwall tomorrow morning.'

'So I hear,' he said, resigned to that fate. 'Are you driving, or shall I?'

She mused, clearly not having thought that far ahead yet. 'Now you mention it, I'd rather you drove. I've got an awful lot to get through while we're en route.'

'So, there won't be much chance for us to talk?'

She gave him a quizzical look. 'I imagine we'll be able to exchange pleasantries.'

'That's not quite what I had in mind.'

She regarded him for several seconds. 'I'd say why don't we talk now, but I have a sneaking feeling I'm going to find it tiresome and tedious.'

'Maybe, but while you've mentioned it, *now* is probably the best time.' He placed his half-finished drink down. 'Can we go somewhere more private?'

Several seconds passed. Eventually, she nodded towards a door standing open atop a nearby fire escape.

Gemma descended the fire escape first, Heck following. They alighted in the side lot, where Heck's Megane was one of the few vehicles parked. No one else was around.

'First, can we drop the formalities?' he said.

She shrugged. 'You're the one who insists on calling me "ma'am" all the time.'

That rather caught him on the hop. 'It's just a term of respect.'

'Agreed. It's not supposed to be a weapon.'

431

'Right, erm . . .' Distracted by that, he struggled to find adequate words. 'I just want to ask you a question. Last month, you said to me that only certain things are keeping us apart.'

'I did?' She didn't sound as if she remembered this.

'Stuff about the job,' he said. 'Namely, the different ways me and you do it.'

She gave him her most frank stare. 'You say "the different ways we do the job", Mark, as if it's a small, non-problematic issue.'

'It is . . . if there's sufficient willpower to overcome it.'

She clearly hadn't expected this response, but said nothing, allowing him to continue.

'Gemma . . .' He felt intensely self-conscious, and already was struggling to remember how he'd decided to phrase this. 'I think it should be pretty obvious that I love you. I know I've not always shown it. I'm not the best at that kind of thing. I didn't even realise I loved you when we were first together. I didn't realise it when we separated . . . and, for the record, I'm well aware that I was the sole instigator of that.'

'That's not quite true,' she said, her tone a touch more conciliatory.

'OK, let's say we both instigated it. Both for selfish reasons.' He averted his eyes downward as he spoke; it felt ridiculous, but it was easier than looking directly at her. 'You didn't want to be attached to someone like me, who was likely to get into trouble. I didn't like the idea of you being more of a high-flyer than I was. It hit my male pride. When I look back on it, I can't believe how pathetic that was. But at the same time, I didn't like the idea of you being at the sharp end either . . .' He glanced up. 'I didn't like the idea of my girl getting hurt.'

'At least that showed you cared,' she said, evidently not having expected this degree of self-effacement. 'Which is something we haven't seen much of in the last few years . . . with your endless liberty-taking, your constantly putting me on the spot.'

He lifted a hand. 'That's what I want to talk about. After we split up, I just toddled on as usual . . . while you soared off into the upper stratosphere of the police service. I was, I dunno . . . peeved, jealous, frustrated. It wasn't that I envied your success. It was just that it seemed to prove everything you'd said. With me, you weren't going anywhere. But when you shook me off, the sky was the limit. We'd made the right decision, plainly . . . but it was hardly something I could be happy about. Given how lonely it left me. I mean, at least for you the endless promotions must've helped . . .'

'Mark . . .'

'I know, I know.' He raised his hand again. 'I've always resisted promotion . . . but in your case, you got the pips without controversy. Each time, the world cheered. In my case, it would only ever have been in exceptional circumstances, and primarily down to *you*. So . . .' He paused, watching her hard, even desperately.

She returned his gaze, intrigued.

'So, you had some consolation,' he said again. 'But I wonder . . . did you still feel lonely? Angry? Like me.'

'Yes,' she said quietly. 'Of course I did. And, for what it's worth, I have no feelings for Jack Reed.'

'I realise that now.'

'Other than that's he's a very capable officer, who will be an exceptional addition to the Serial Crimes Unit now that our future is assured. On top of that, he's pretty easy on the eye. But that's all.'

'So, what does all this mean?' he asked. 'I mean for us?'

'Mark . . .' She rubbed at her forehead.

'I wouldn't keep asking you this, Gemma, if I didn't think I already knew the answer. If I thought it was going to be

"Get out of my damn face once and for all!" . . . I'd do exactly that. But the truth is, deep down, I think it's the opposite.'

'Haven't we reached this point before?' She shook her head. 'We've discussed this thing so many times, and we always come up against the same wall.'

'I'm leaving SCU,' he said abruptly.

'I . . . *what?*'

'Ma'am . . . *Gemma*. If that's what it takes, I'm leaving.'

Her mouth dropped partly open.

It was a rare occasion indeed when Gemma Piper was rendered speechless. It didn't last, not that she recovered quickly. 'And . . . where are you going?'

'Not very far as it happens. Believe it or not, Bob Hunter's offered me Ray Marciano's old desk at the Flying Squad.'

'You're going to the Sweeney?' Her incredulity grew steadily. 'Isn't that a bit low-brow?'

'At least it's still in London. But the main thing is I won't be in your face all day . . .'

'Hang on!' Her cheeks now coloured. 'You're taking Ray Marciano's old job?'

'I know it's a bit tasteless. But the truth is I was offered it before we knew Ray was up to no good . . .'

'How many times have I offered you a promotion to DI?'

'Ah . . . I've lost count.'

'Yeah, so have I. But then Bob Hunter comes waddling along . . .'

'Trust me, it's nothing to do with Bob. He's the dodgiest character in the job, and the first time he offered it to me, I wasn't particularly interested. But the circs have changed. Gemma, don't you get it? It means you won't have my disruptive presence in the office. You won't need to be pulling rank on me all day.'

'I bet Bob Hunter won't either!' She laughed bitterly.

'Because everyone down at the Flying Squad does exactly the same thing as you.'

'Gemma, are you hearing me?'

'Yes, I'm hearing you.' She walked away a few yards, hands on hips.

Heck watched her warily. It hadn't been an easy decision, but all things considered, it wouldn't be a huge sacrifice. The Flying Squad had elite status; they were at the heart of London's battle against heavy crime. There were many worse alternatives.

'And when does this wonderful new phase of your life start?' she asked, her back turned.

'Well . . . if you want me to work some kind of notice, I will. I mean, we're still in the middle of Sledgehammer. There are several names that haven't yet been accounted for. If you want me to work those . . .'

'I'd be some kind of boss, holding you to that, considering how much you've done already.'

'Well, in that case . . . I want it to happen as soon as possible.'

She looked at him almost reproachfully.

'So that I can ask you out on a date,' he added hurriedly. 'A proper date. You know . . . the flicks, a bite to eat, a couple of drinks. Afterwards, we go back to our respective digs, and you consider long and hard whether my request to see you again has got legs. To all intents and purposes, we could be strangers. We certainly won't have any mutual stress hanging over us from our shared working day.'

Her expression remained vexed. She walked around, hands still on hips.

'Well . . . at least you've not said "no",' he ventured.

She swung to face him. 'And the price of this date is that I lose my best detective?'

'And I lose the best boss I've ever worked under. Which means we should make it worth both our whiles.'

When she came at him, he barely even saw it. But the next thing Heck knew, she'd grabbed him by the tie and planted her mouth on his.

It took his breath away in all senses of the phrase. Her soft tongue, sweetened by the flavoured alcohol, entwined with his. Her left arm crooked around the back of his neck, to draw him closer, crushing him to her, melding her shapely body into his own. When Heck had recovered from the shock, he embraced her equally tightly, wrapping his arms around her back, lifting her off the ground. She arced with pleasure, her ankles locking together at the backs of her knees. For lingering, blissful seconds, they were as hungry for each other as teenagers, all those endless years of pent-up waiting, watching, wondering and aching now released, flooding through the pair of them in a torrent of passion and desire . . .

So absorbed were they that neither initially noticed when the fireworks started, the rattling *BOOM* of successive explosions, the flickering light show dancing over them and all across the pub car park.

Except . . . fireworks in September? Heck was the first to pull away and glance at the empty sky. And then to turn his head left and focus on the windows to the function room.

Which were filled with thunder and lightning.

Now Gemma saw too.

She broke away from him.

They stood agog – before Gemma reached for the pocket of the coat she wasn't wearing. She turned to Heck, wild-eyed. 'My phone's upstairs.'

'Mine too.' He dashed back across the lot.

'Mark . . . wait! What are you . . .?'

It was a valid question, and it brought him to a sliding

halt before he even reached the foot of the fire-escape stair. He gazed up at it, face bathed in icy sweat.

Briefly, the shooting stopped – no doubt so that a new magazine could be fitted. In that brief, ear-pummelling silence, a dirge of moans and cries replaced the gunfire, only to be lost again as it resumed: a demonic strobe-like flashing and cacophonous roar, the latter amplified a hundred times as stray rounds punched out the windows and cascades of jangling shards fell into the car park.

For the first time in as long as he'd been a cop, Heck did not know what to do.

His limbs had locked; his spine was a strip of ice. When Gemma grabbed his shoulder, he almost jumped out of his skin.

'This way,' she panted. 'This way.'

He was so numbed that he didn't know what she meant. But then he realised that she was leading him away from the foot of the staircase, at the top of which a figure had appeared.

It was Charlie Finnegan, and he stood there swaying, his face a rictus of pain, his torso somehow misshapen, his hips misaligned. Even as they watched him, his white sports shirt turned slowly red from top to bottom. When he fell forward, it was heavily, clumsily. He turned head over heels, coming to a rest halfway down, limbs tangled with the metal rungs.

Stumbling, brain reeling, Heck continued to retreat.

More flashes filled that upper room; more thunderous, rattling gunfire; more windows erupting outward. There were no longer screams, though; nor shouts.

They were thirty yards from the fire escape, still able to see twisting crimson ribbons where blood drained from Finnegan's shattered corpse, when Heck realised that they'd come up level with the next corner. Here, Gemma released him. She was ice-pale, that lovely mouth of hers helplessly agape as though she couldn't draw sufficient air through it to breathe. Tears flooded her eyes as she turned and tottered along the front of the building.

'Gemma . . .?'

'Gotta . . . gotta put a call out,' she stammered over her shoulder. 'Must be a landline . . .'

Too numb to argue, Heck went after her.

They arrived at the pub's main doors, through which the few customers who were downstairs had already fled and were now scattering across the front car park like frightened rabbits.

Blundering into the main bar, they were confronted by a room that was empty except for the two barmaids, who were still behind the bar, white-faced with fear and shock, one of them frozen like a waxwork, the other on the landline, engaged in what was presumably a 999 call. Gemma hurried over, shouting that she was a police officer and wrestling the phone from the startled girl's hand. Heck turned back to the foot of the internal staircase. From this position, he could just about hear the din of the attack, though now it had reduced to the hard, flat reports of separate, individual shots. He knew what this meant. Whoever they were, they were prowling the flotsam, picking off survivors.

He'd never really understood the meaning of that term, 'rooted to the spot' – until now.

Abruptly, even the single shots ceased.

Whoever it was, they'd most likely use the fire escape as the quickest way to the outside and the getaway car. Meanwhile, Gemma leaned on the bar as she tried to fully explain what was happening, tears dripping from her face.

This the best we can do? Seriously?

Heck turned again to the stairs. Slowly, woodenly, like a mannequin creaking to life, he walked towards them and began to ascend.

'Mark!' It was a frantic shout from behind. 'Mark . . . *wait!*'

He ignored her, but he wasn't being brave. He knew there was no danger upstairs. Not any more. Not that he wished to see what remained, but he had no choice. Skulking below went against his whole ethos.

When he reached the door to the function room, he halted, nostrils wrinkling at the stench of cordite, eyes straining to penetrate the pall of gun smoke hanging shroud-like over the carnage of smashed furniture and bloodied, enmeshed forms.

The worst thing perhaps was the lack of movement in there.

Not a twitch, not a shudder, not even a faint, dying whimper to disturb the rancid air.

Then he heard it, the clanging of boots descending the fire escape, and a coarse, rage-filled voice, a curse delivered in a foreign tongue. Heck didn't understand what it said, but he knew what it meant. Charlie Finnegan's corpse had got in the way, and no doubt now was being unceremoniously kicked aside.

With a bellow of bull-like fury, Heck charged across the room.

As he ran, he tried not to look at what he trod and slipped in, even if glimpses of certain upturned faces were unavoidable. Though shattered and streaked with gore, he recognised some of them: Andy Rawlins, Burt Cunliffe . . . Jack Reed, for Christ's sake!

Again, he heard Gemma's voice calling him.

But before he could respond, he'd reached the door at the top of the fire escape and peered down it just in time to see a dark-clad figure leaping into a rumbling white Subaru XV, which must already have someone behind the wheel – because no sooner had the assassin vanished into the front passenger seat than it tore away across the car park and out onto the street at such reckless speed that a passing Hyundai spun off the road.

Heck clattered down the stairs. As he'd suspected, the body of Charlie Finnegan had been thrown inelegantly aside. The treads below were slick with his blood, but Heck leapt over them, landing with stinging blows on the soles of both feet, but jerking himself upright and running towards his own car.

'*Heck!*' he heard Gemma cry.

In his sidelong vision, she emerged around the corner of the pub. But he didn't stop, diving into his Megane, starting it up and swinging it round in a demented, tyre-screeching circle.

As he hurled it at the entrance to the car park, Gemma stepped into his path.

'For Christ's sake!' he roared, flinging the wheel left, almost hitting the gatepost.

Before he could readjust position and take off again, Gemma yanked open his rear offside door and scrambled inside.

'What the hell do you think you're doing?' she yelled.

'Spotted the bastards! White Subaru XV! Two targets minimum.'

'So . . . where the hell are we going now?'

'They're not going to stay in that motor.' He swerved onto the blacktop, hitting the gas for all he was worth. 'We've got to tail them till they make the switch. We don't, they get clean away.'

'OK . . . OK . . .' She had no objection; it made perfect sense.

'Gemma, they . . .' His voice half-broke as he struggled to stay focused. 'They got all of them. Everyone . . .'

'*All* of them?' Her voice was cold, flat.

'Never . . . seen anything like it. Bloody massacre.'

'There!' she shouted, consciously distracting herself. '*THERE!*'

Eighty-odd yards ahead, a white vehicle blazed through

the Ferny Hill junction. It galvanised Heck to greater efforts. He slammed his foot to the floor, hitting sixty in a forty zone. At the next roundabout, he veered, almost spinning out of control as he followed his quarry onto Waggon Road, still clamping his foot to the floor.

'Who's coming?' he shouted.

'Everyone,' she replied. 'I called everyone . . . trouble is, as long as we keep moving, I can't update them on where we are. You didn't think to grab your phone . . .'

'No . . . *fuck!*' Heck cursed.

'It doesn't matter,' she said, 'just make sure you stay in touch with the car.'

He nodded. Now that the red mist was clearing, this was all he actually could do. He'd come across too many automatic weapons for his own liking in the previous weeks. The last time, he'd been armed with something that was no more than a pea-shooter in comparison. This time he had nothing at all.

But even staying in touch wouldn't be easy.

The Subaru, which was clearly aware they were pursuing, hit 70mph as it tore through Hadley Wood, making crazy manoeuvres to overtake the slower-moving cars in front of it. Even cars in the opposite carriageway went careering off the blacktop, many of them suffering heavy impacts.

'The stupidest woodentops in the job can follow this trail of madness,' Gemma said. 'Heck . . .' Her voice quavered. 'You don't mean *all* of them? Not *all* of them?'

He nodded, struggling to nail his attention on the Subaru and put everything else from his mind. But he was successful at this simply because the white vehicle was proving so incredibly elusive.

On Dancers Hill Road, it accelerated to something approaching 90mph, taking corners with such rash abandon that it screeched repeatedly into the opposing lane. Thankfully, there were fewer and fewer vehicles the further it penetrated into the countryside. At last, on a road called Trotters Bottom, there was nothing coming the other way at all, which made it all the more bewildering when the Subaru suddenly cut sharp left down a much narrower road with leafy copses to either side.

'Hang on!' Heck shouted, swinging his Megane in pursuit.

All four tyres travelled sideways across the tarmac, surely losing centimetres of tread. Gemma, who wasn't yet belted in, yelped as she flew from one side of the vehicle to the other.

This next route was unlit, and the trees, clustered up to either verge and standing behind six-foot-high stone-built walls, made it even darker. Heck banged his headlights up to full, but the twists and turns gave him no vantage further ahead than thirty or forty yards.

The Subaru was lost to view.

'Shit, shit!' he muttered. 'Can't see them . . . they haven't turned off somewhere else?'

'Heck, I don't like this!' Gemma warned. 'This isn't natural . . . there's no escape this way.'

That made sense to Heck, but already he was screeching around the next bend onto an open stretch – and some eighty yards ahead, they regained sight of the Subaru. It had halted on the left side of the narrow road, directly behind a heavy goods vehicle, the rear ramp to which had been lowered, revealing a hollow interior.

'Got 'em!' Heck shouted, ramming his foot down again.

But less than a millisecond later, he spotted two dark figures, one to either side of the Subaru, both facing towards him. Another millisecond, and he sighted the weapons they were squinting along. He hit his brakes, projecting the Megane into a terrifying skid, but dazzling, strobe-like flashes already filled his windscreen, peppering it with explosive impacts, before busting the whole thing inward.

Heck swung sharp right, aiming for a wooden farm gate, which he struck at full force.

The Megane was heavy, but this was a mighty obstacle. It flew apart under the impact, but the jolt was terrific. Fleetingly, the wheels lost traction and velocity, allowing the machine gunners to rake the car down its nearside flank, juddering hammer blows hitting every part of it, before it ploughed into the wooded area, where it went through a tangle of fibrous undergrowth, a chaos of leaves and broken twigs surging through the smashed windscreen, and slammed full-on into the trunk of an elm tree.

The impact was tremendous, the sound like a bomb blast.

Heck was jarred forward into his airbag.

What seemed like an age of vague, dim awareness followed. Every one of his senses too numbed to respond. The car was dead, and darkness engulfed him. The only sound he could hear was the tinkle of glass as it trickled from the shattered windows. But then he heard something else as well: the slamming of boots on tarmac, rapidly drawing closer.

'Gemma,' he murmured, nothing really making sense, though some concept of alarm was growing on him. And, in a rush, it all fell back into place. '*Gemma, get out!*'

He unclipped his belt and kicked repeatedly at his door, which had buckled in its frame. The rear-offside passenger door opened, and from the corner of his eye, he saw Gemma lurch out and throw herself flat into the undergrowth. In contrast, his own door only budged by millimetres. Horribly aware that they were a handful of yards from the road, he fought furiously with it, battering it with his shoulders, his elbows, his knees.

The footfalls came nearer.

Heck risked a glance backward.

Through an opening in the trees, he could see twenty yards' worth of stone wall. There was no sign of anyone there yet. He swung back to the door, and with a snarl of effort which all but ruptured his throat, he flung his entire body forward, and with a *CRACK!* of straining metal, the door burst open. He fell through the gap, along with the champagne bottle, which had been thrown across the interior of the car during the crash.

He glanced around. Gemma was still lying low, but there was no time to speak with her.

Snatching the bottle by its neck, he scuttled around the front of his car and the massive tree trunk that had staved it in, scrambled to the wall and hunkered down in its shadow.

In no time, feet arrived on the other side.

The barrel of an automatic rifle projected over the top of the wall, directly above him. With a rattle of blistering, deafening fire, it drilled another salvo into the smashed and twisted Megane, turning its bodywork to Swiss cheese, taking out all the remaining windows, blowing the bonnet lid off, raking the interior back and forth.

It only ceased when the magazine was spent – which was when Heck made his move.

He launched himself upward, grabbing the barrel with one hand, red-hot though it was, and swinging the champagne in a massive overhead arc.

The figure on the other side of the wall, a well-built guy, wearing dark clothes with pale, bearded features framed inside a white woollen balaclava, was taken completely by surprise, especially when the heavy glass bottle exploded on his cranium.

Heck yanked the empty gun from his faltering grasp and threw it out of reach into the undergrowth, at the same time trying to drag him over the wall. The gunman, already tottering, blood welling through his balaclava, tried to pull back. Heck snatched his wrist with his left hand, and with his right brought down the remaining bottleneck over and over again. As good as any blade, he plunged it repeatedly into the gunman's left shoulder and the left side of his neck.

A shout caught Heck's attention; it was wild, incoherent, and it came from further up the road. More footfalls sounded as the second of the gunmen ran their way.

Heck saw him coming. He was burlier than the first, also bearded and wearing dark clothes, with his hair tucked under a black woollen cap. Only when the first one dropped to the road, through shock and blood loss, did this second one open fire.

Slugs screamed along the top of the wall, kicking out fist-sized chunks of stone and mortar. Heck ducked and rolled into the foliage. Dropping the blood-slimed bottleneck, he scampered away on all fours, heading as deep into the cover of the trees as he could. He made thirty-odd yards before leaping up and running, weaving between the trunks, trusting that the blackness of night would also conceal him.

Thirty yards became forty, became fifty, became sixty . . . but Heck knew that if the other bastard simply sprayed this woodland with slugs, he still had a good chance of hitting his target.

And yet that didn't happen.

Instead, Heck heard a gabble of muffled voices. By the sounds of it, the second guy was now attending to the first, because one of those voices was a pain-racked gibber. Heck circled an oak and slammed his back to it. He stood there rigid, drenched with sweat, straining to hear, though he couldn't make head nor tail of what they were saying. Not even enough to distinguish whether they were speaking English, though he was certain they hadn't been when he'd heard them back at the pub.

'Who the hell . . .?' he said under his breath.

Whoever they were, they didn't hang around. What sounded like a stumbling run, no doubt the one assisting the

445

other, diminished away along the road again. Then he heard a car engine jar to life. It was the Subaru.

Heck was torn with indecision. His heart told him to return to the road. If they got that motor inside the lorry, whose make and registration number he hadn't yet noted, they were clean away. But his head told him that this could be a ruse to draw him out into the open.

His heart won – but only after a potentially catastrophic delay. As he wove his way back, he heard the louder rumble of an HGV coming to life.

'Shit!'

He ran faster, reaching the wall a dozen yards along it from the point where he'd fought with the first gunman. But the lorry was already out of sight, its tail lights dwindling to pinpoints of red in the distant darkness, before winking out altogether.

Heck leaned against the stonework, gasping, head drooped.

Only with an effort did he push himself away, and hobble back towards his car, passing a section of wall whose entire parapet had been sheared off by gunfire. His adrenaline was flagging fast, and suddenly he felt weary beyond belief. A hundred different strains and sprains nagged at him. Even the cut over his brow had opened again and was leaking.

That was when he realised that he was clutching something in his left hand. A bracelet of some sort, which he'd yanked loose from the first bastard's wrist.

Initially, he only glanced at it, but that was enough to stop him in his tracks.

He held it up in the half-light, to check it out properly – and there was no mistake. It was a leather bangle dangling with tiny, Gothic adornments: skulls, inverted crucifixes, wolf heads. Even in the midst of this whole overwhelming calamity, Heck's own haunting words came back to him like bullets in their own right:

I don't think this'll be the last we hear from these guys.
And when we do hear . . . it's going to be seriously nasty.

His breath struggling out in ragged sobs, he staggered on.

He'd known it. He'd said it all along. If only he'd insisted
. . . but no, there was no time for futile self-recrimination.
There wasn't even time to find an evidence bag. For the
moment, he had no choice but to slide the bracelet into the
pocket of his trousers. It would be as safe there as anywhere.

'Gemma?' he called, as his Megane came into sight through
the bushes. It was little more than a smoking, devastated
hulk – but that was hardly a surprise.

'Gemma?' he said. 'Gemma . . . you OK?'

He rounded the rear of the car, picking through the shattered timbers of the gate, at which point he saw that she
was still keeping low in the undergrowth.

'Gemma, they've gone. But, you won't believe . . .' His
words tailed off. 'Gemma . . .?'

She wasn't keeping low as much as lying on her left side.
Unmoving.

Heck threw himself onto his knees next to her.

The blood soaking thickly into her blouse both front and
back was a horrifying shock.

'G . . . Gemma?' Thoughts whirling, he fought to get the
words out. 'Come on . . . come on, darling . . .'

At first, he hardly dared touch her. When he finally did,
it was her bare right arm, the flesh of which was cooling
fast.

'Gemma . . . *NO!*'

Frantic, disregarding all rules, because no rules he knew
would help them now, he turned her over and hoisted her
up into his arms. Even cradled, she lay elegantly, knees
together under her denim skirt, the toes of her pretty shoes
turned slightly inward. But her head lolled back. When he
slid an arm underneath it, to raise it up, her eyelids fluttered.

'That's it . . . yeah, that's it. Come on, darling . . . just, stay with me, yeah!' He looked wildly around, but there hadn't been a vehicle past in the last few minutes, let alone anyone on foot who might hear him shout.

He shouted anyway: 'Someone . . . anyone! *HELP US, PLEASE!*'

'Mark . . .' she breathed.

He looked down, hope surging. Her eyes had opened slightly, but the expression on her face was strangely serene. Hurt though she was, she'd managed to raise her right hand and now touched his cheek with it.

'Come on, Gemma,' he coaxed her gently. 'Come on, darling. It'll be OK.'

She smiled at him for a second or two, before her eyes closed again.

When her hand dropped away, the howl that ripped from his chest split the night apart, lingering for what seemed like minutes on the light summer breeze.

Get back to where it all started with book one of the series, where Heck takes on the most brutal of killers...

Dark, terrifying and unforgettable.
Stalkers will keep fans of Stuart MacBride and M.J. Arlidge looking over their shoulder.

A vicious serial killer is holding the country to ransom, publicly – and gruesomely – murdering his victims.

A heart-stopping and unforgettable thriller that you won't be able to put down, from bestseller Paul Finch.

DS Mark 'Heck' Heckenburg is used to bloodbaths. But nothing will prepare him for this.

Brace yourself as you turn the pages of a living nightmare.

Welcome to The Killing Club.

As a brutal winter takes hold of the Lake District, a prolific serial killer stalks the fells. And for Heck, the signs are all too familiar...

The fourth unputdownable book in the DS Mark Heckenburg series. A killer thriller for fans of Stuart MacBride and *Luther*.

Heck needs to watch his back. Because someone's watching him...

Get hooked on Heck: the maverick cop who knows no boundaries. A grisly whodunit, perfect for fans of Stuart MacBride and *Luther*.

A stranger is just a killer you
haven't met yet...

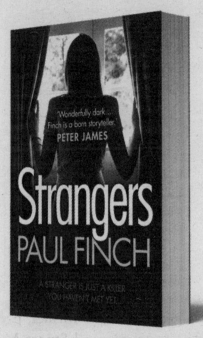

Meet Paul Finch's new heroine in the first
of the PC Lucy Clayburn series. Read the
Sunday Times bestseller now.

Is your home safe?

An unforgettable crime thriller, perfect for fans of M.J. Arlidge and Stuart MacBride. Read the *Sunday Times* bestseller now.

Do you know who's watching you?

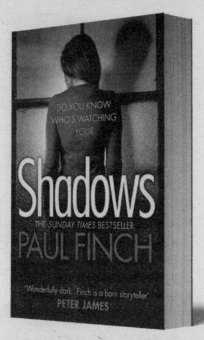

PC Lucy Clayburn faces one of the toughest cases
of her life – and one which will prove
once and for all whether blood really is
thicker than water...